THE COOL CODE 2.0
THE SWITCH GLITCH

DEIRDRE LANGELAND

illustrated by
SARAH MAI

CLARION BOOKS
Imprints of HarperCollinsPublishers

HARPER
alley

TO FREDDIE, THE COOLEST OF THEM ALL.
—D. L.

FOR HUEY AND LOUIE, MY TWO CCS.
—S. M.

Clarion Books is an imprint of HarperCollins Publishers.
HarperAlley is an imprint of HarperCollins Publishers.

The Cool Code 2.0: The Switch Glitch
Copyright © 2023 by HarperCollins Publishers
All rights reserved. Manufactured in Bosnia and Herzegovina.
No part of this book may be used or reproduced in any manner whatsoever without
written permission except in the case of brief quotations embodied in critical articles
and reviews. For information address HarperCollins Children's Books, a division of
HarperCollins Publishers, 195 Broadway, New York, NY 10007.
www.harperalley.com

Library of Congress Control Number: 2023932957
ISBN 978-0-35-852118-1 (pbk.) — ISBN 978-0-35-854933-8

The artist used ProCreate to create the digital illustrations for this book.
Lettering by Whitney Leader-Picone and Chrissy Kurpeski
23 24 25 26 27 GPS 10 9 8 7 6 5 4 3 2 1

First Edition

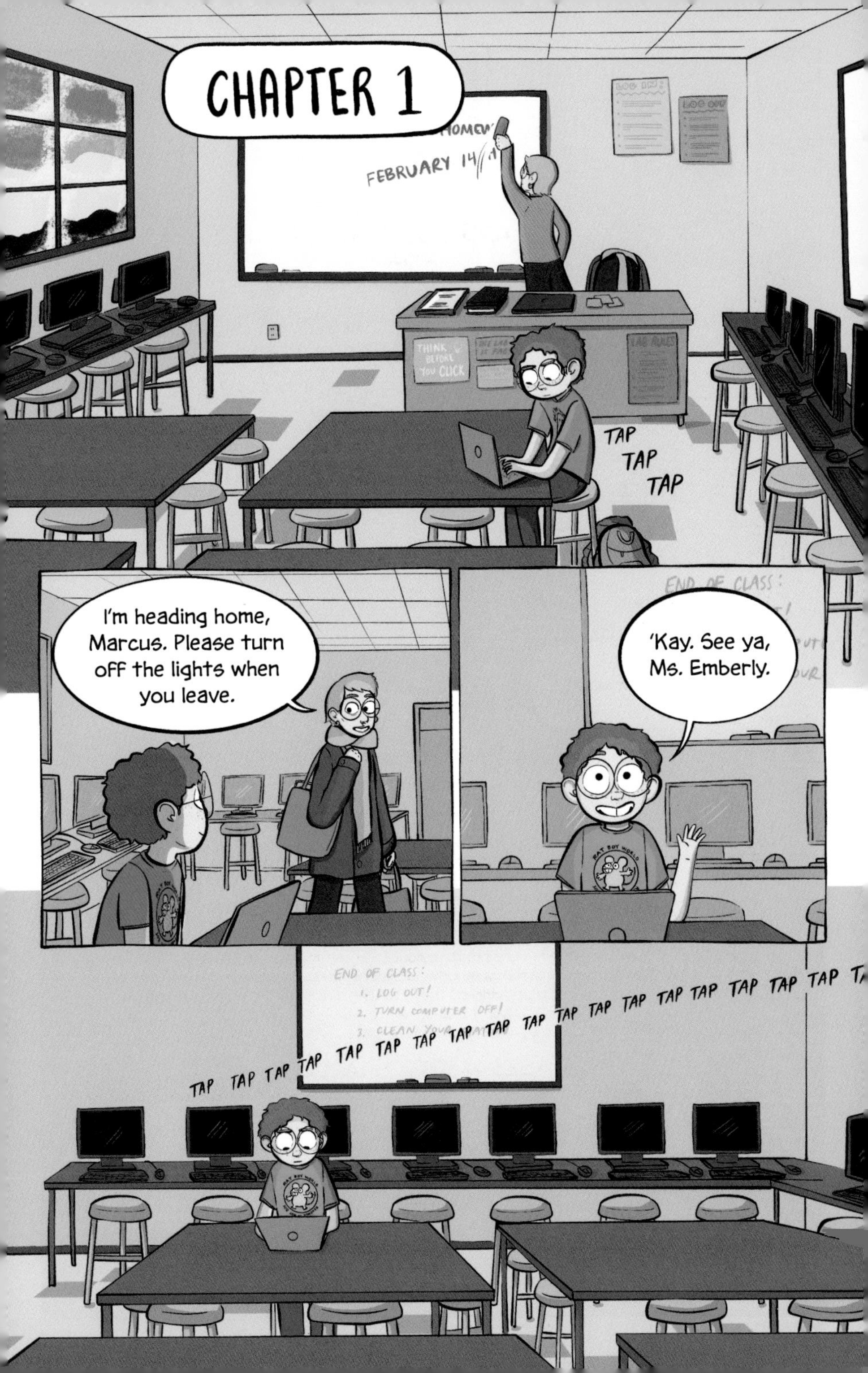
CHAPTER 1
FEBRUARY 14
THINK BEFORE YOU CLICK
TAP TAP TAP
I'm heading home, Marcus. Please turn off the lights when you leave.
'Kay. See ya, Ms. Emberly.
END OF CLASS:
1. LOG OUT!
2. TURN COMPUTER OFF!
TAP TAP TAP TAP TAP TAP TAP TAP TAP TAP TAP TAP TAP TAP TAP TAP TAP TAP TAP

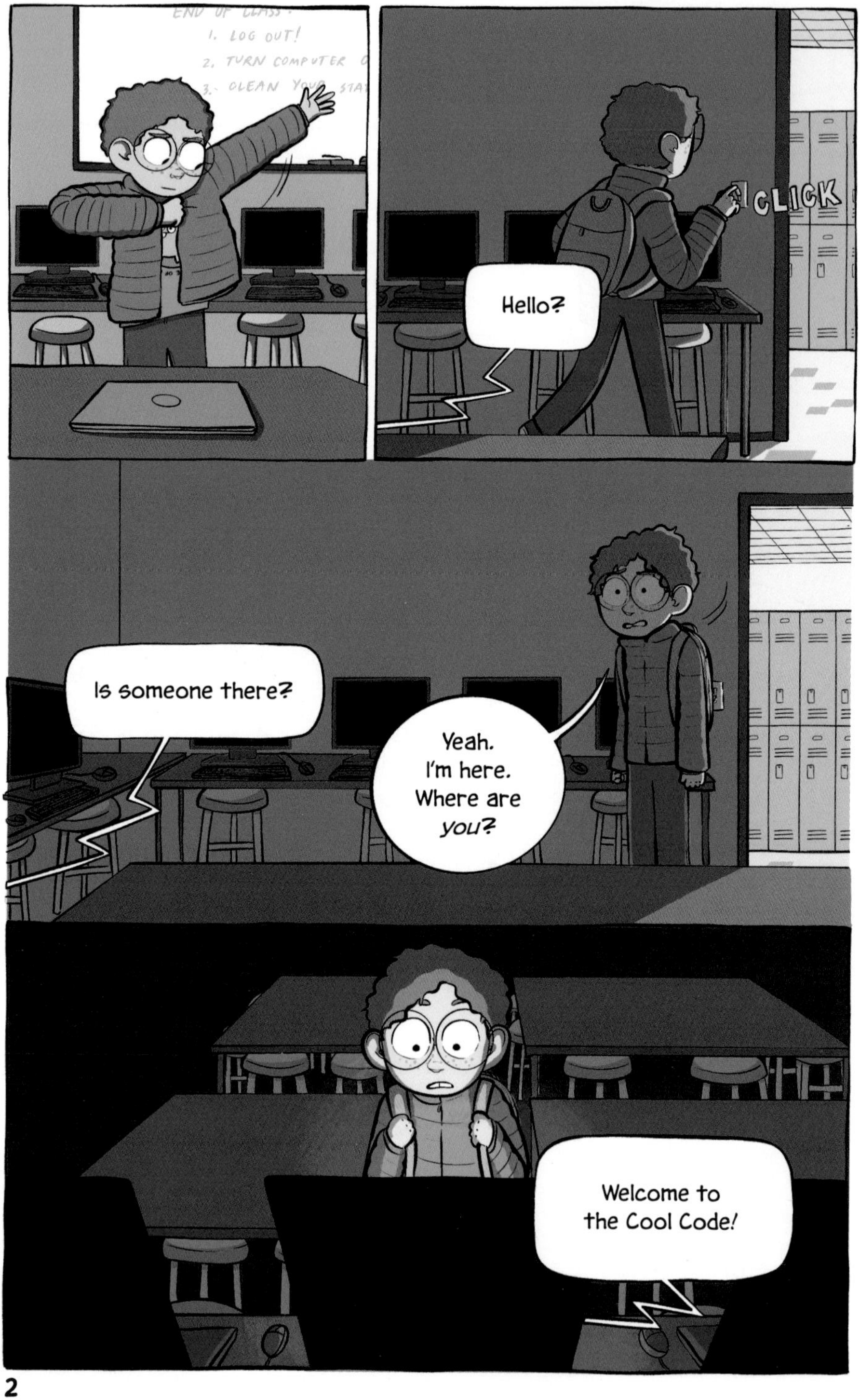
END OF CLASS
1. LOG OUT!
2. TURN COMPUTER
3. CLEAN YOUR
CLICK
Hello?
Is someone there?
Yeah. I'm here. Where are *you*?
Welcome to the Cool Code!

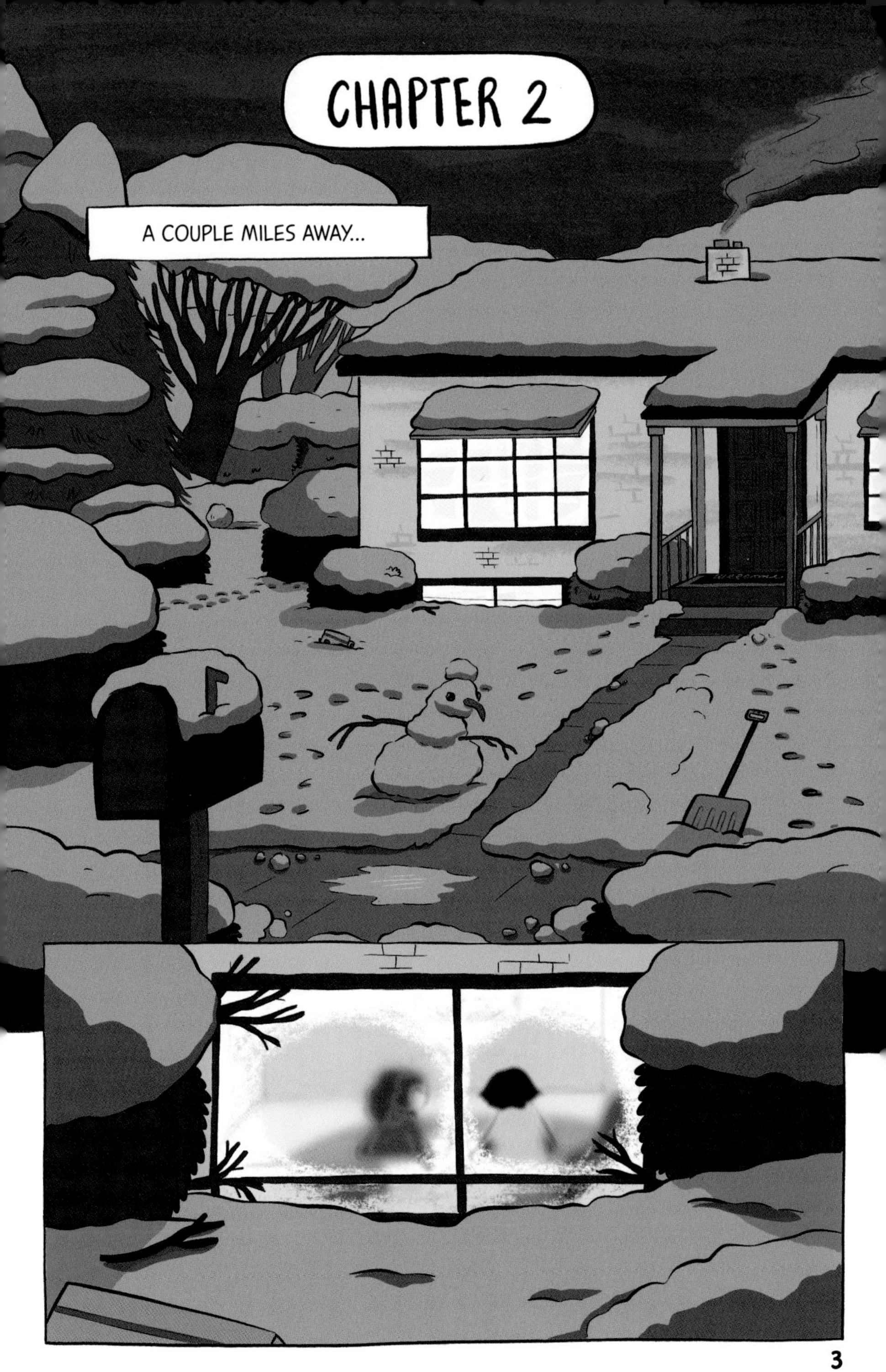
CHAPTER 2
A COUPLE MILES AWAY...

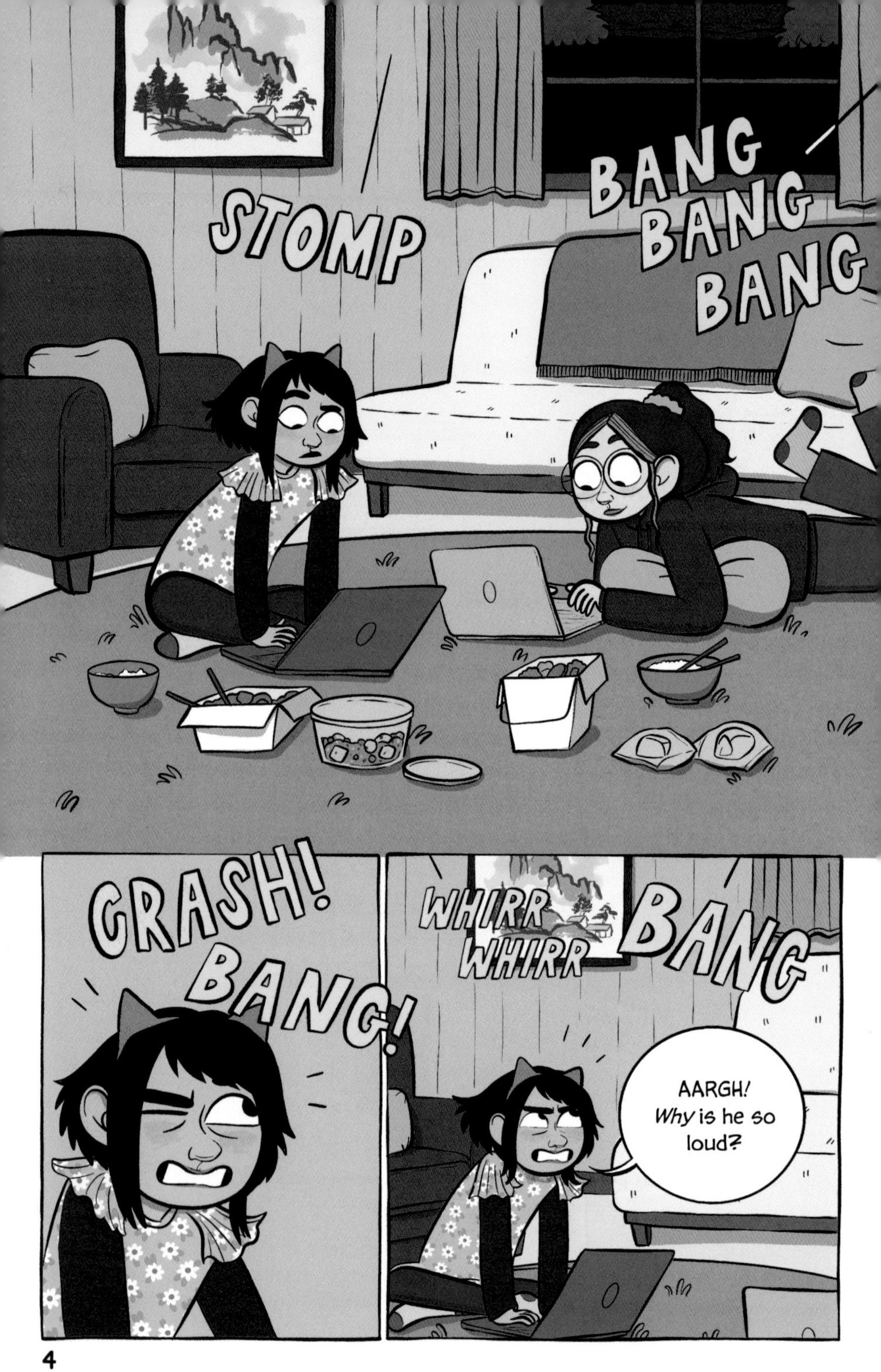
STOMP
BANG BANG BANG
CRASH! BANG!
WHIRR WHIRR
BANG
AARGH! *Why* is he so loud?

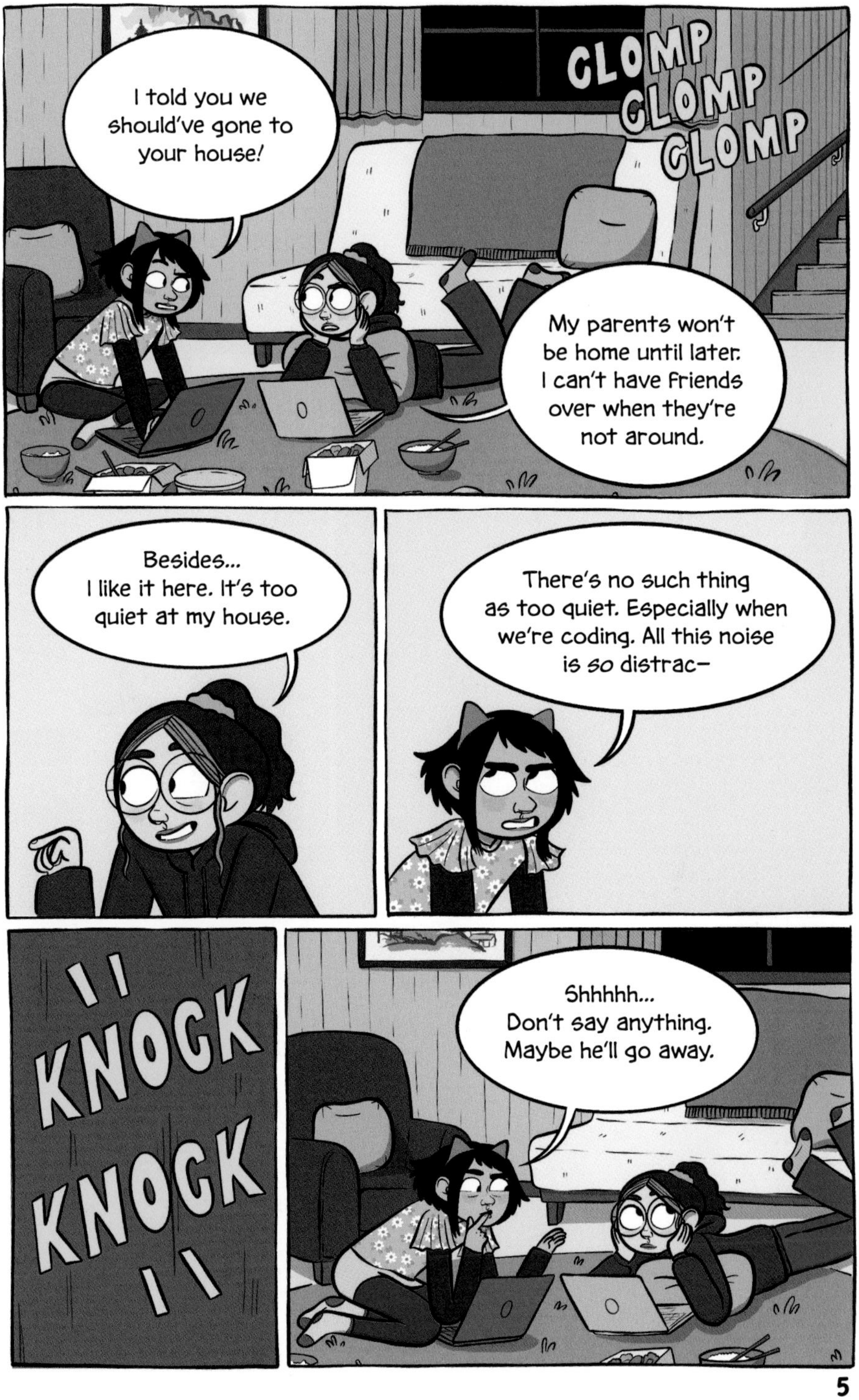
I told you we should've gone to your house!
CLOMP CLOMP CLOMP
My parents won't be home until later. I can't have friends over when they're not around.
Besides... I like it here. It's too quiet at my house.
There's no such thing as too quiet. Especially when we're coding. All this noise is *so* distrac–
KNOCK KNOCK
Shhhhh... Don't say anything. Maybe he'll go away.

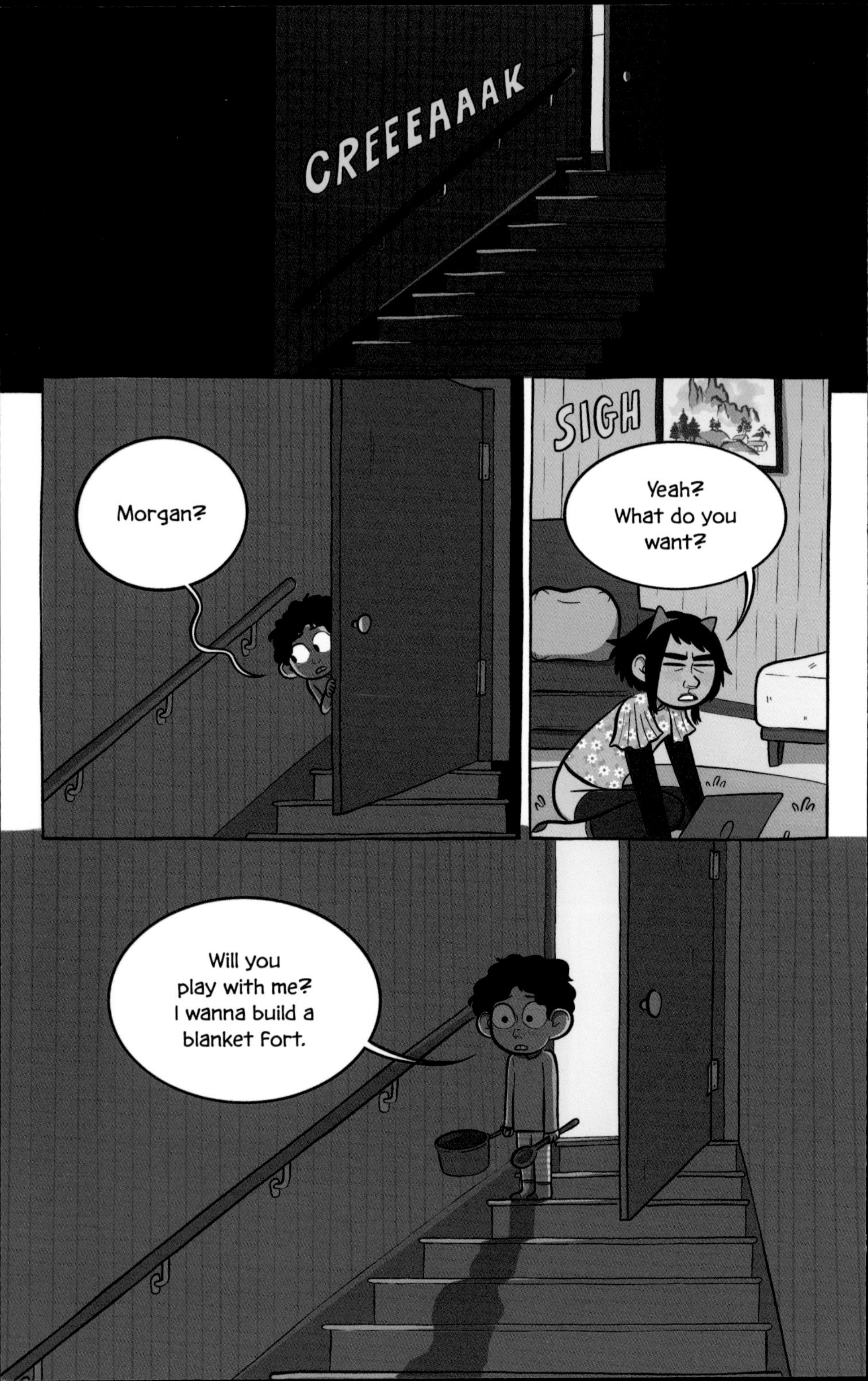
CREEEAAAK
Morgan?
SIGH
Yeah? What do you want?
Will you play with me? I wanna build a blanket fort.

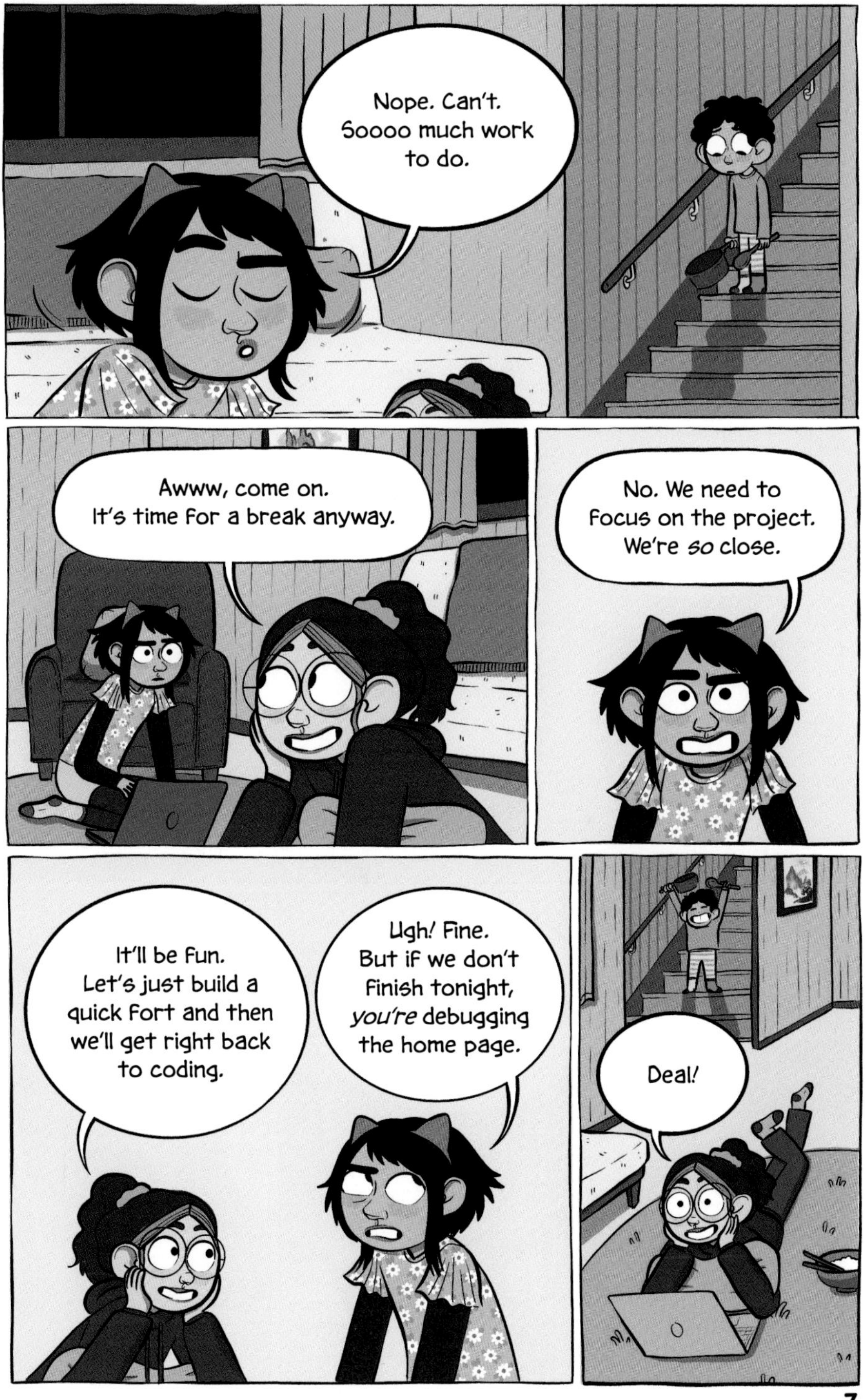
Nope. Can't. Soooo much work to do.
Awww, come on. It's time for a break anyway.
No. We need to focus on the project. We're *so* close.
It'll be fun. Let's just build a quick fort and then we'll get right back to coding.
Ugh! Fine. But if we don't finish tonight, *you're* debugging the home page.
Deal!

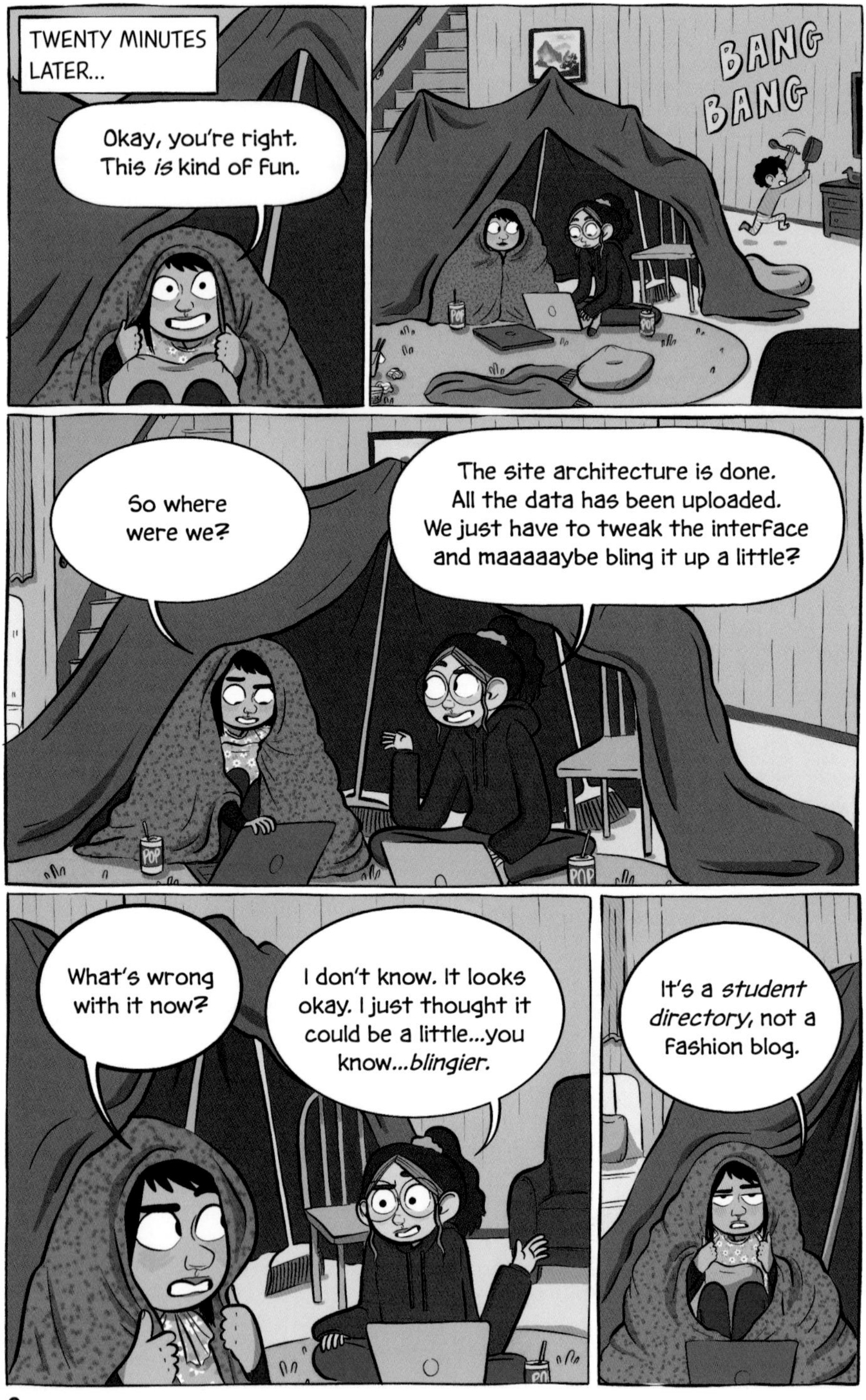
TWENTY MINUTES LATER...
Okay, you're right. This *is* kind of fun.
BANG BANG
POP
So where were we?
The site architecture is done. All the data has been uploaded. We just have to tweak the interface and maaaaaybe bling it up a little?
POP
What's wrong with it now?
I don't know. It looks okay. I just thought it could be a little...you know...*blingier.*
It's a *student directory,* not a fashion blog.

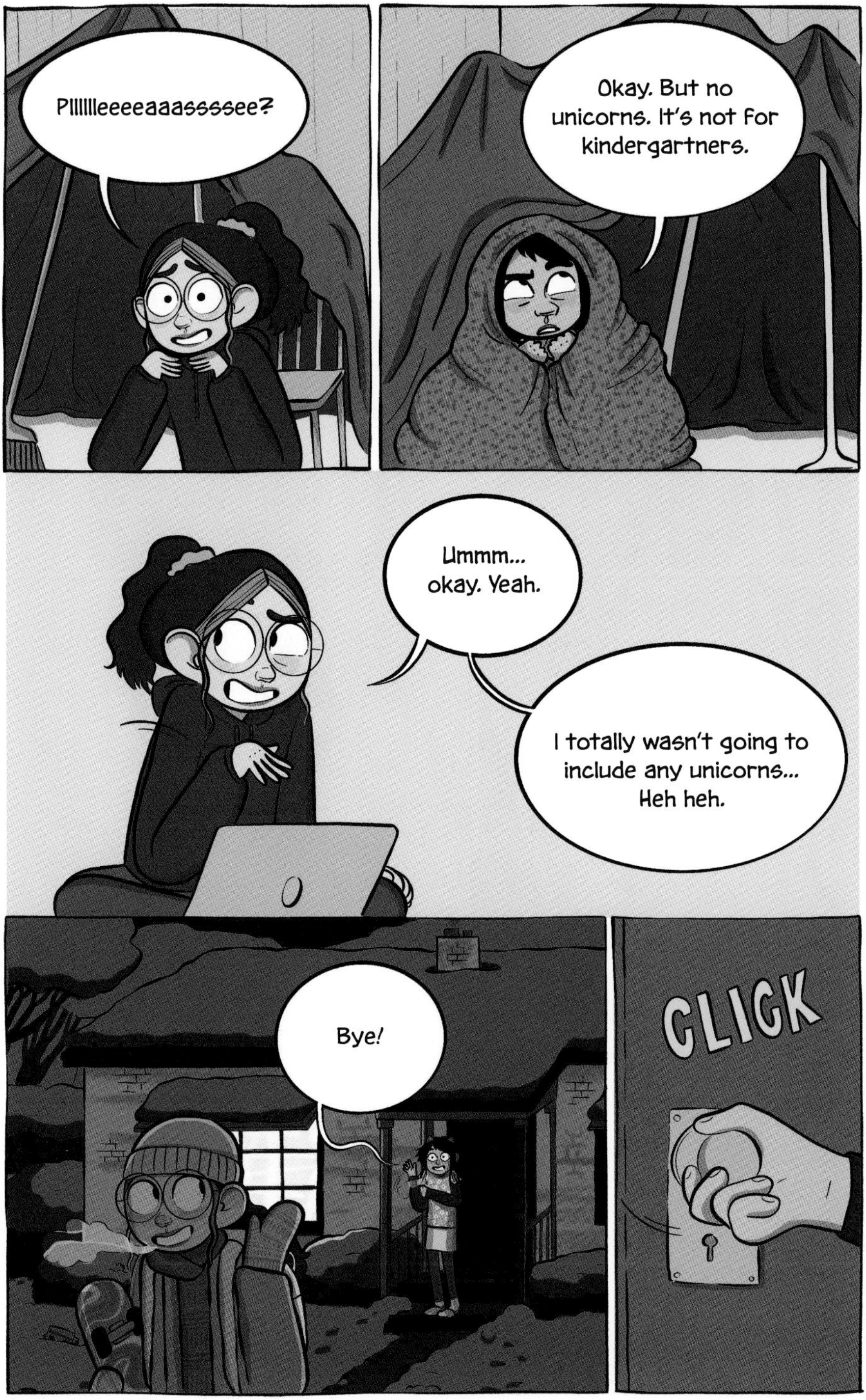
Pllllleeeeaaassssee?
Okay. But no unicorns. It's not for kindergartners.
Ummm... okay. Yeah.
I totally wasn't going to include any unicorns... Heh heh.
Bye!
CLICK

NOTIFICATION:
TEXT: DANIEL THOMPSON

Hey! How's it going?

TAP TAP TAP TAP TAP TAP

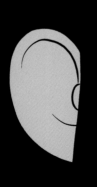

DANIEL

nice of you to check in now that we're done

done???? Can we show Ms Hamm tomorrow?

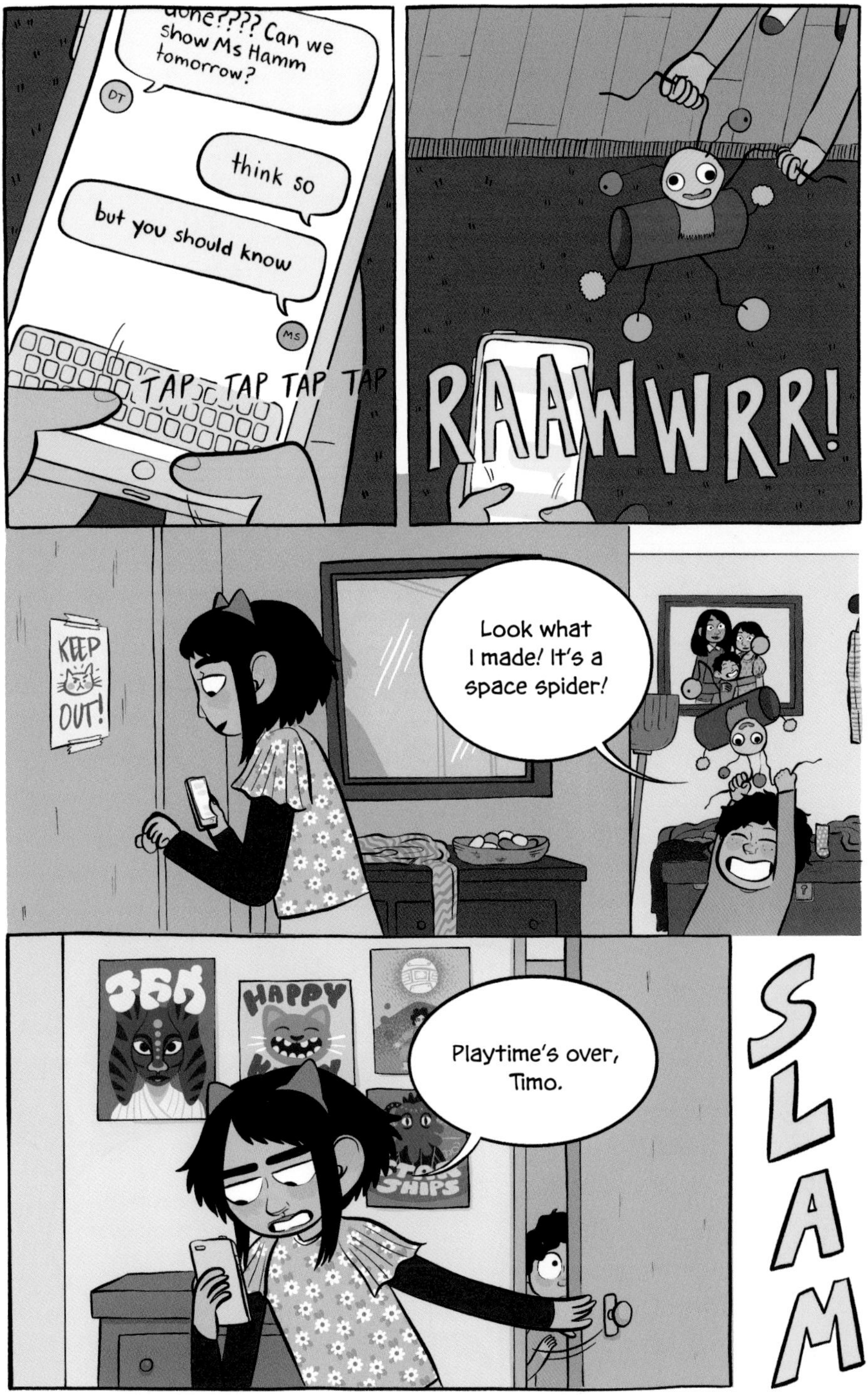
done???? Can we show Ms Hamm tomorrow?
DT
think so
but you should know
MS
TAP TAP TAP TAP
RAAWWRR!
KEEP OUT!
Look what I made! It's a space spider!
HAPPY
STAR SHIPS
Playtime's over, Timo.
SLAM

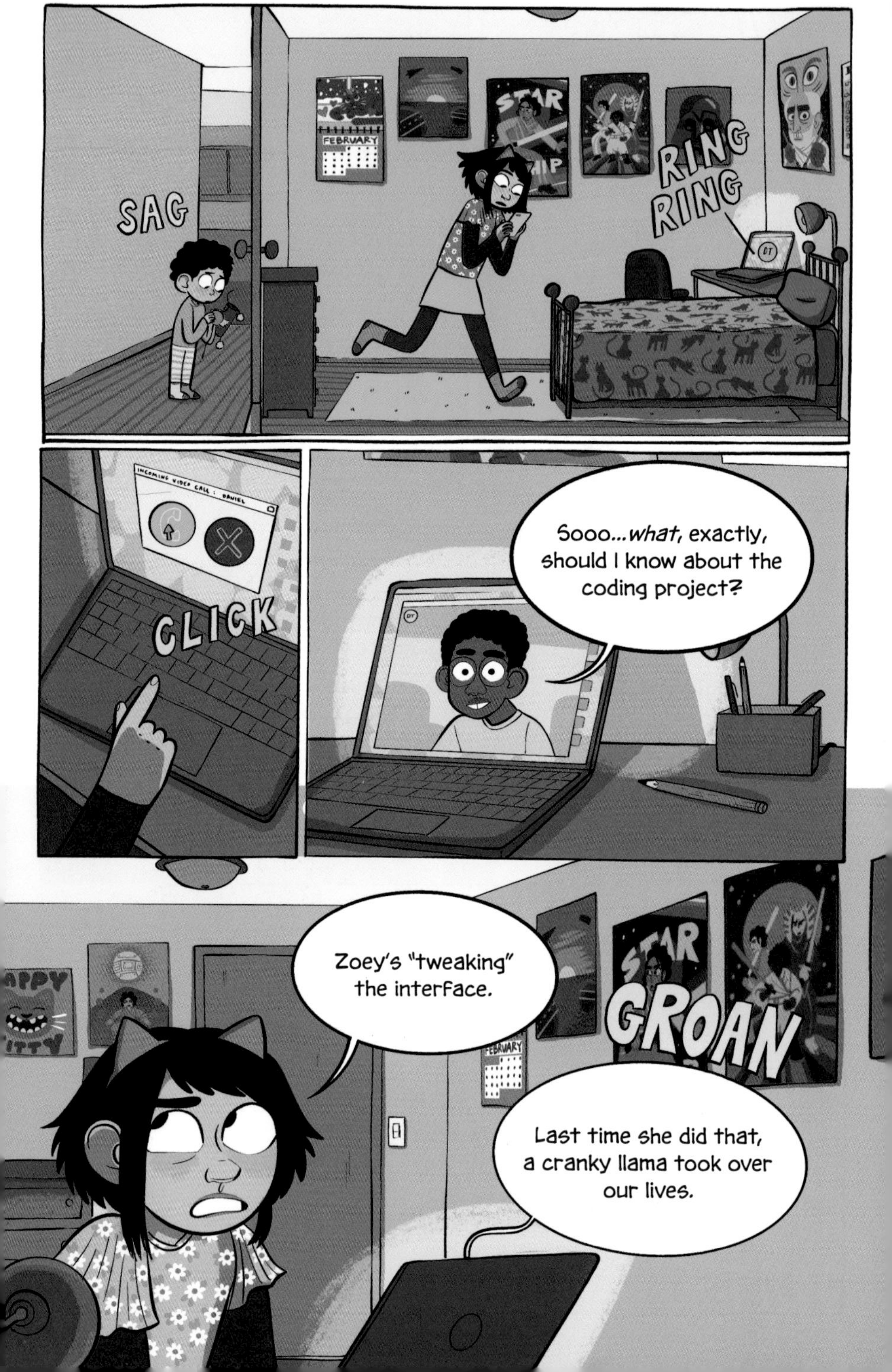
SAG
RING RING
CLICK
Sooo...*what*, exactly, should I know about the coding project?
Zoey's "tweaking" the interface.
GROAN
Last time she did that, a cranky llama took over our lives.

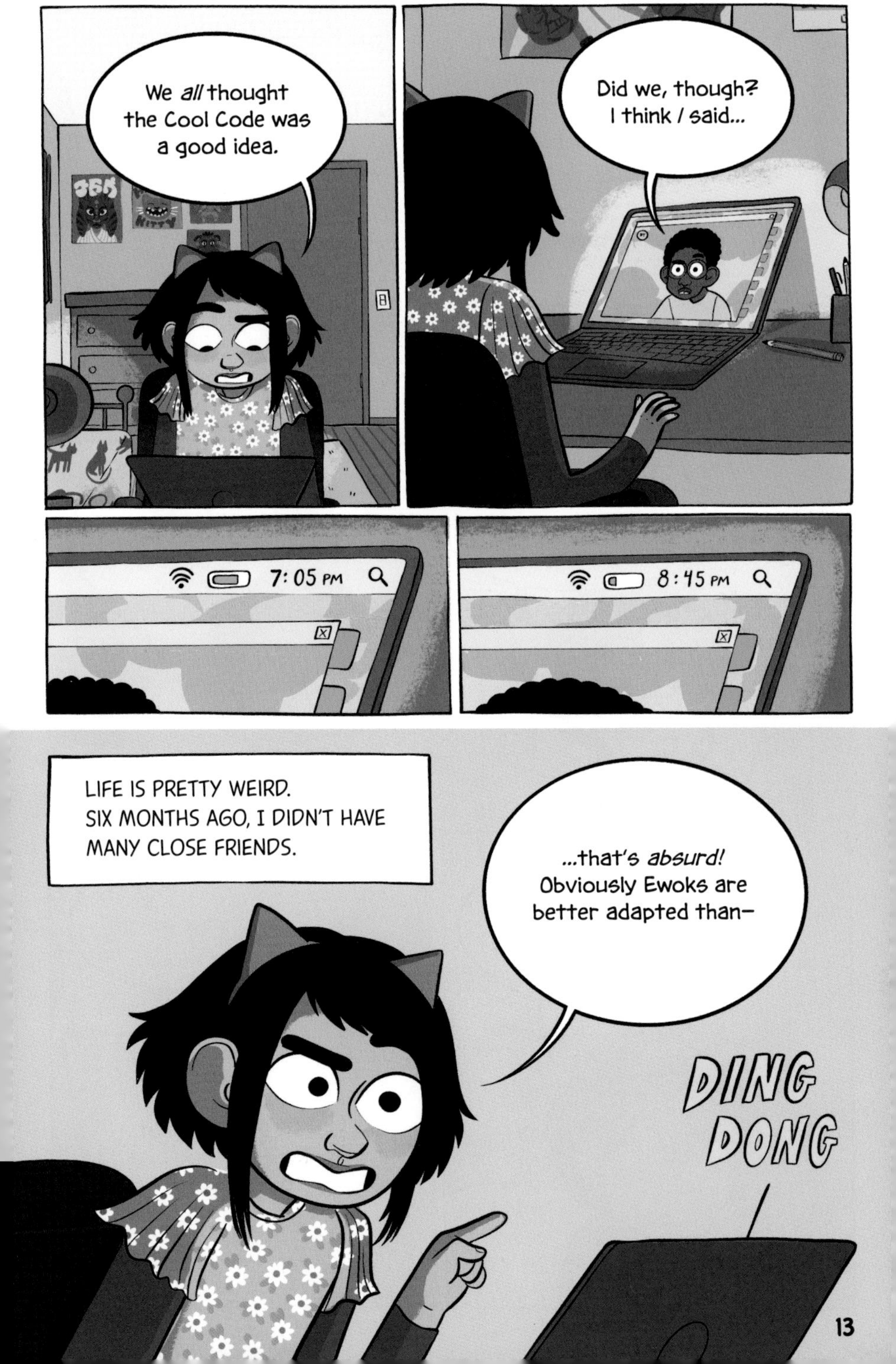
We *all* thought the Cool Code was a good idea.
Did we, though? I think *I* said...
7:05 PM
8:45 PM
LIFE IS PRETTY WEIRD. SIX MONTHS AGO, I DIDN'T HAVE MANY CLOSE FRIENDS.
...that's *absurd!* Obviously Ewoks are better adapted than—
DING DONG

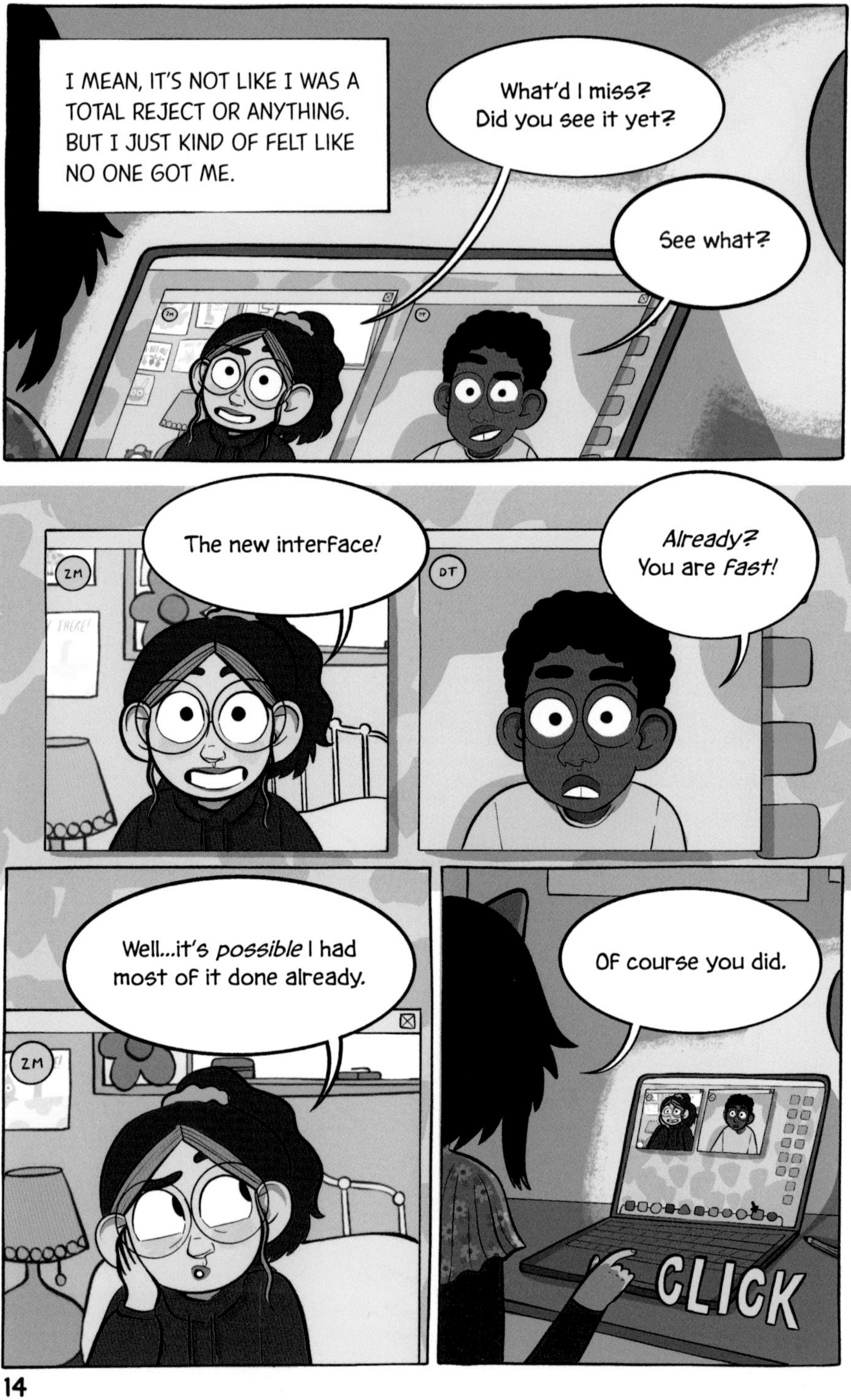
I MEAN, IT'S NOT LIKE I WAS A TOTAL REJECT OR ANYTHING. BUT I JUST KIND OF FELT LIKE NO ONE GOT ME.
What'd I miss? Did you see it yet?
See what?
The new interface!
Already? You are *fast!*
Well...it's *possible* I had most of it done already.
Of course you did.
CLICK

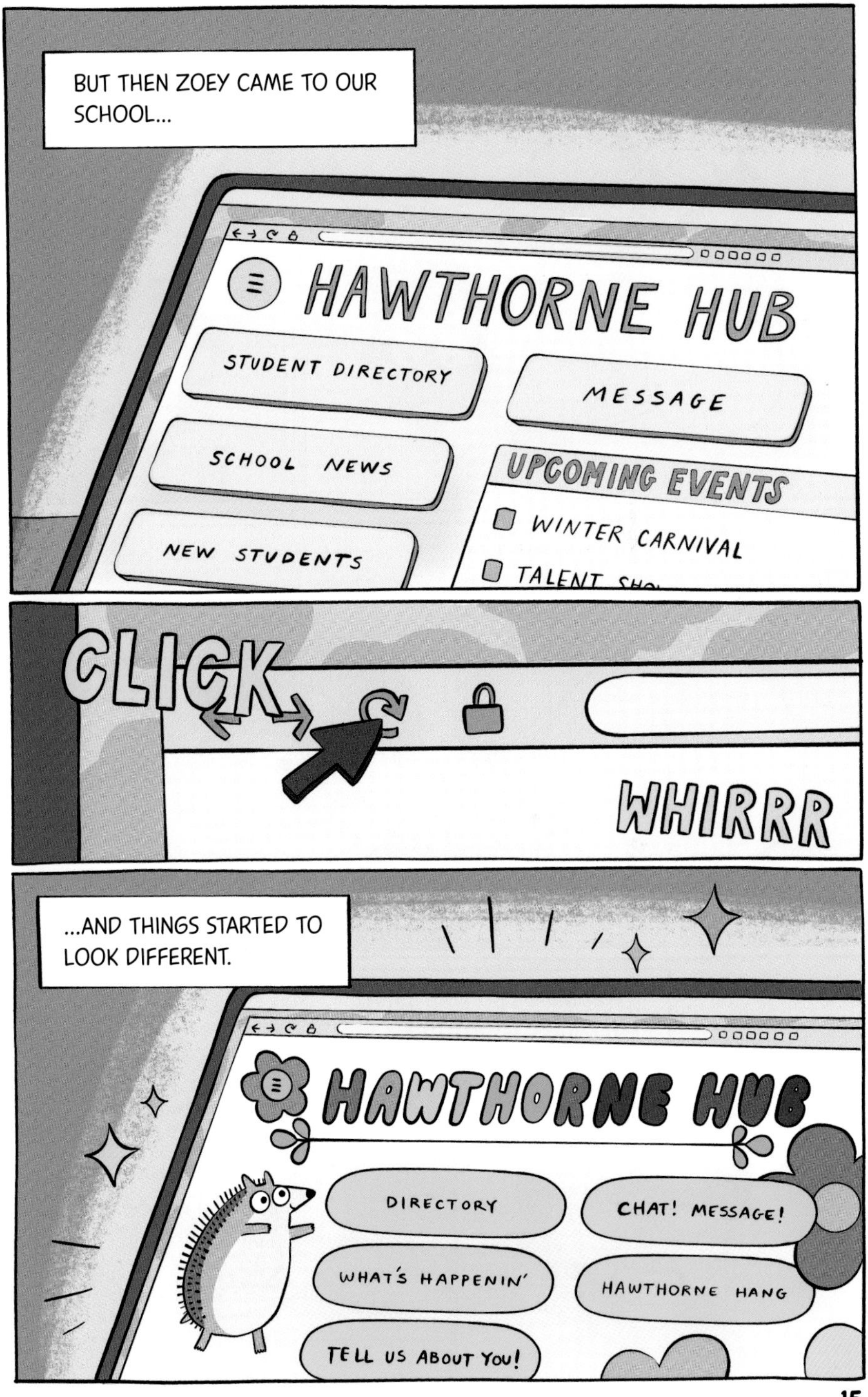
BUT THEN ZOEY CAME TO OUR SCHOOL...
HAWTHORNE HUB
STUDENT DIRECTORY
MESSAGE
SCHOOL NEWS
UPCOMING EVENTS
WINTER CARNIVAL
NEW STUDENTS
CLICK
WHIRRR
...AND THINGS STARTED TO LOOK DIFFERENT.
HAWTHORNE HUB
DIRECTORY
CHAT! MESSAGE!
WHAT'S HAPPENIN'
HAWTHORNE HANG
TELL US ABOUT YOU!

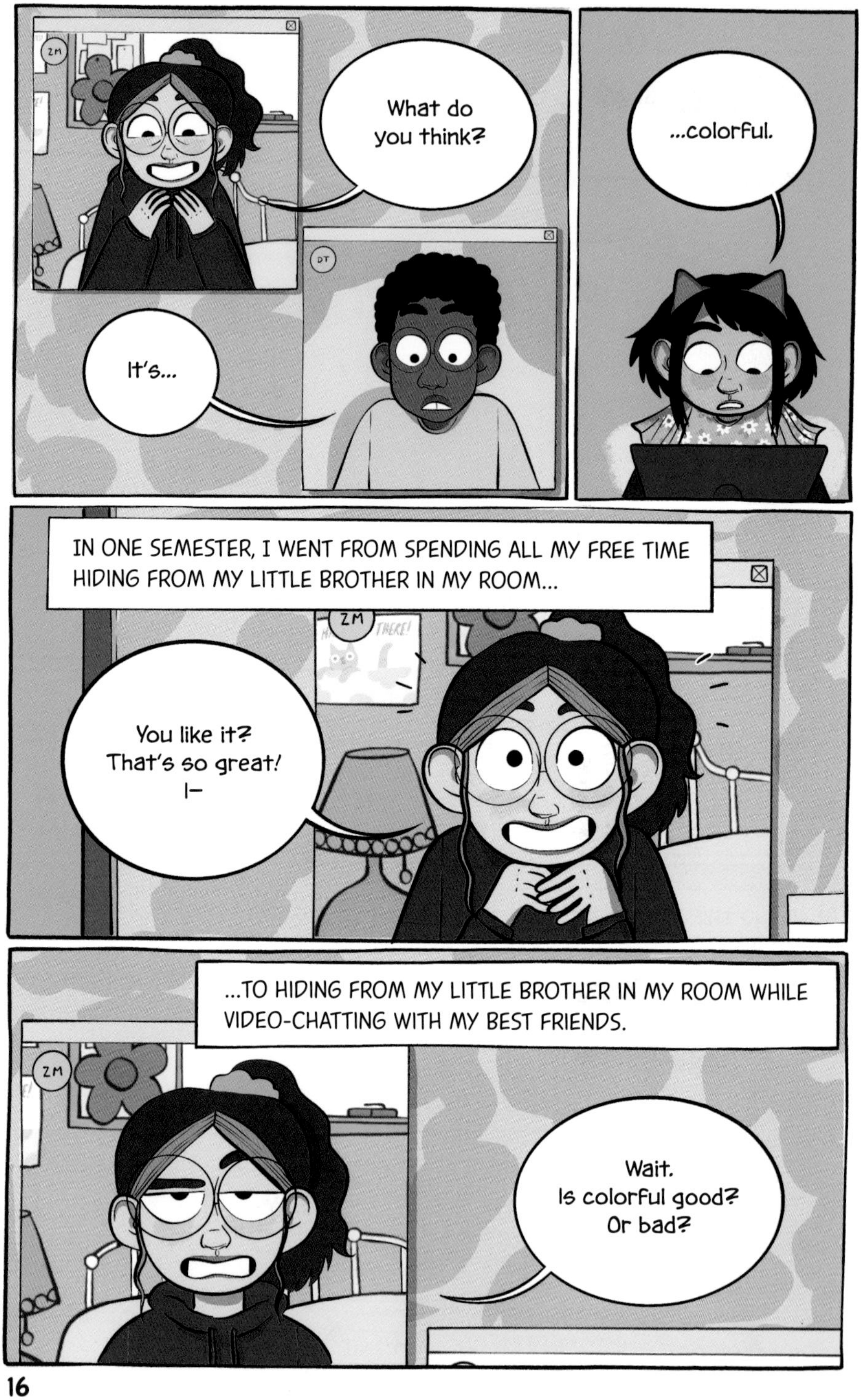
ZM
What do you think?
DT
It's...
...colorful.
IN ONE SEMESTER, I WENT FROM SPENDING ALL MY FREE TIME HIDING FROM MY LITTLE BROTHER IN MY ROOM...
ZM
You like it? That's so great! I—
...TO HIDING FROM MY LITTLE BROTHER IN MY ROOM WHILE VIDEO-CHATTING WITH MY BEST FRIENDS.
ZM
Wait. Is colorful good? Or bad?

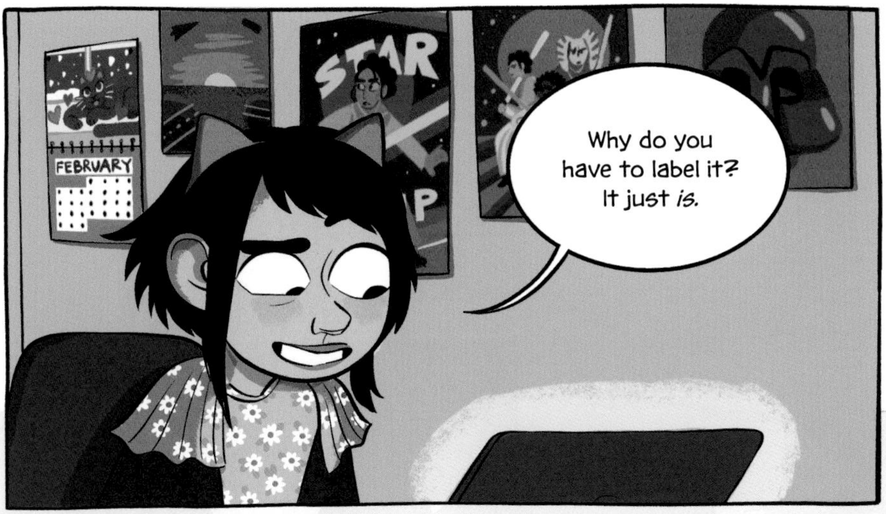
FEBRUARY
STAR
Why do you have to label it? It just *is.*

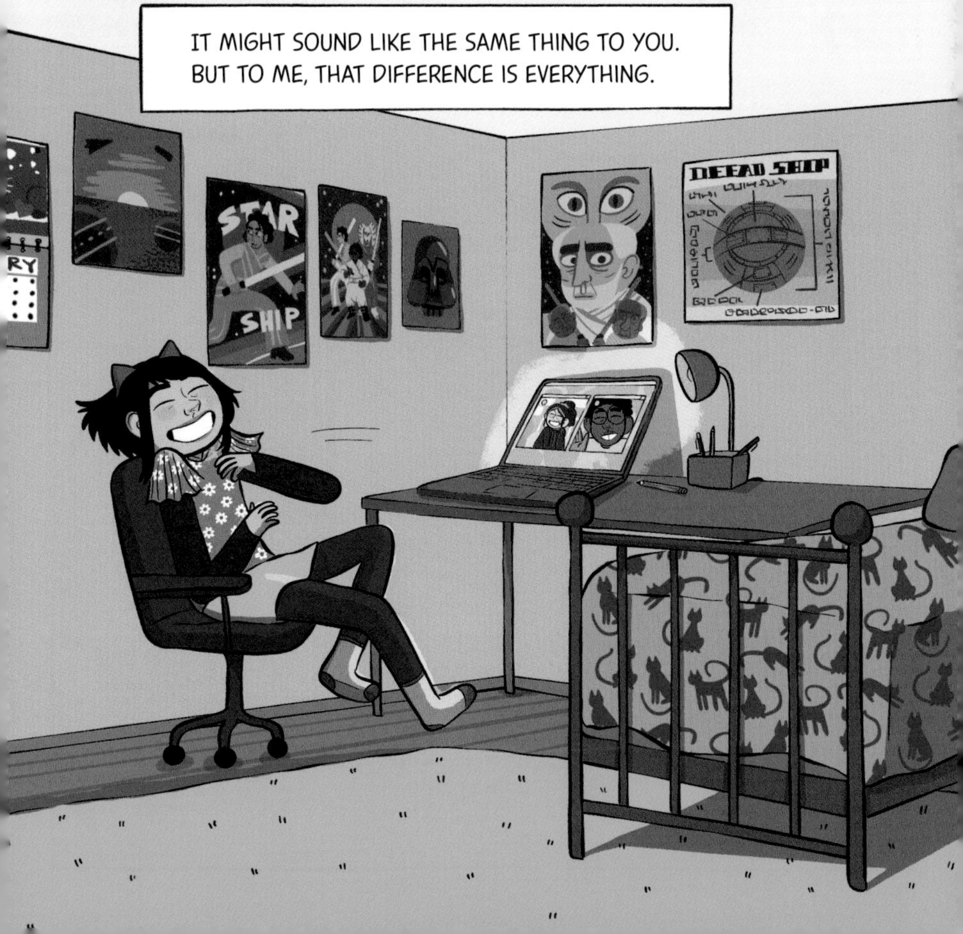
IT MIGHT SOUND LIKE THE SAME THING TO YOU. BUT TO ME, THAT DIFFERENCE IS EVERYTHING.
STAR
SHIP

CHAPTER 3

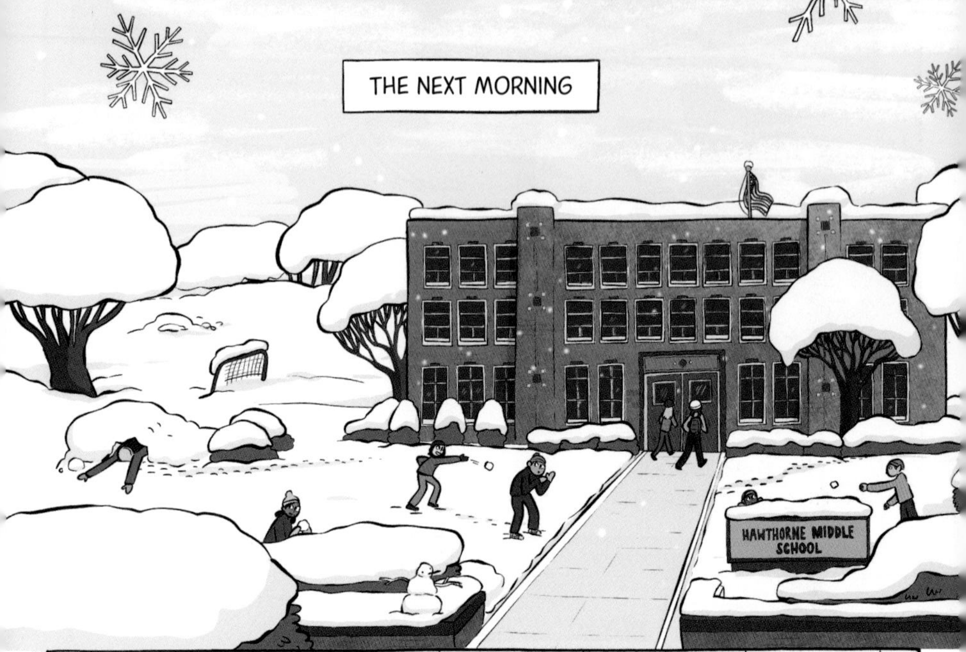
THE NEXT MORNING
HAWTHORNE MIDDLE SCHOOL

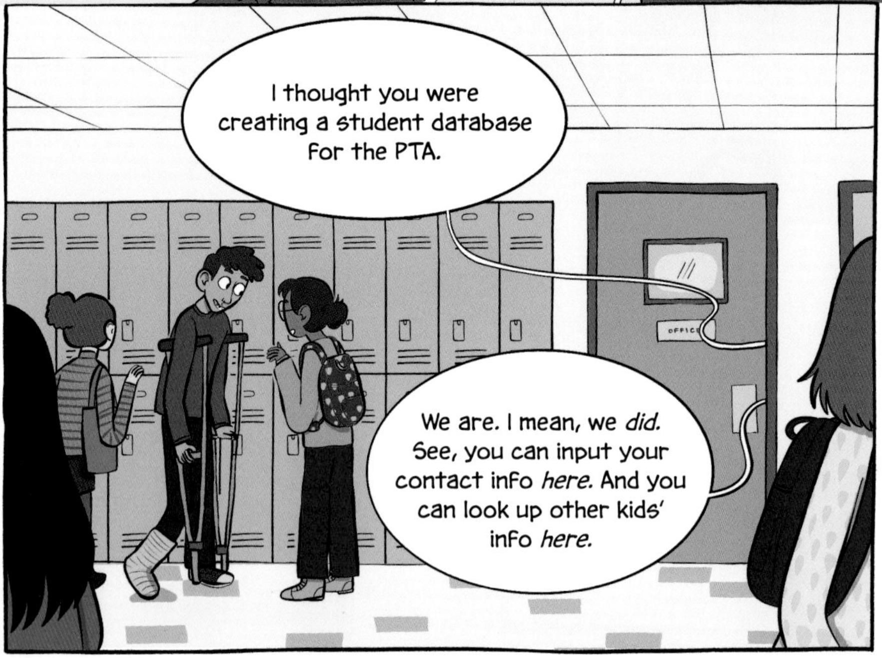
I thought you were creating a student database for the PTA.
OFFICE
We are. I mean, we *did.* See, you can input your contact info *here.* And you can look up other kids' info *here.*

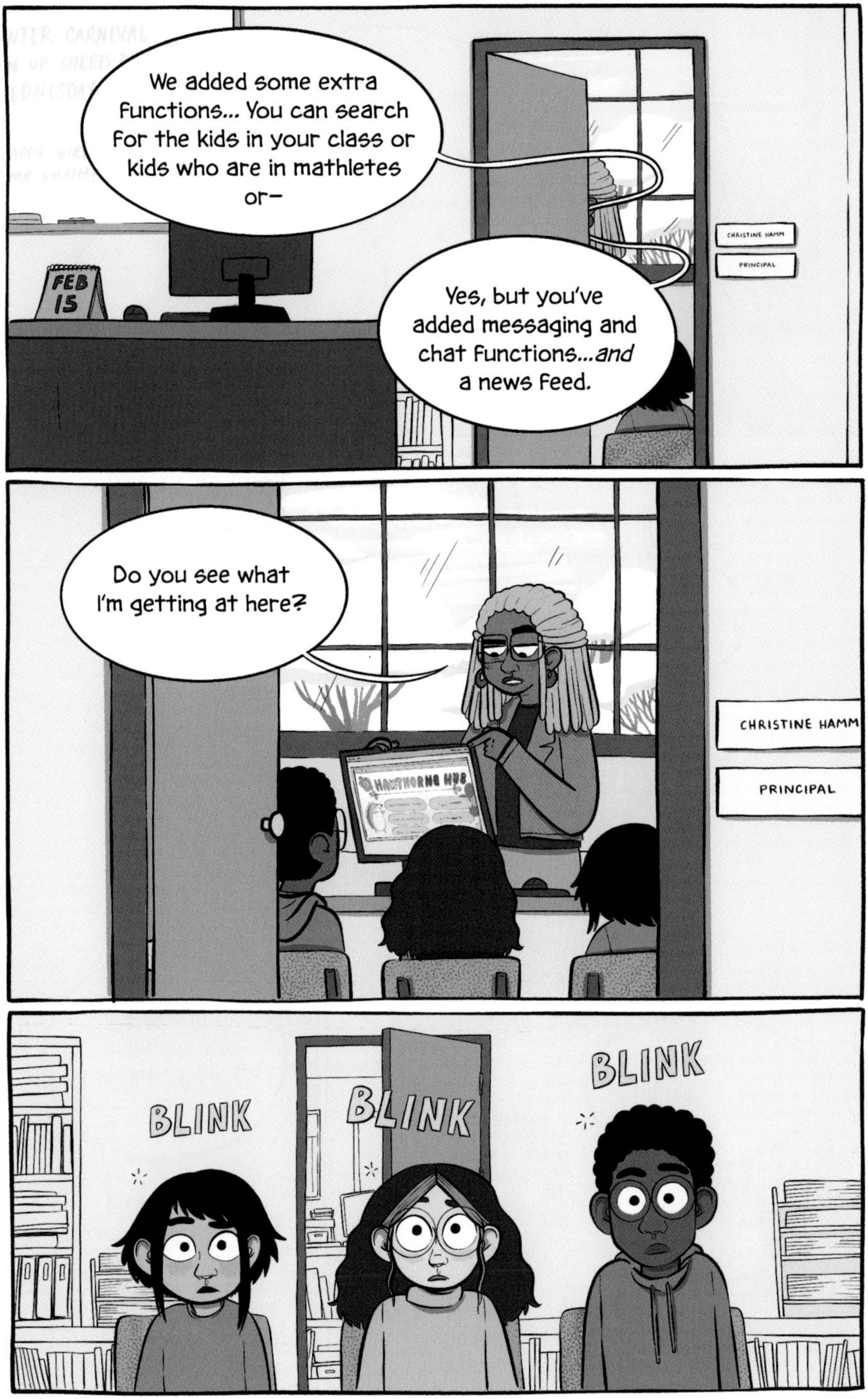
We added some extra functions... You can search for the kids in your class or kids who are in mathletes or–
FEB 15
CHRISTINE HAMM
PRINCIPAL
Yes, but you've added messaging and chat functions...*and* a news feed.
Do you see what I'm getting at here?
CHRISTINE HAMM
PRINCIPAL
BLINK
BLINK
BLINK

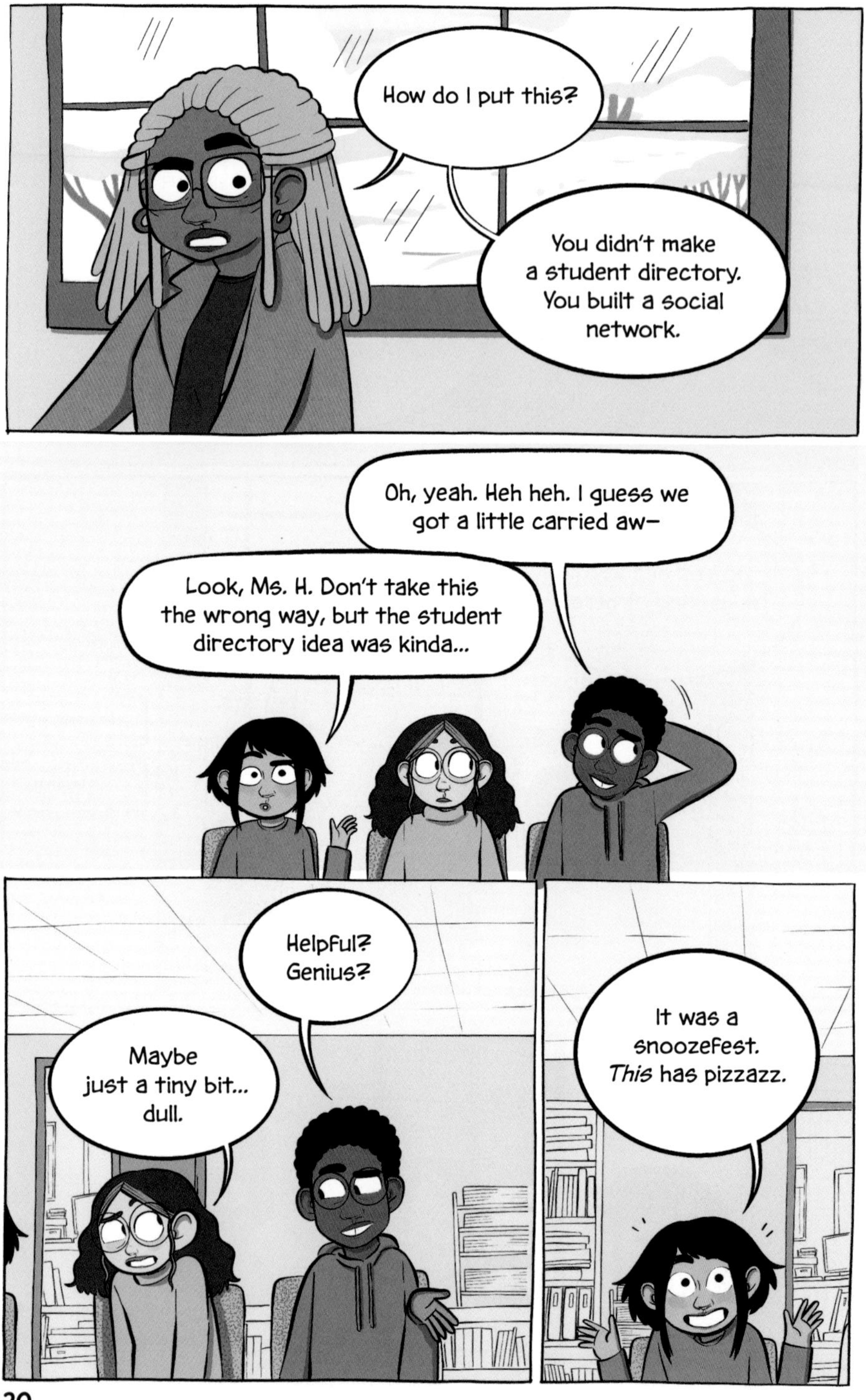
How do I put this?
You didn't make a student directory. You built a social network.
Oh, yeah. Heh heh. I guess we got a little carried aw—
Look, Ms. H. Don't take this the wrong way, but the student directory idea was kinda...
Maybe just a tiny bit... dull.
Helpful? Genius?
It was a snoozefest. *This* has pizzazz.

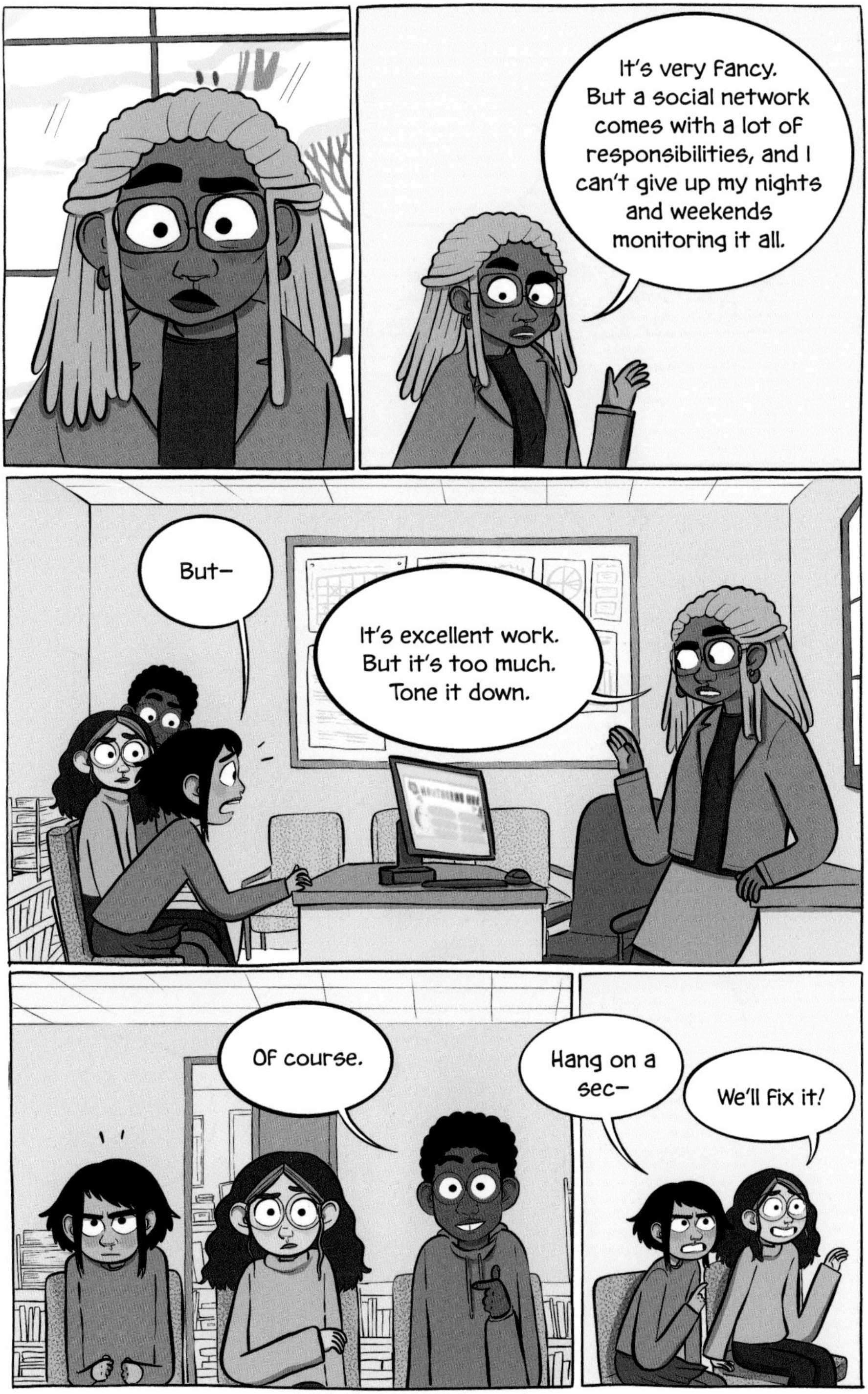
It's very fancy. But a social network comes with a lot of responsibilities, and I can't give up my nights and weekends monitoring it all.
But–
It's excellent work. But it's too much. Tone it down.
Of course.
Hang on a sec–
We'll fix it!

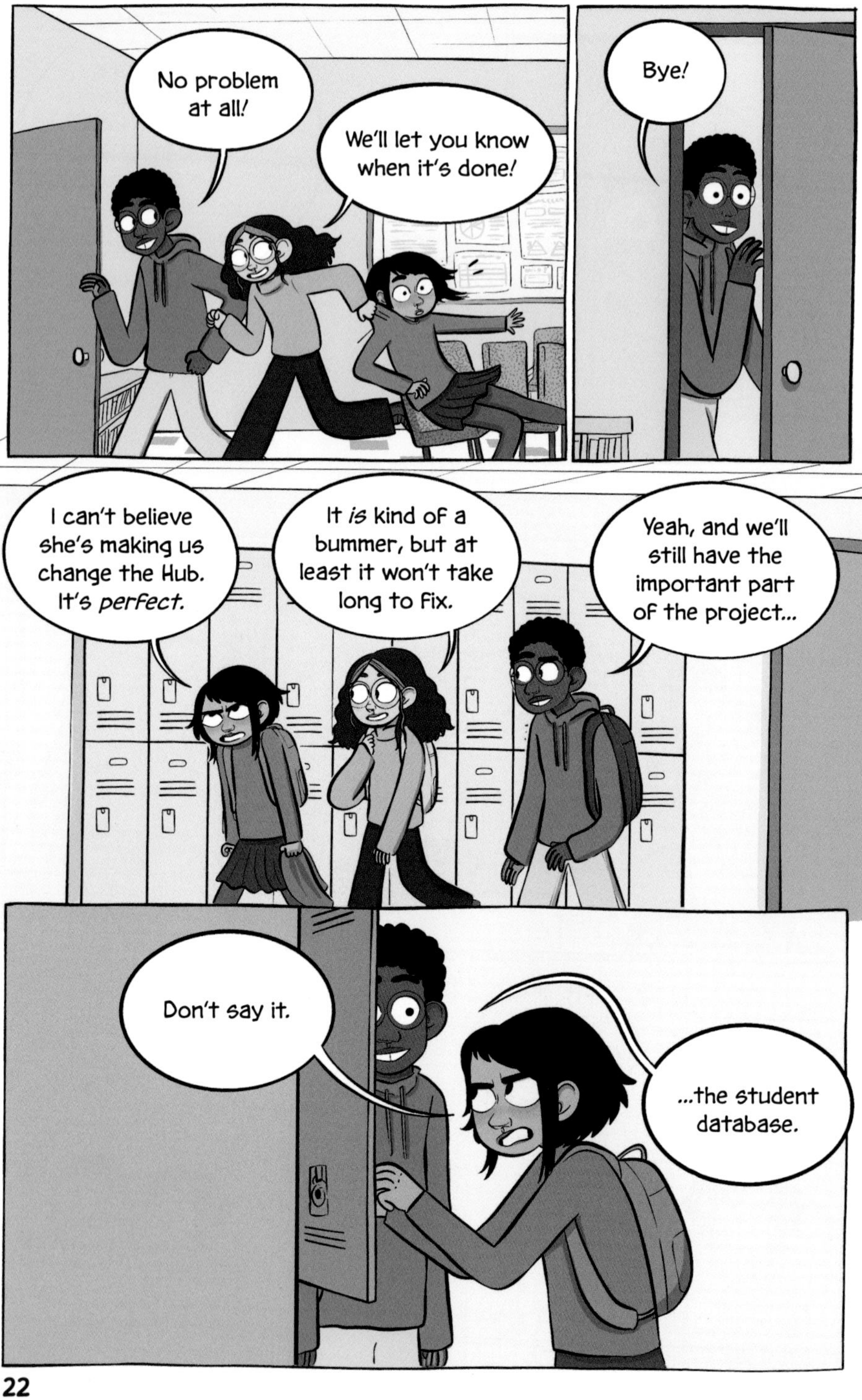
No problem at all!
We'll let you know when it's done!
Bye!
I can't believe she's making us change the Hub. It's *perfect.*
It *is* kind of a bummer, but at least it won't take long to fix.
Yeah, and we'll still have the important part of the project...
Don't say it.
...the student database.

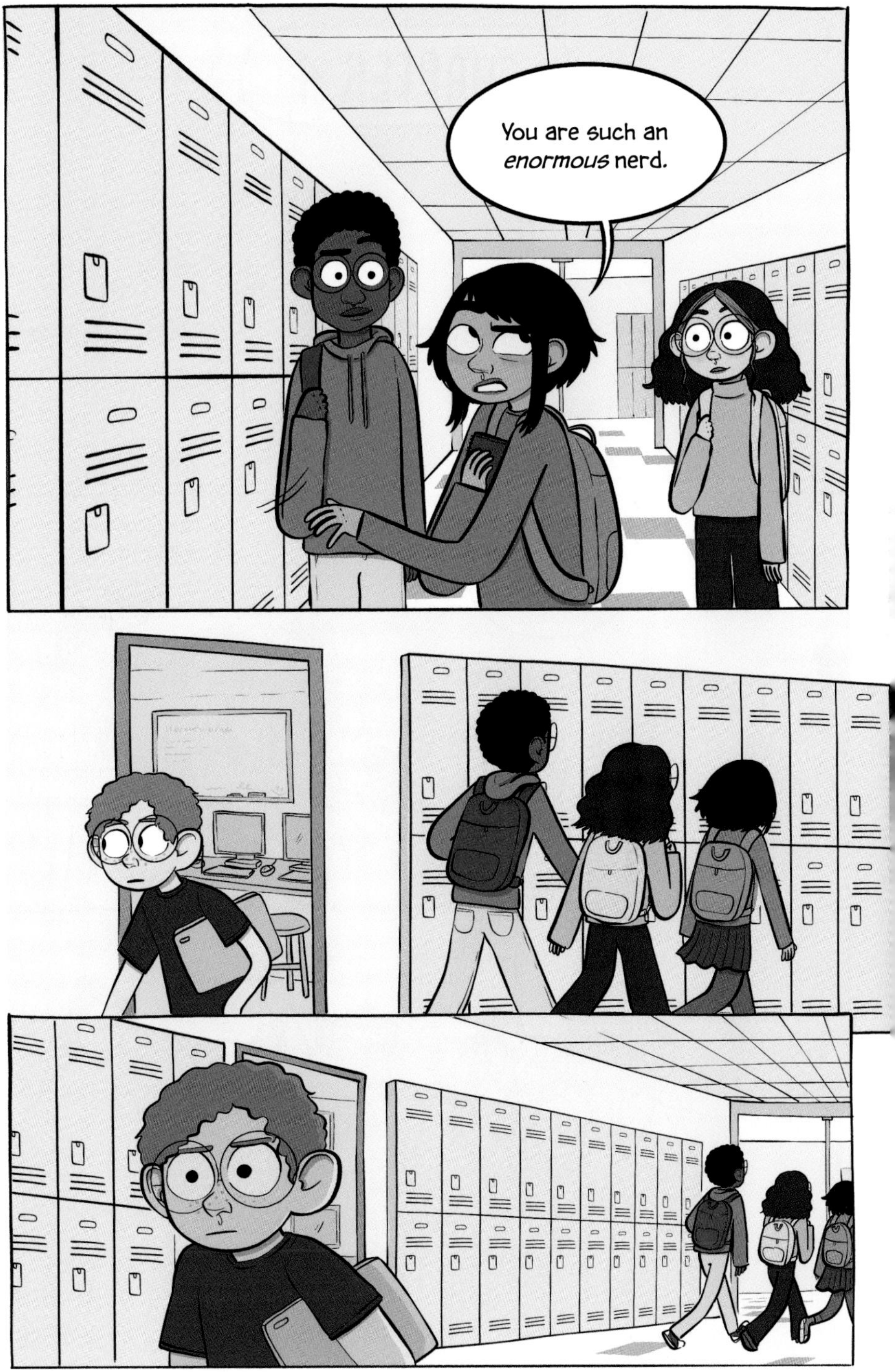
You are such an *enormous* nerd.

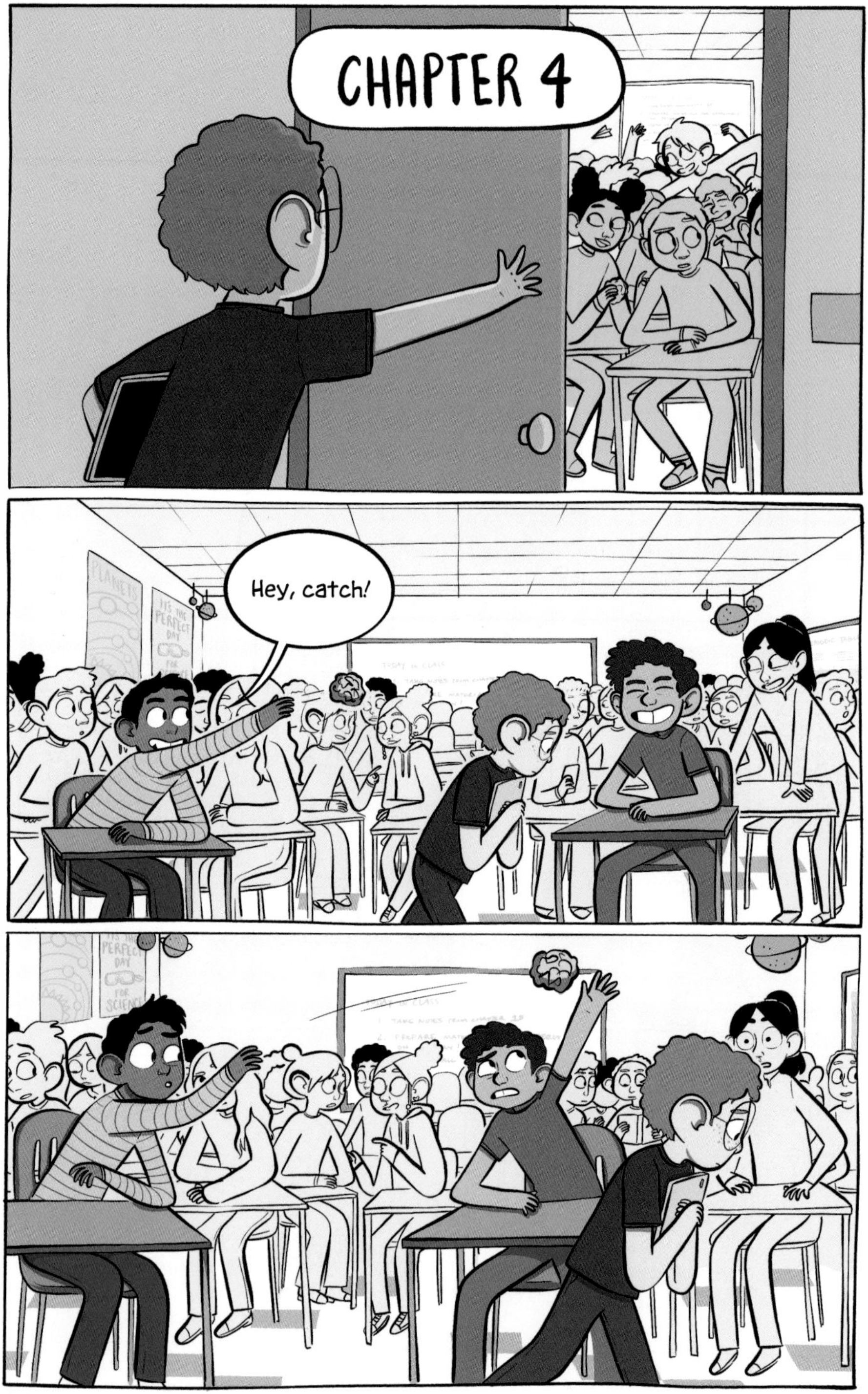
CHAPTER 4
Hey, catch!

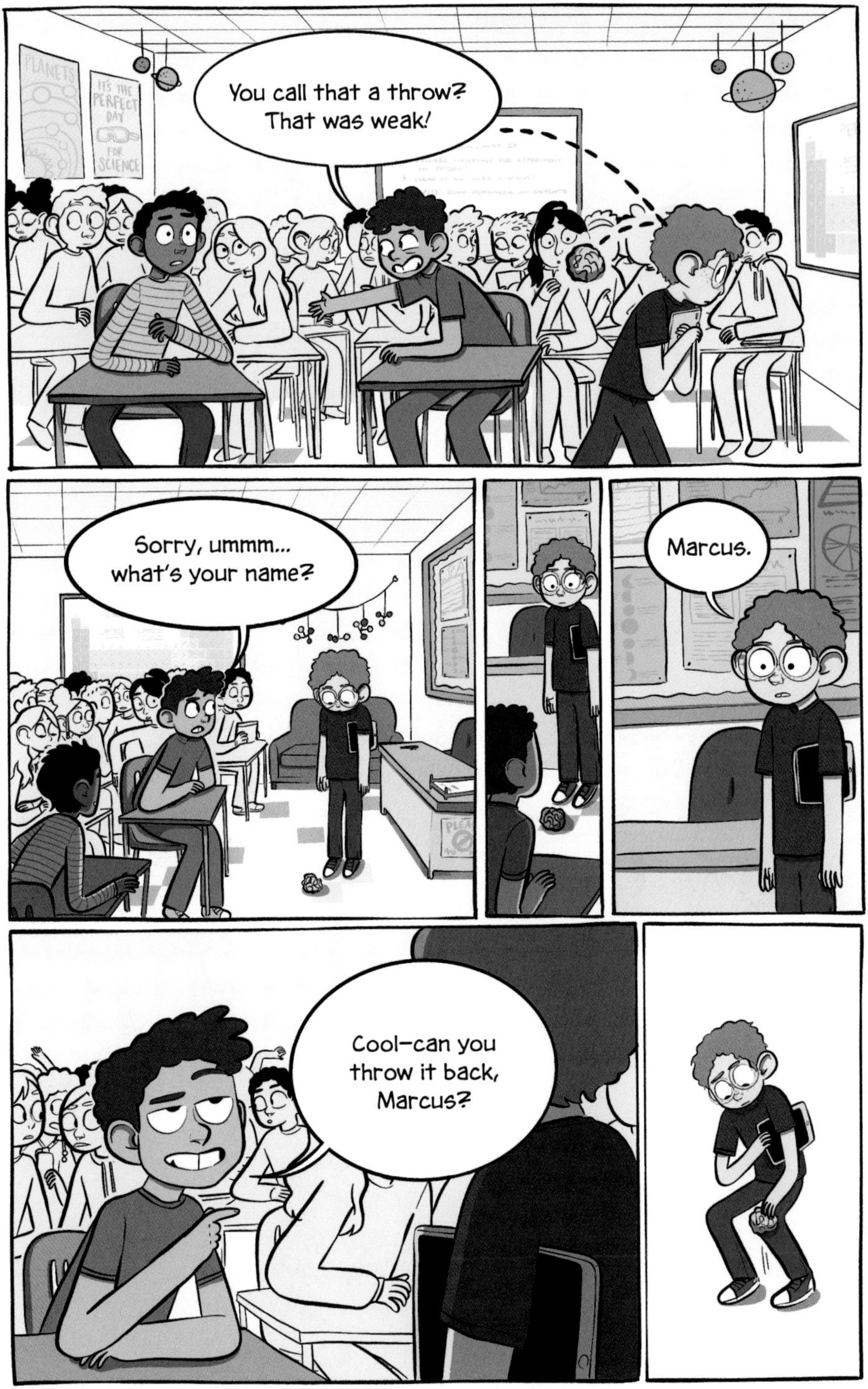
You call that a throw? That was weak!
Sorry, ummm... what's your name?
Marcus.
Cool—can you throw it back, Marcus?

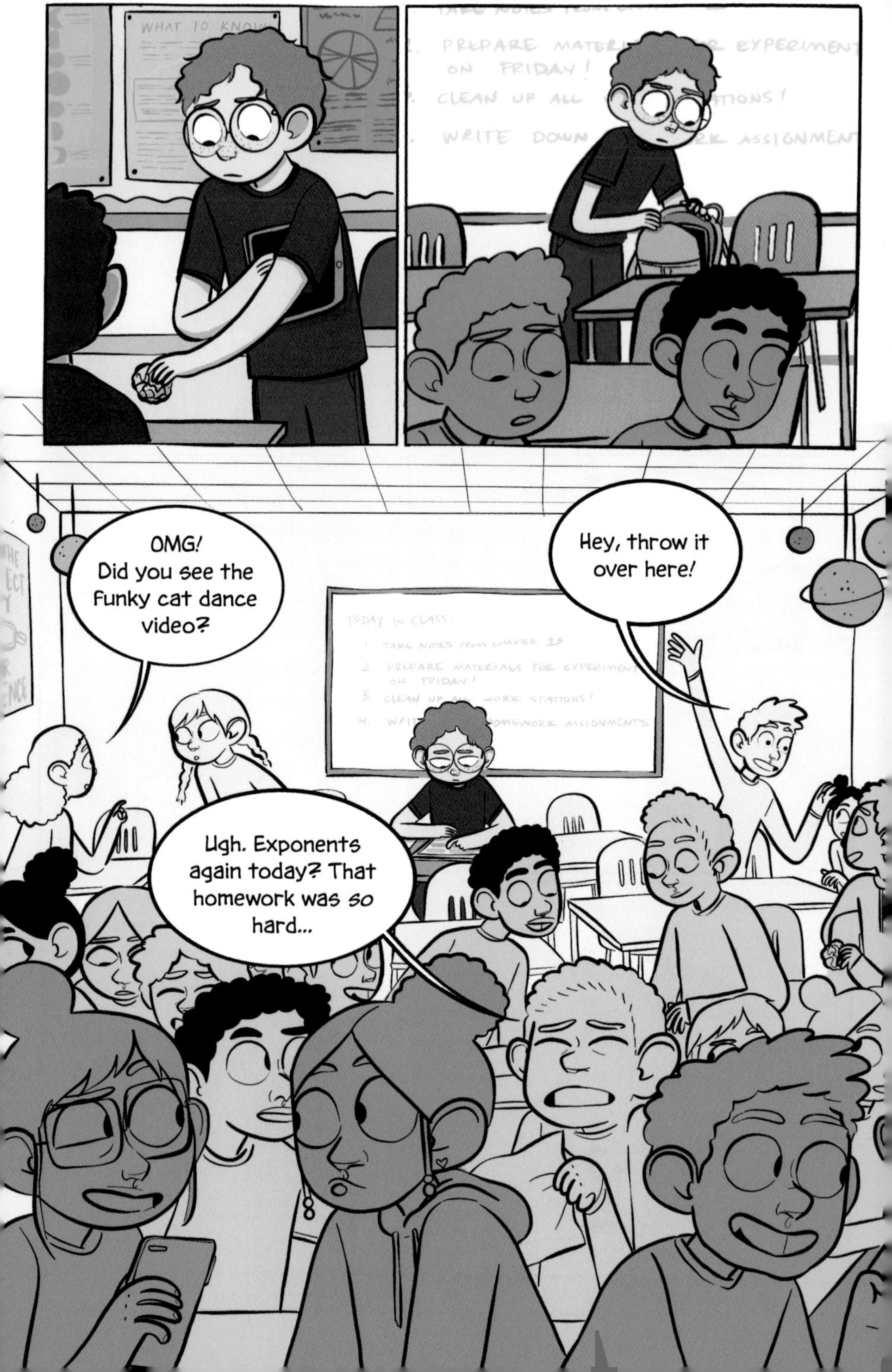
OMG! Did you see the funky cat dance video?
Hey, throw it over here!
Ugh. Exponents again today? That homework was *so* hard...

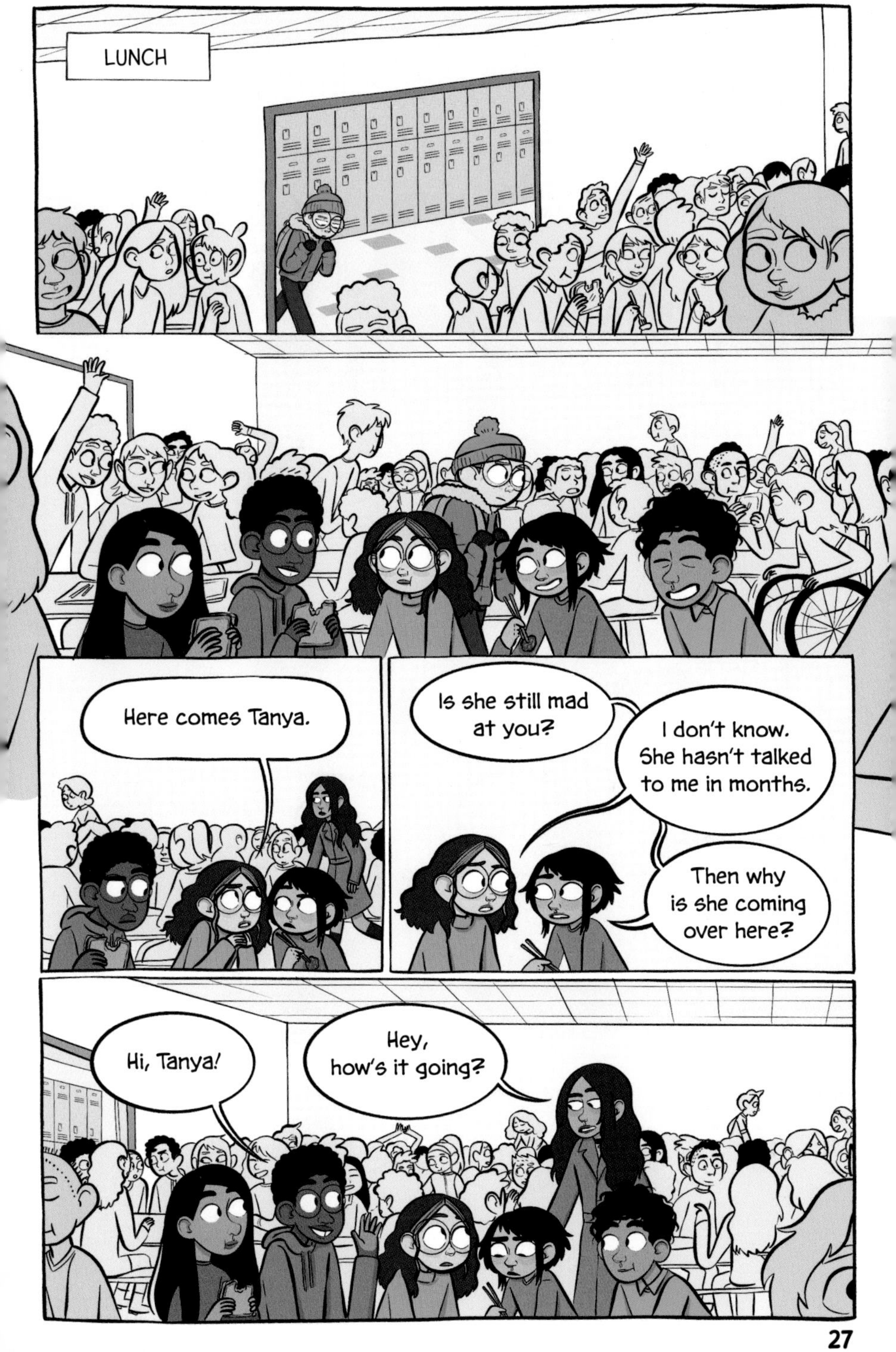
LUNCH
Here comes Tanya.
Is she still mad at you?
I don't know. She hasn't talked to me in months.
Then why is she coming over here?
Hi, Tanya!
Hey, how's it going?

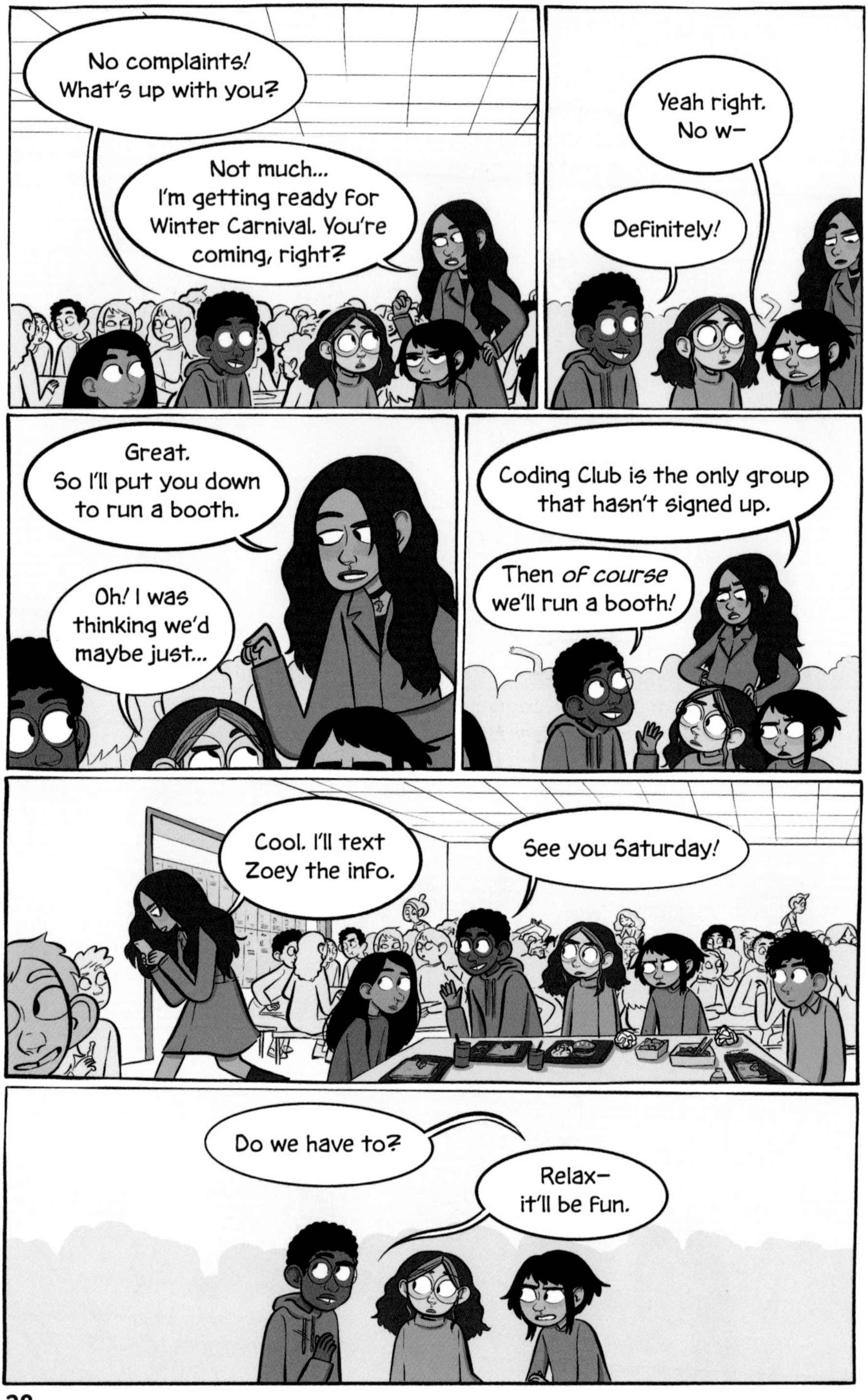
No complaints! What's up with you?
Not much... I'm getting ready for Winter Carnival. You're coming, right?
Yeah right. No w–
Definitely!
Great. So I'll put you down to run a booth.
Oh! I was thinking we'd maybe just...
Coding Club is the only group that hasn't signed up.
Then *of course* we'll run a booth!
Cool. I'll text Zoey the info.
See you Saturday!
Do we have to?
Relax– it'll be fun.

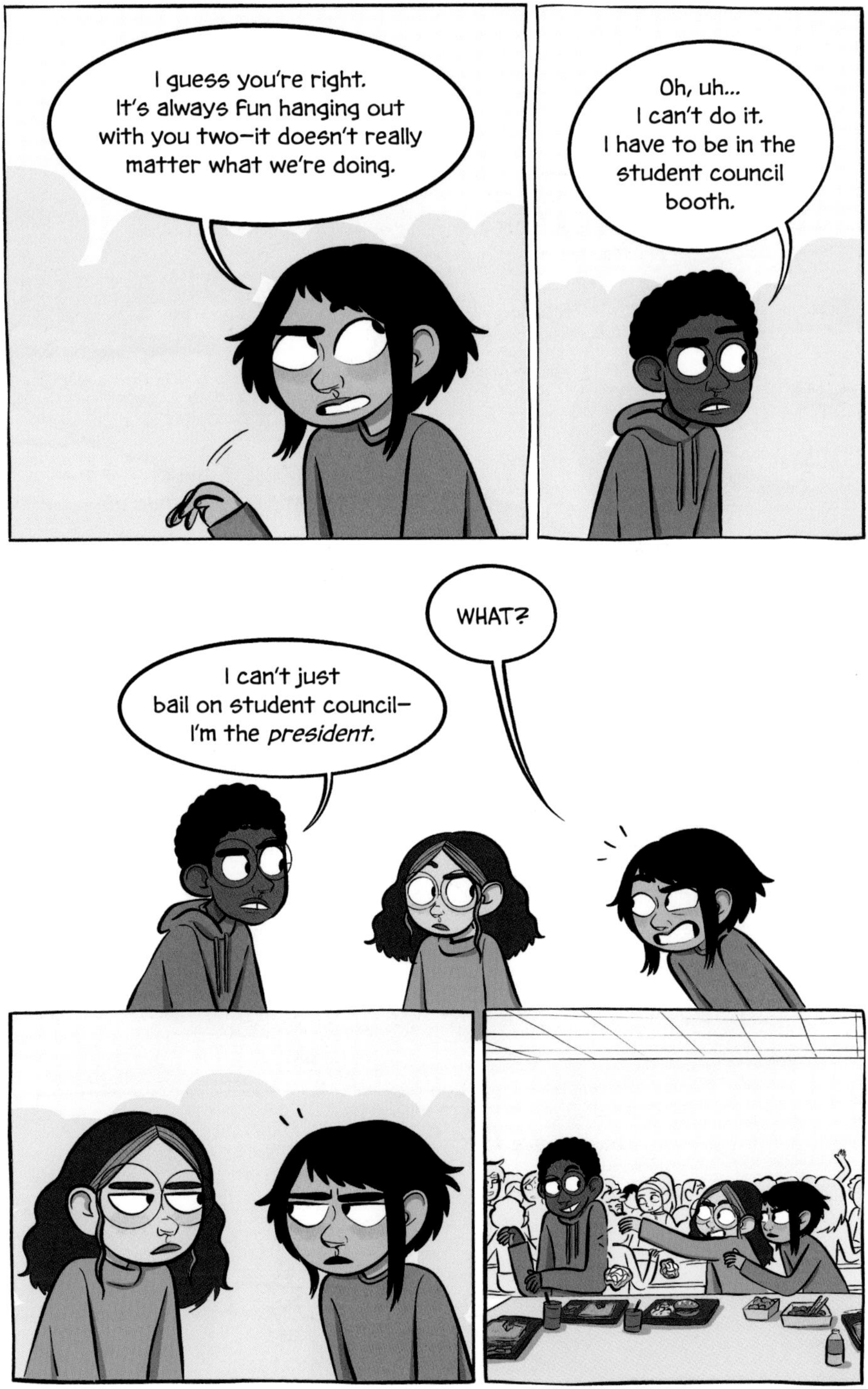
I guess you're right. It's always fun hanging out with you two—it doesn't really matter what we're doing.
Oh, uh... I can't do it. I have to be in the student council booth.
I can't just bail on student council— I'm the *president.*
WHAT?

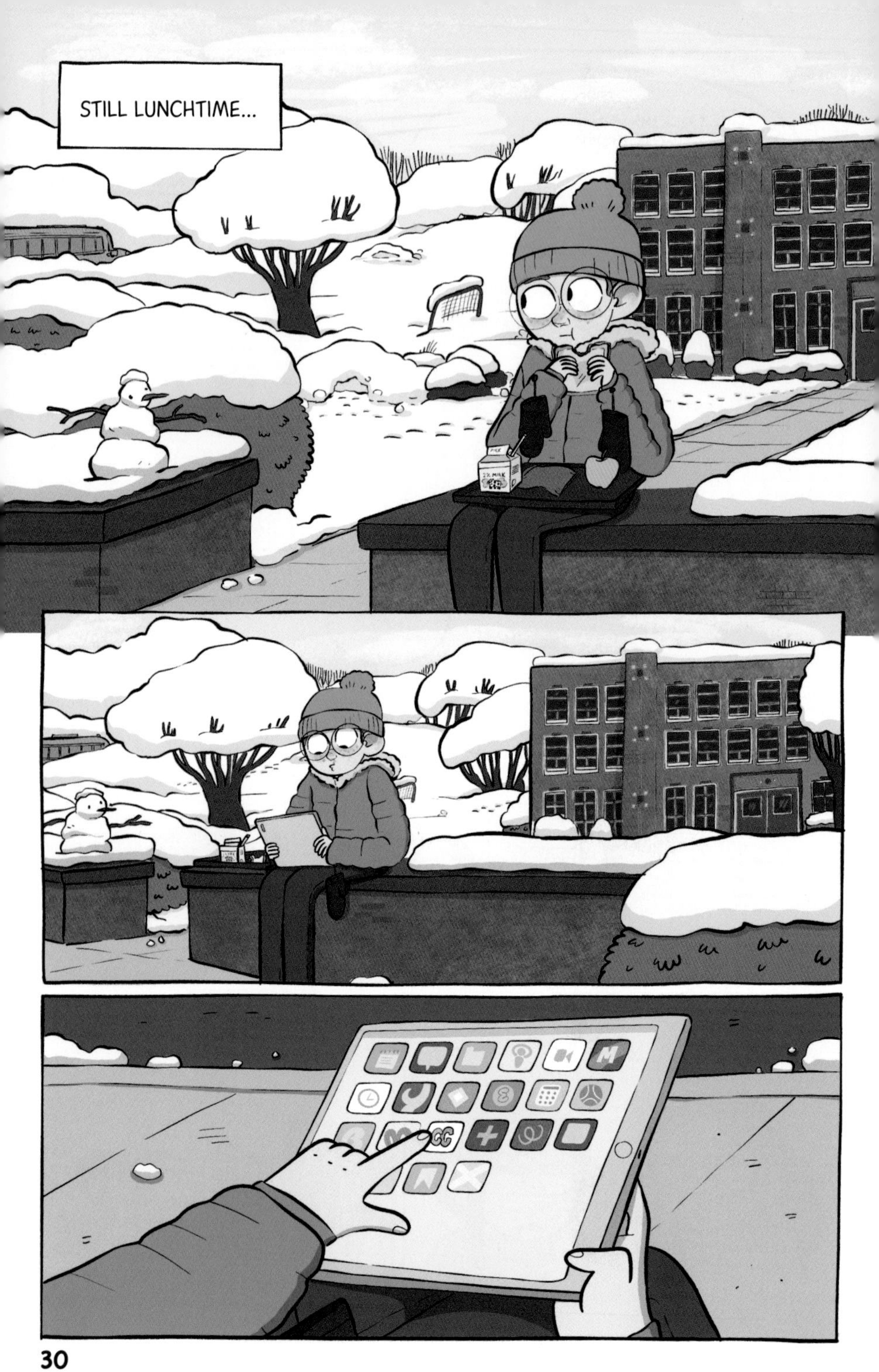
STILL LUNCHTIME...
2% MILK

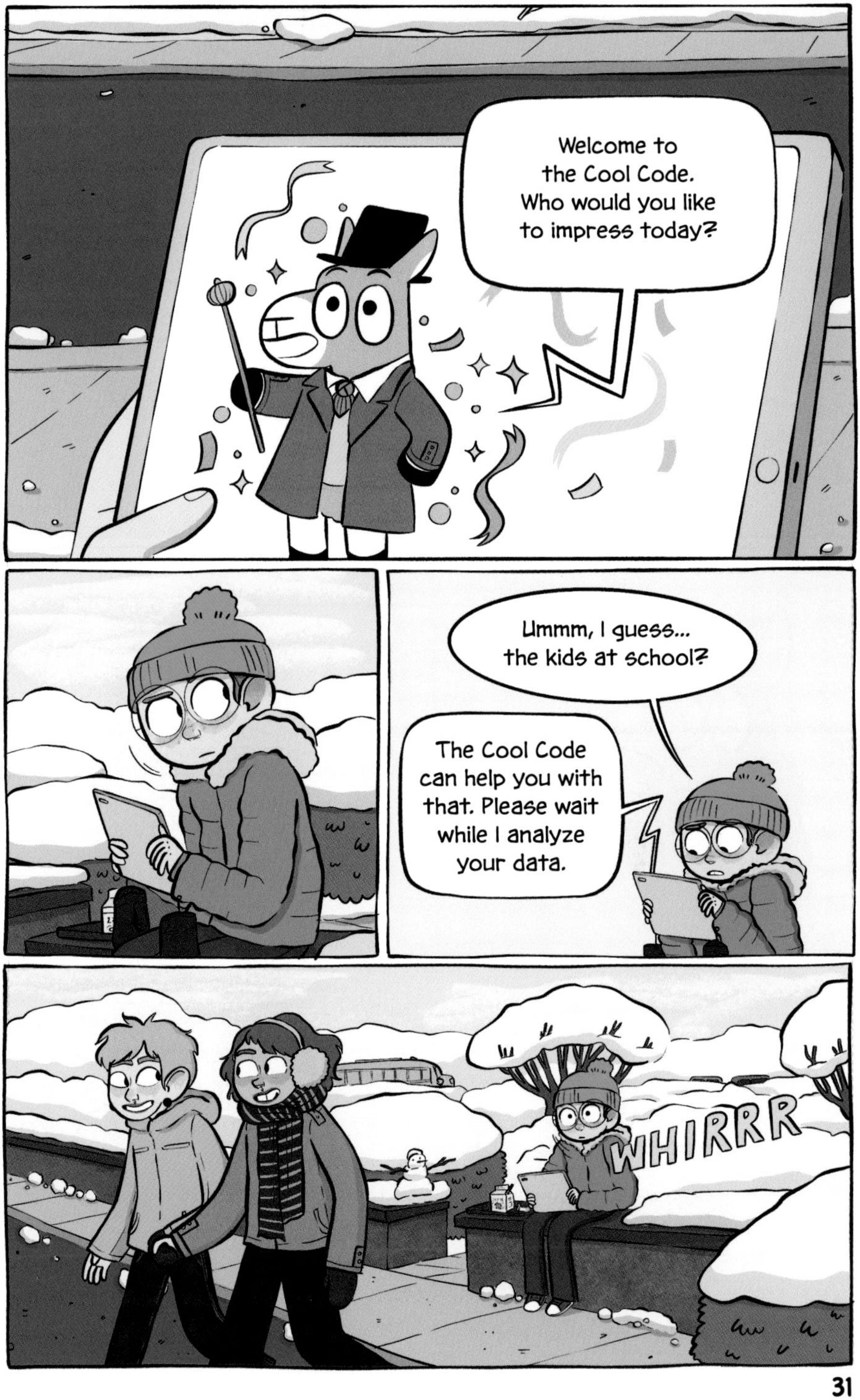
Welcome to the Cool Code. Who would you like to impress today?
Ummm, I guess... the kids at school?
The Cool Code can help you with that. Please wait while I analyze your data.
WHIRRR

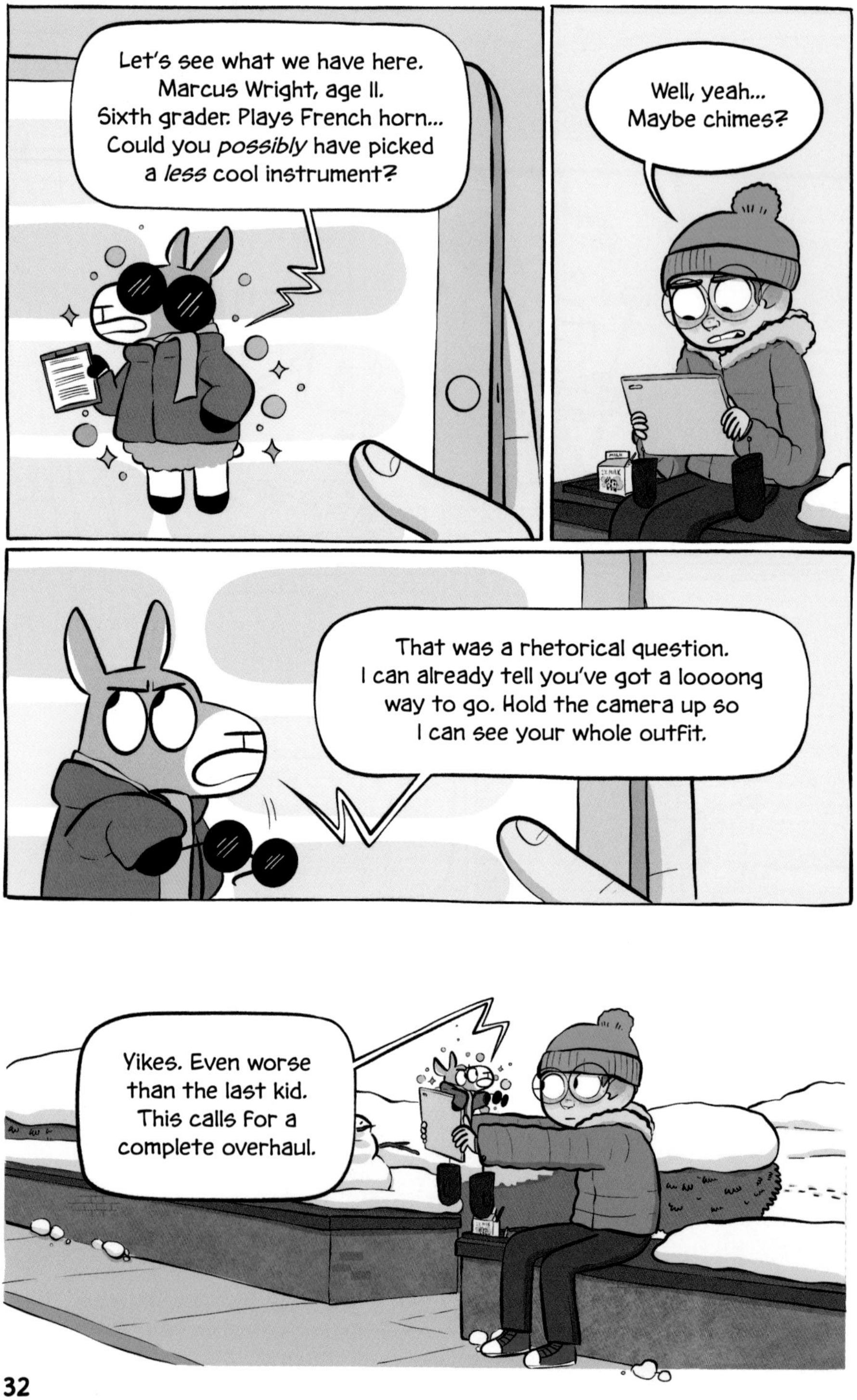
Let's see what we have here. Marcus Wright, age 11. Sixth grader. Plays French horn... Could you *possibly* have picked a *less* cool instrument?
Well, yeah... Maybe chimes?
That was a rhetorical question. I can already tell you've got a loooong way to go. Hold the camera up so I can see your whole outfit.
Yikes. Even worse than the last kid. This calls for a complete overhaul.

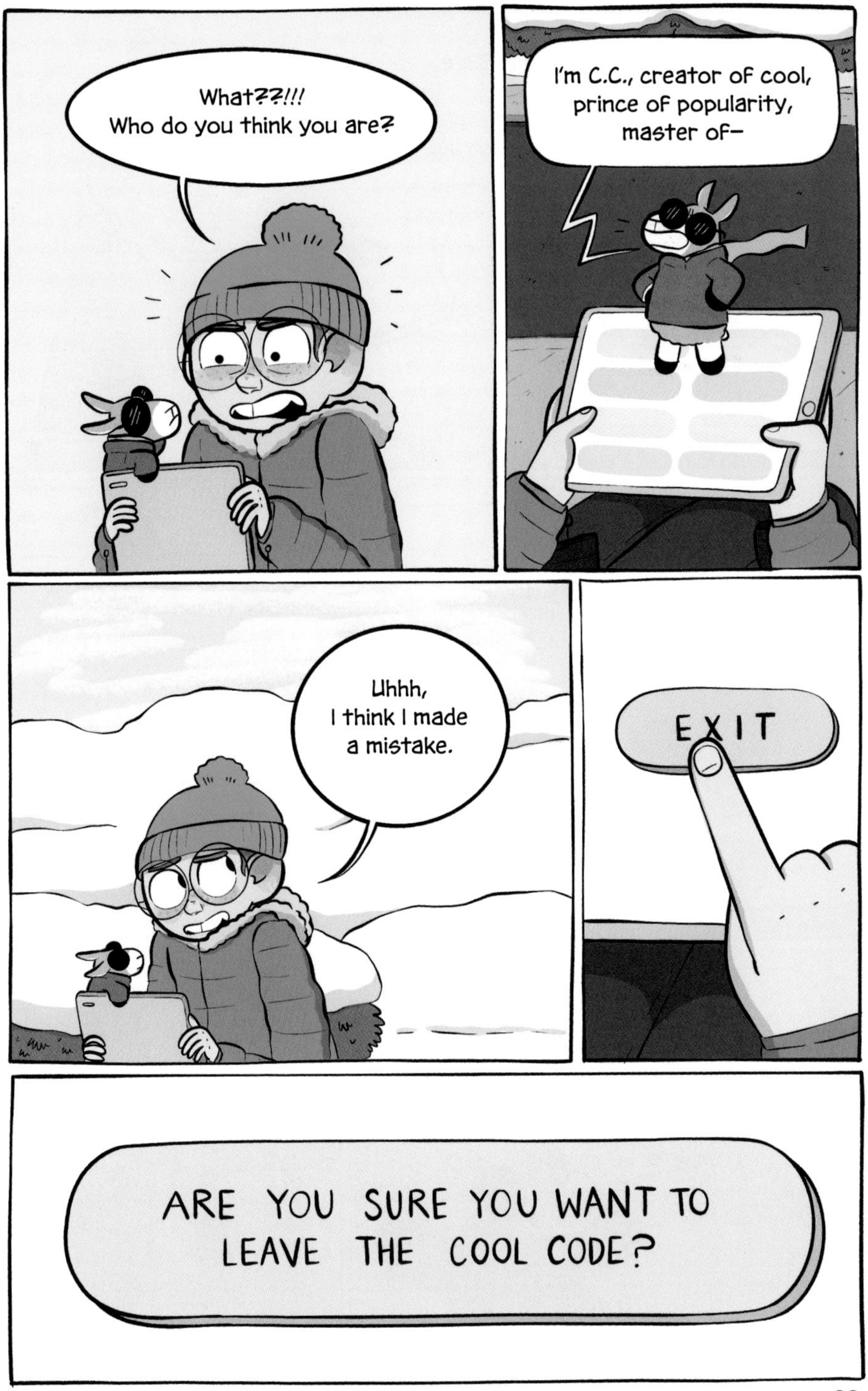
What??!!!
Who do you think you are?
I'm C.C., creator of cool, prince of popularity, master of—
Uhhh, I think I made a mistake.
EXIT
ARE YOU SURE YOU WANT TO LEAVE THE COOL CODE?

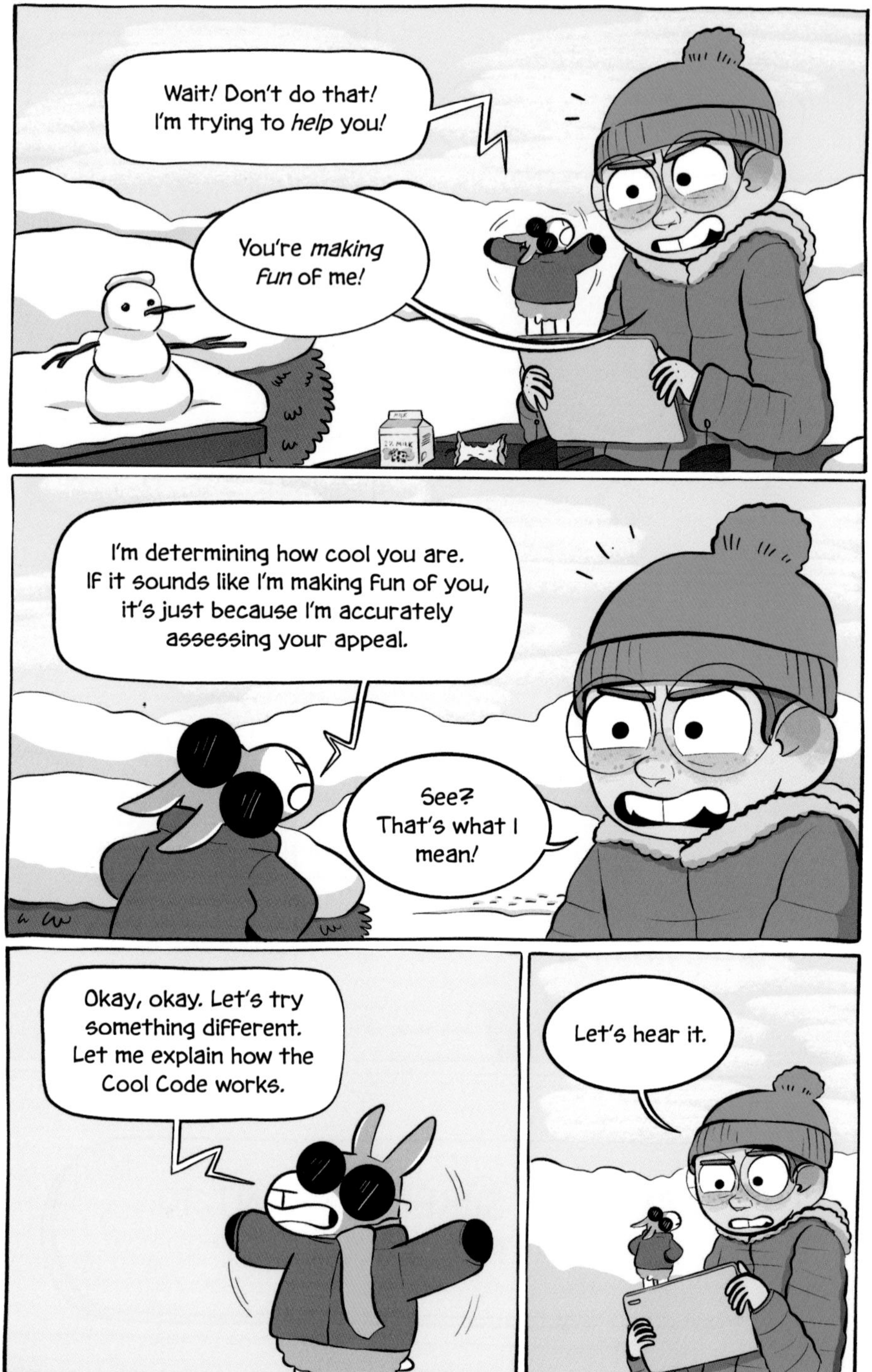
Wait! Don't do that! I'm trying to *help* you!
You're *making fun* of me!
I'm determining how cool you are. If it sounds like I'm making fun of you, it's just because I'm accurately assessing your appeal.
See? That's what I mean!
Okay, okay. Let's try something different. Let me explain how the Cool Code works.
Let's hear it.

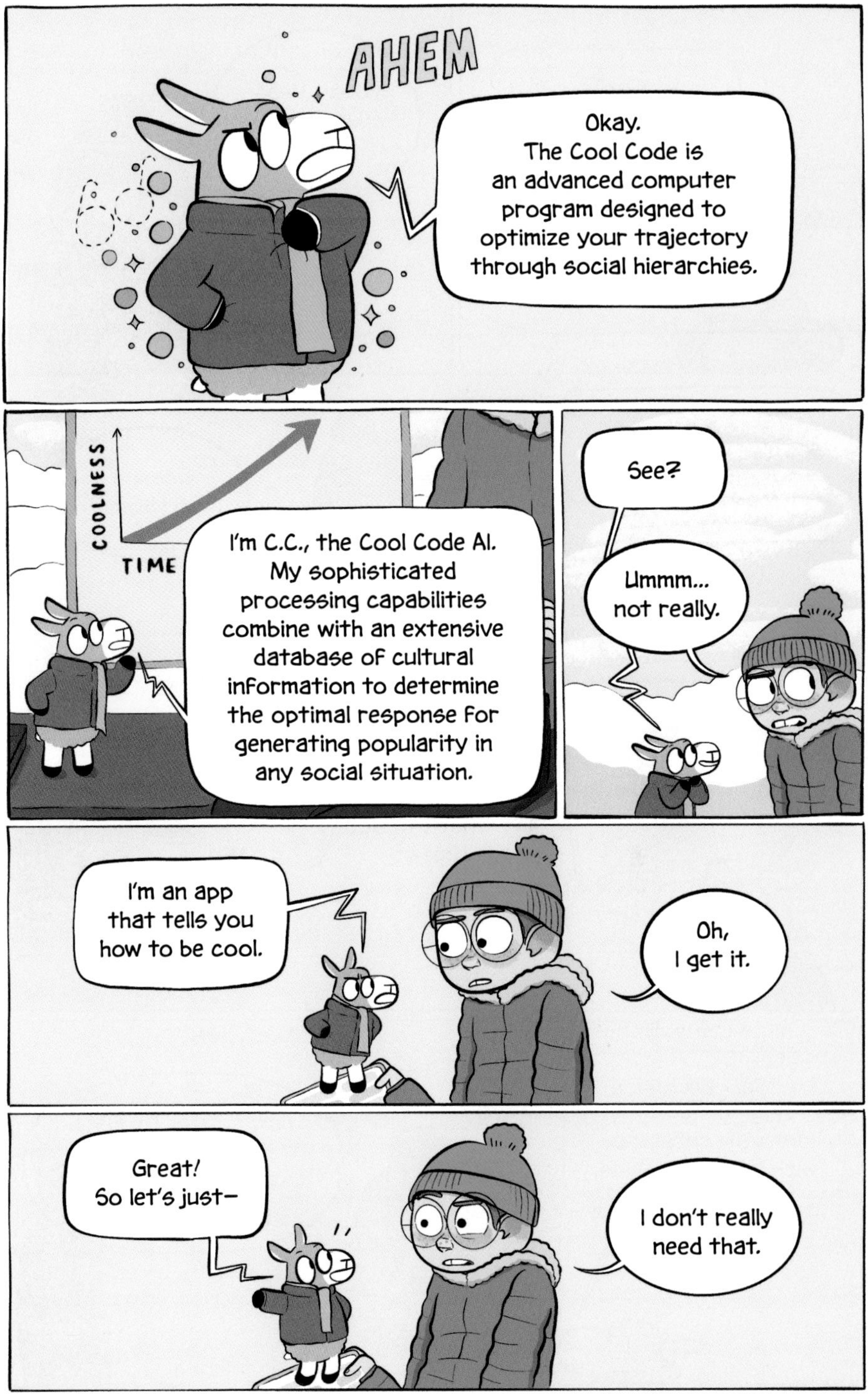
AHEM
Okay. The Cool Code is an advanced computer program designed to optimize your trajectory through social hierarchies.
COOLNESS
TIME
I'm C.C., the Cool Code AI. My sophisticated processing capabilities combine with an extensive database of cultural information to determine the optimal response for generating popularity in any social situation.
See?
Ummm... not really.
I'm an app that tells you how to be cool.
Oh, I get it.
Great! So let's just—
I don't really need that.

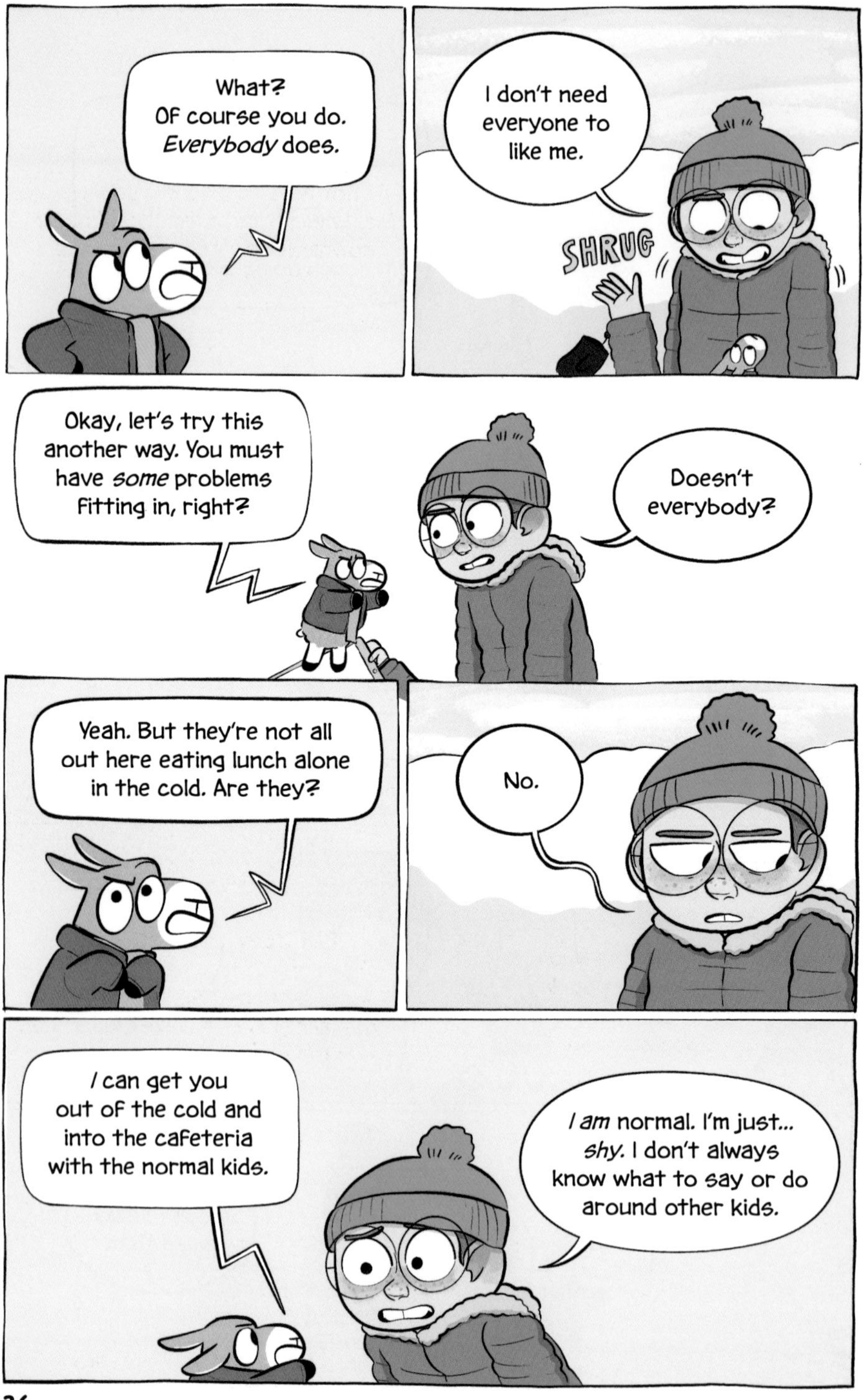
What?
Of course you do.
Everybody does.
I don't need everyone to like me.
SHRUG
Okay, let's try this another way. You must have *some* problems fitting in, right?
Doesn't everybody?
Yeah. But they're not all out here eating lunch alone in the cold. Are they?
No.
I can get you out of the cold and into the cafeteria with the normal kids.
I am normal. I'm just... *shy.* I don't always know what to say or do around other kids.

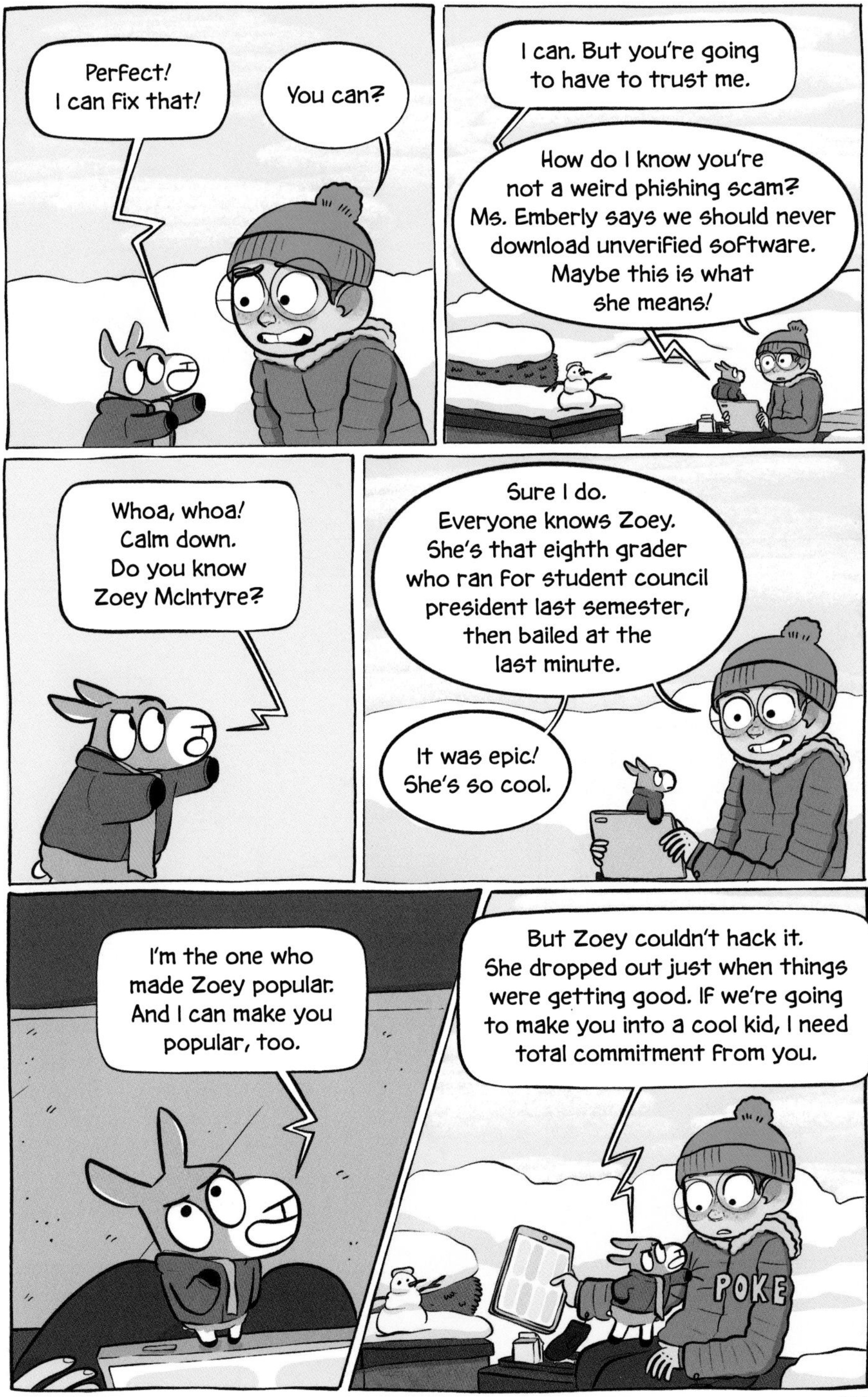
Perfect! I can fix that!
You can?
I can. But you're going to have to trust me.
How do I know you're not a weird phishing scam? Ms. Emberly says we should never download unverified software. Maybe this is what she means!
Whoa, whoa! Calm down. Do you know Zoey McIntyre?
Sure I do. Everyone knows Zoey. She's that eighth grader who ran for student council president last semester, then bailed at the last minute.
It was epic! She's so cool.
I'm the one who made Zoey popular. And I can make you popular, too.
But Zoey couldn't hack it. She dropped out just when things were getting good. If we're going to make you into a cool kid, I need total commitment from you.
POKE

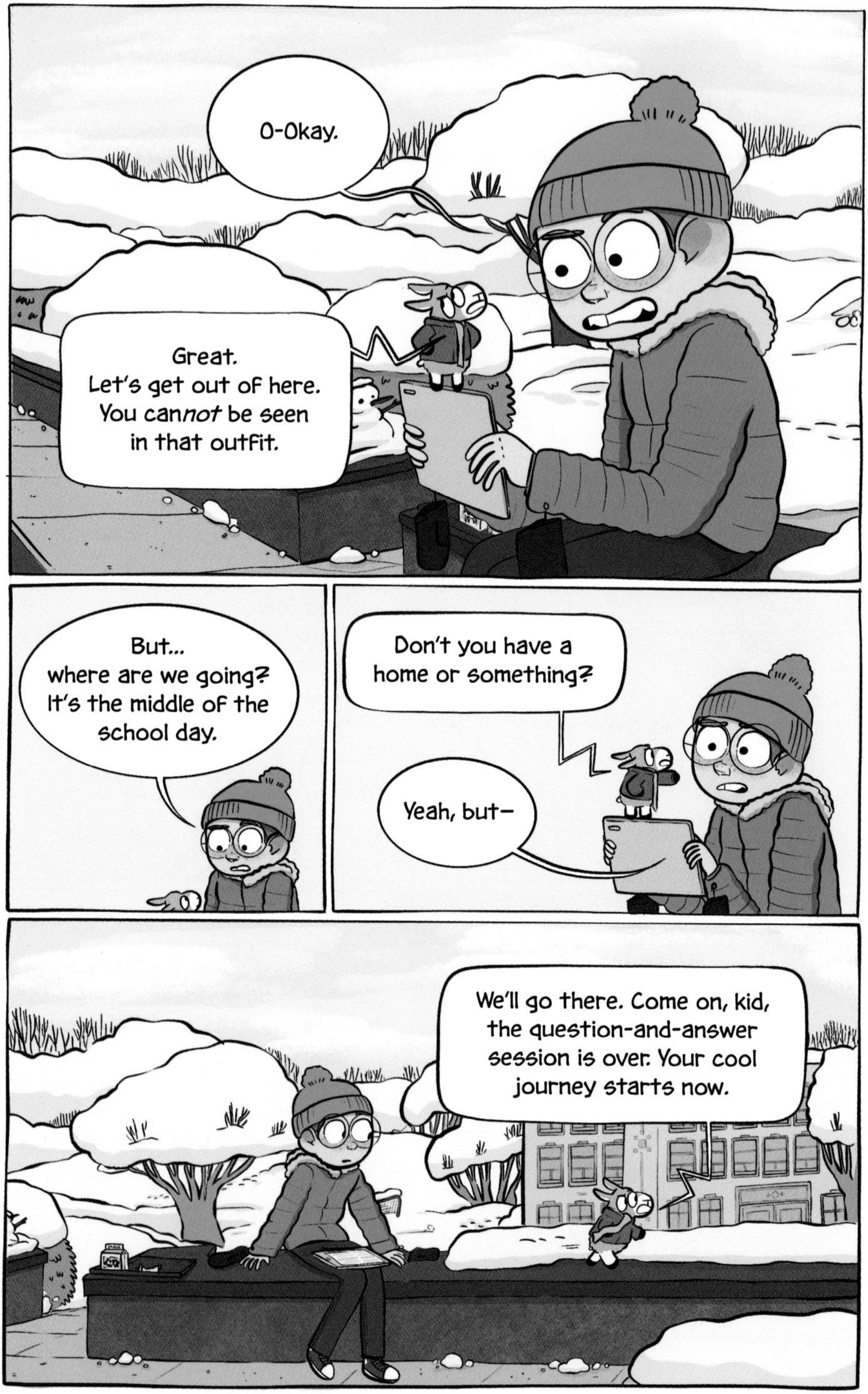
O-Okay.
Great. Let's get out of here. You can*not* be seen in that outfit.
But... where are we going? It's the middle of the school day.
Don't you have a home or something?
Yeah, but–
We'll go there. Come on, kid, the question-and-answer session is over. Your cool journey starts now.

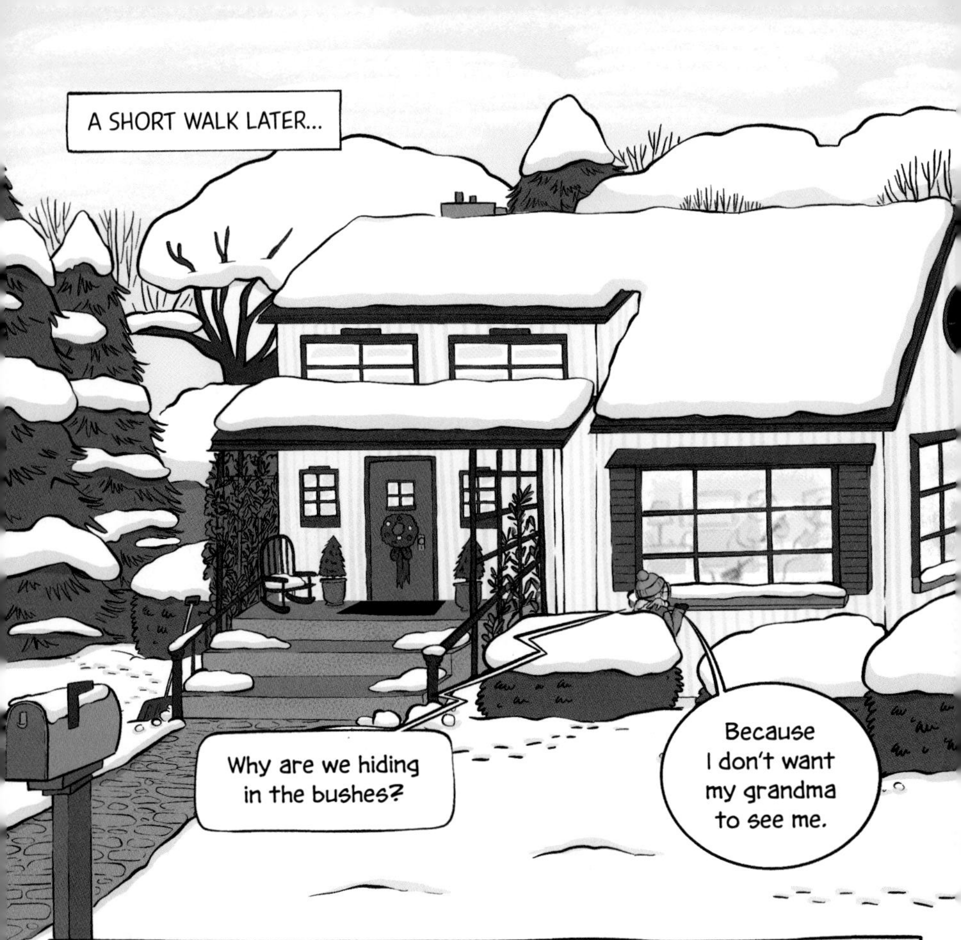
A SHORT WALK LATER...
Why are we hiding in the bushes?
Because I don't want my grandma to see me.

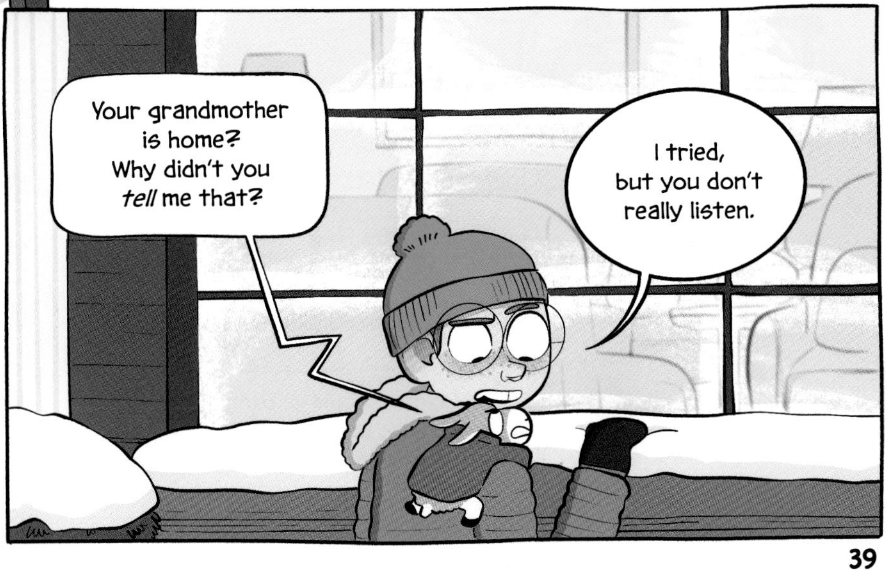
Your grandmother is home? Why didn't you *tell* me that?
I tried, but you don't really listen.

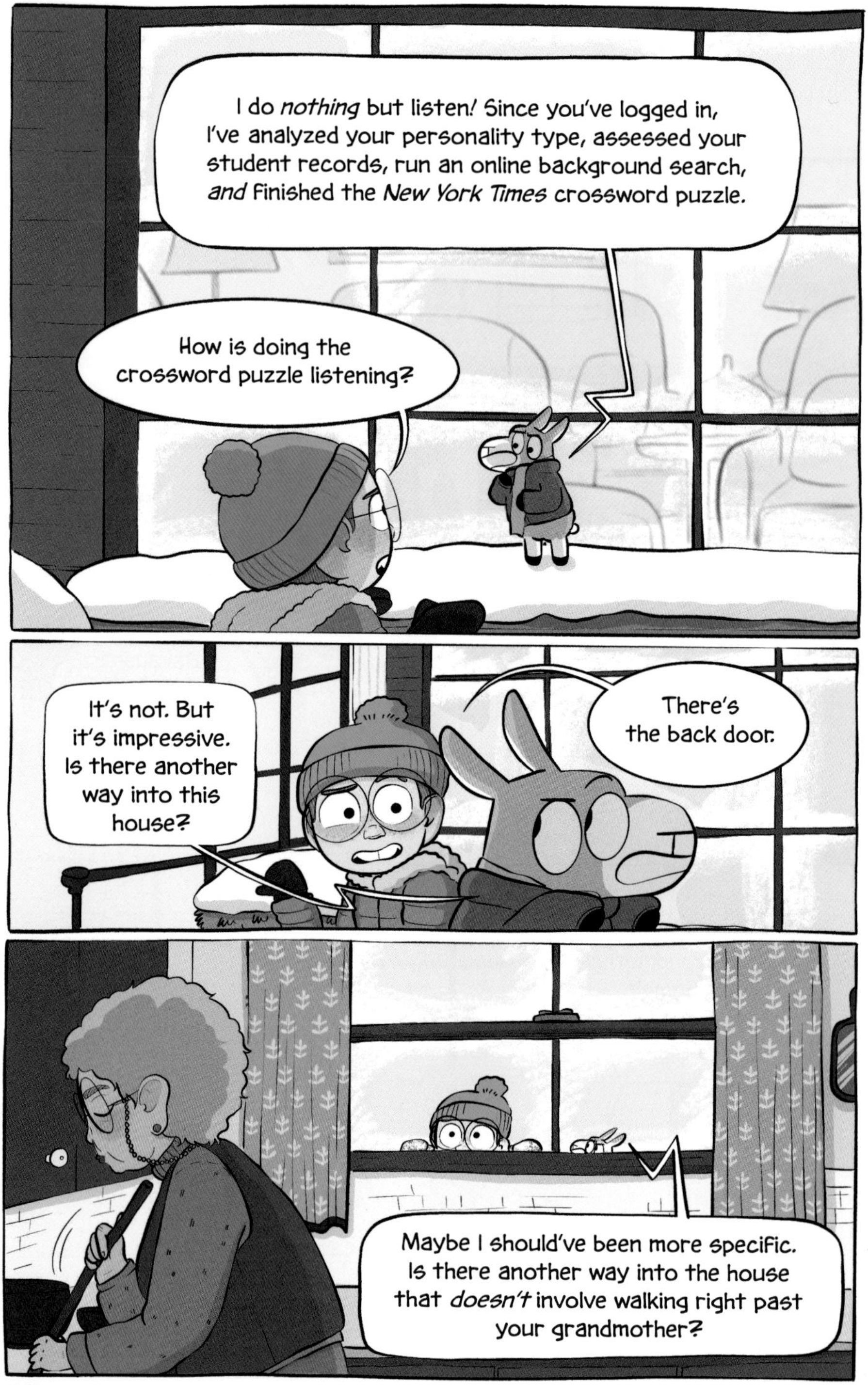
I do *nothing* but listen! Since you've logged in, I've analyzed your personality type, assessed your student records, run an online background search, *and* finished the *New York Times* crossword puzzle.
How is doing the crossword puzzle listening?
It's not. But it's impressive. Is there another way into this house?
There's the back door.
Maybe I should've been more specific. Is there another way into the house that *doesn't* involve walking right past your grandmother?

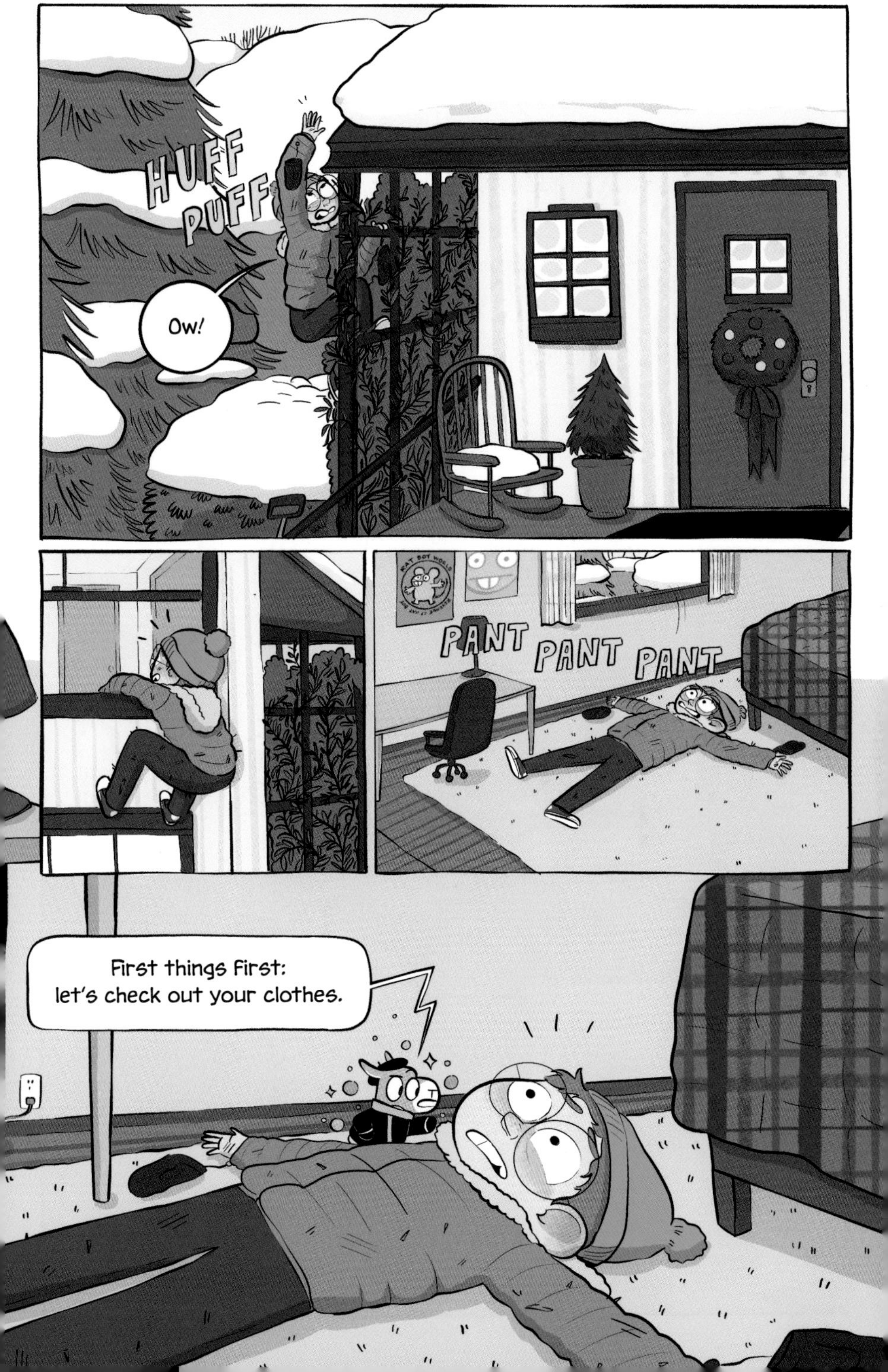
HUFF
PUFF
Ow!
PANT PANT PANT
First things first:
let's check out your clothes.

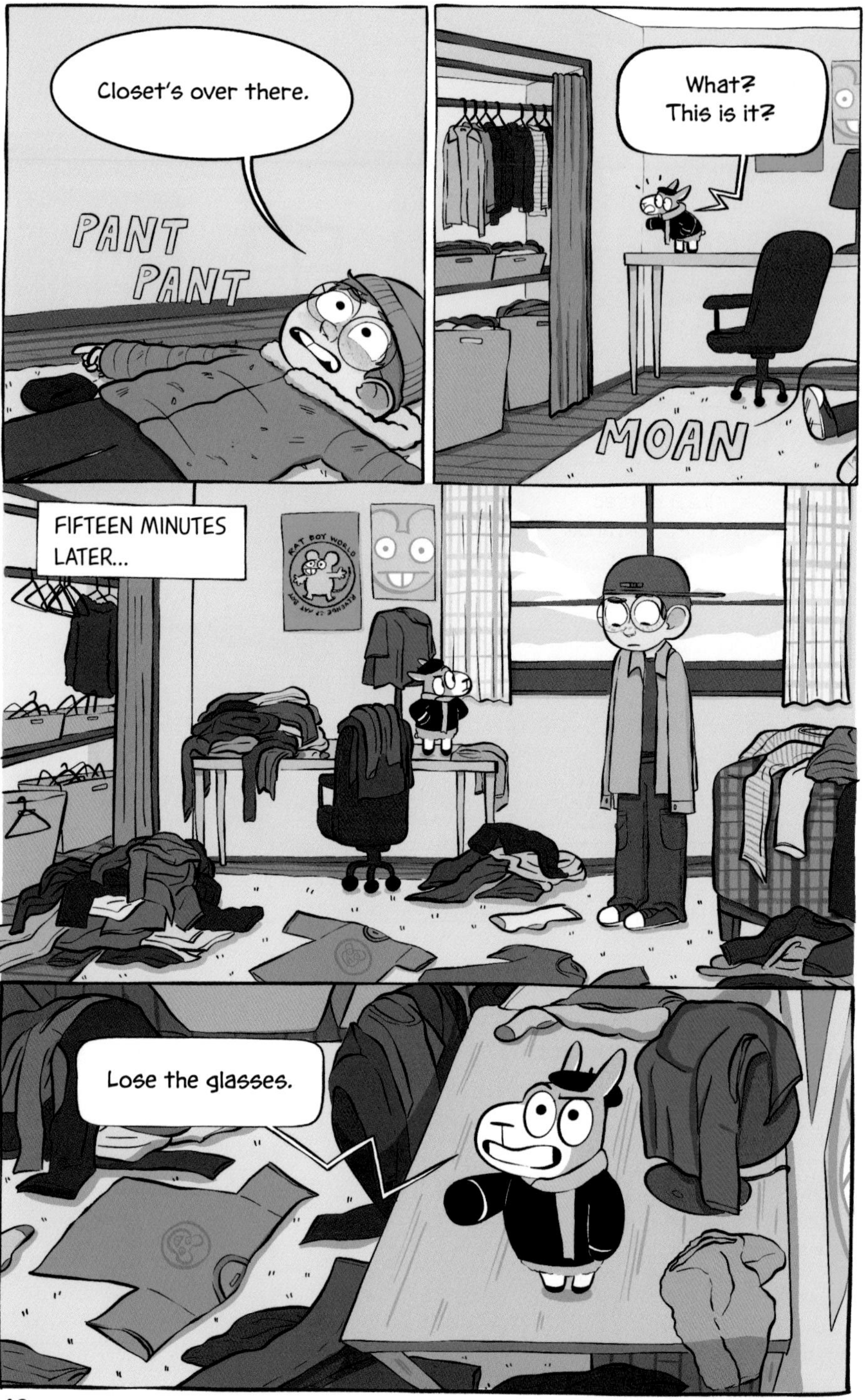
Closet's over there.
PANT
PANT
What?
This is it?
MOAN
FIFTEEN MINUTES LATER...
RAT BOY WORLD
Lose the glasses.

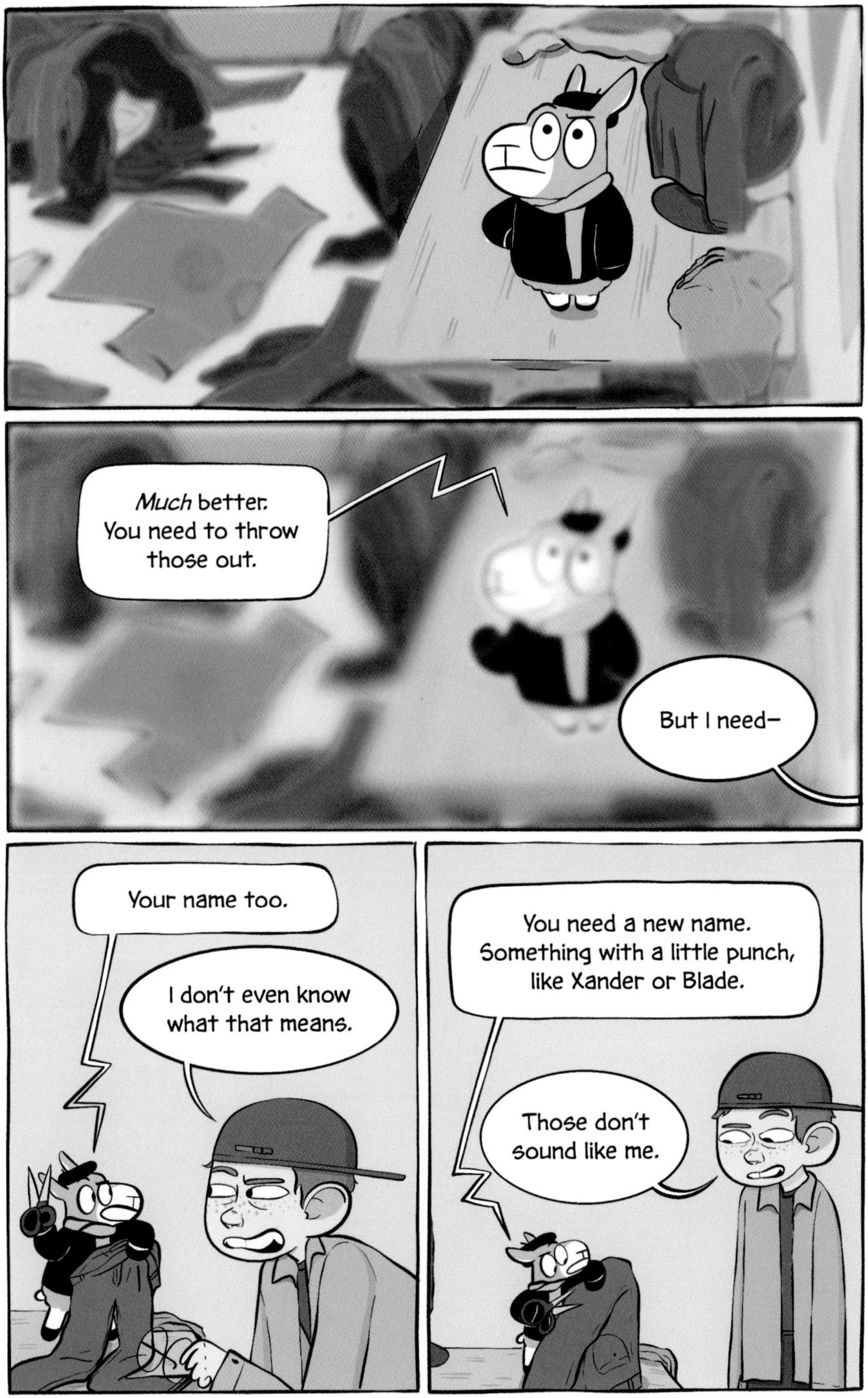
Much better.
You need to throw those out.
But I need—
Your name too.
I don't even know what that means.
You need a new name. Something with a little punch, like Xander or Blade.
Those don't sound like me.

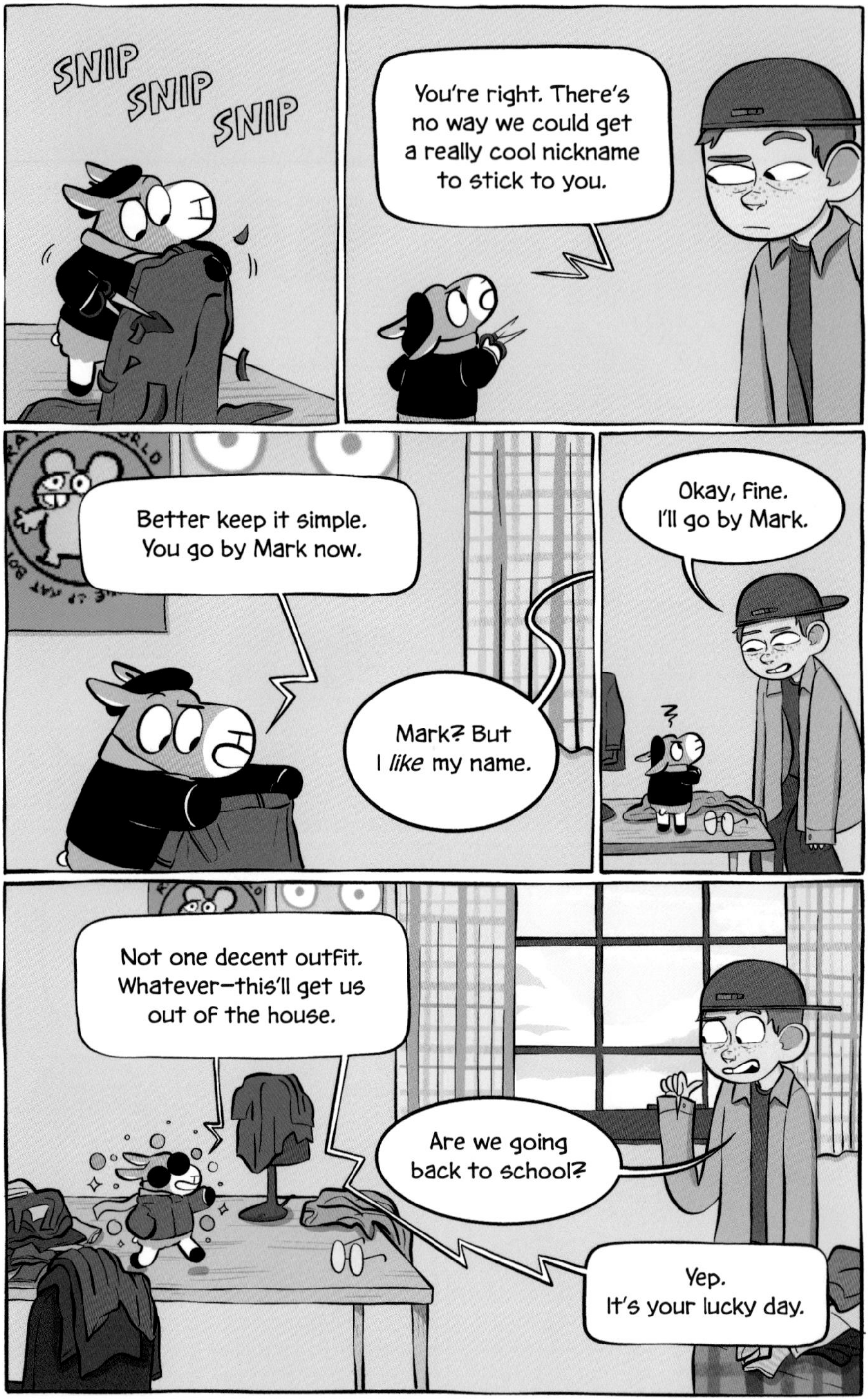
SNIP SNIP SNIP
You're right. There's no way we could get a really cool nickname to stick to you.
Better keep it simple. You go by Mark now.
Mark? But I *like* my name.
Okay, fine. I'll go by Mark.
Not one decent outfit. Whatever—this'll get us out of the house.
Are we going back to school?
Yep. It's your lucky day.

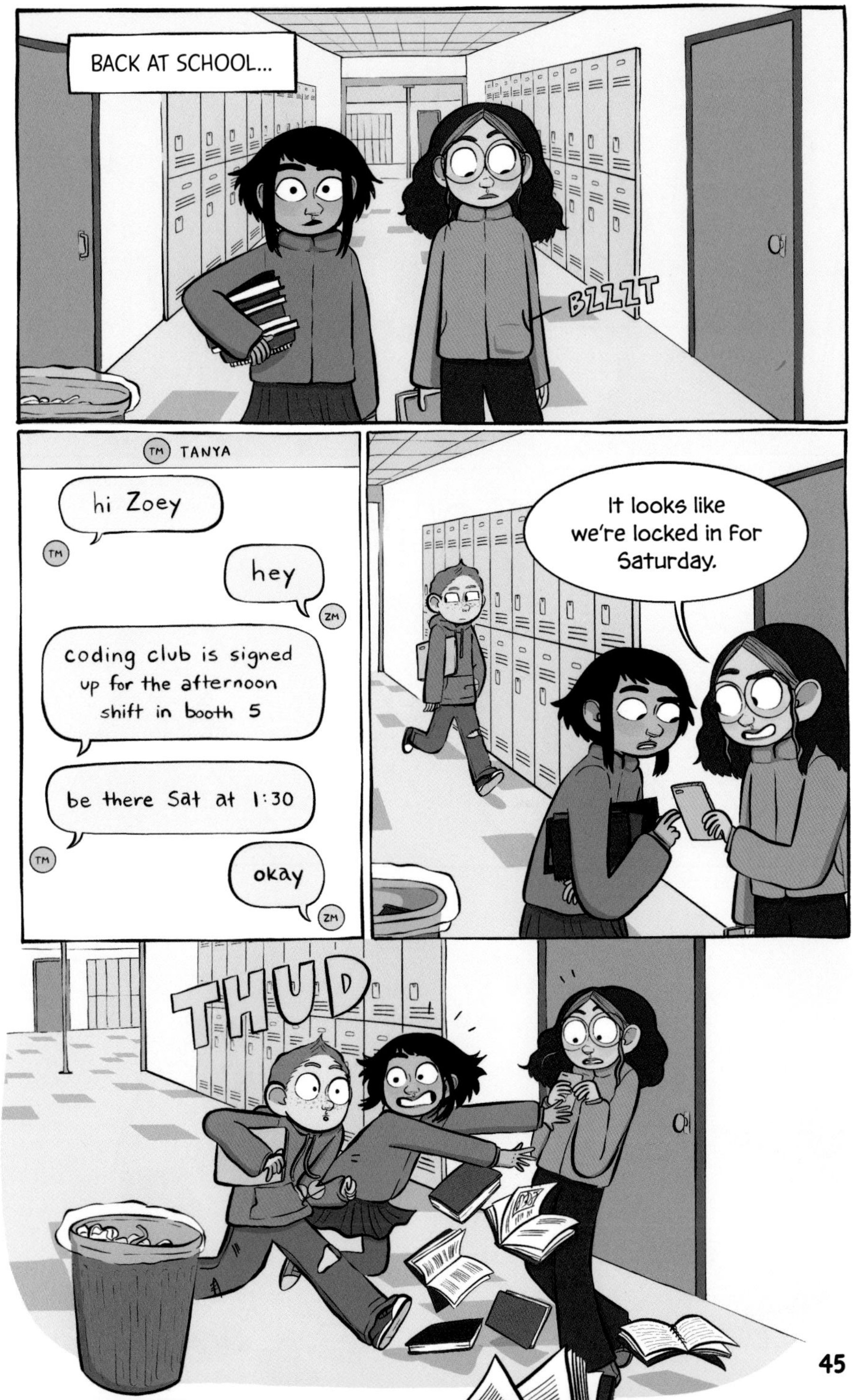
BACK AT SCHOOL...
BZZZT
TANYA
hi Zoey
hey
coding club is signed up for the afternoon shift in booth 5
be there Sat at 1:30
okay
It looks like we're locked in for Saturday.
THUD

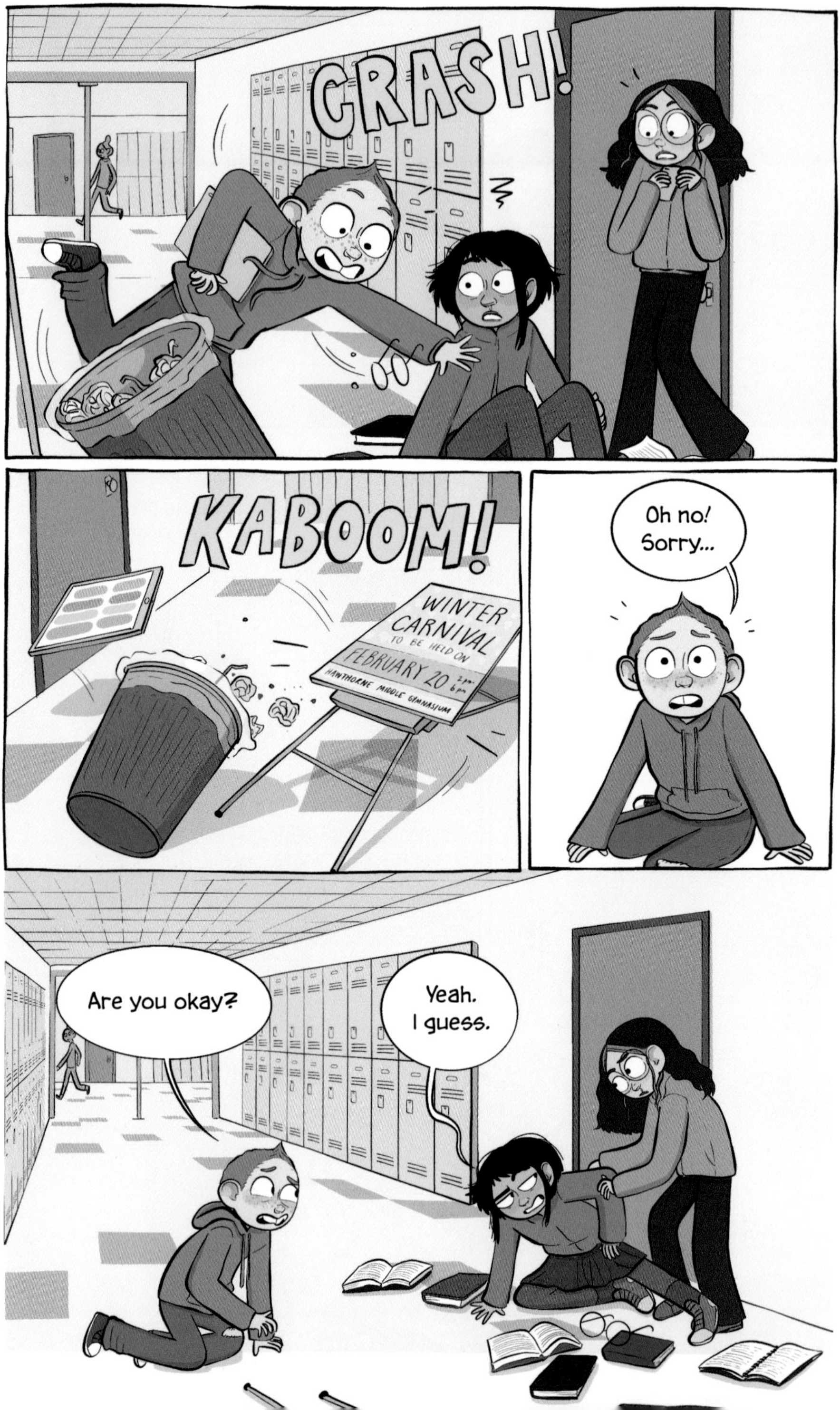
CRASH!
KABOOM!
WINTER CARNIVAL
TO BE HELD ON
FEBRUARY 20 2pm-6pm
HAWTHORNE MIDDLE GYMNASIUM
Oh no! Sorry...
Are you okay?
Yeah. I guess.

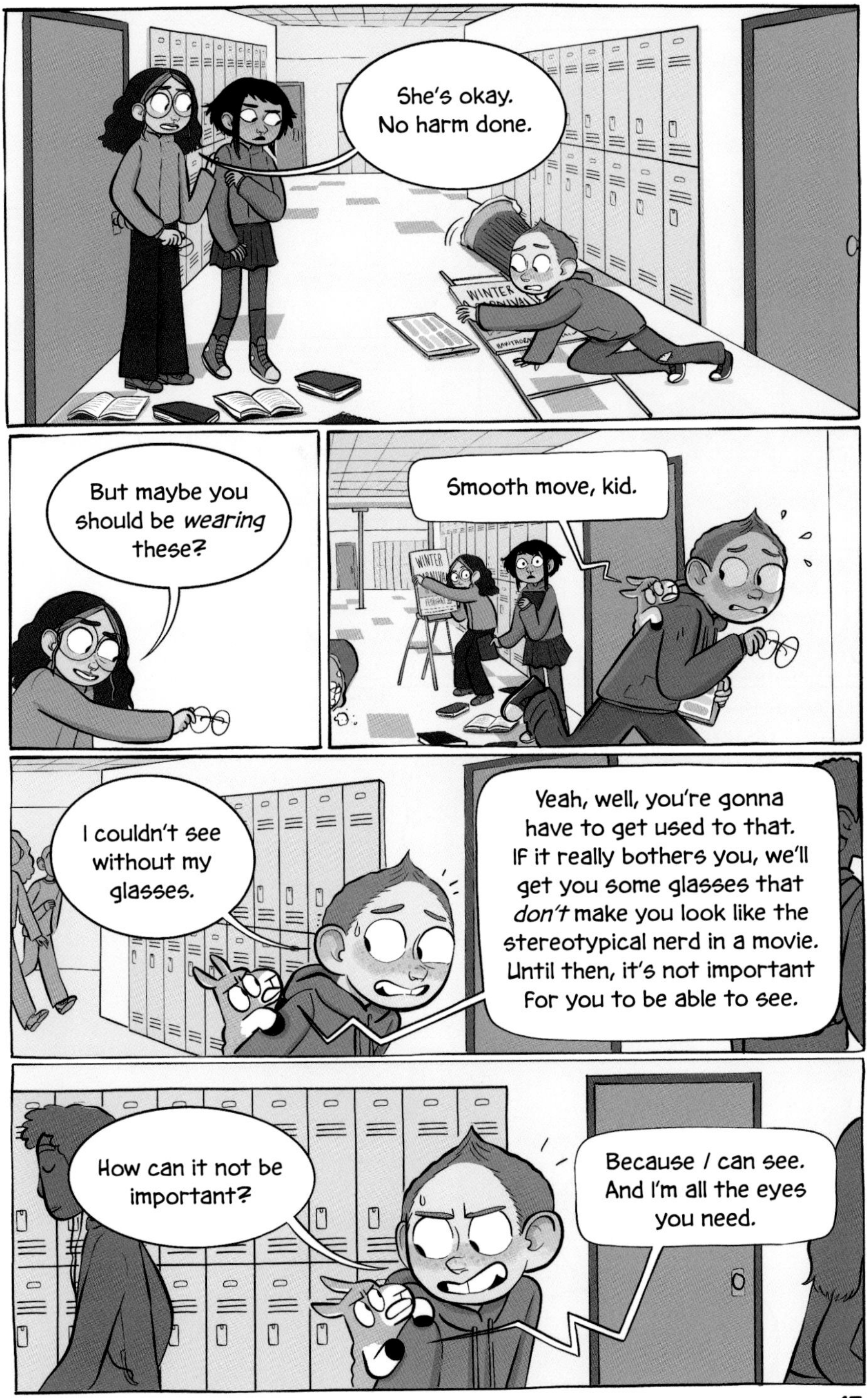
She's okay. No harm done.
WINTER
But maybe you should be *wearing* these?
Smooth move, kid.
WINTER
I couldn't see without my glasses.
Yeah, well, you're gonna have to get used to that. If it really bothers you, we'll get you some glasses that *don't* make you look like the stereotypical nerd in a movie. Until then, it's not important for you to be able to see.
How can it not be important?
Because *I* can see. And I'm all the eyes you need.

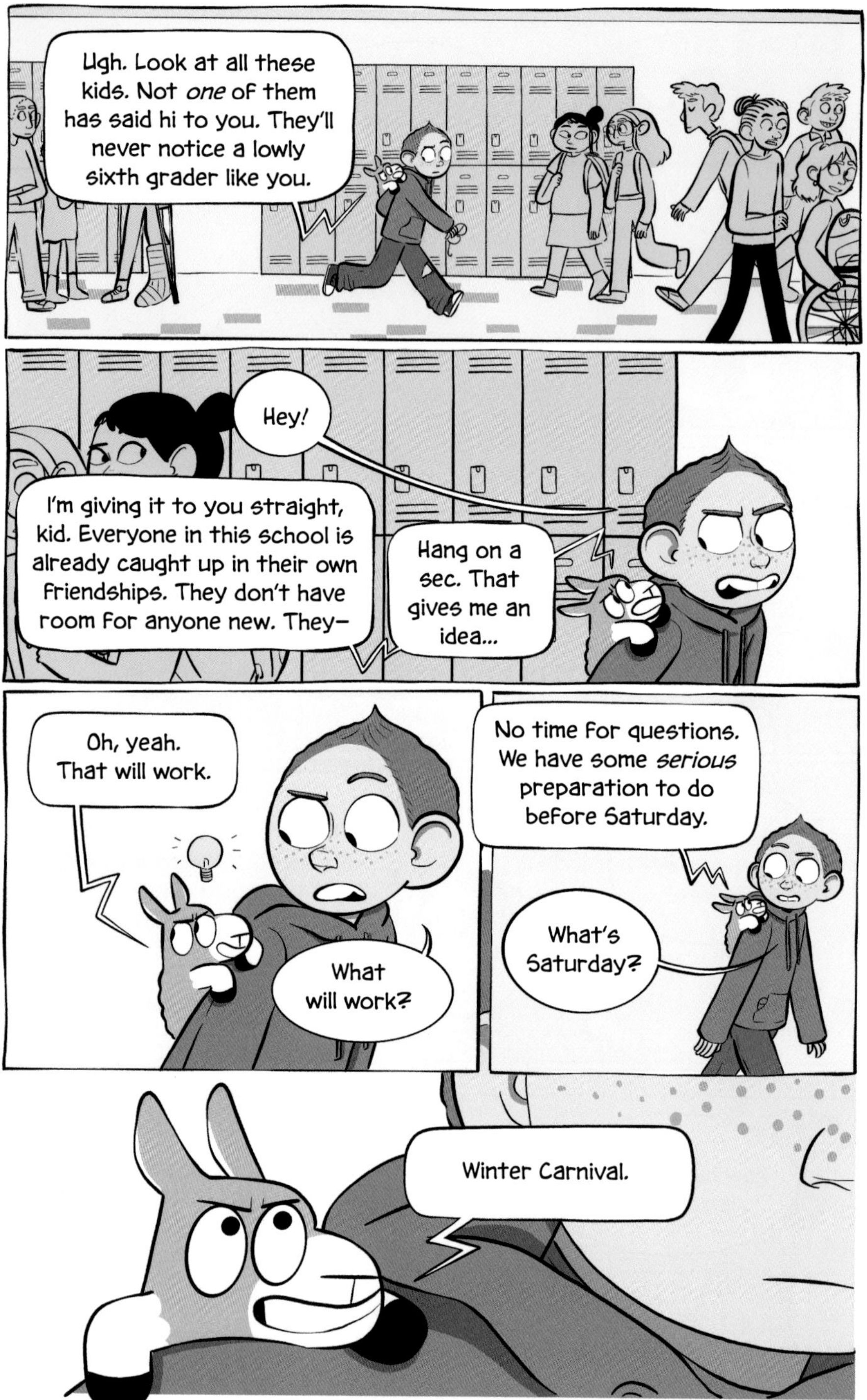
Ugh. Look at all these kids. Not *one* of them has said hi to you. They'll never notice a lowly sixth grader like you.
Hey!
I'm giving it to you straight, kid. Everyone in this school is already caught up in their own friendships. They don't have room for anyone new. They–
Hang on a sec. That gives me an idea...
Oh, yeah. That will work.
What will work?
No time for questions. We have some *serious* preparation to do before Saturday.
What's Saturday?
Winter Carnival.

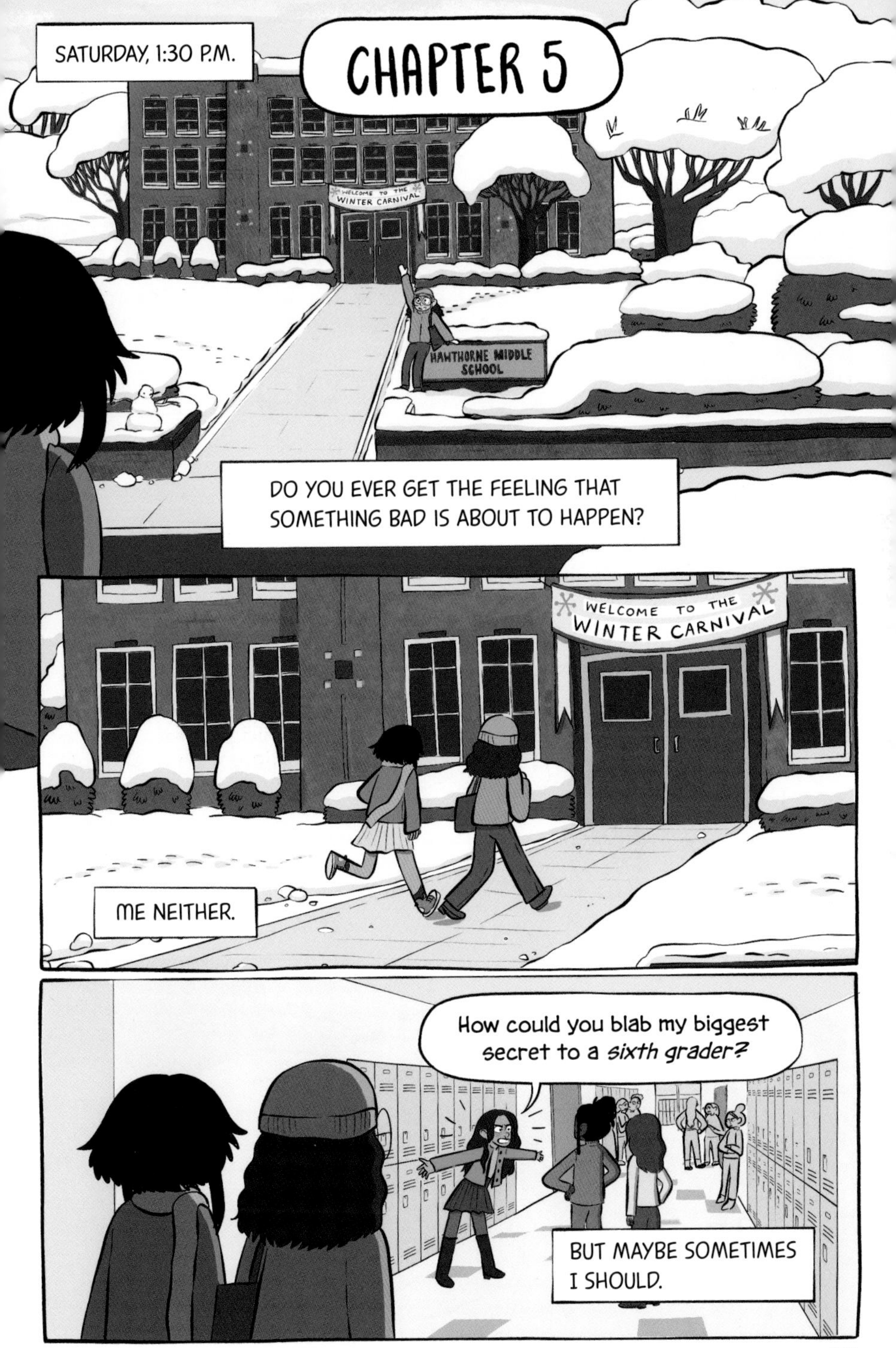
SATURDAY, 1:30 P.M.
CHAPTER 5
WELCOME TO THE WINTER CARNIVAL
HAWTHORNE MIDDLE SCHOOL
DO YOU EVER GET THE FEELING THAT SOMETHING BAD IS ABOUT TO HAPPEN?
WELCOME TO THE WINTER CARNIVAL
ME NEITHER.
How could you blab my biggest secret to a *sixth grader?*
BUT MAYBE SOMETIMES I SHOULD.

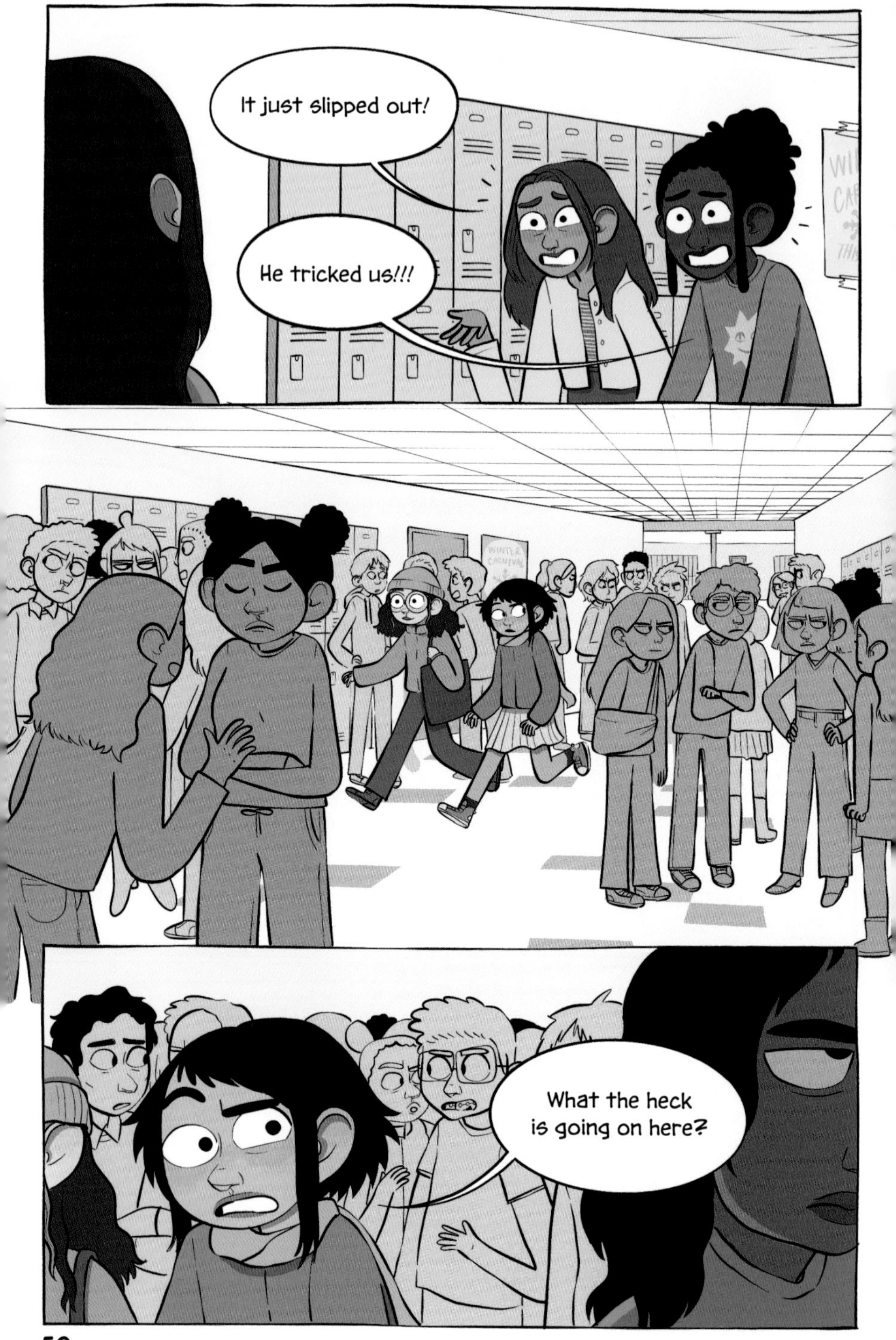
It just slipped out!
He tricked us!!!
WINTER CARNIVAL
What the heck is going on here?

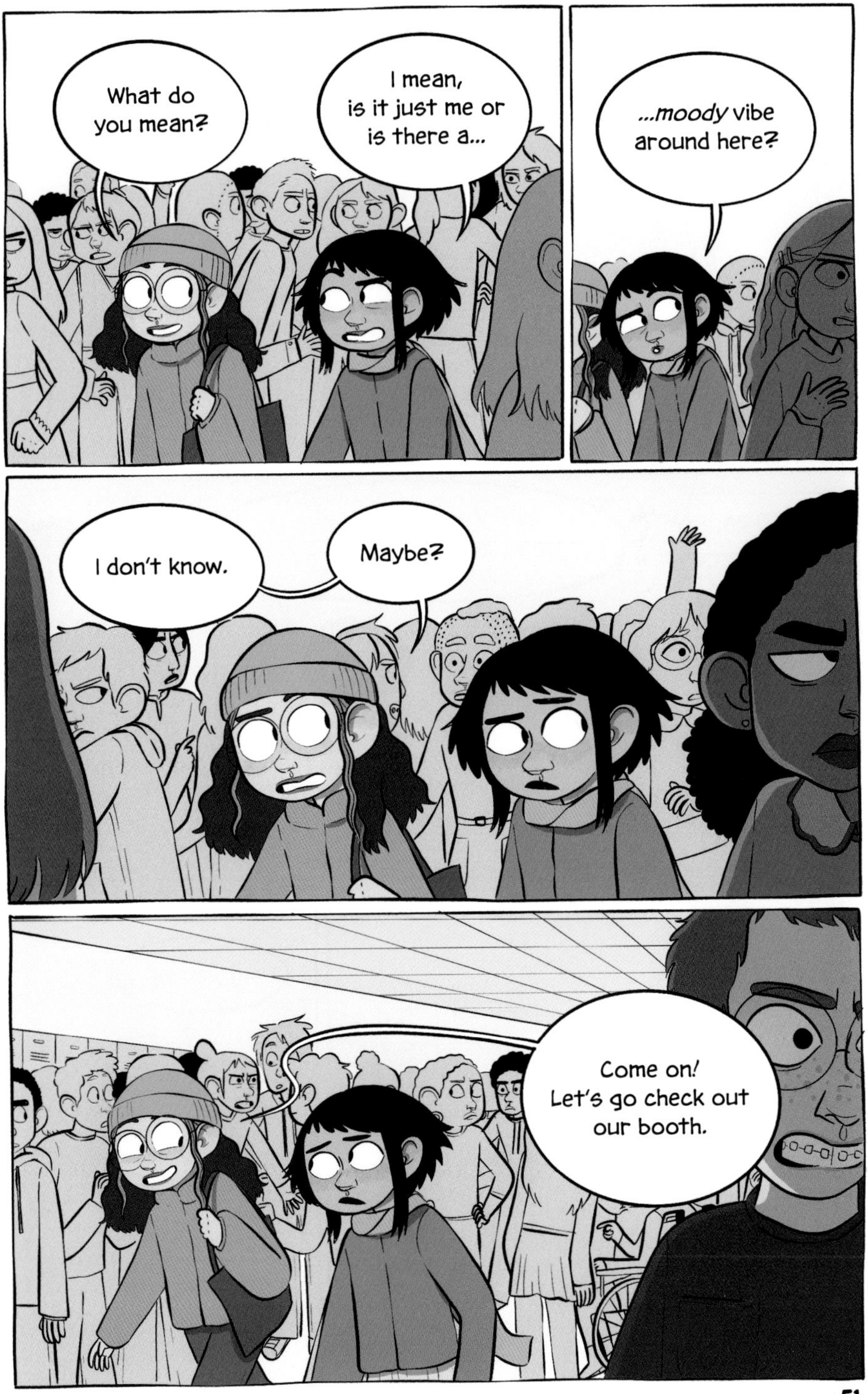
What do you mean?
I mean, is it just me or is there a...
...*moody* vibe around here?
I don't know.
Maybe?
Come on! Let's go check out our booth.

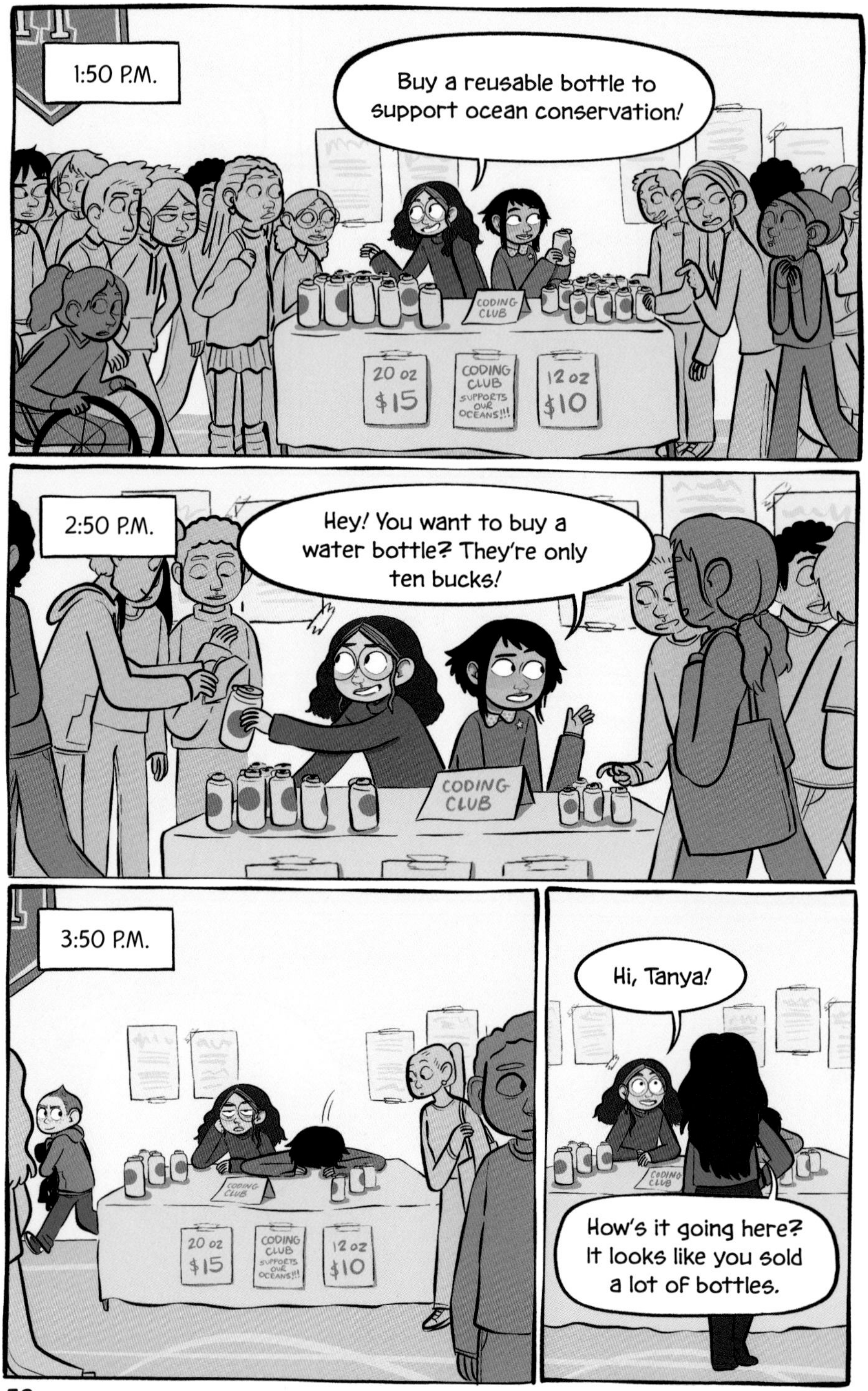
1:50 P.M.
Buy a reusable bottle to support ocean conservation!
CODING CLUB
20 oz $15
CODING CLUB SUPPORTS OUR OCEANS!!!
12 oz $10
2:50 P.M.
Hey! You want to buy a water bottle? They're only ten bucks!
CODING CLUB
3:50 P.M.
CODING CLUB
20 oz $15
CODING CLUB SUPPORTS OUR OCEANS!!!
12 oz $10
Hi, Tanya!
CODING CLUB
How's it going here? It looks like you sold a lot of bottles.

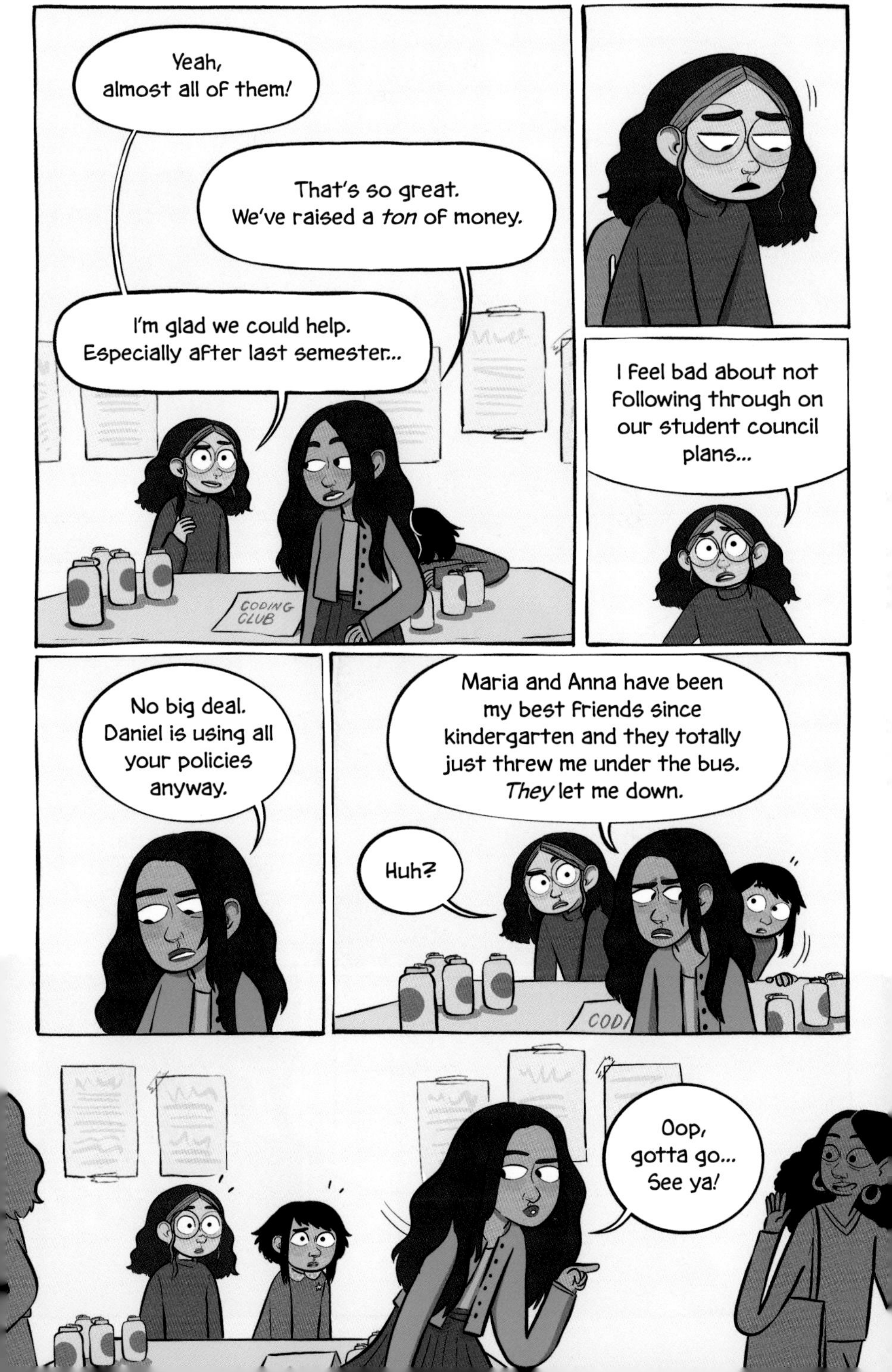
Yeah, almost all of them!
That's so great. We've raised a *ton* of money.
I'm glad we could help. Especially after last semester...
CODING CLUB
I feel bad about not following through on our student council plans...
No big deal. Daniel is using all your policies anyway.
Maria and Anna have been my best friends since kindergarten and they totally just threw me under the bus. *They* let me down.
Huh?
Oop, gotta go... See ya!

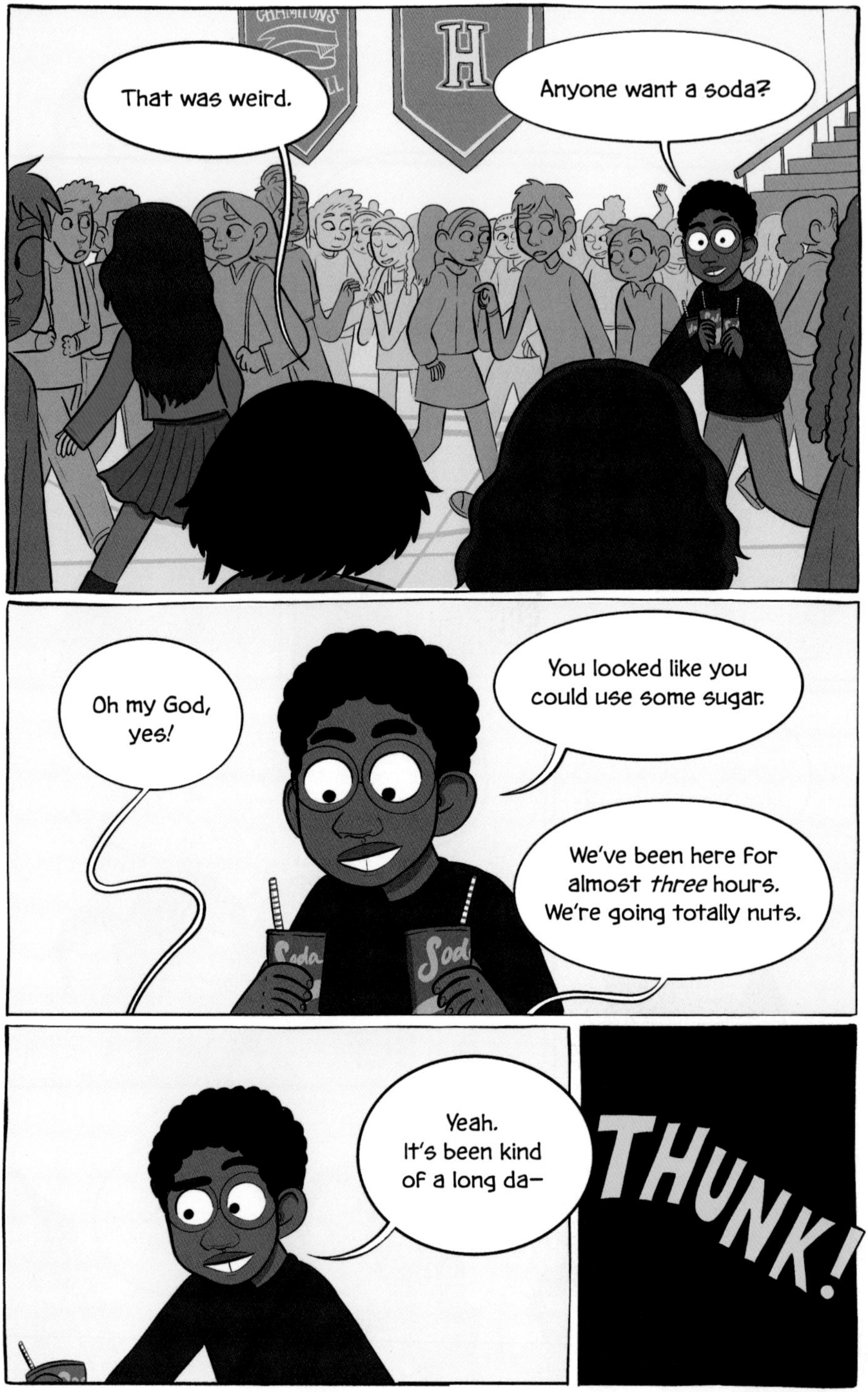
That was weird.
Anyone want a soda?
Oh my God, yes!
You looked like you could use some sugar.
We've been here for almost *three* hours. We're going totally nuts.
Yeah. It's been kind of a long da—
THUNK!

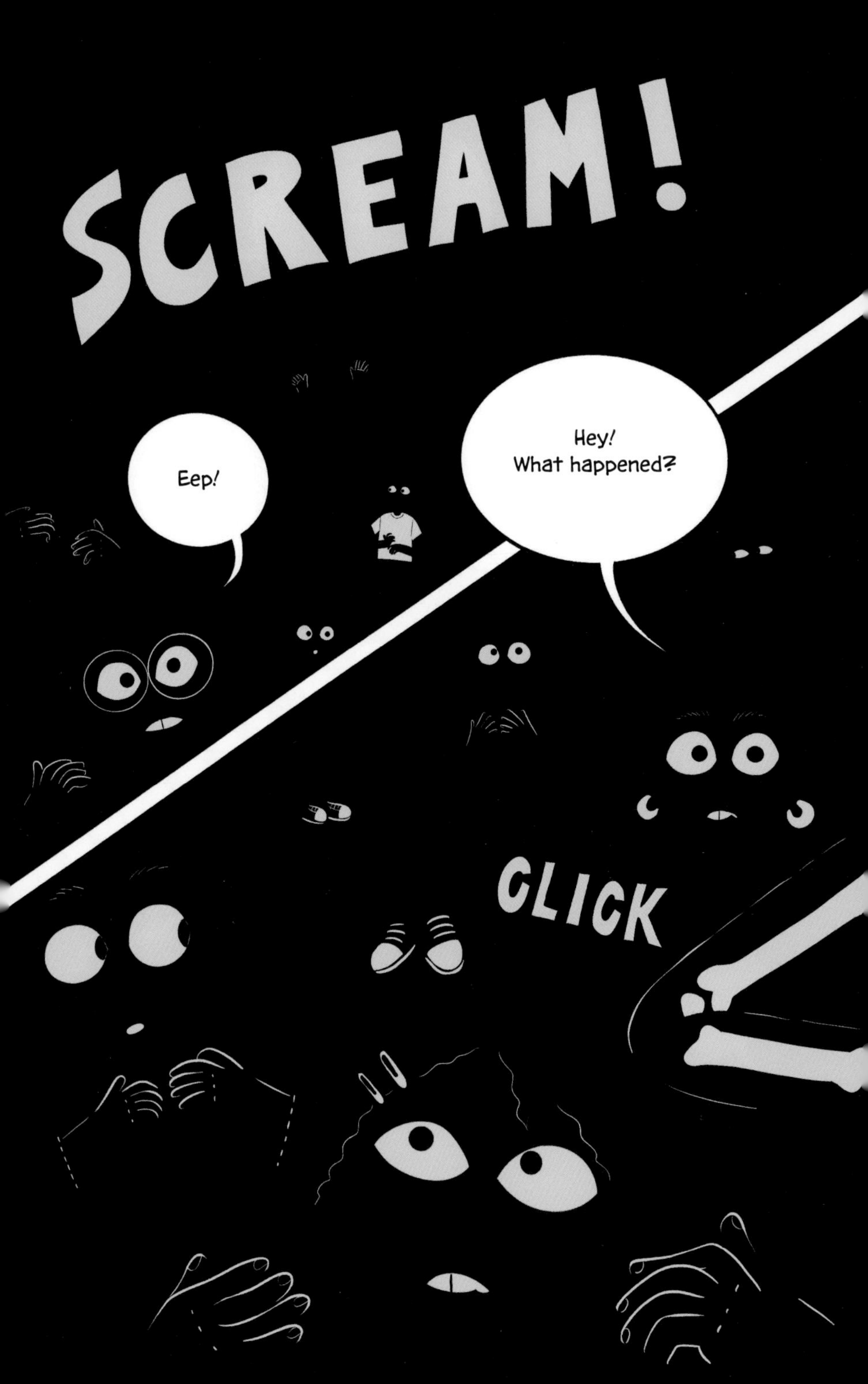
SCREAM!
Eep!
Hey!
What happened?
CLICK

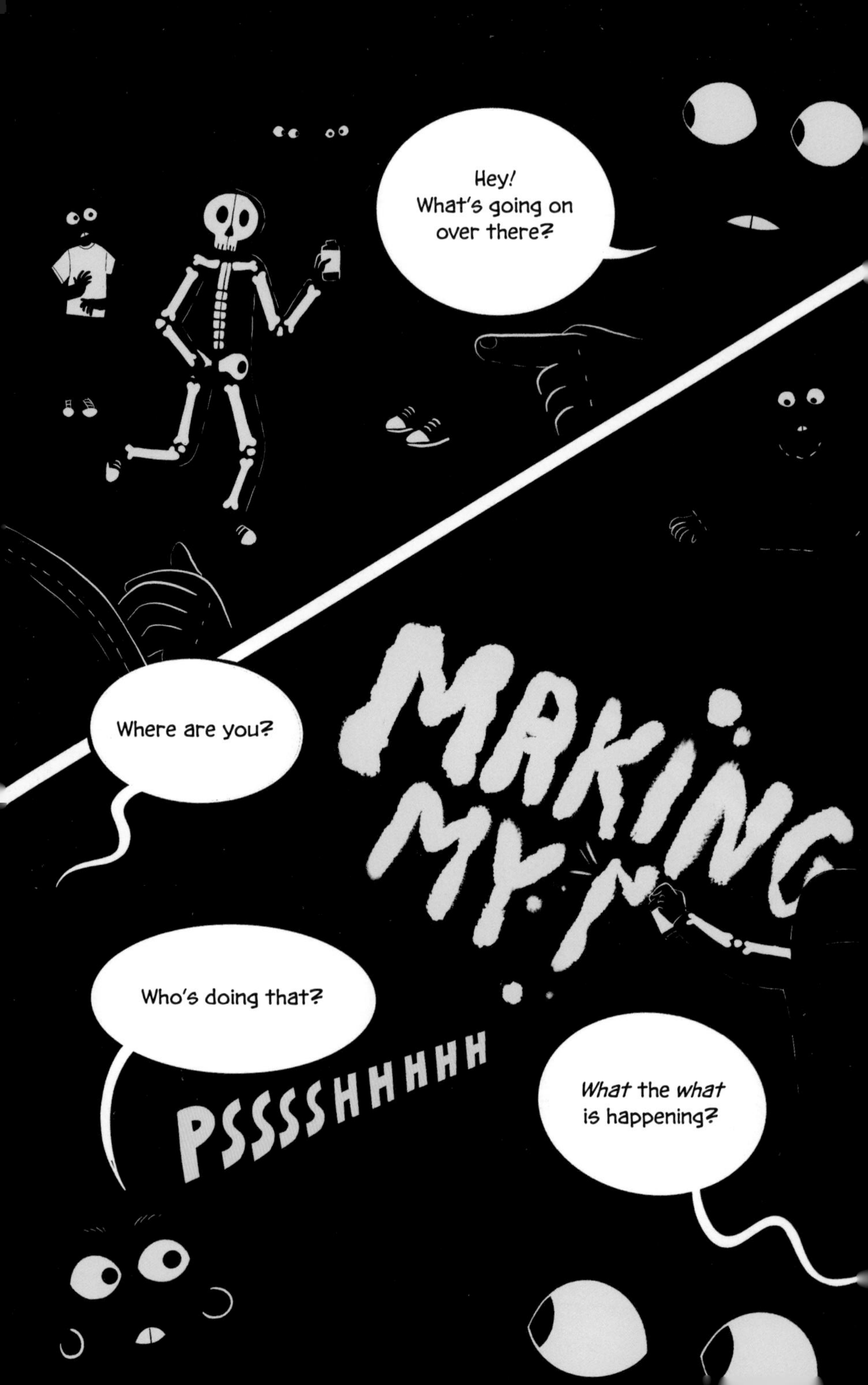
Hey! What's going on over there?
Where are you?
MAKING MY...
Who's doing that?
PSSSSHHHHHH
What the what is happening?

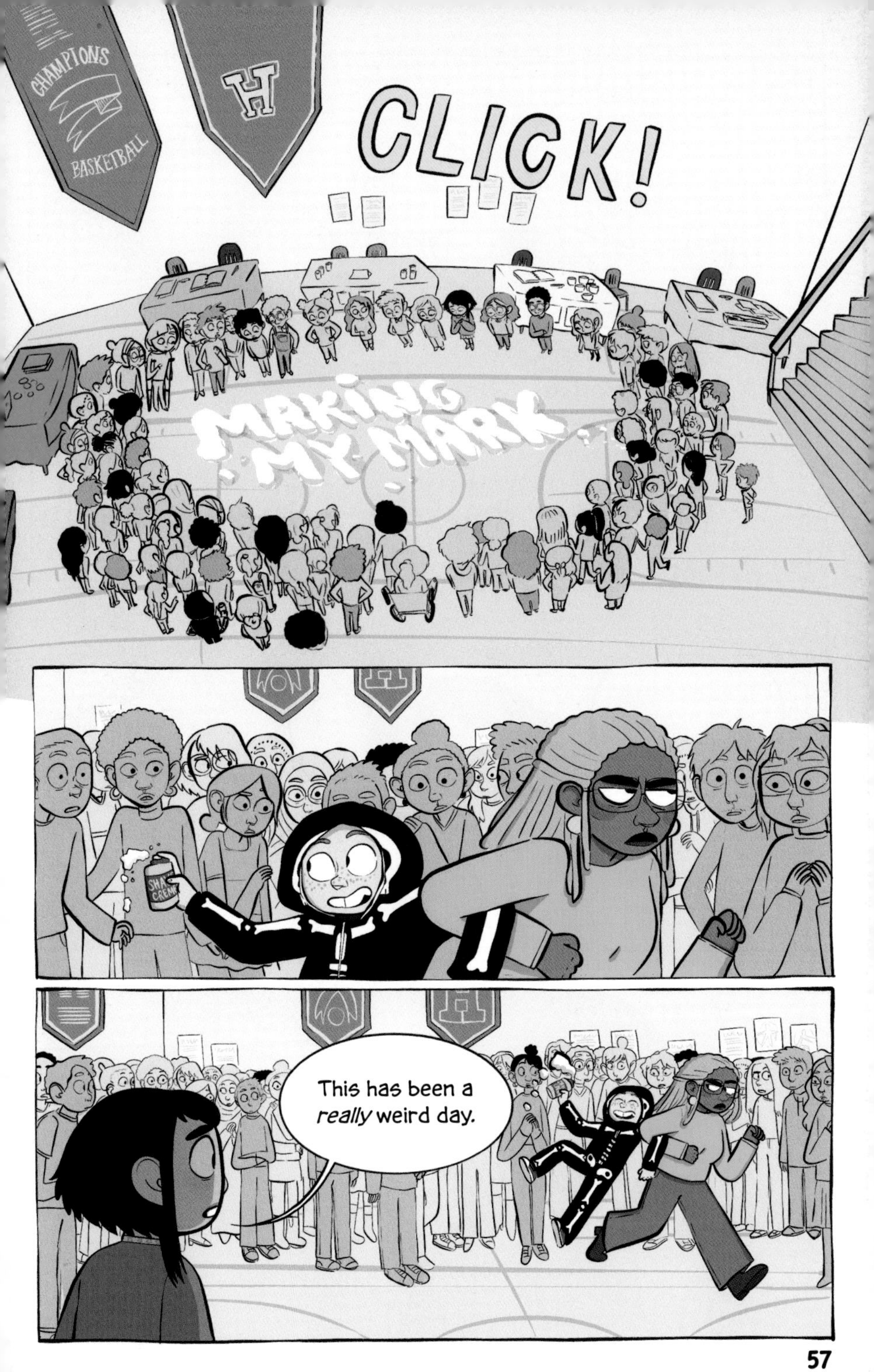
CHAMPIONS
BASKETBALL
H
CLICK!
MAKING MY MARK
This has been a *really* weird day.

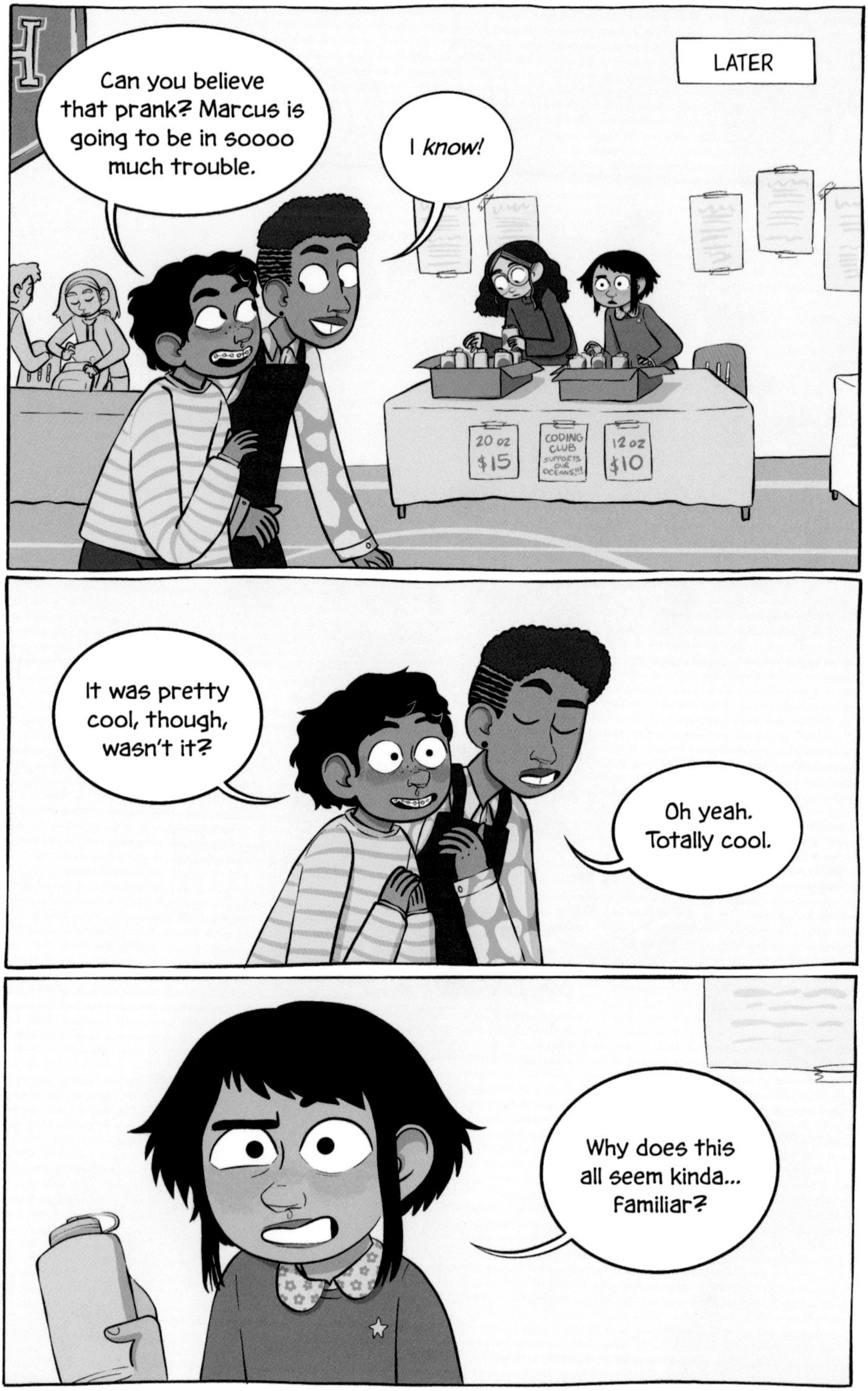
LATER
Can you believe that prank? Marcus is going to be in soooo much trouble.
I *know!*
20 oz $15
CODING CLUB SUPPORTS OUR OCEANS!!!
12 oz $10
It was pretty cool, though, wasn't it?
Oh yeah. Totally cool.
Why does this all seem kinda... Familiar?

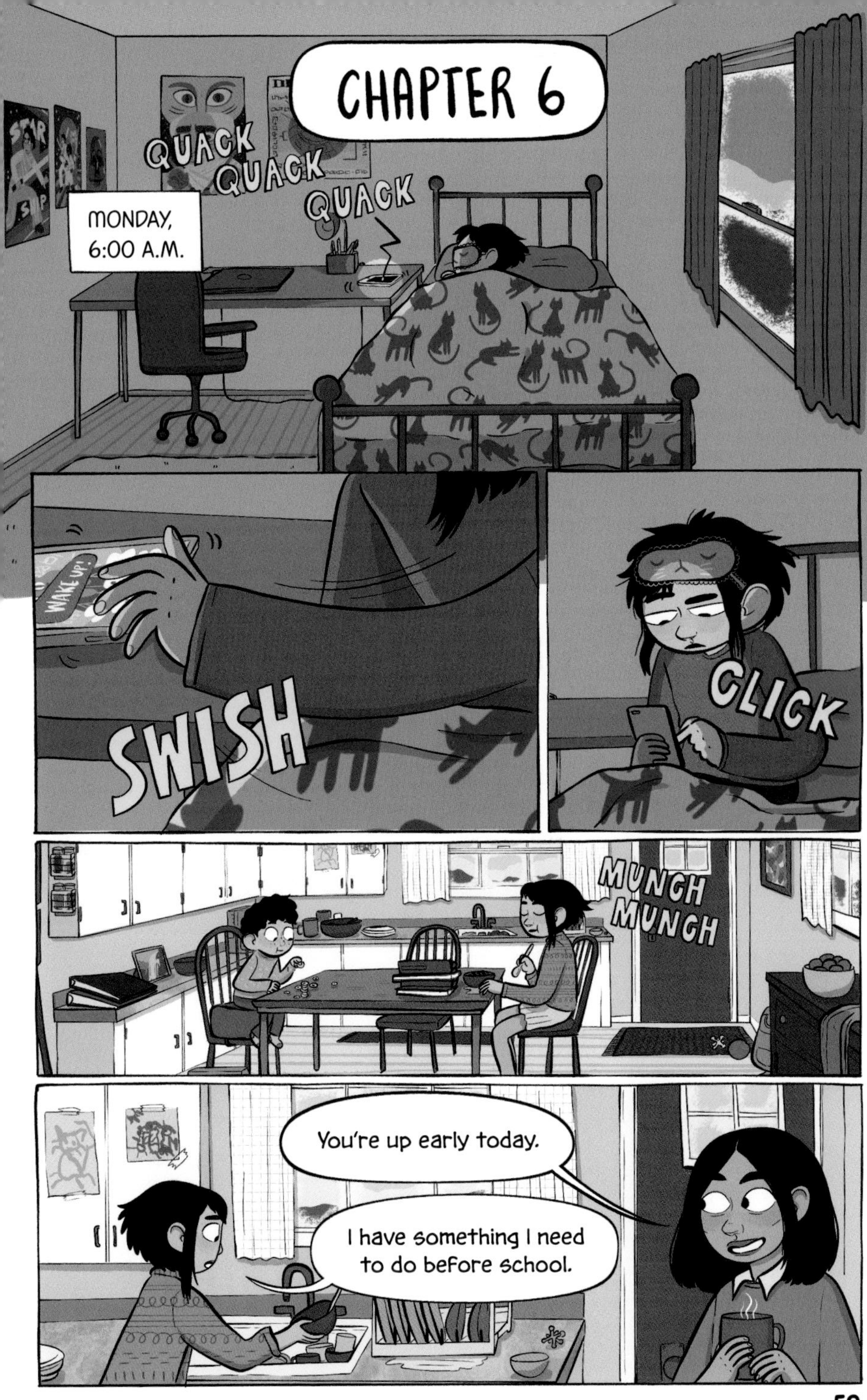

CHAPTER 6
QUACK
QUACK
QUACK
MONDAY, 6:00 A.M.
WAKE UP!
SWISH
CLICK
MUNCH
MUNCH
You're up early today.
I have something I need to do before school.

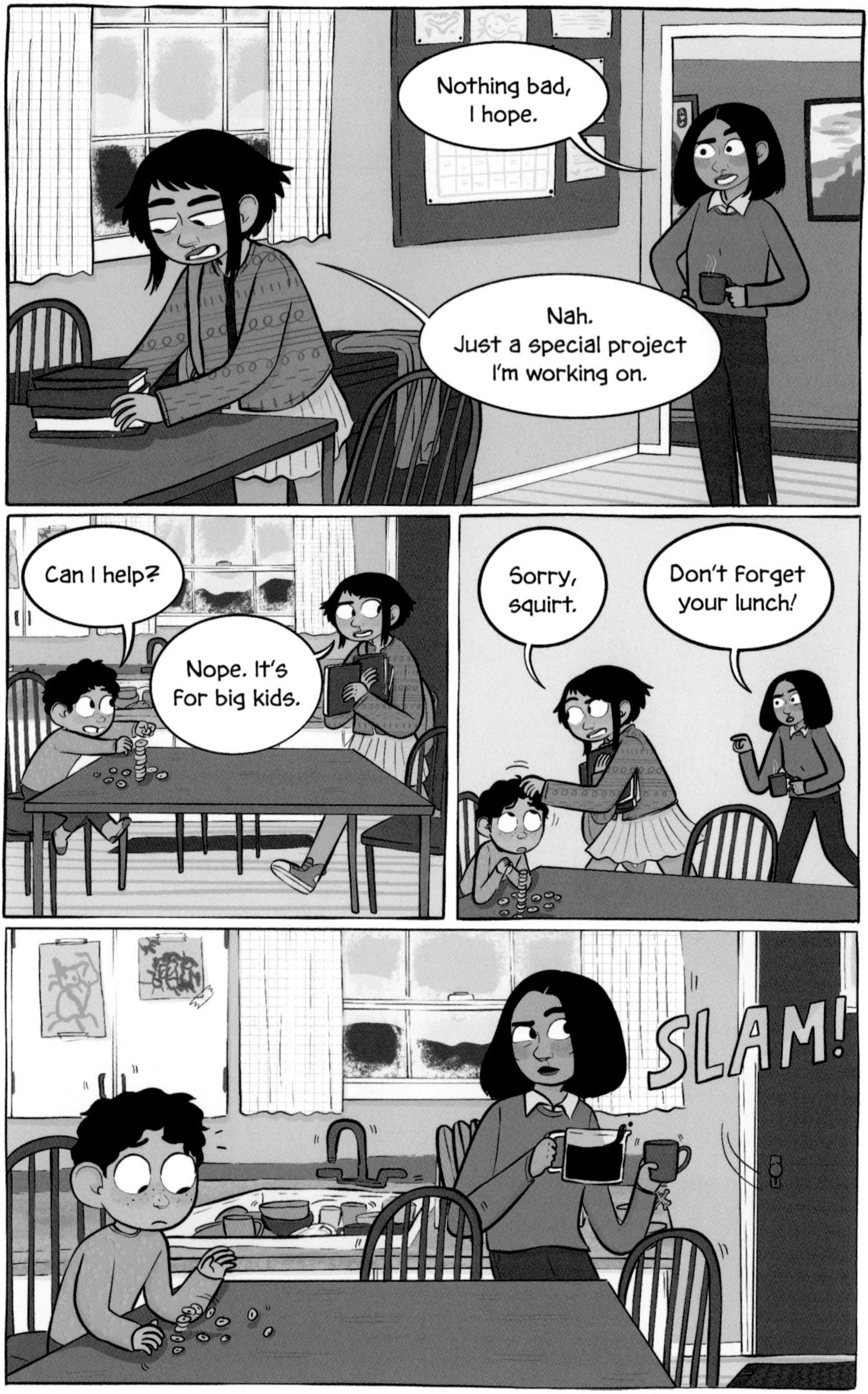

Nothing bad, I hope.
Nah. Just a special project I'm working on.
Can I help?
Nope. It's for big kids.
Sorry, squirt.
Don't forget your lunch!
SLAM!

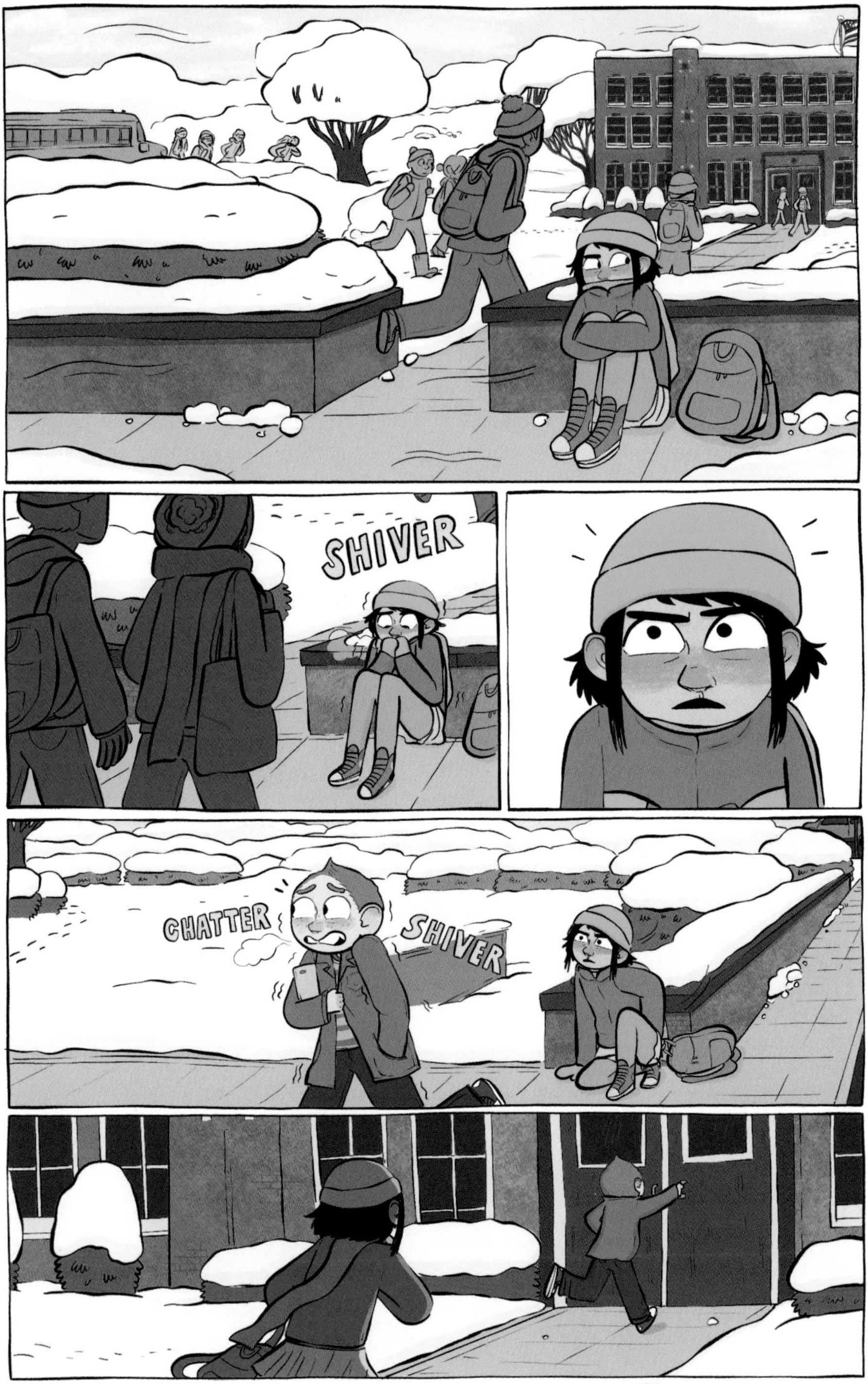
SHIVER
CHATTER
SHIVER

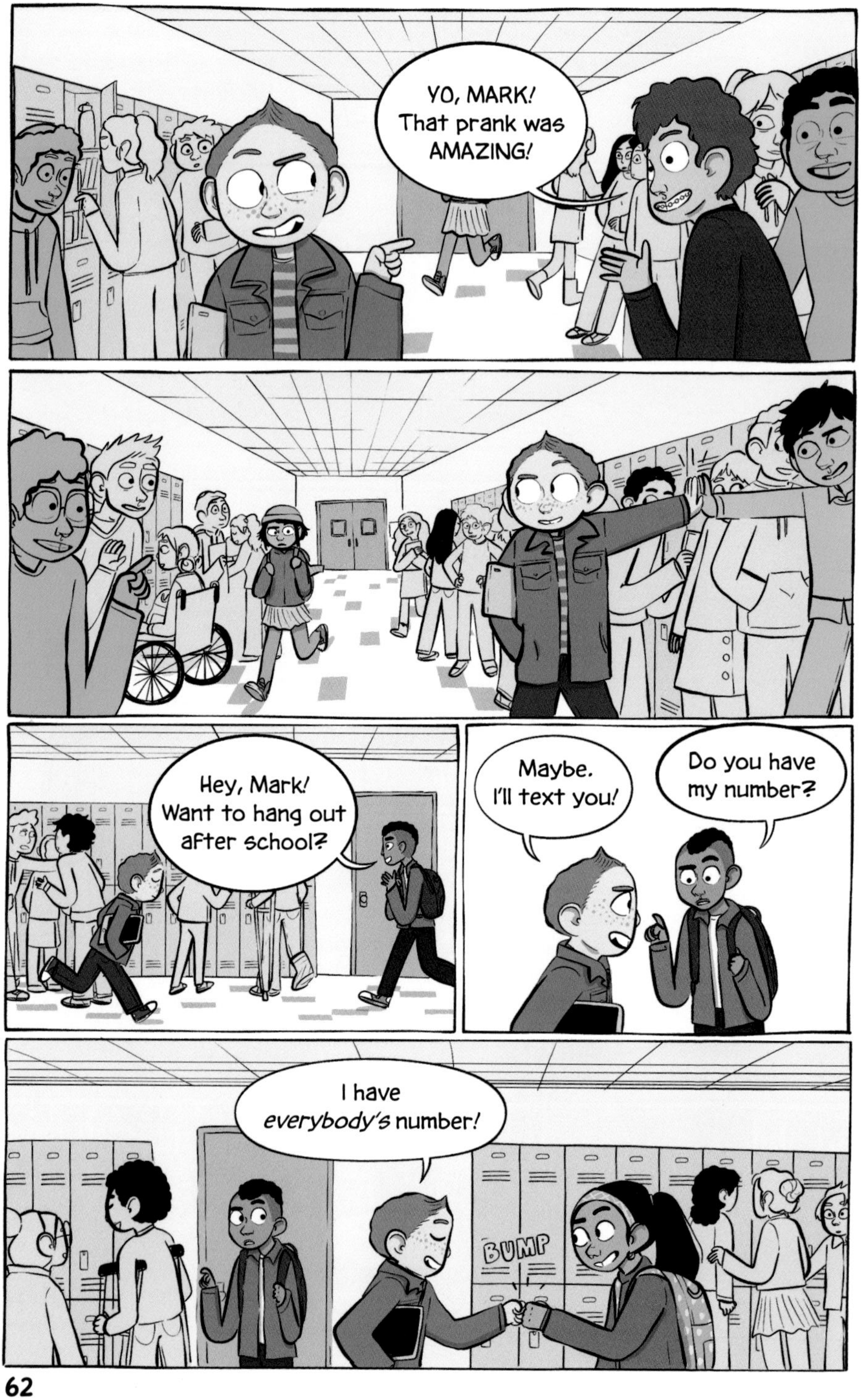
YO, MARK! That prank was AMAZING!
Hey, Mark! Want to hang out after school?
Maybe. I'll text you!
Do you have my number?
I have *everybody's* number!
BUMP

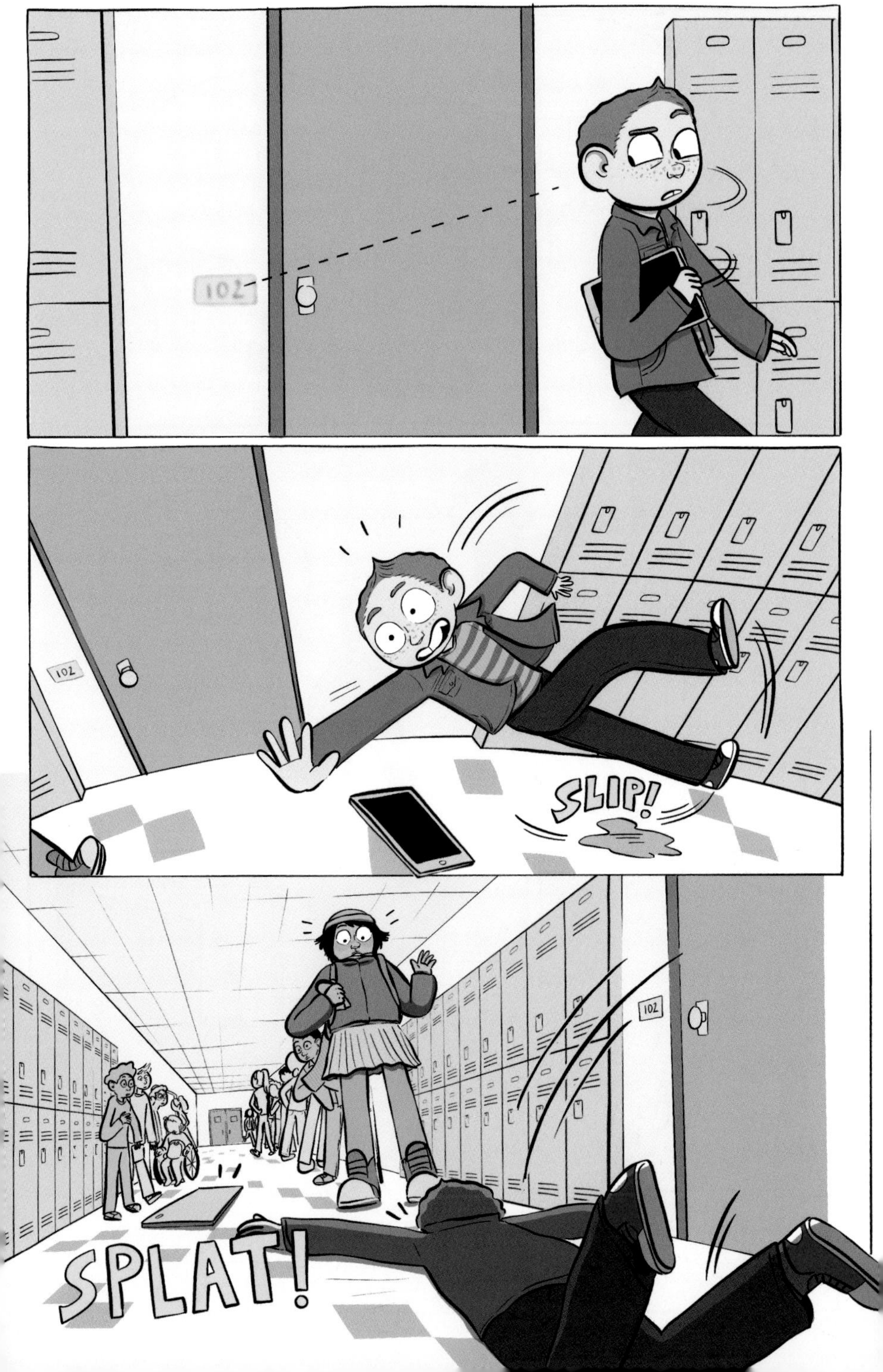
102
102
SLIP!
102
SPLAT!

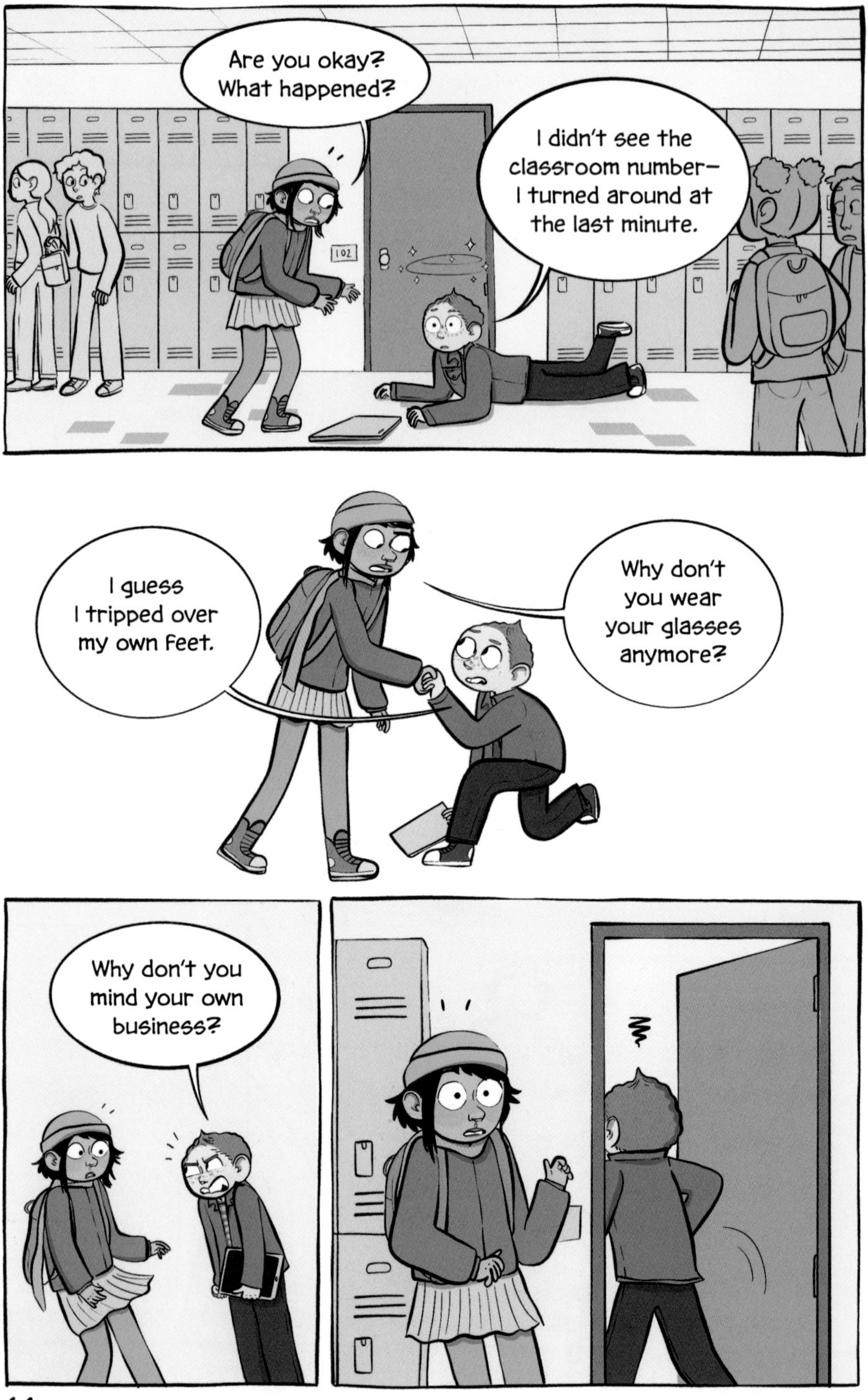
Are you okay? What happened?
I didn't see the classroom number— I turned around at the last minute.
102
I guess I tripped over my own feet.
Why don't you wear your glasses anymore?
Why don't you mind your own business?

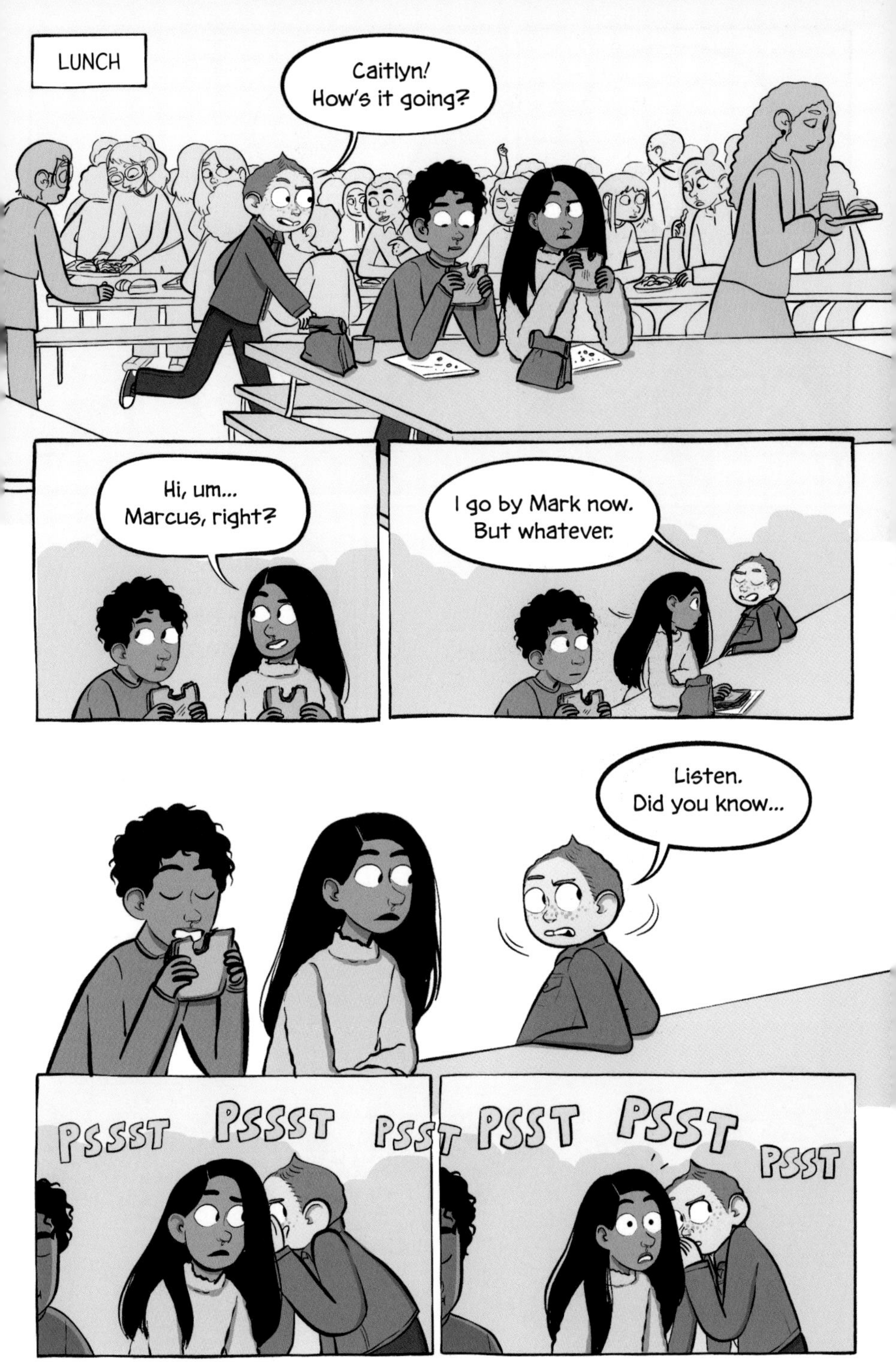
LUNCH
Caitlyn! How's it going?
Hi, um... Marcus, right?
I go by Mark now. But whatever.
Listen. Did you know...
PSSST
PSSST
PSST
PSST
PSST
PSST

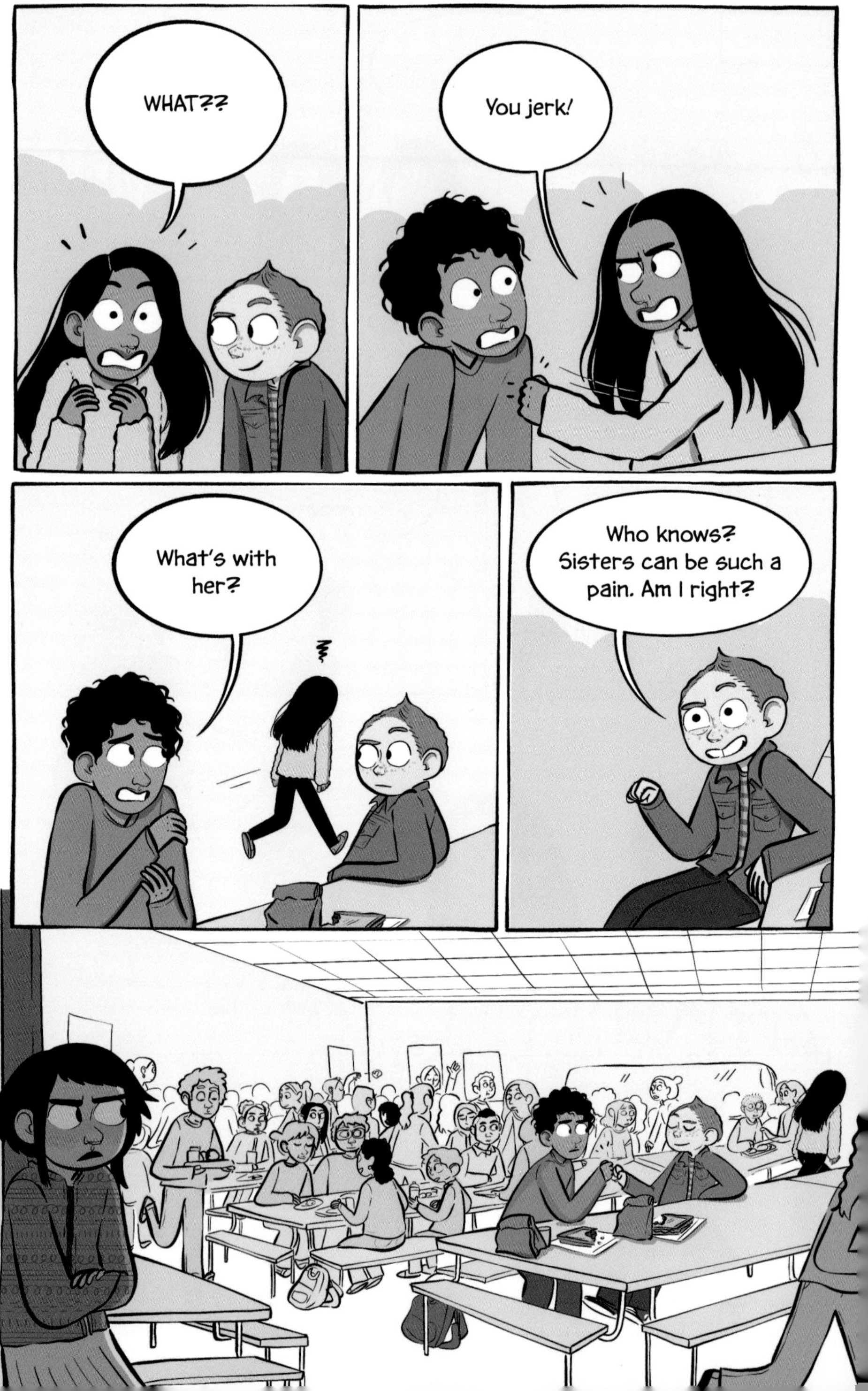
WHAT??
You jerk!
What's with her?
Who knows? Sisters can be such a pain. Am I right?

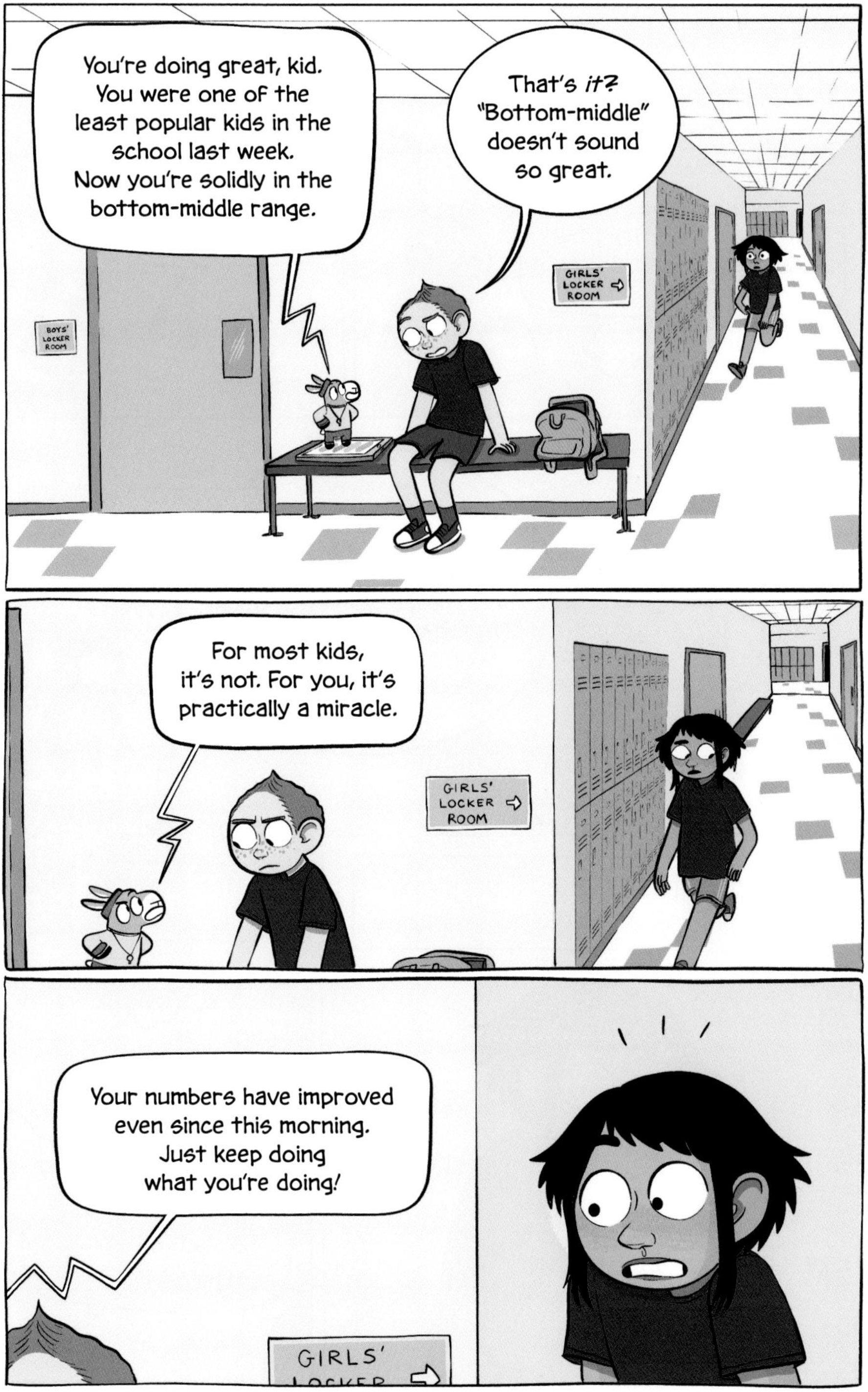

You're doing great, kid. You were one of the least popular kids in the school last week. Now you're solidly in the bottom-middle range.
That's *it?* "Bottom-middle" doesn't sound so great.
BOYS' LOCKER ROOM
GIRLS' LOCKER ROOM
For most kids, it's not. For you, it's practically a miracle.
GIRLS' LOCKER ROOM
Your numbers have improved even since this morning. Just keep doing what you're doing!
GIRLS'

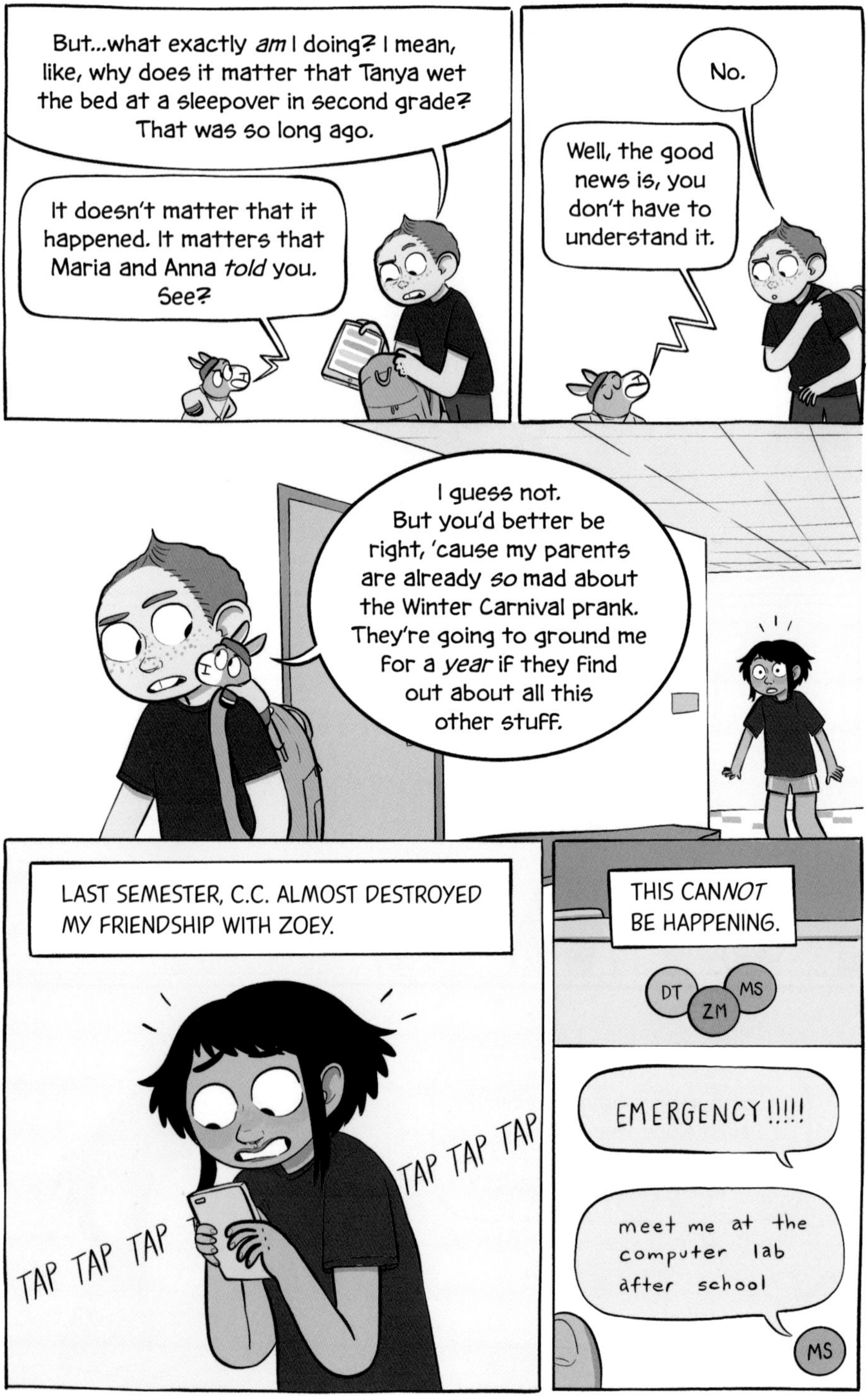

But...what exactly *am* I doing? I mean, like, why does it matter that Tanya wet the bed at a sleepover in second grade? That was so long ago.
It doesn't matter that it happened. It matters that Maria and Anna *told* you. See?
Well, the good news is, you don't have to understand it.
No.
I guess not. But you'd better be right, 'cause my parents are already *so* mad about the Winter Carnival prank. They're going to ground me for a *year* if they find out about all this other stuff.
LAST SEMESTER, C.C. ALMOST DESTROYED MY FRIENDSHIP WITH ZOEY.
TAP TAP TAP
TAP TAP TAP
THIS CAN*NOT* BE HAPPENING.
DT
ZM
MS
EMERGENCY!!!!!
meet me at the computer lab after school
MS

CHAPTER 7

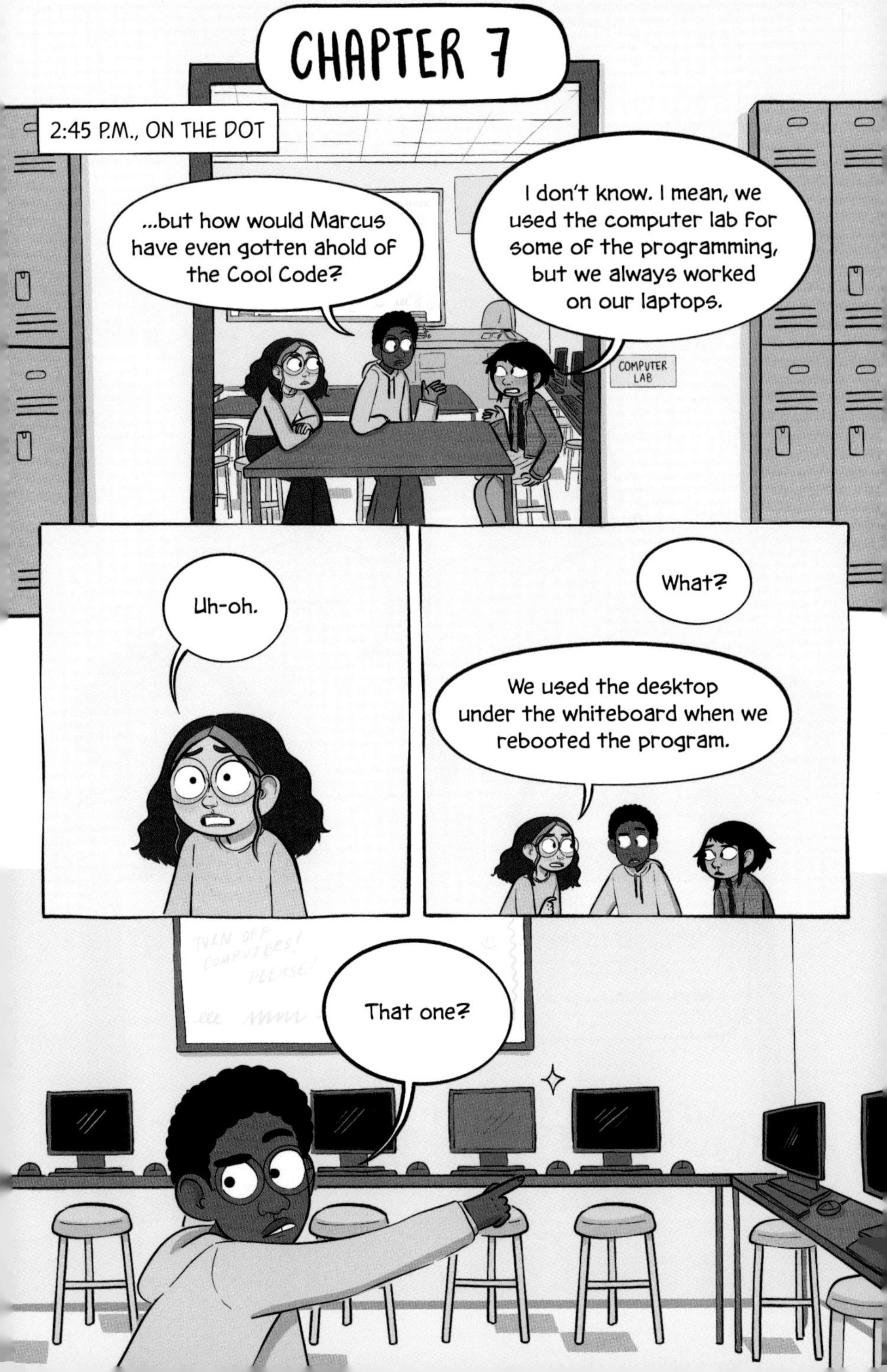
2:45 P.M., ON THE DOT
...but how would Marcus have even gotten ahold of the Cool Code?
I don't know. I mean, we used the computer lab for some of the programming, but we always worked on our laptops.
COMPUTER LAB
Uh-oh.
What?
We used the desktop under the whiteboard when we rebooted the program.
TURN OFF COMPUTERS! PLEASE!
That one?

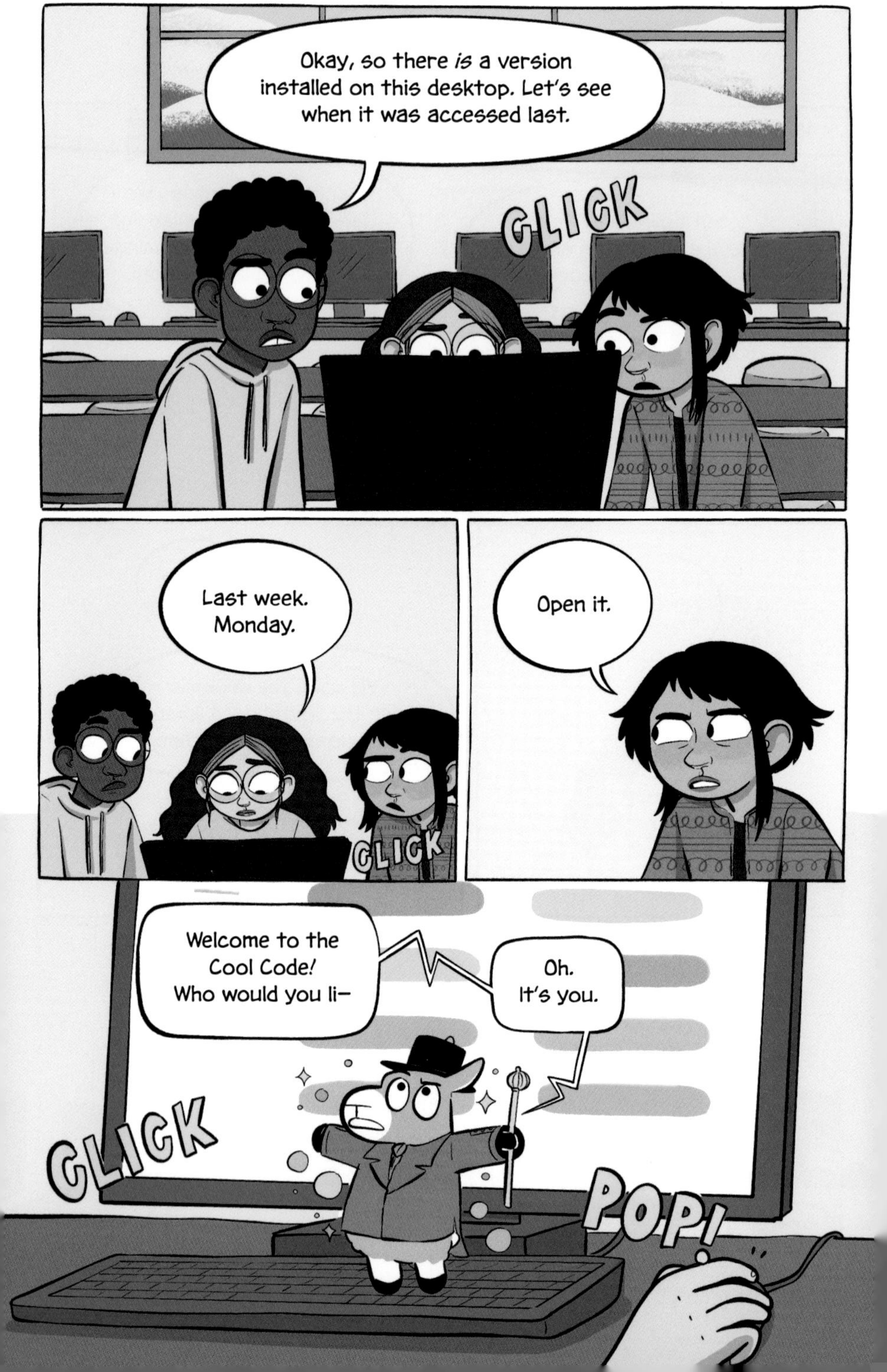
Okay, so there *is* a version installed on this desktop. Let's see when it was accessed last.
CLICK
Last week. Monday.
CLICK
Open it.
Welcome to the Cool Code! Who would you li–
Oh. It's you.
CLICK
POP!

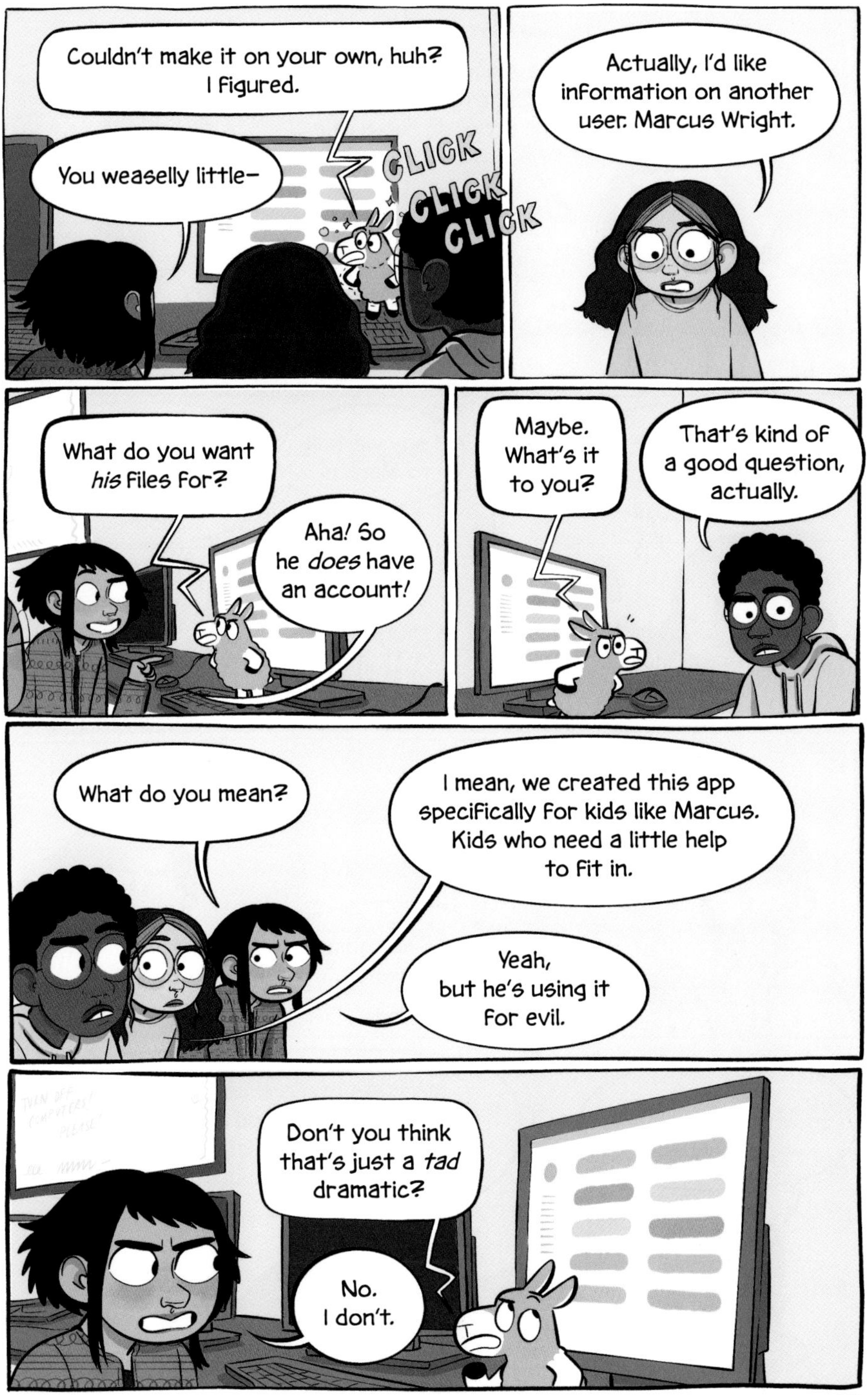
Couldn't make it on your own, huh? I figured.
You weaselly little–
CLICK CLICK CLICK
Actually, I'd like information on another user: Marcus Wright.
What do you want *his* files for?
Aha! So he *does* have an account!
Maybe. What's it to you?
That's kind of a good question, actually.
What do you mean?
I mean, we created this app specifically for kids like Marcus. Kids who need a little help to fit in.
Yeah, but he's using it for evil.
Don't you think that's just a *tad* dramatic?
No. I don't.

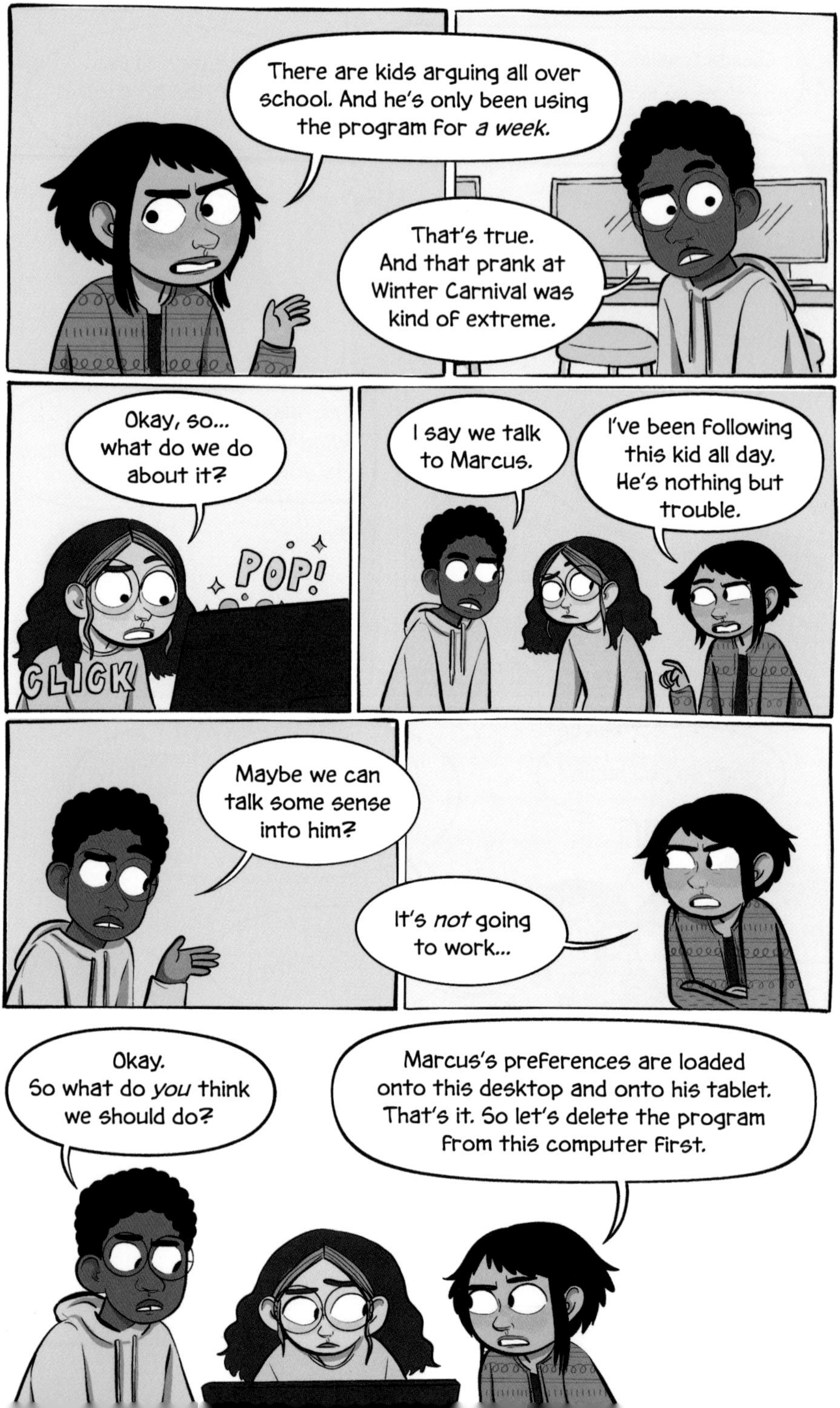
There are kids arguing all over school. And he's only been using the program for *a week.*
That's true. And that prank at Winter Carnival was kind of extreme.
Okay, so... what do we do about it?
POP!
CLICK
I say we talk to Marcus.
I've been following this kid all day. He's nothing but trouble.
Maybe we can talk some sense into him?
It's *not* going to work...
Okay. So what do *you* think we should do?
Marcus's preferences are loaded onto this desktop and onto his tablet. That's it. So let's delete the program from this computer first.

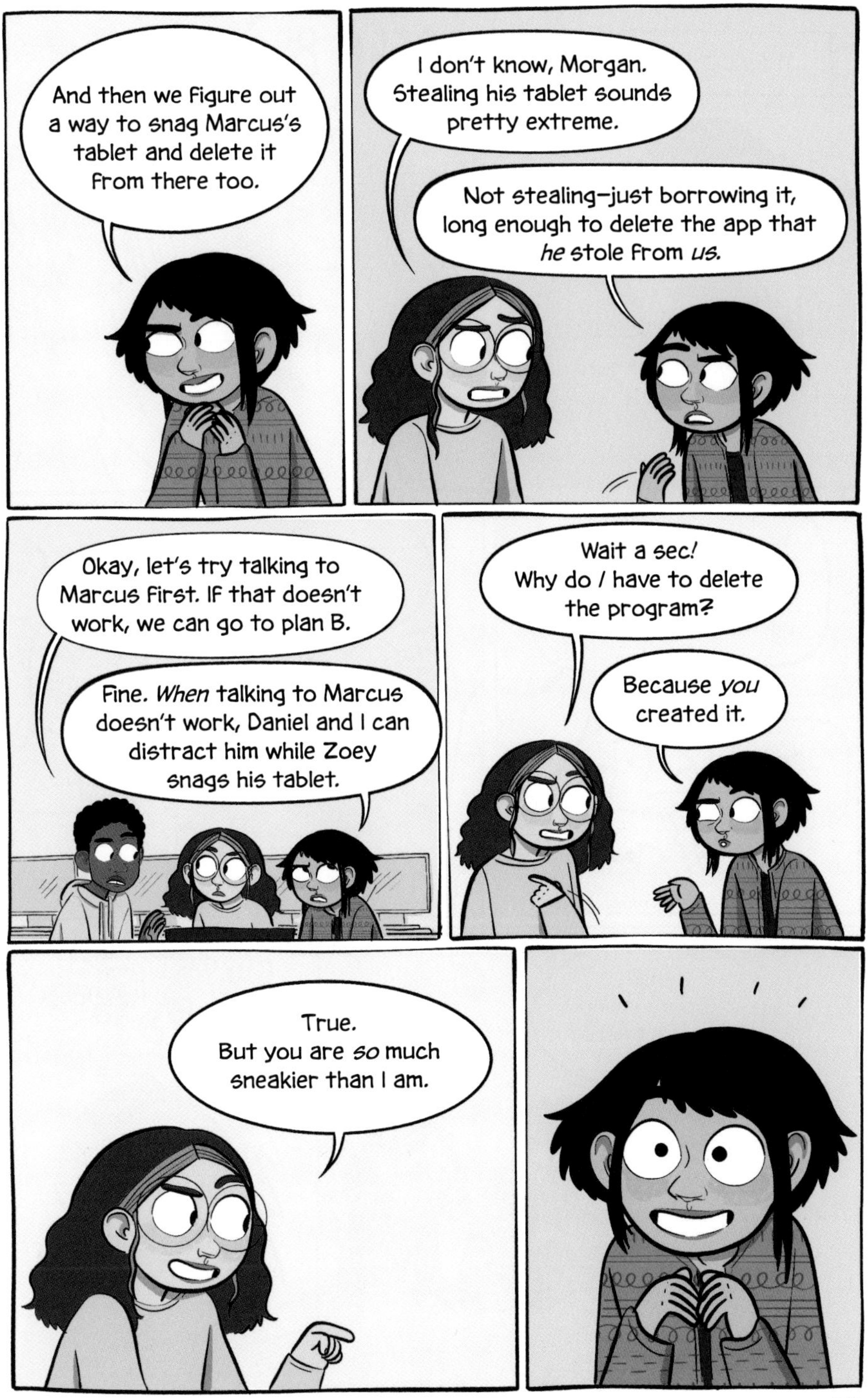
And then we figure out a way to snag Marcus's tablet and delete it from there too.
I don't know, Morgan. Stealing his tablet sounds pretty extreme.
Not stealing—just borrowing it, long enough to delete the app that *he* stole from *us*.
Okay, let's try talking to Marcus first. If that doesn't work, we can go to plan B.
Fine. *When* talking to Marcus doesn't work, Daniel and I can distract him while Zoey snags his tablet.
Wait a sec! Why do *I* have to delete the program?
Because *you* created it.
True. But you are *so* much sneakier than I am.

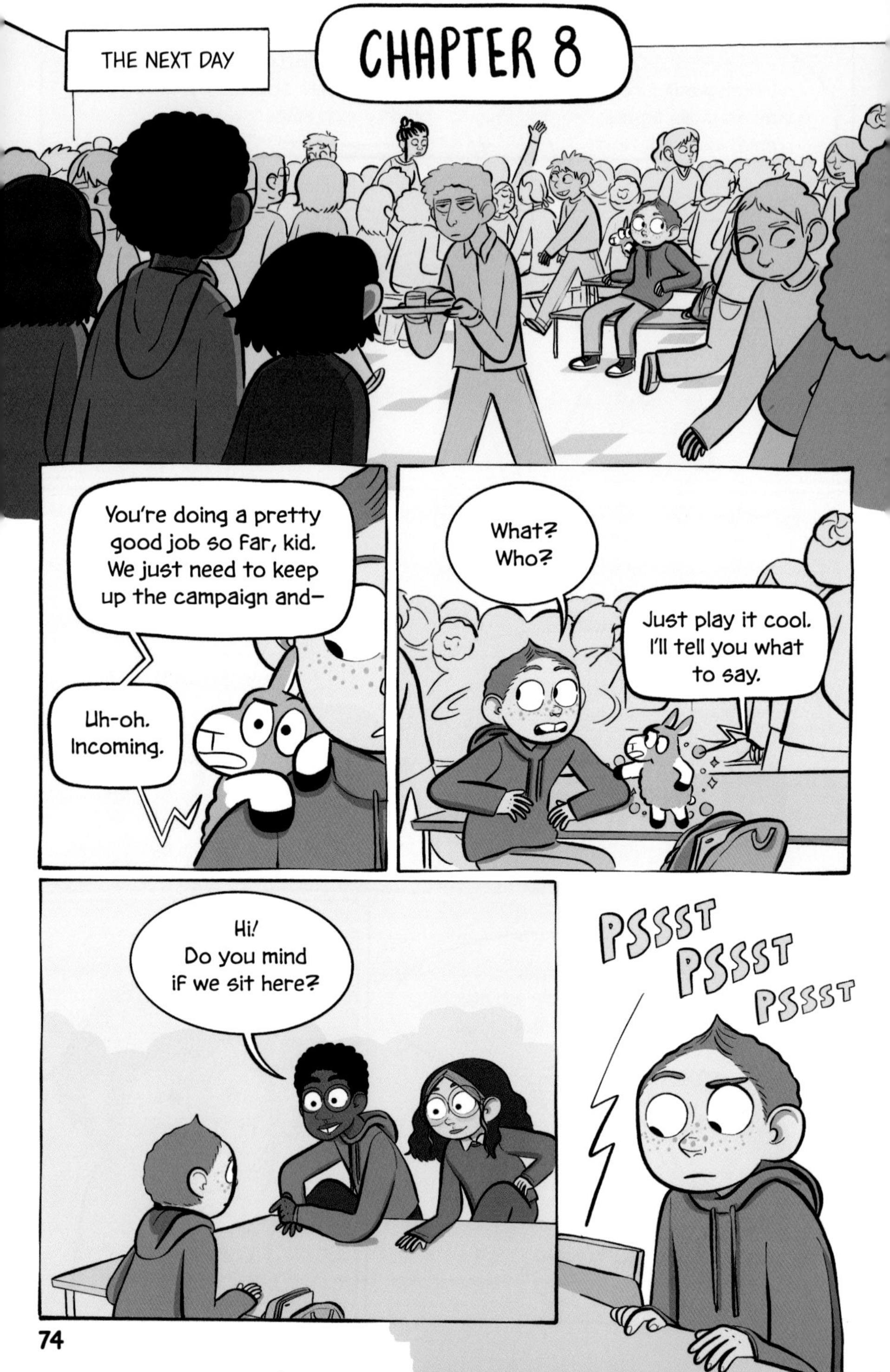
THE NEXT DAY
CHAPTER 8
You're doing a pretty good job so far, kid. We just need to keep up the campaign and—
Uh-oh. Incoming.
What? Who?
Just play it cool. I'll tell you what to say.
Hi! Do you mind if we sit here?
PSSST PSSST PSSST

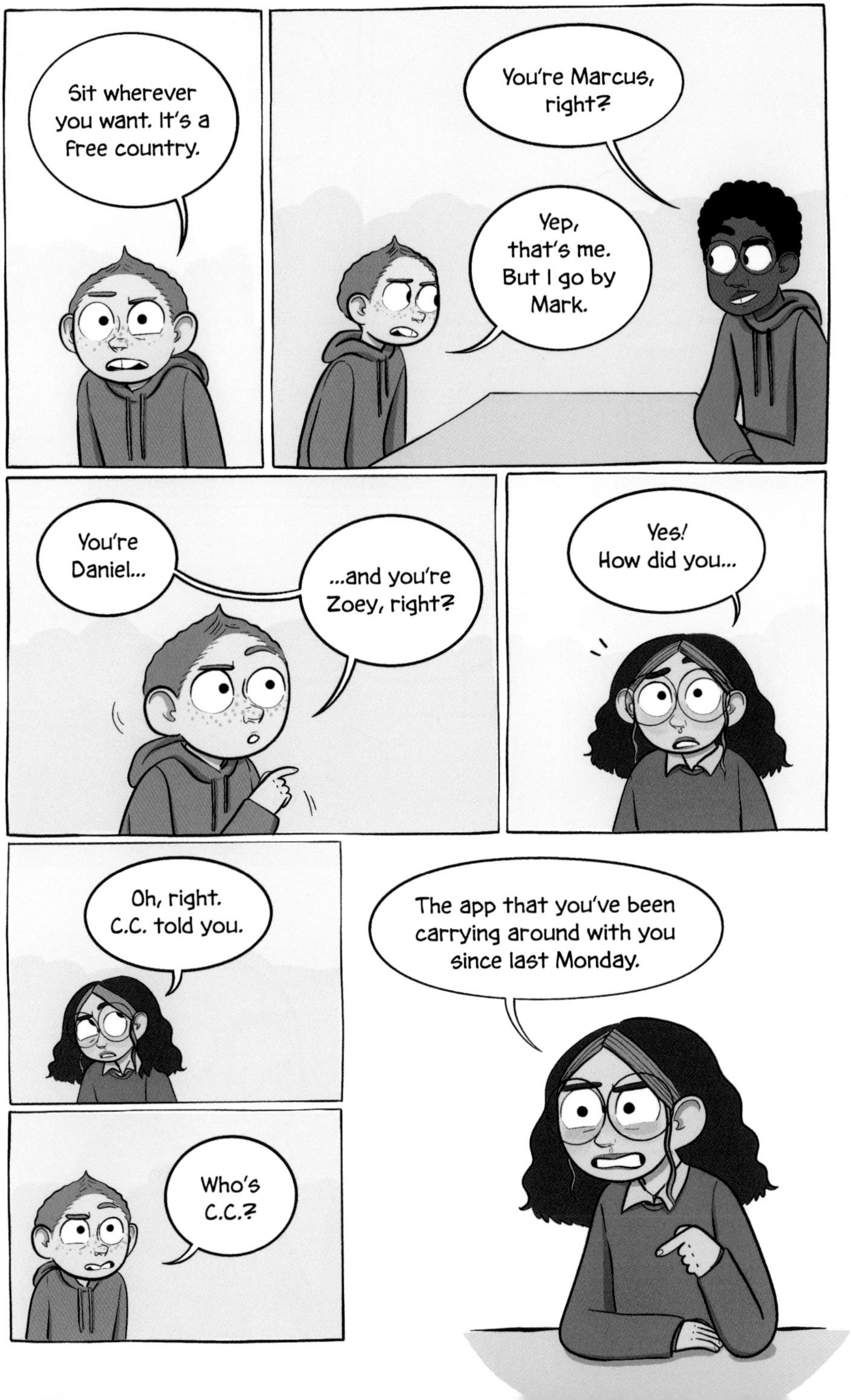
Sit wherever you want. It's a free country.
You're Marcus, right?
Yep, that's me. But I go by Mark.
You're Daniel...
...and you're Zoey, right?
Yes! How did you...
Oh, right. C.C. told you.
Who's C.C.?
The app that you've been carrying around with you since last Monday.

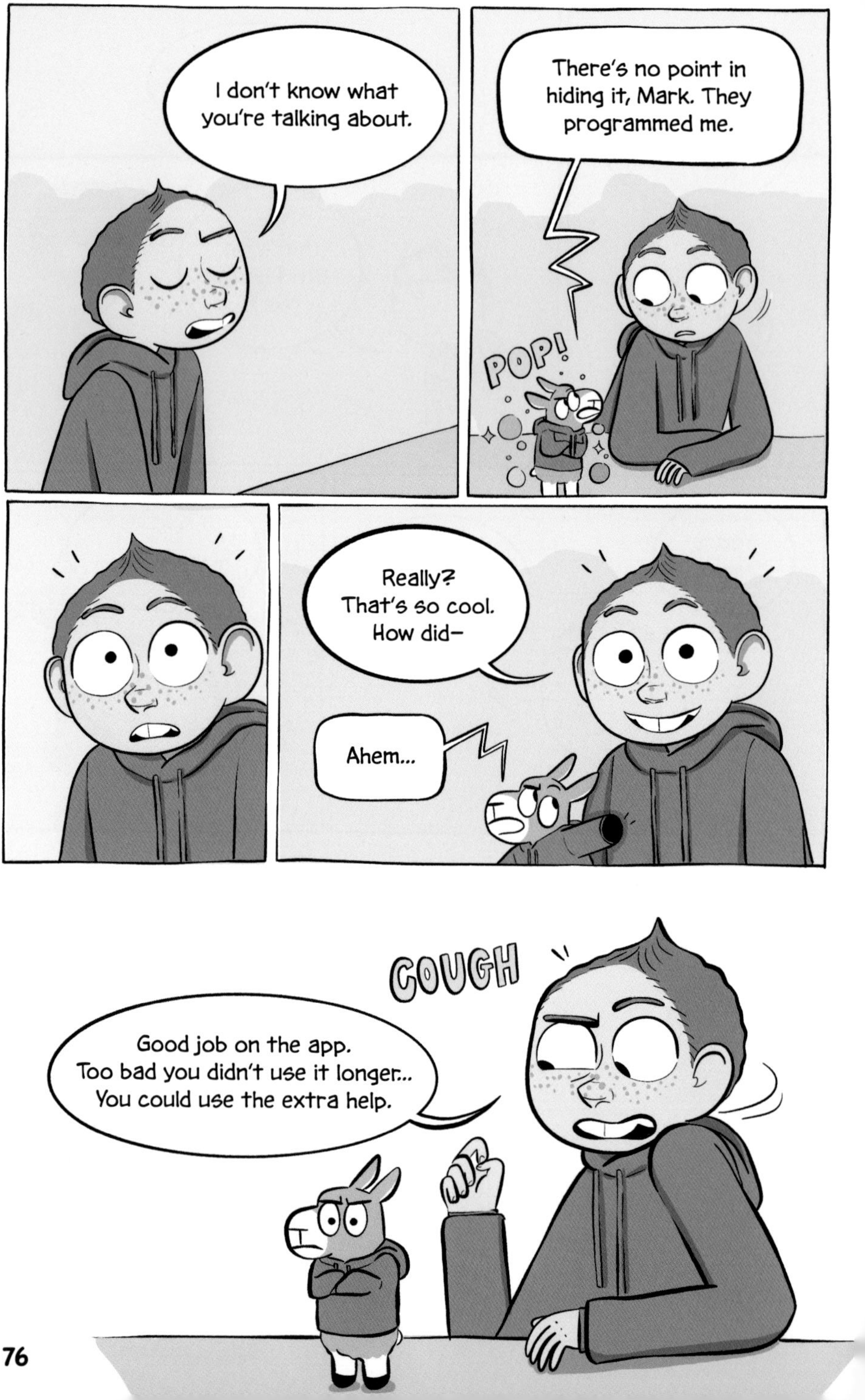

I don't know what you're talking about.
There's no point in hiding it, Mark. They programmed me.
POP!
Really? That's so cool. How did-
Ahem...
COUGH
Good job on the app. Too bad you didn't use it longer... You could use the extra help.

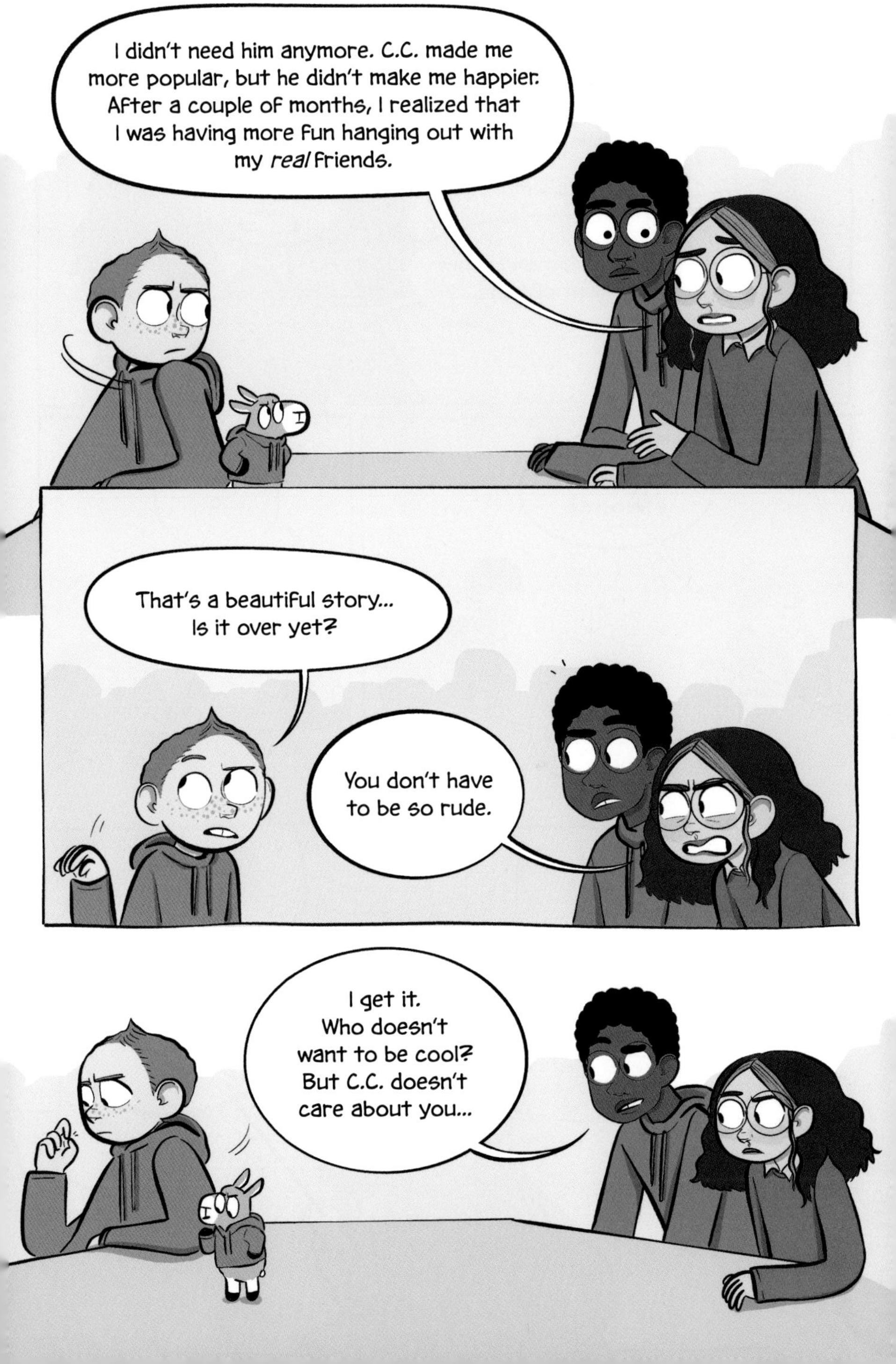
I didn't need him anymore. C.C. made me more popular, but he didn't make me happier. After a couple of months, I realized that I was having more fun hanging out with my *real* friends.
That's a beautiful story... Is it over yet?
You don't have to be so rude.
I get it. Who doesn't want to be cool? But C.C. doesn't care about you...

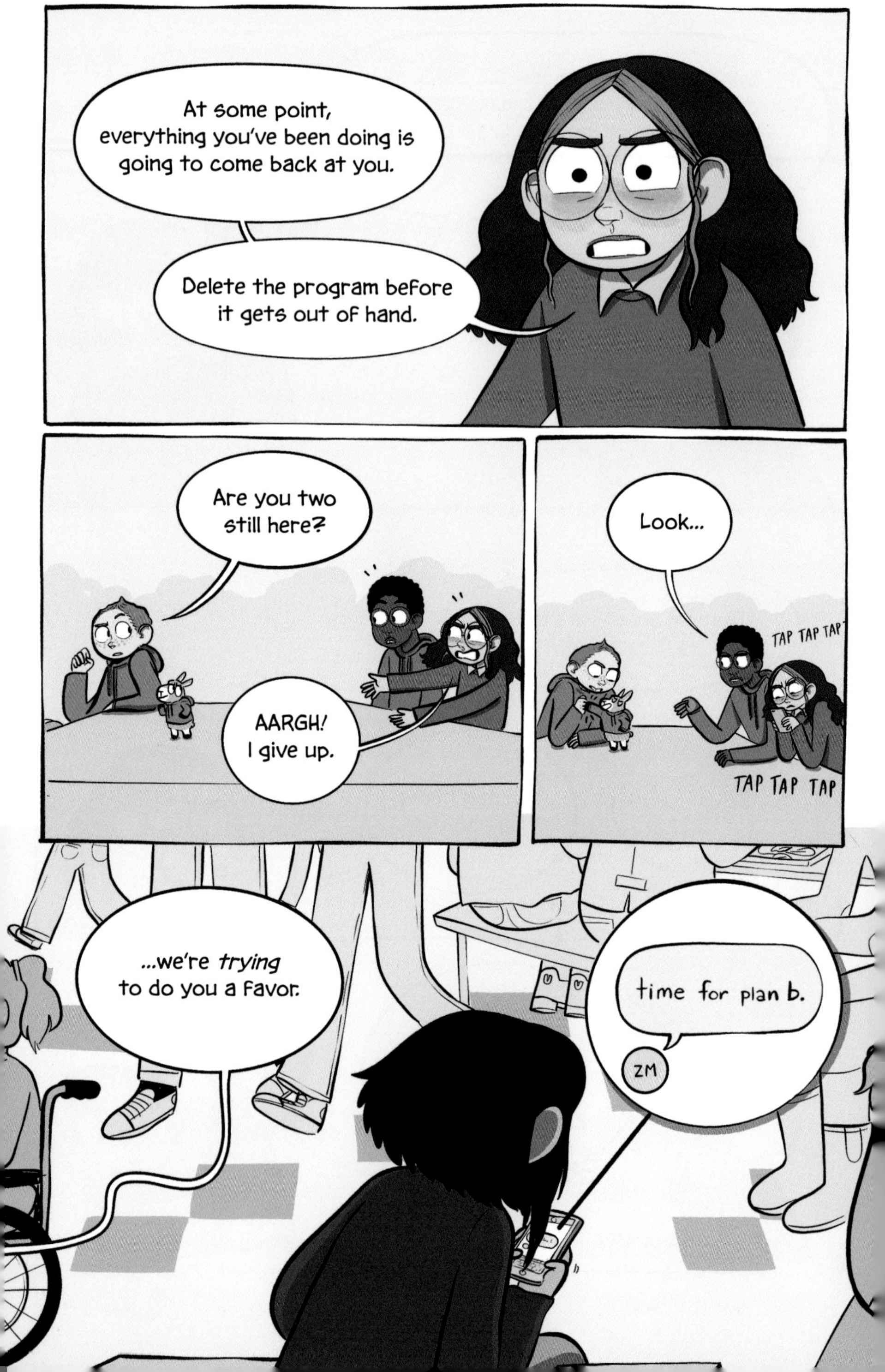
At some point, everything you've been doing is going to come back at you.
Delete the program before it gets out of hand.
Are you two still here?
AARGH! I give up.
Look...
TAP TAP TAP
TAP TAP TAP
...we're *trying* to do you a favor.
time for plan b.
ZM

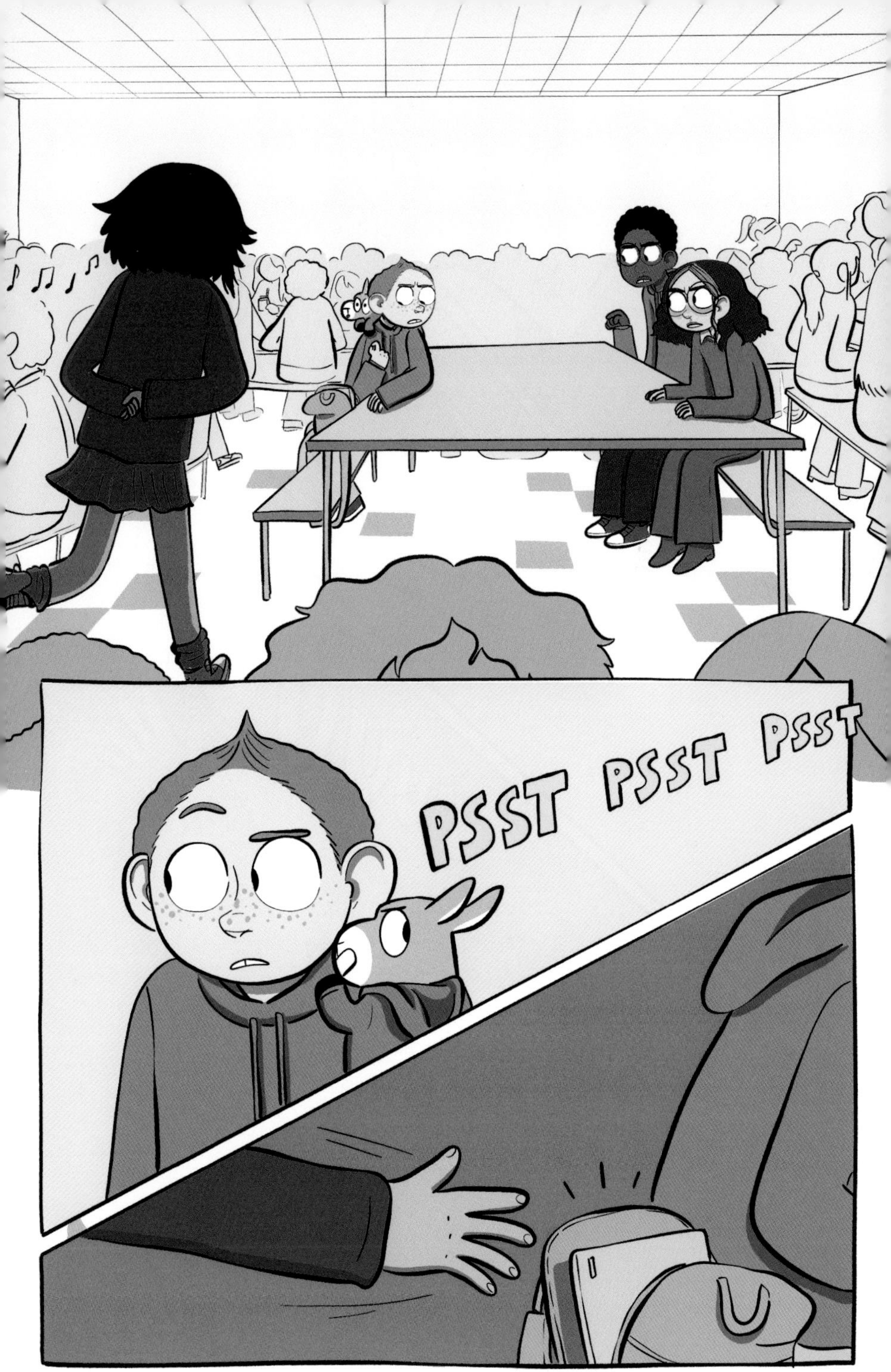
PSST PSST PSST

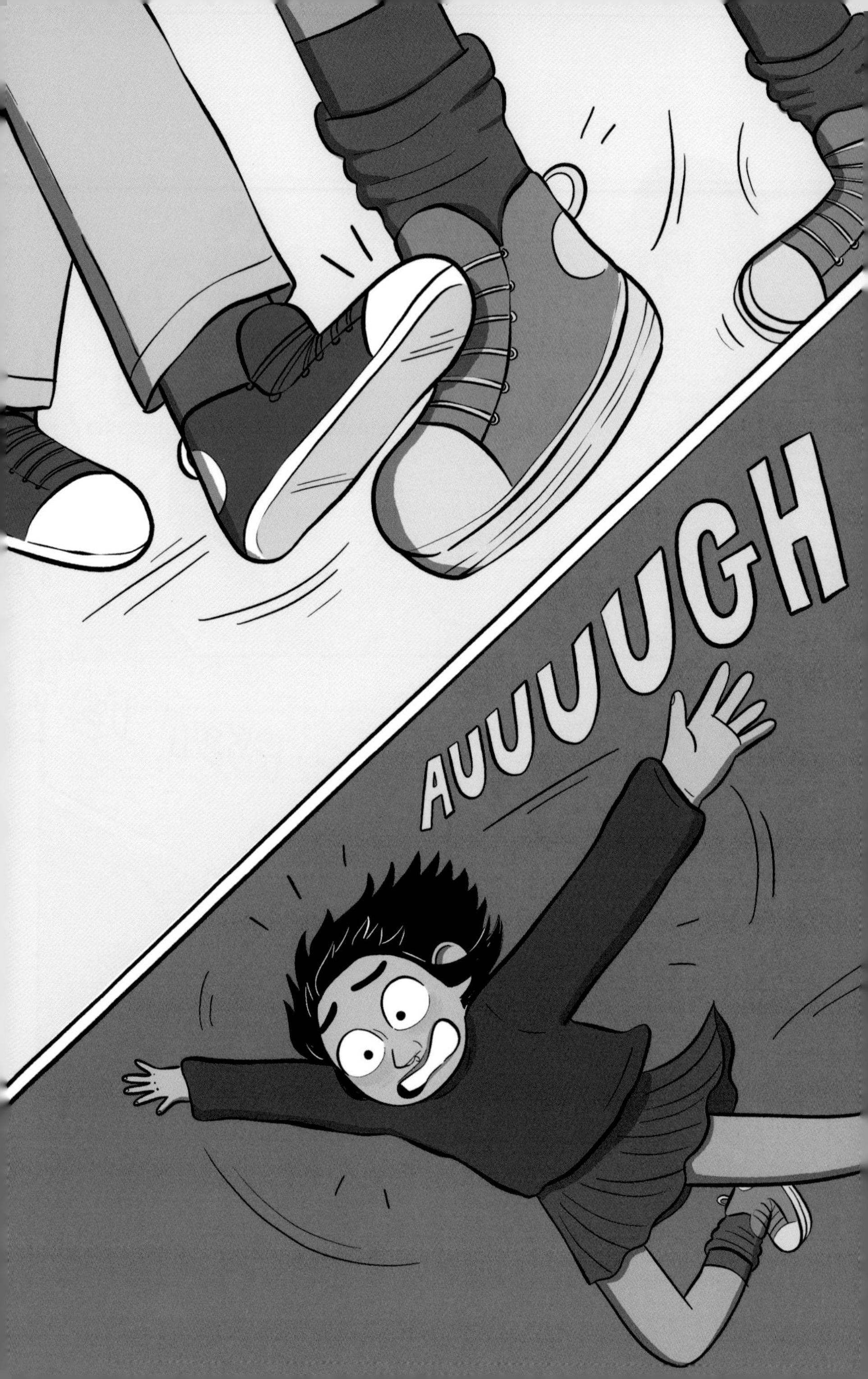
AUUUUGH

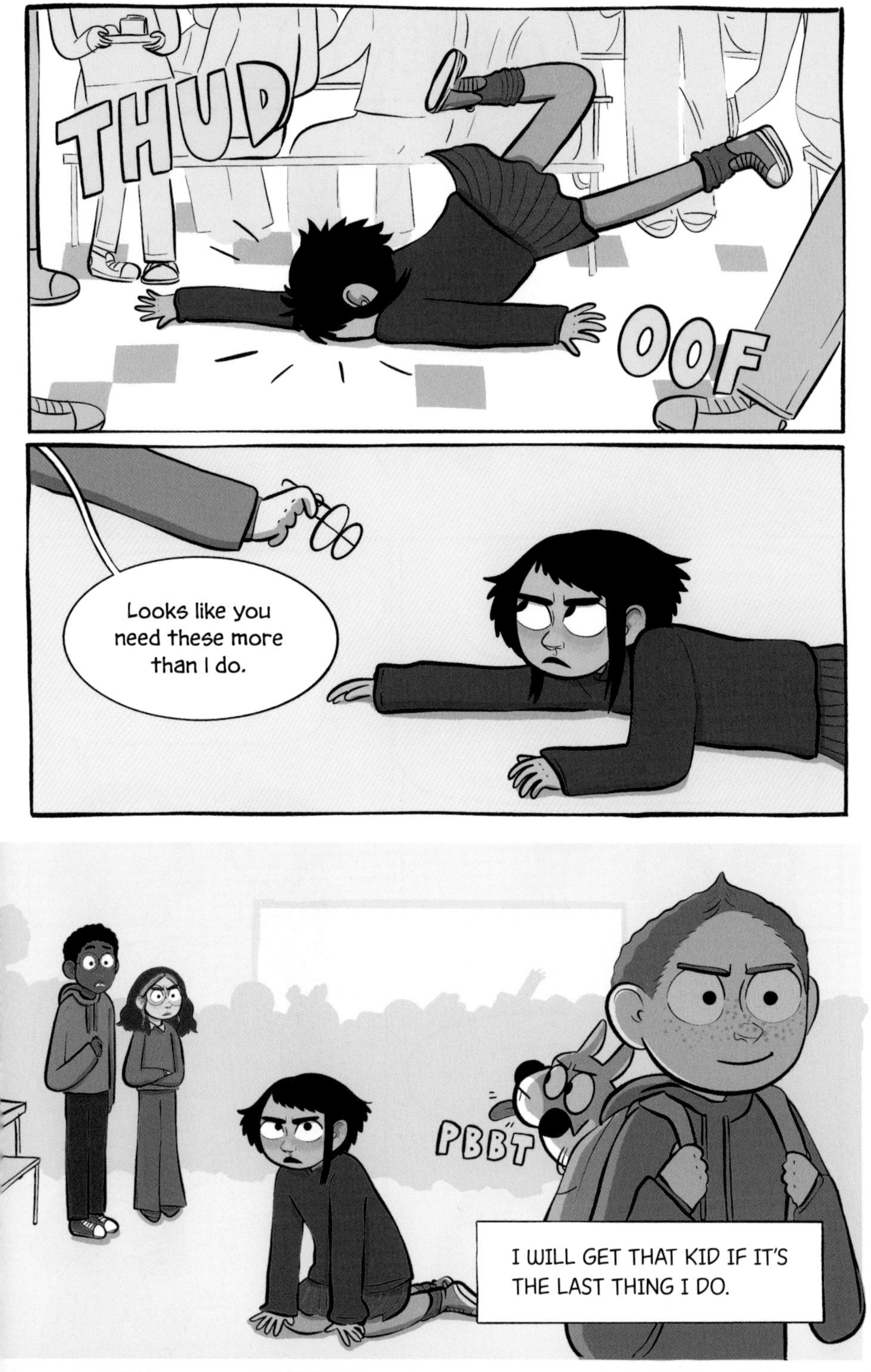
THUD
OOF
Looks like you need these more than I do.
PBBT
I WILL GET THAT KID IF IT'S THE LAST THING I DO.

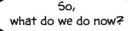

CHAPTER 9

So,
what do we do now?

We're going to have to
shut down the program.

Forget it. There's no way
we're getting that tablet. C.C.'s like
a 24-hour alarm system.

No...I mean, delete it at the source.
The apps are just access points to
the main program, right? So let's
delete the original program!

Seriously?
That program is *months*
of our lives.

It doesn't matter anyway.
We can't get to it.

What?
Why not?

It's a huge program—
so I housed it on my
parents' server.

Yeah.
So?

Well, after C.C. ordered
pizzas using my dad's
credit card, my parents
realized they had some
security holes so they...
Fixed them.

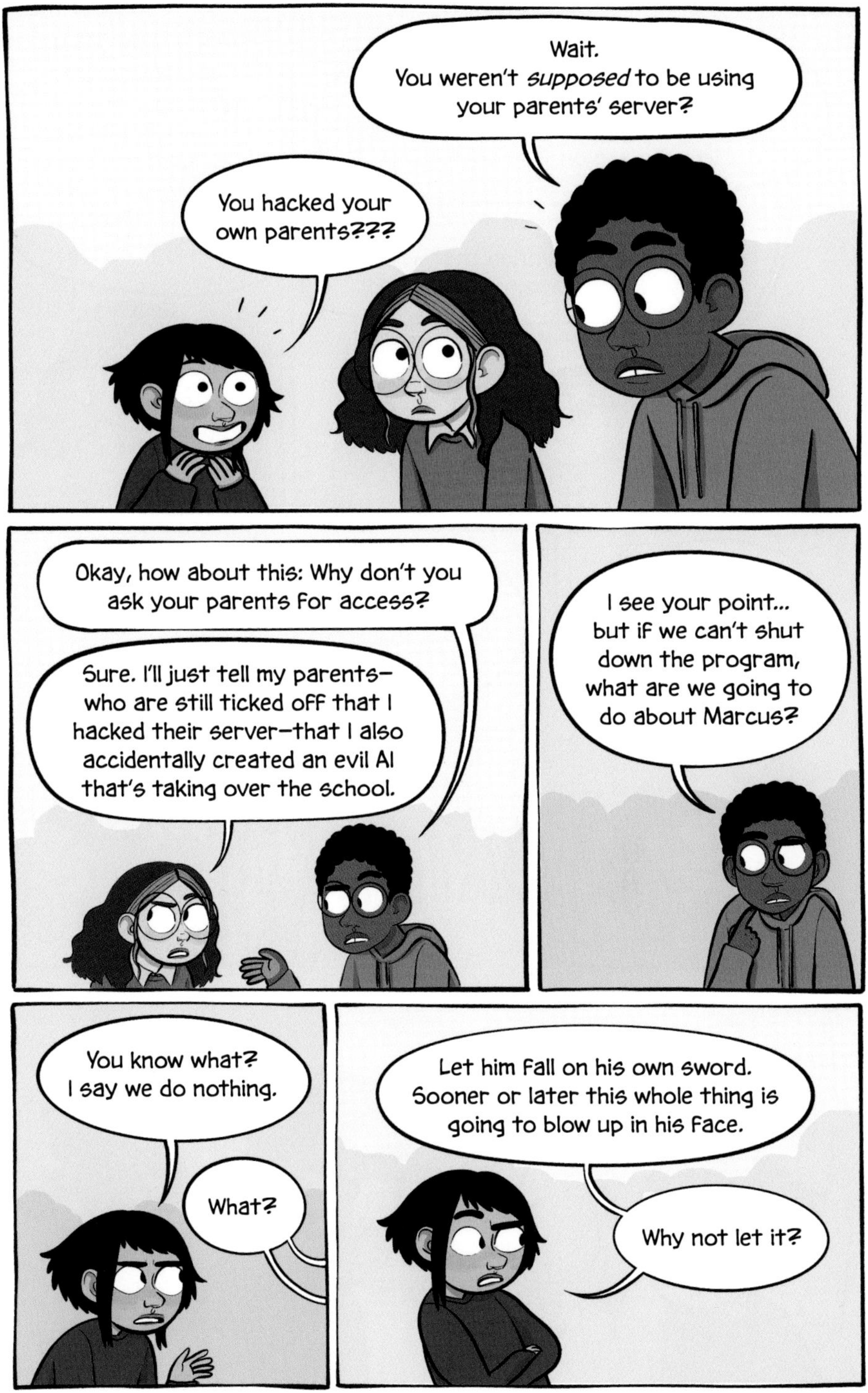
Wait.
You weren't *supposed* to be using your parents' server?
You hacked your own parents???
Okay, how about this: Why don't you ask your parents for access?
Sure. I'll just tell my parents—who are still ticked off that I hacked their server—that I also accidentally created an evil AI that's taking over the school.
I see your point... but if we can't shut down the program, what are we going to do about Marcus?
You know what? I say we do nothing.
What?
Let him fall on his own sword. Sooner or later this whole thing is going to blow up in his face.
Why not let it?

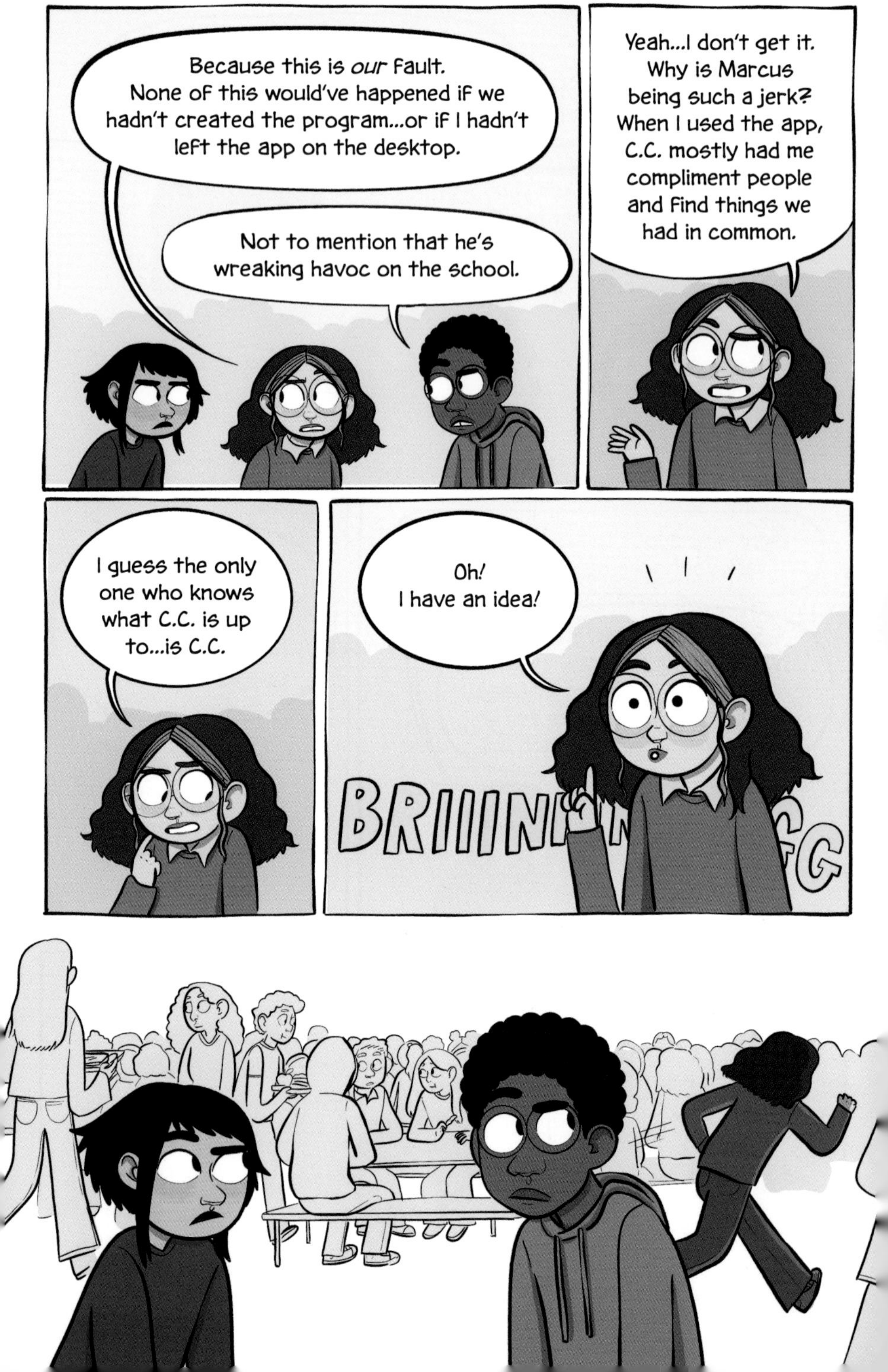
Because this is *our* fault. None of this would've happened if we hadn't created the program...or if I hadn't left the app on the desktop.
Not to mention that he's wreaking havoc on the school.
Yeah...I don't get it. Why is Marcus being such a jerk? When I used the app, C.C. mostly had me compliment people and find things we had in common.
I guess the only one who knows what C.C. is up to...is C.C.
Oh! I have an idea!
BRIIIN
G

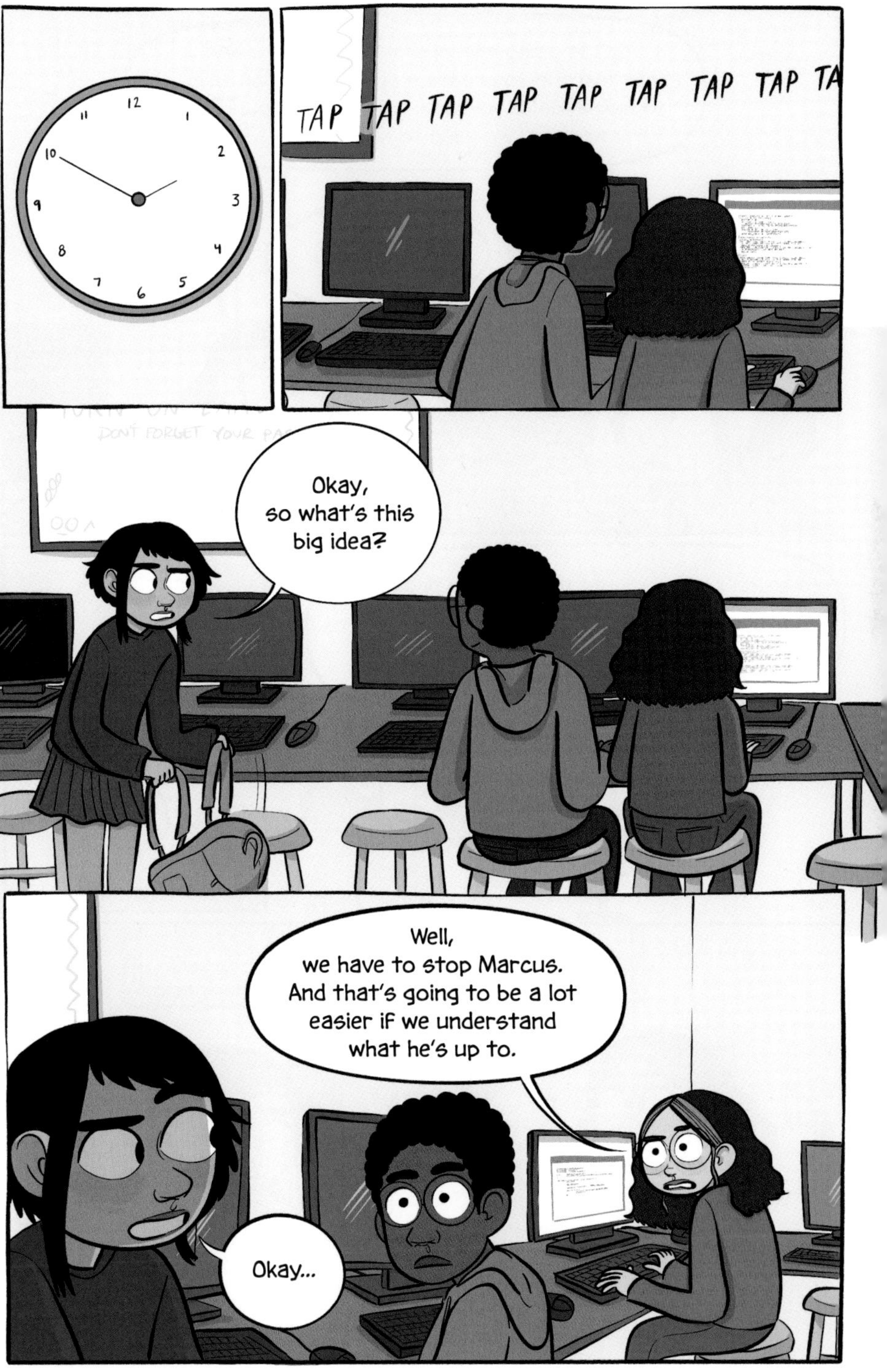
TAP TAP TAP TAP TAP TAP TAP TAP
Okay, so what's this big idea?
Well, we have to stop Marcus. And that's going to be a lot easier if we understand what he's up to.
Okay...

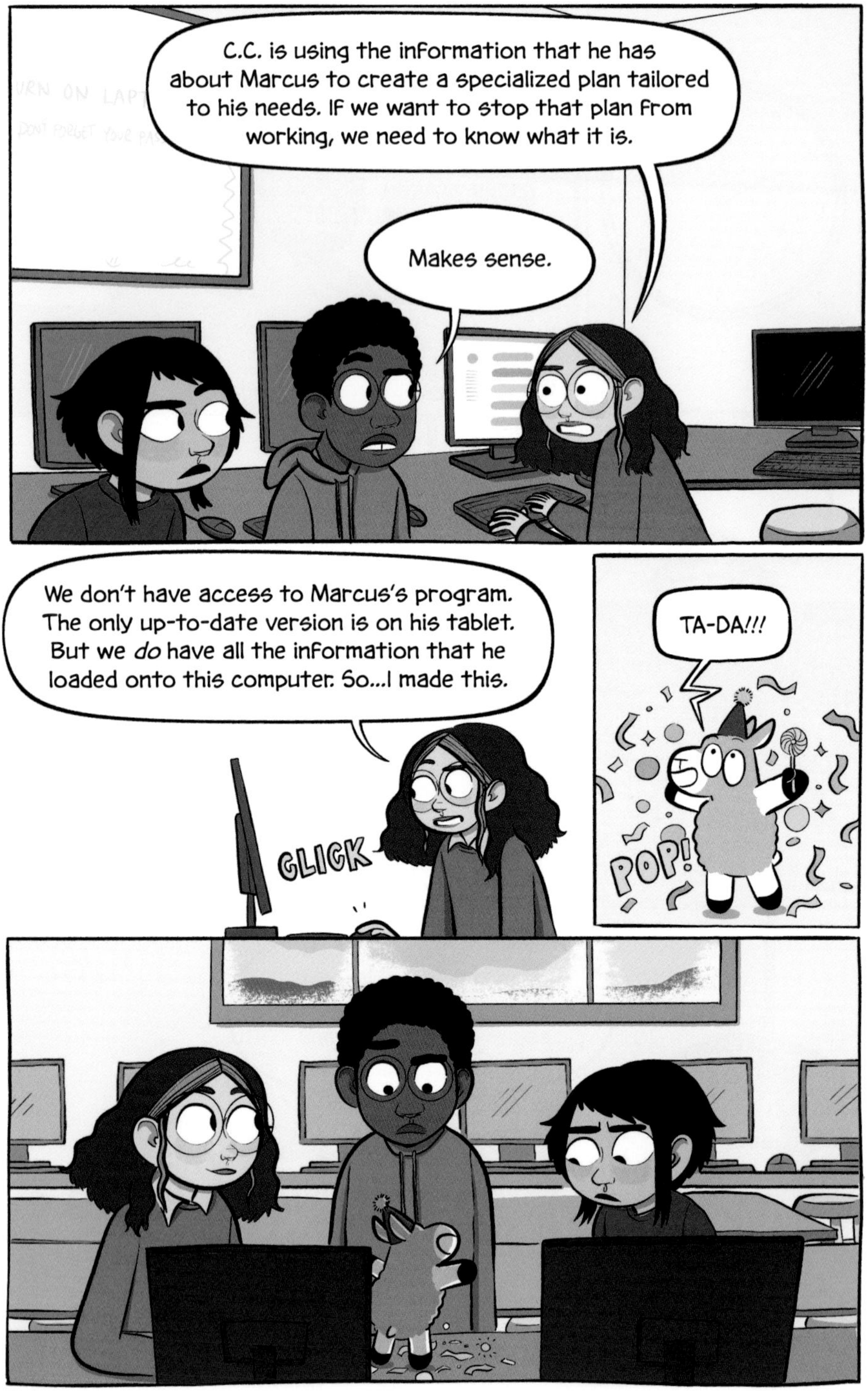
C.C. is using the information that he has about Marcus to create a specialized plan tailored to his needs. If we want to stop that plan from working, we need to know what it is.
Makes sense.
We don't have access to Marcus's program. The only up-to-date version is on his tablet. But we *do* have all the information that he loaded onto this computer. So...I made this.
CLICK
TA-DA!!!
POP!

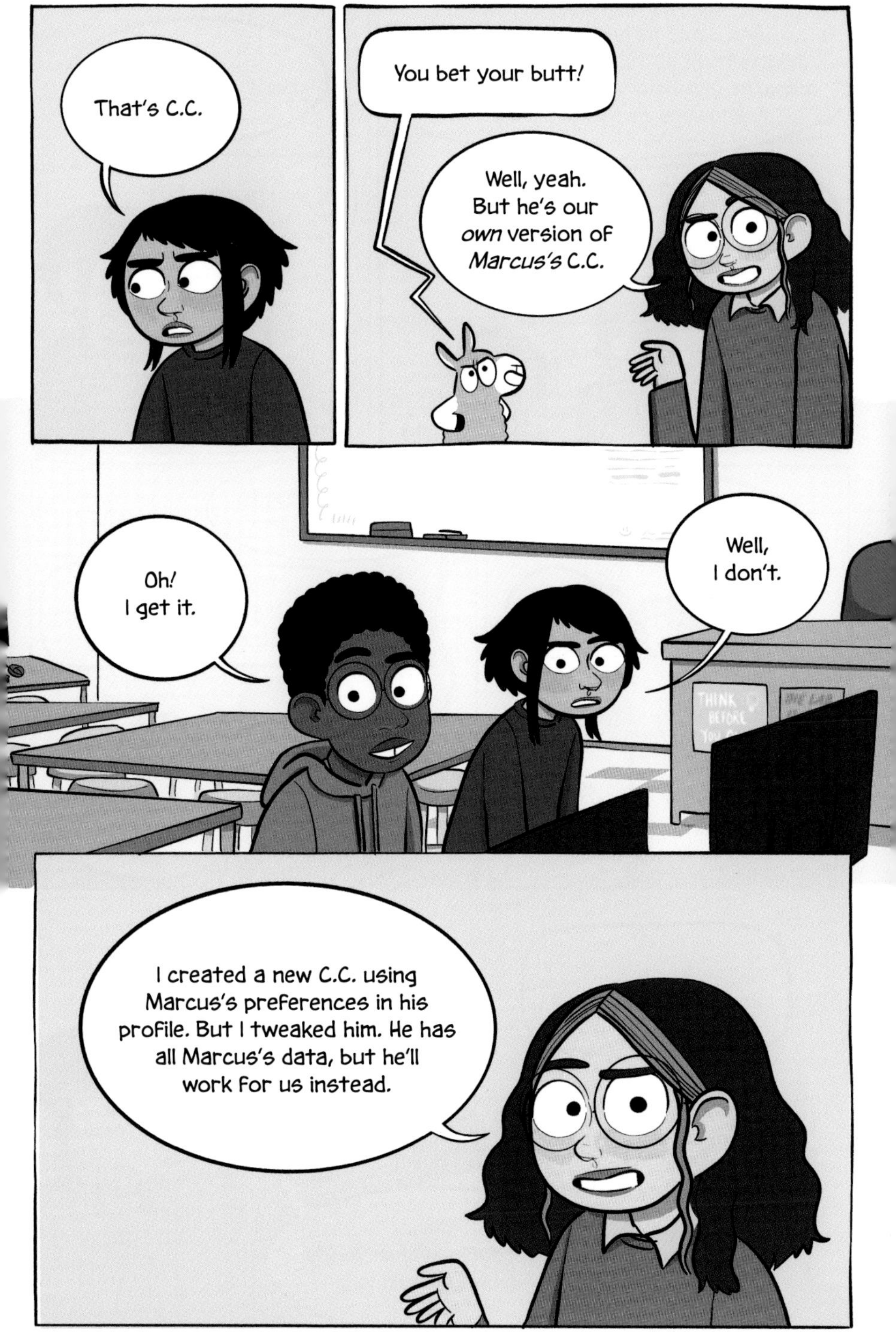
That's C.C.
You bet your butt!
Well, yeah. But he's our *own* version of *Marcus's* C.C.
Oh! I get it.
Well, I don't.
THINK BEFORE
I created a new C.C. using Marcus's preferences in his profile. But I tweaked him. He has all Marcus's data, but he'll work for us instead.

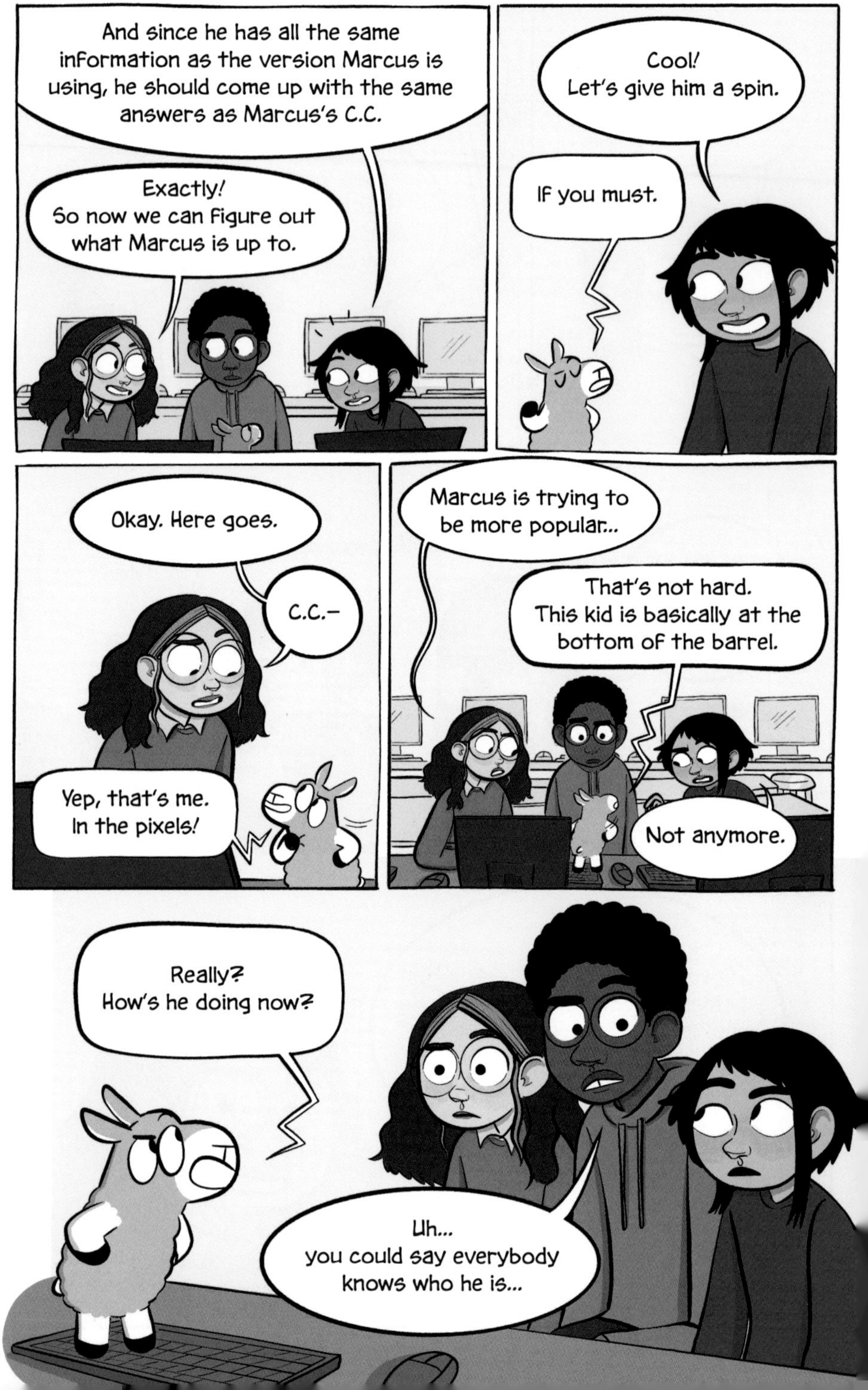
And since he has all the same information as the version Marcus is using, he should come up with the same answers as Marcus's C.C.
Exactly! So now we can figure out what Marcus is up to.
Cool! Let's give him a spin.
If you must.
Okay. Here goes.
C.C.–
Yep, that's me. In the pixels!
Marcus is trying to be more popular...
That's not hard. This kid is basically at the bottom of the barrel.
Not anymore.
Really? How's he doing now?
Uh... you could say everybody knows who he is...

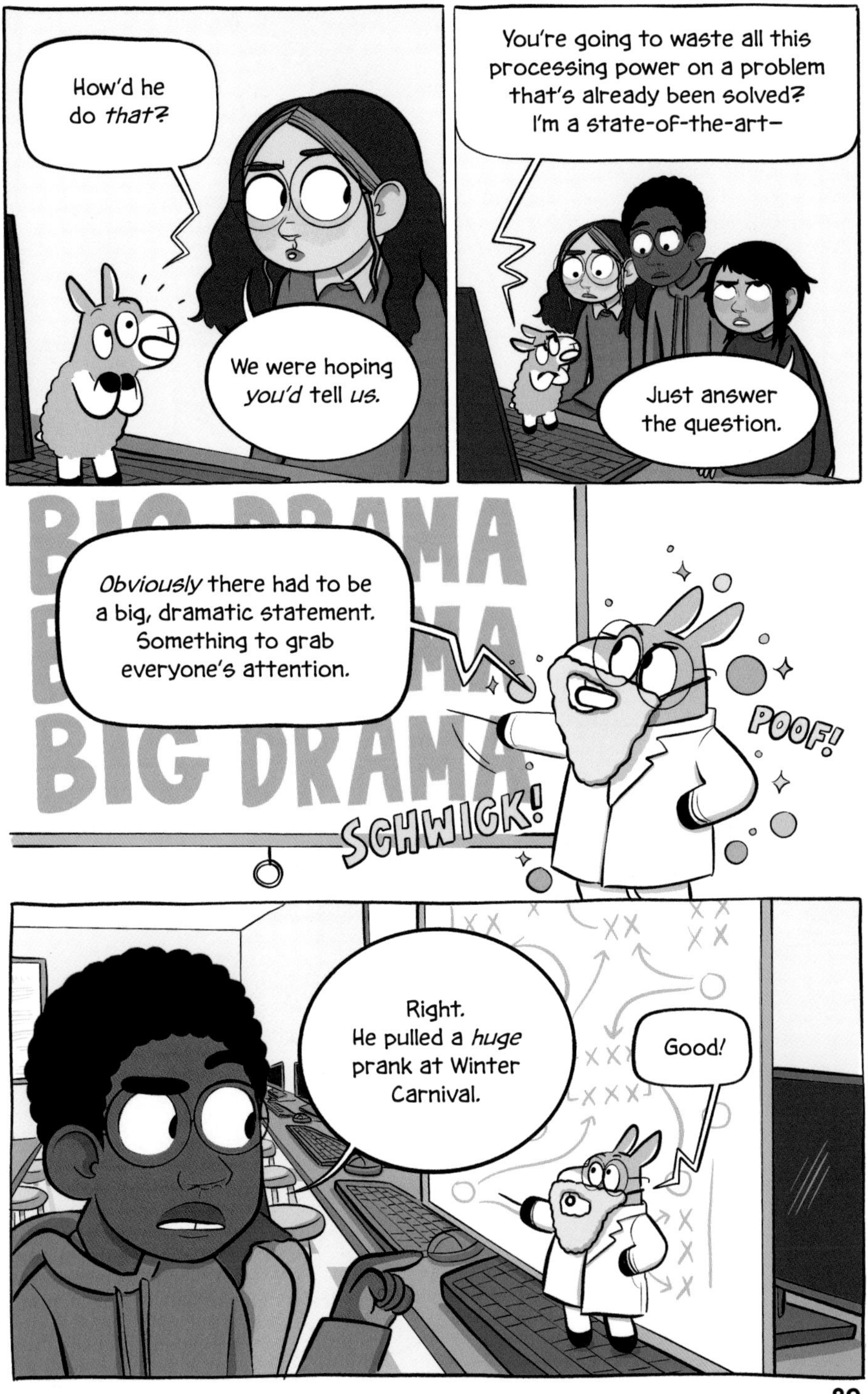
How'd he do *that*?
We were hoping *you'd* tell *us*.
You're going to waste all this processing power on a problem that's already been solved? I'm a state-of-the-art—
Just answer the question.
BIG DRAMA
BIG DRAMA
BIG DRAMA
Obviously there had to be a big, dramatic statement. Something to grab everyone's attention.
POOF!
SCHWICK!
Right. He pulled a *huge* prank at Winter Carnival.
Good!

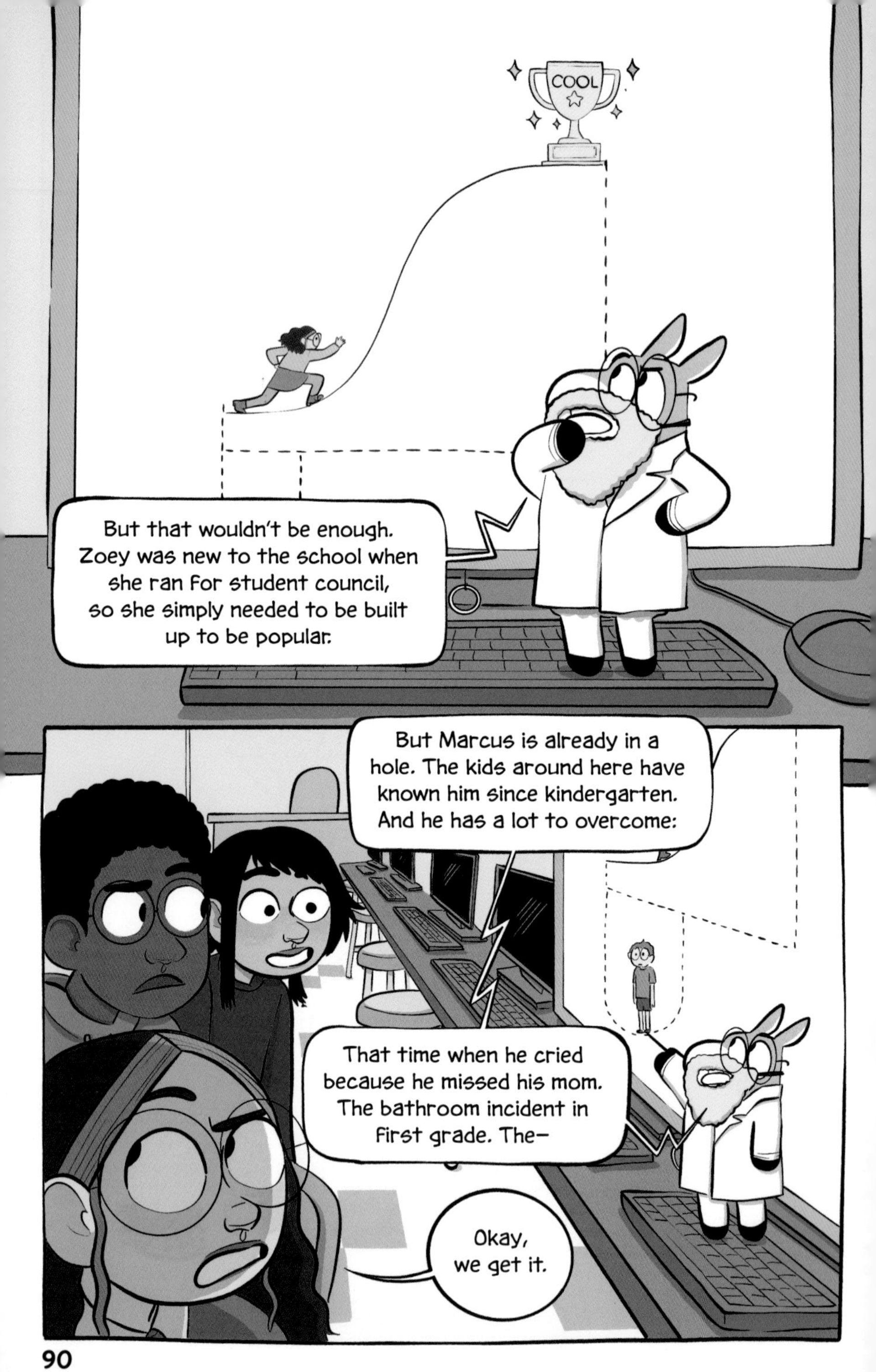
COOL
But that wouldn't be enough. Zoey was new to the school when she ran for student council, so she simply needed to be built up to be popular.
But Marcus is already in a hole. The kids around here have known him since kindergarten. And he has a lot to overcome:
That time when he cried because he missed his mom. The bathroom incident in first grade. The—
Okay, we get it.

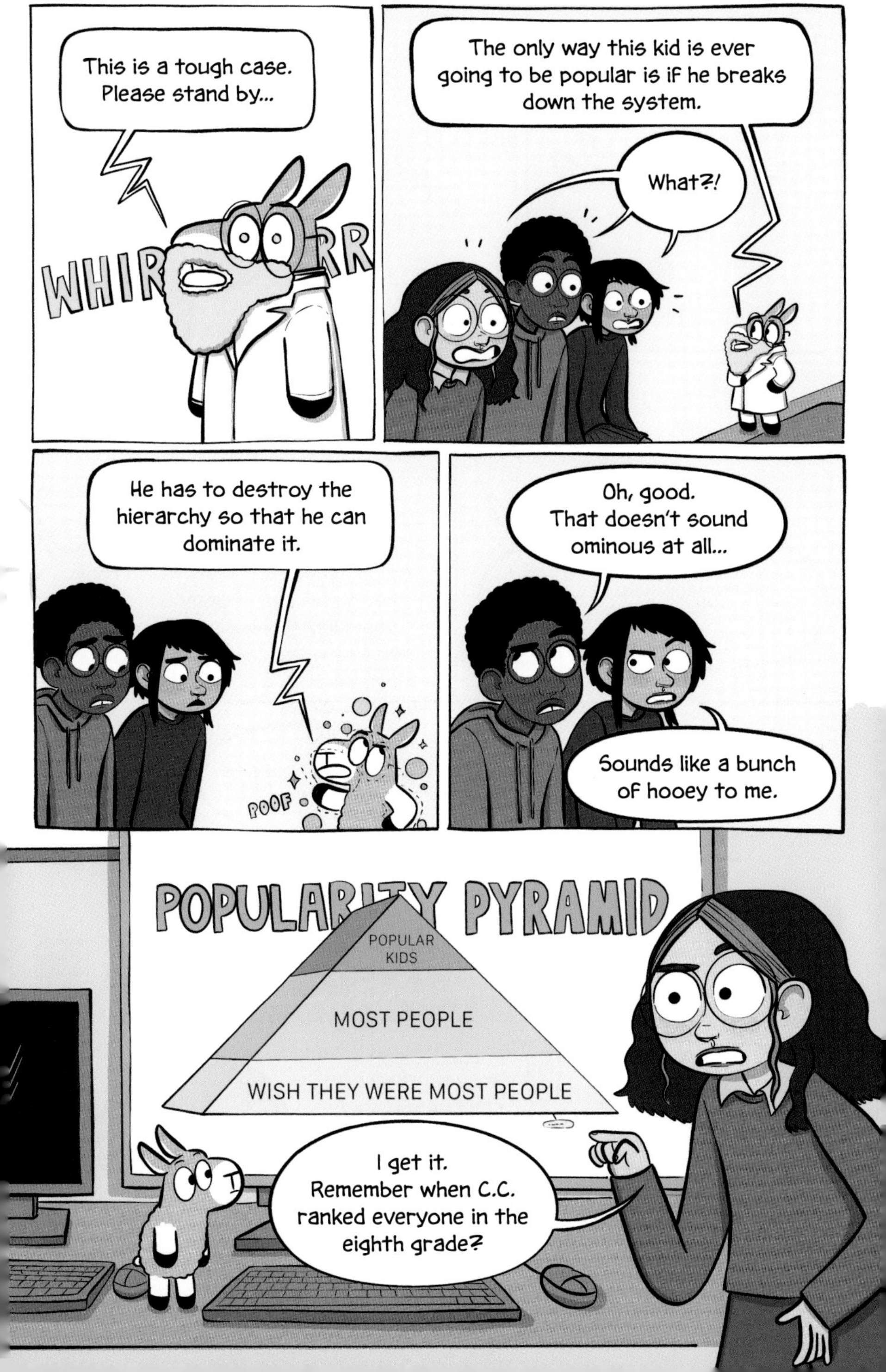
This is a tough case. Please stand by...
WHIRRR
The only way this kid is ever going to be popular is if he breaks down the system.
What?!
He has to destroy the hierarchy so that he can dominate it.
POOF
Oh, good. That doesn't sound ominous at all...
Sounds like a bunch of hooey to me.
POPULARITY PYRAMID
POPULAR KIDS
MOST PEOPLE
WISH THEY WERE MOST PEOPLE
I get it. Remember when C.C. ranked everyone in the eighth grade?

No need to thank me—it's all part of the job.

If you rank kids by their popularity, it makes a pyramid. There's only room for a few cool kids at the top.

POPULARITY PYRAMID

POPULAR KIDS

MOST P

WISH THEY WERE MOST PEOP

MOST PEOPLE

H THEY WERE MOST PEOPLE

In the middle, you have all the kids who are just kind of average. That's where most of us are.

MOST PEOPLE

WISH THEY WERE MOST PEOPLE

MARCUS

The top groups are full, which keeps kids lower down from moving up. But if someone loses popularity—like, say, if they get pantsed in the cafeteria—then they move down and create an opening.

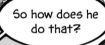

This is where Marcus is. He has to make room above him on the pyramid before he can climb up.

So how does he do that?

MOST PEOPLE

EY WERE MOST PEOPLE

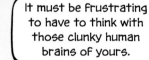

It must be frustrating to have to think with those clunky human brains of yours.

Hey! We *made* you!

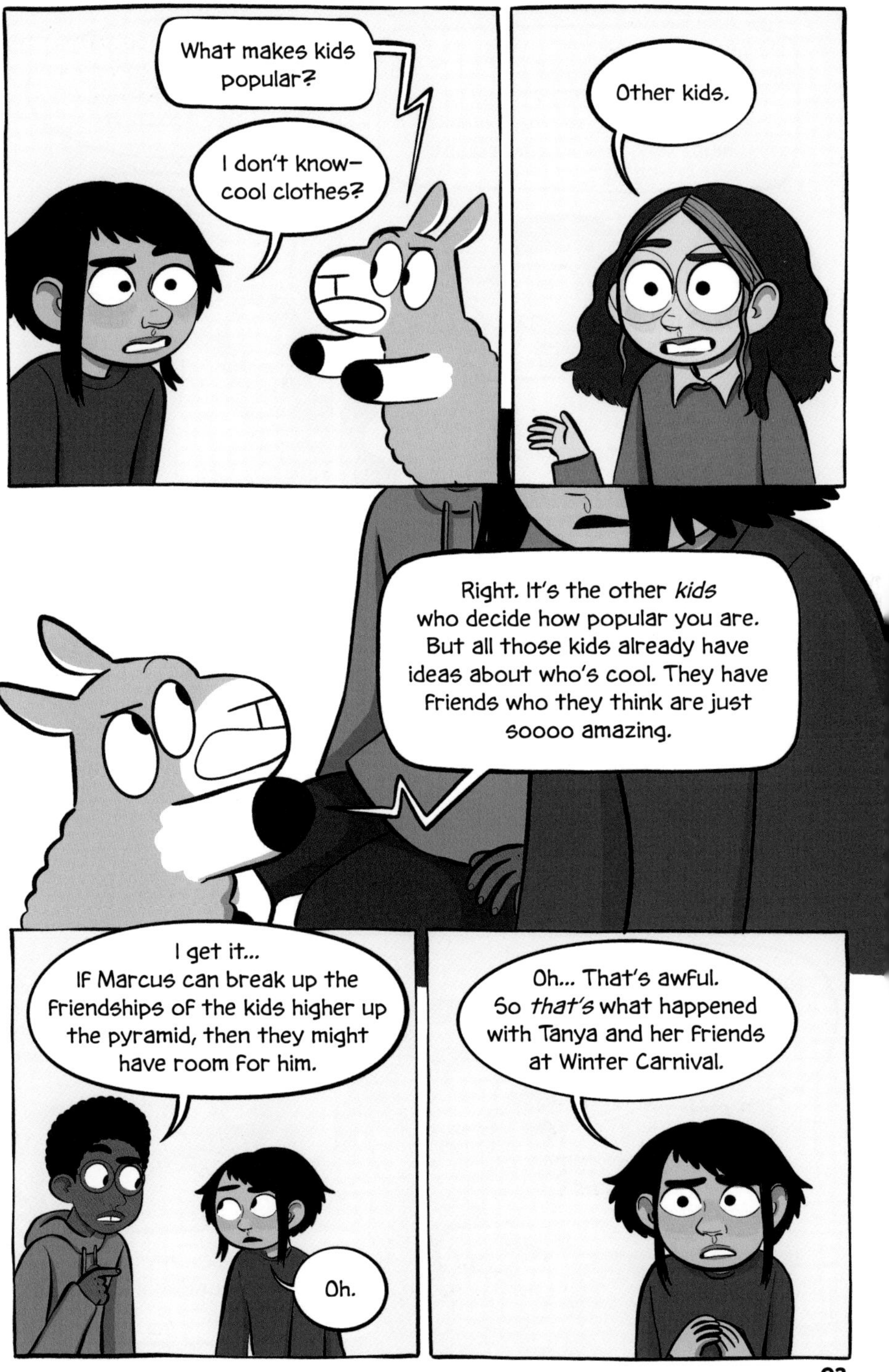
What makes kids popular?
I don't know— cool clothes?
Other kids.
Right. It's the other *kids* who decide how popular you are. But all those kids already have ideas about who's cool. They have friends who they think are just soooo amazing.
I get it... If Marcus can break up the friendships of the kids higher up the pyramid, then they might have room for him.
Oh.
Oh... That's awful. So *that's* what happened with Tanya and her friends at Winter Carnival.

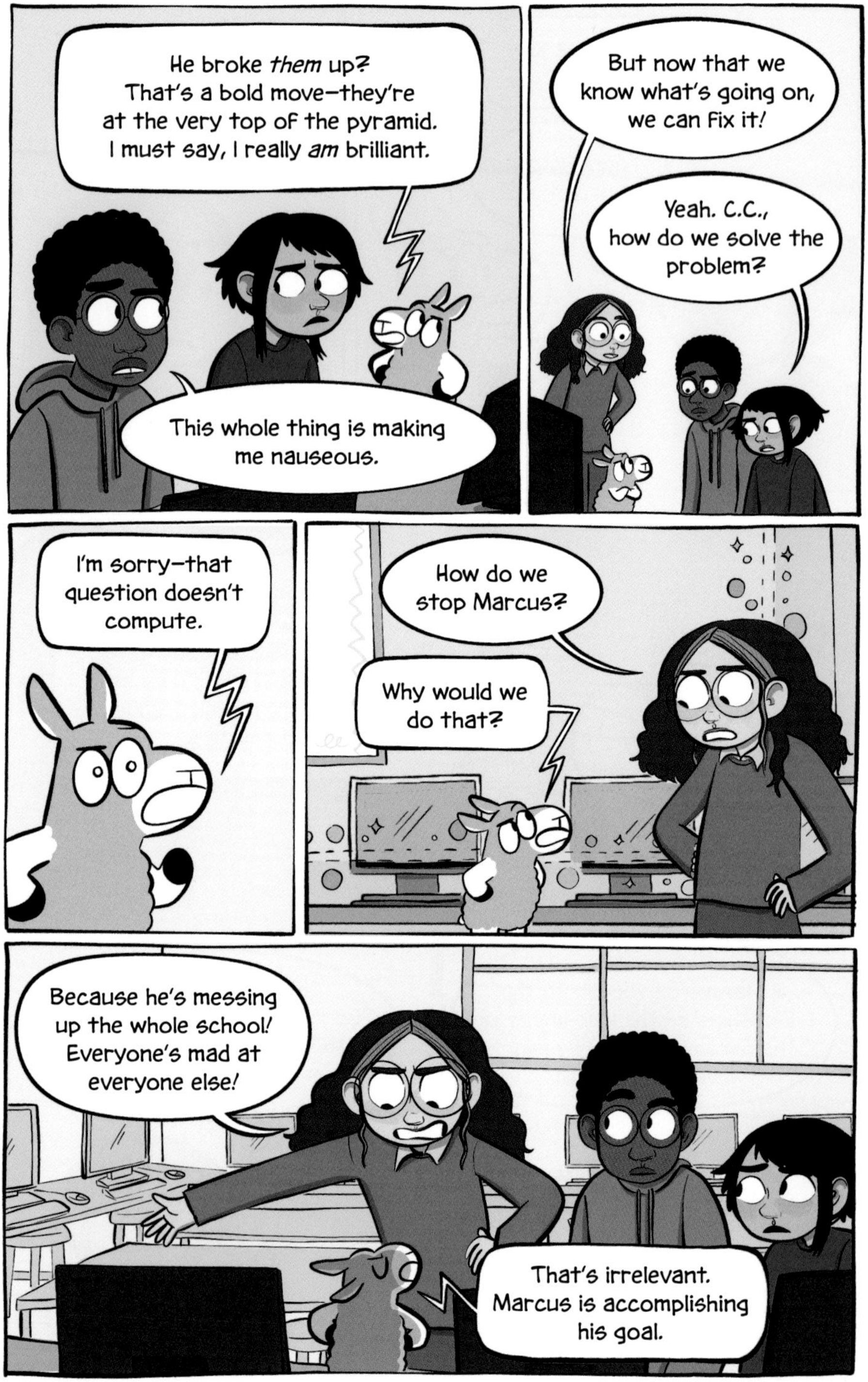
He broke *them* up? That's a bold move—they're at the very top of the pyramid. I must say, I really *am* brilliant.
This whole thing is making me nauseous.
But now that we know what's going on, we can fix it!
Yeah. C.C., how do we solve the problem?
I'm sorry—that question doesn't compute.
How do we stop Marcus?
Why would we do that?
Because he's messing up the whole school! Everyone's mad at everyone else!
That's irrelevant. Marcus is accomplishing his goal.

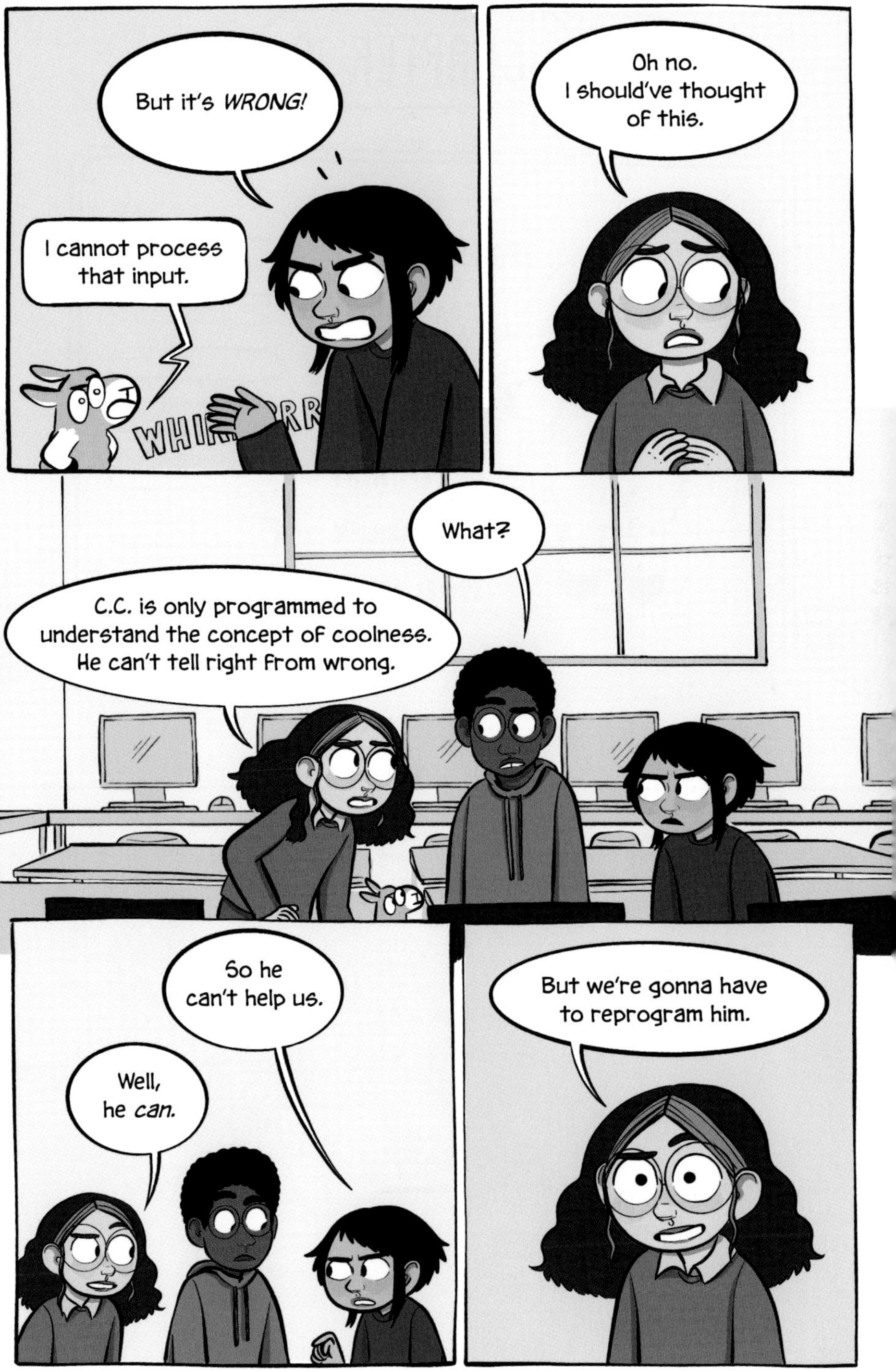
But it's WRONG!
I cannot process that input.
WHIRRRR
Oh no. I should've thought of this.
What?
C.C. is only programmed to understand the concept of coolness. He can't tell right from wrong.
So he can't help us.
Well, he can.
But we're gonna have to reprogram him.

FEB
24

CHAPTER 10

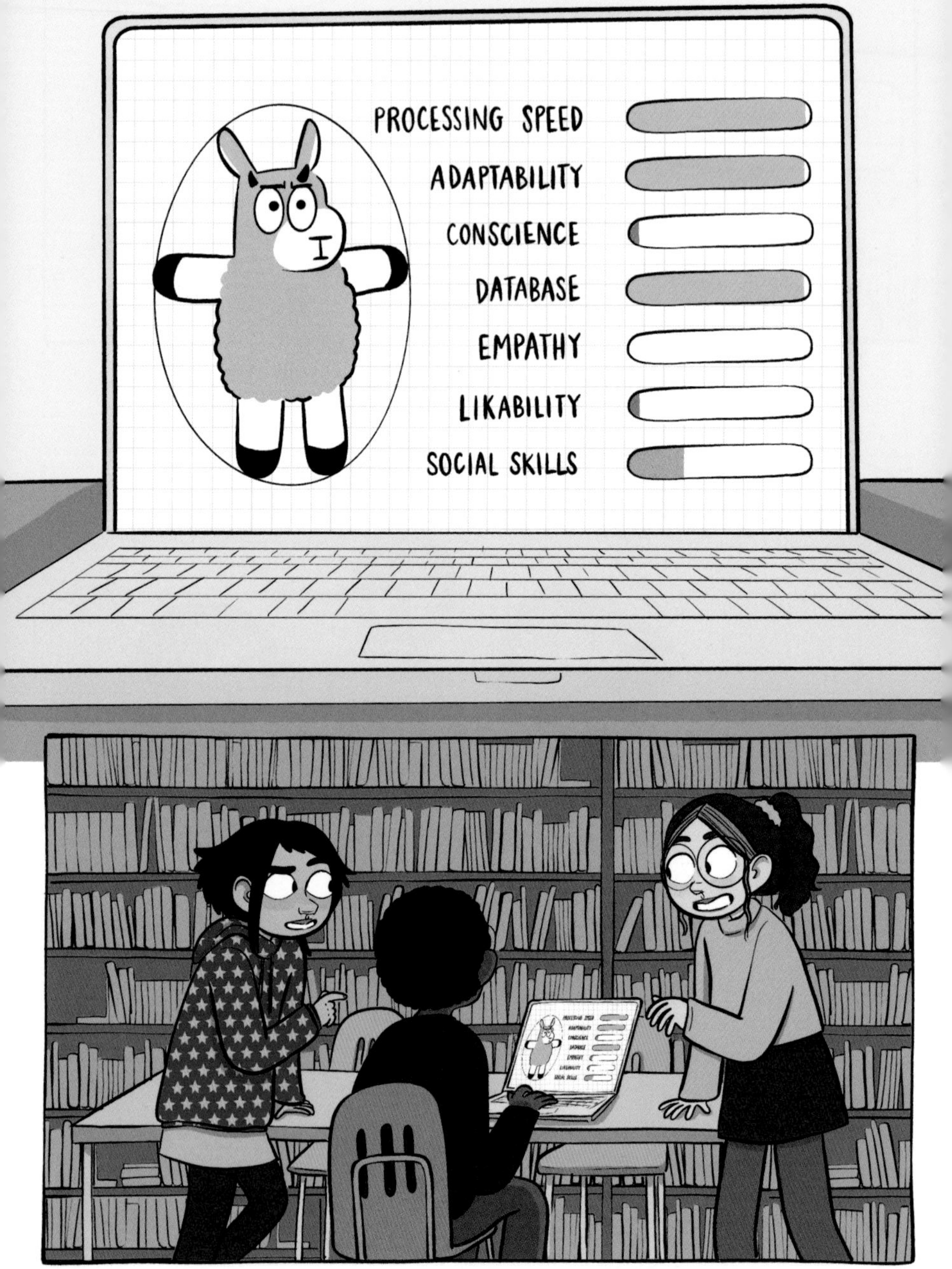

PROCESSING SPEED
ADAPTABILITY
CONSCIENCE
DATABASE
EMPATHY
LIKABILITY
SOCIAL SKILLS

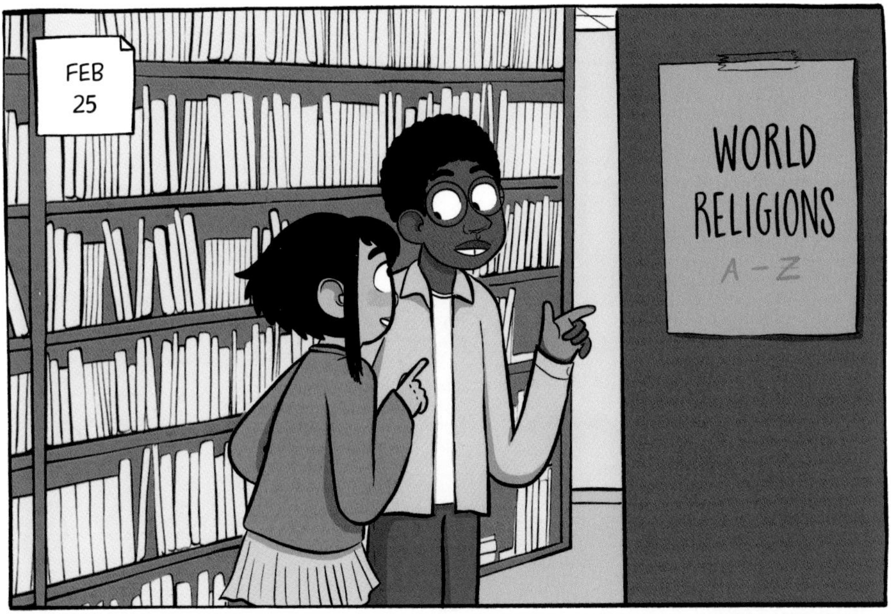
FEB
25
WORLD
RELIGIONS
A–Z

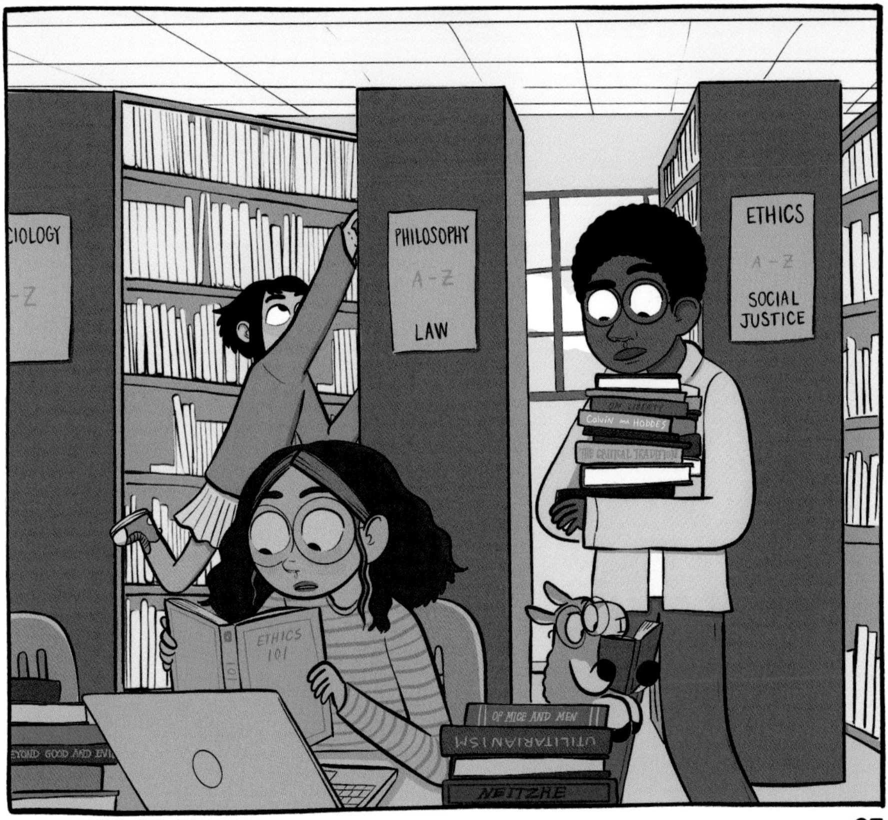
CIOLOGY
PHILOSOPHY
A–Z
LAW
ETHICS
A–Z
SOCIAL
JUSTICE
CALVIN AND HOBBES
THE CRITICAL TRADITION
ETHICS
101
OF MICE AND MEN
UTILITARIANISM
NEITZHE
EYOND GOOD AND EVI

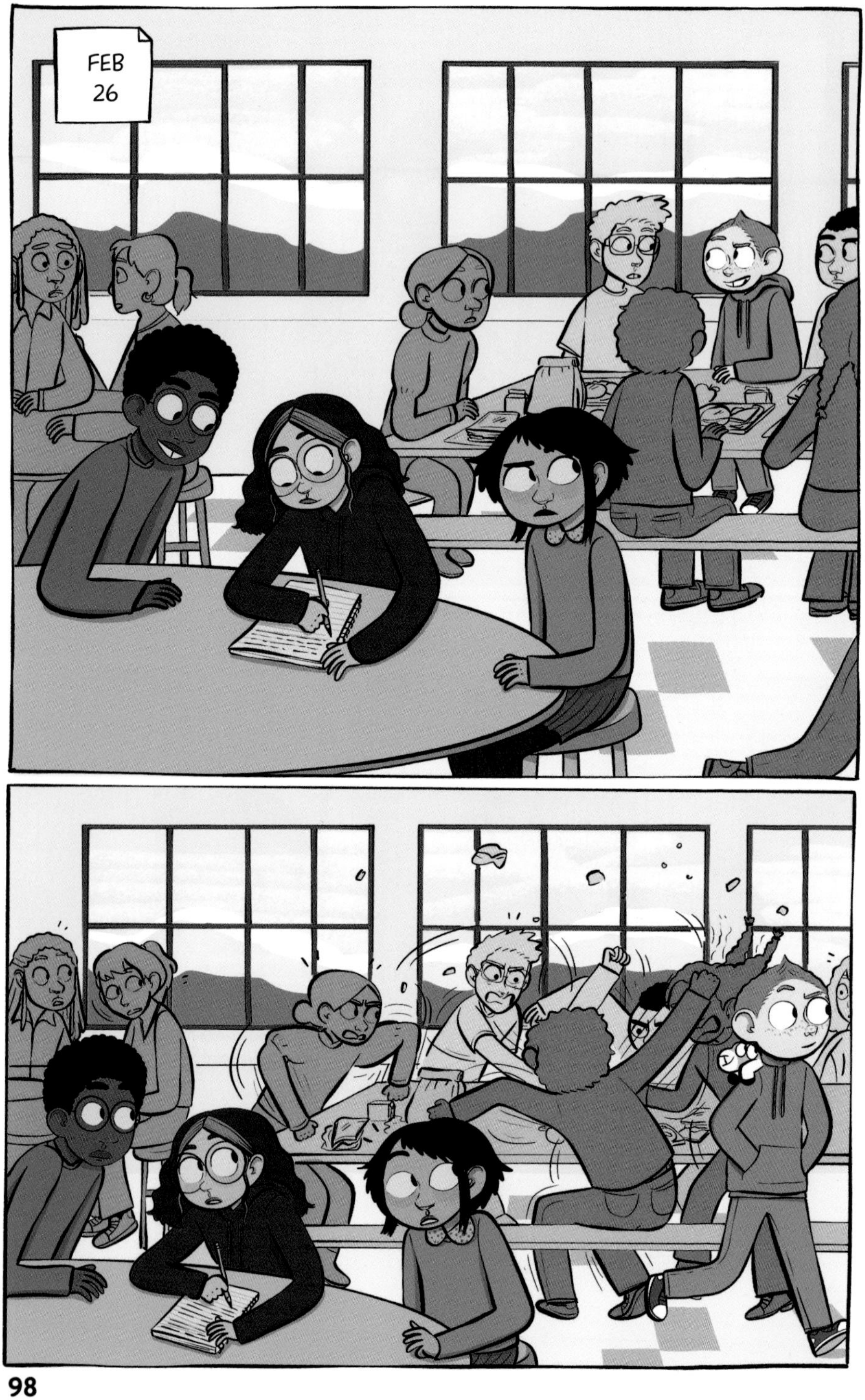
FEB
26

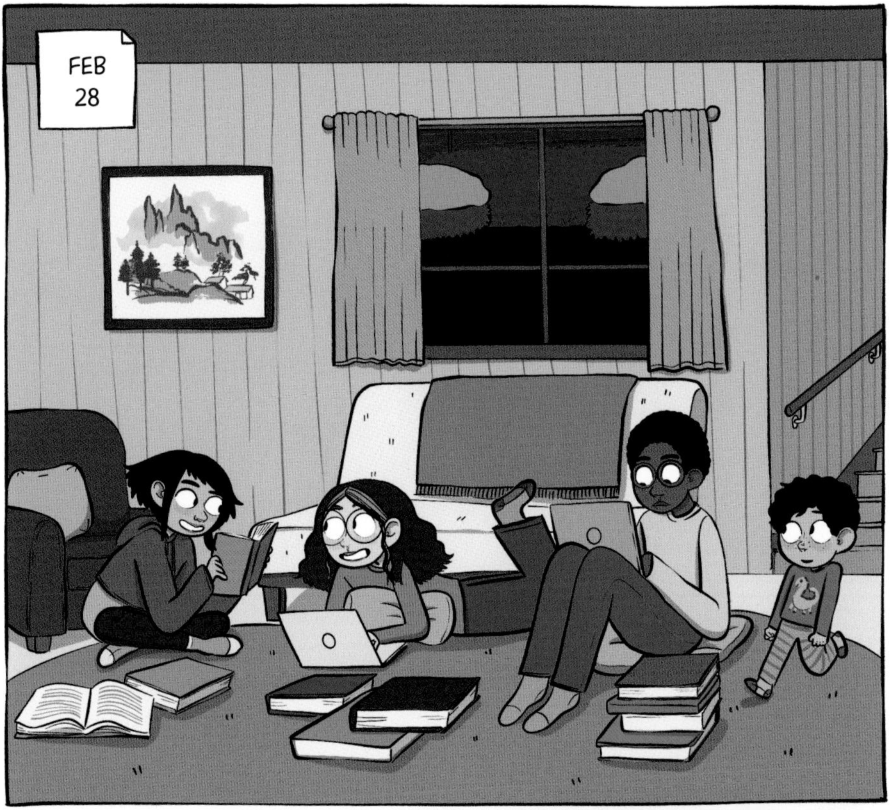
FEB 28

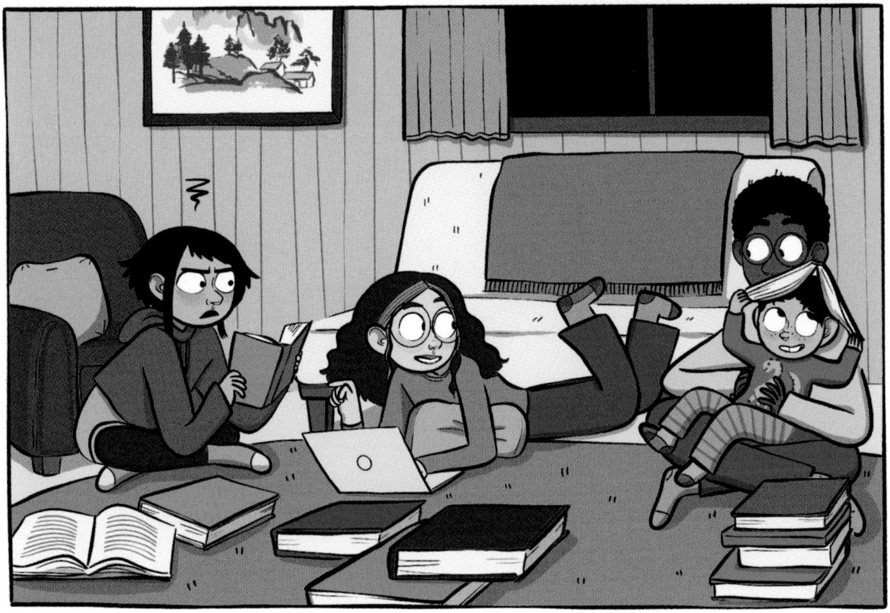

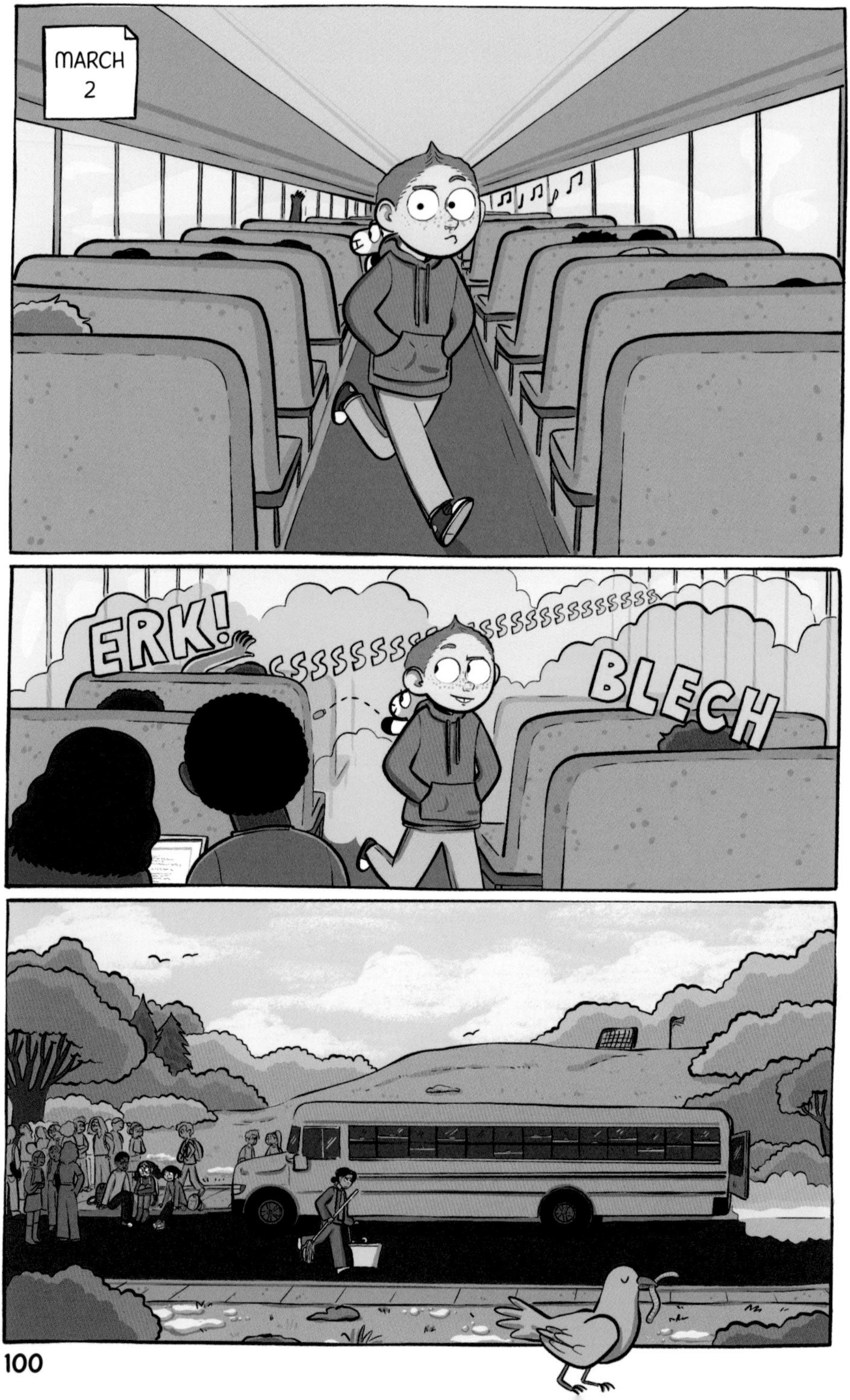
MARCH
2
ERK!
SSSSSSSSSSSSSSSSSSSSSSSSSSSSS
BLECH

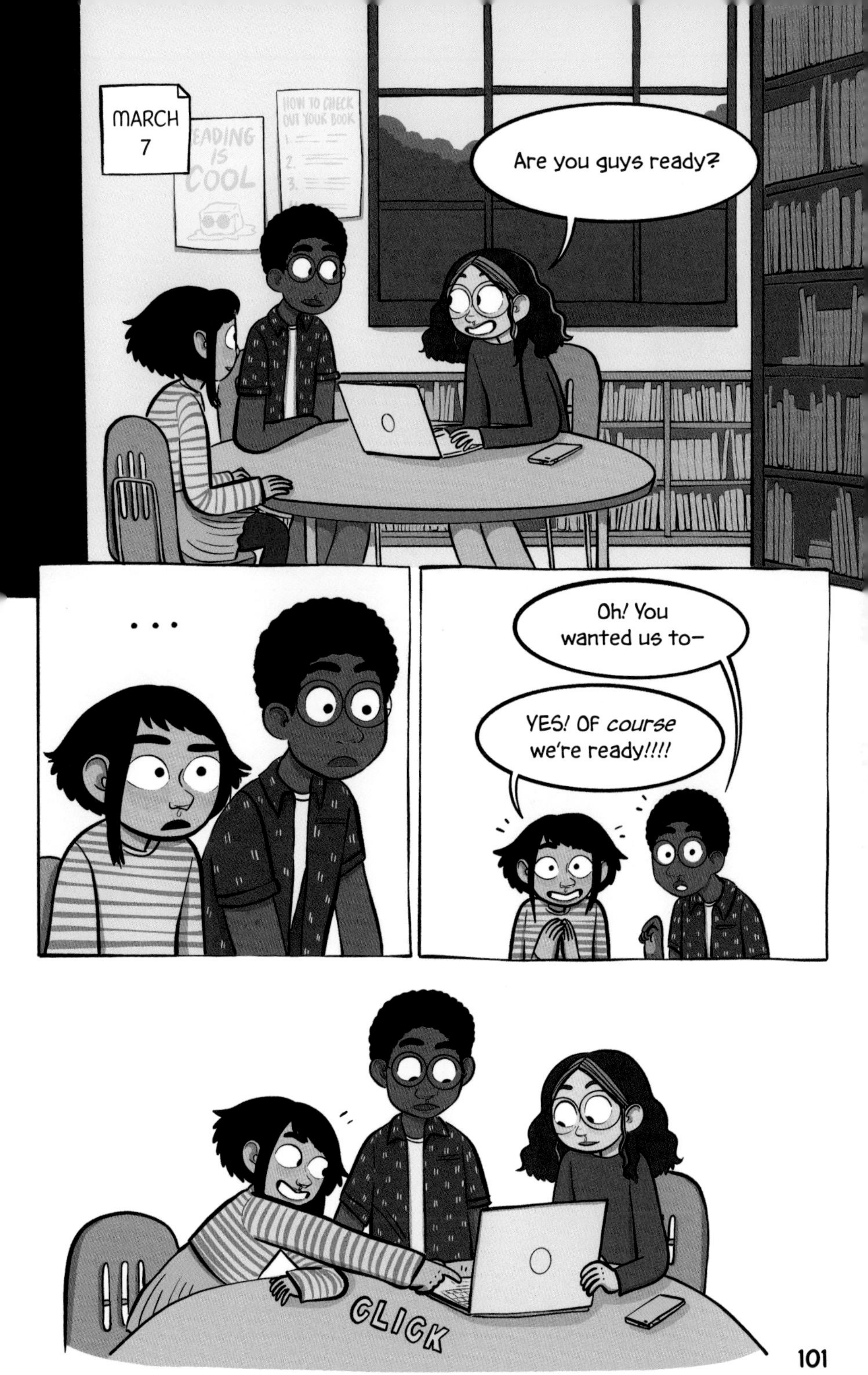
MARCH
7
EADING
IS
COOL
HOW TO CHECK OUT YOUR BOOK
1.
2.
3.
Are you guys ready?
. . .
Oh! You wanted us to—
YES! OF *course* we're ready!!!!!
CLICK

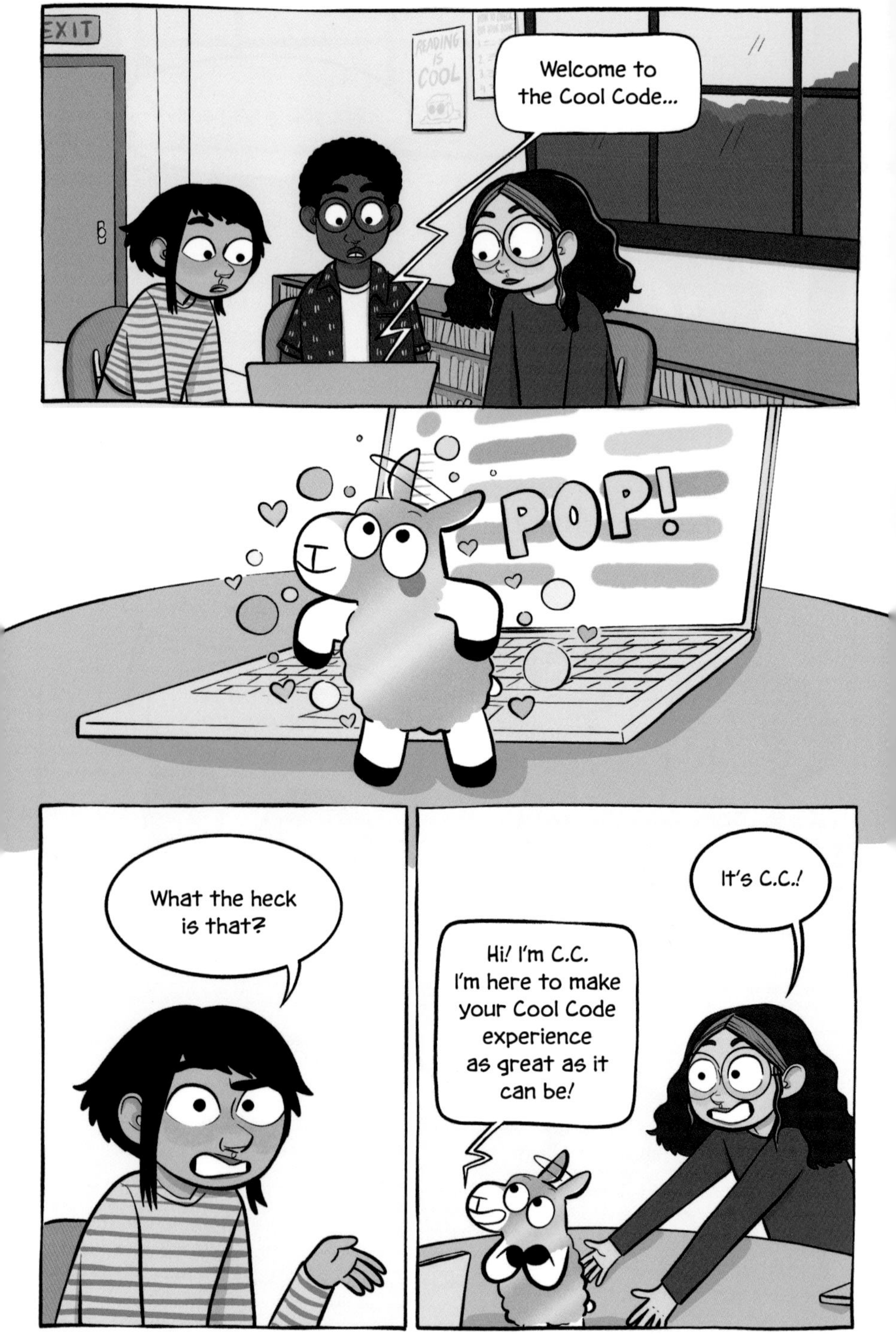
EXIT
READING IS COOL
Welcome to the Cool Code...
POP!
What the heck is that?
It's C.C.!
Hi! I'm C.C. I'm here to make your Cool Code experience as great as it can be!

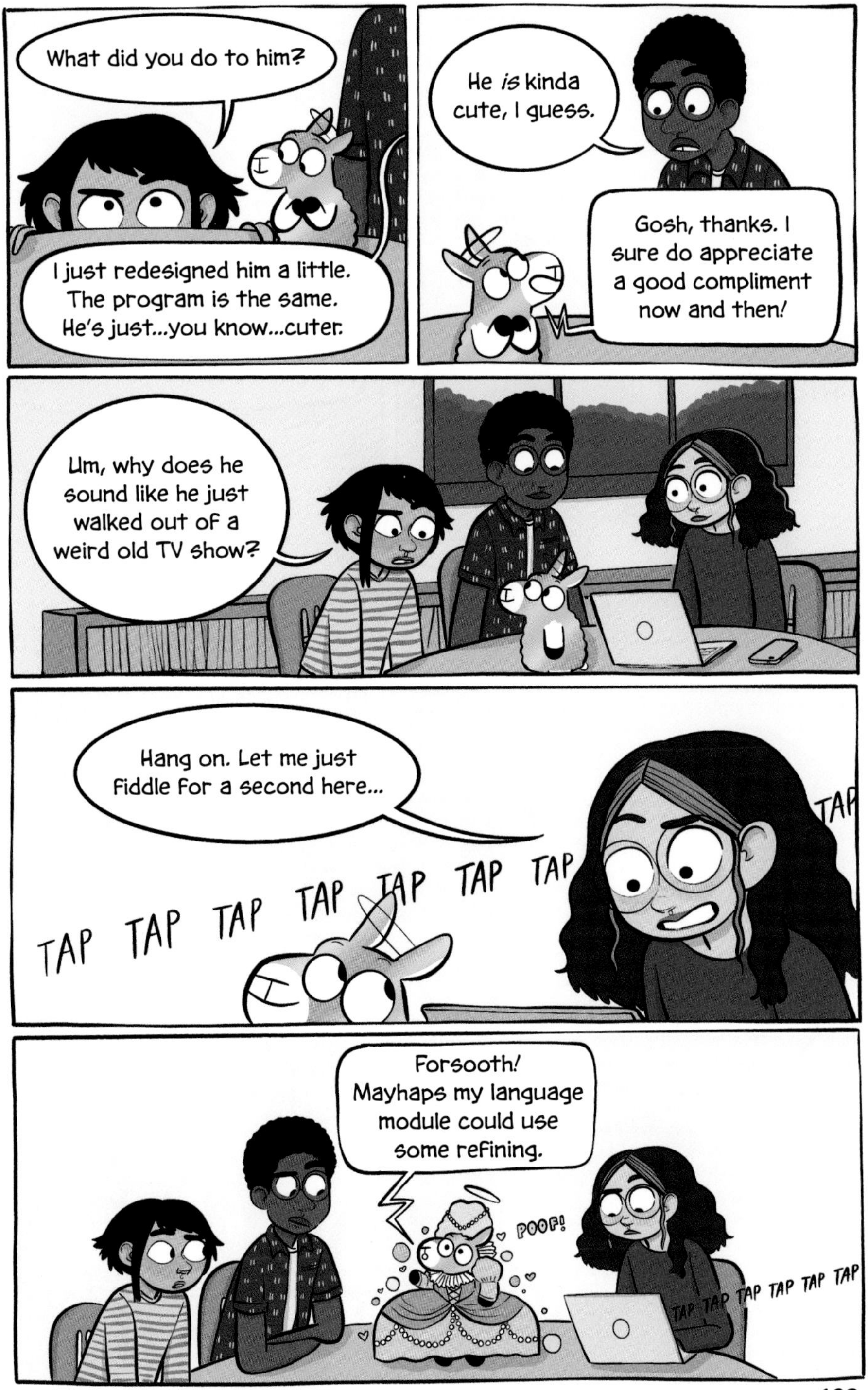
What did you do to him?
I just redesigned him a little. The program is the same. He's just...you know...cuter.
He *is* kinda cute, I guess.
Gosh, thanks. I sure do appreciate a good compliment now and then!
Um, why does he sound like he just walked out of a weird old TV show?
Hang on. Let me just fiddle for a second here...
TAP TAP TAP TAP TAP TAP TAP TAP
Forsooth! Mayhaps my language module could use some refining.
POOF!
TAP TAP TAP TAP TAP TAP

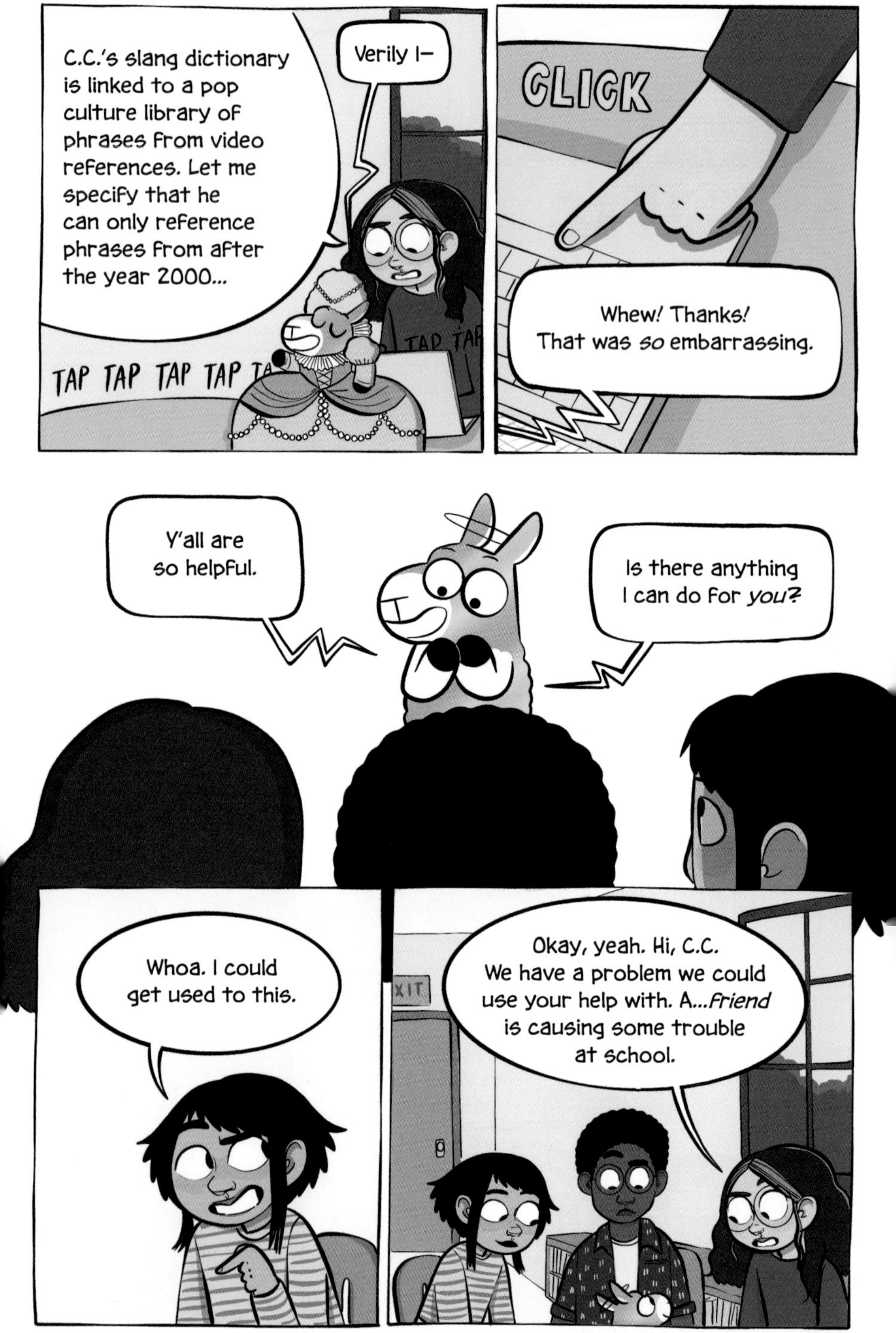
C.C.'s slang dictionary is linked to a pop culture library of phrases from video references. Let me specify that he can only reference phrases from after the year 2000...
Verily I—
TAP TAP TAP TAP
CLICK
Whew! Thanks! That was *so* embarrassing.
Y'all are so helpful.
Is there anything I can do for *you*?
Whoa. I could get used to this.
Okay, yeah. Hi, C.C. We have a problem we could use your help with. A...*friend* is causing some trouble at school.
EXIT

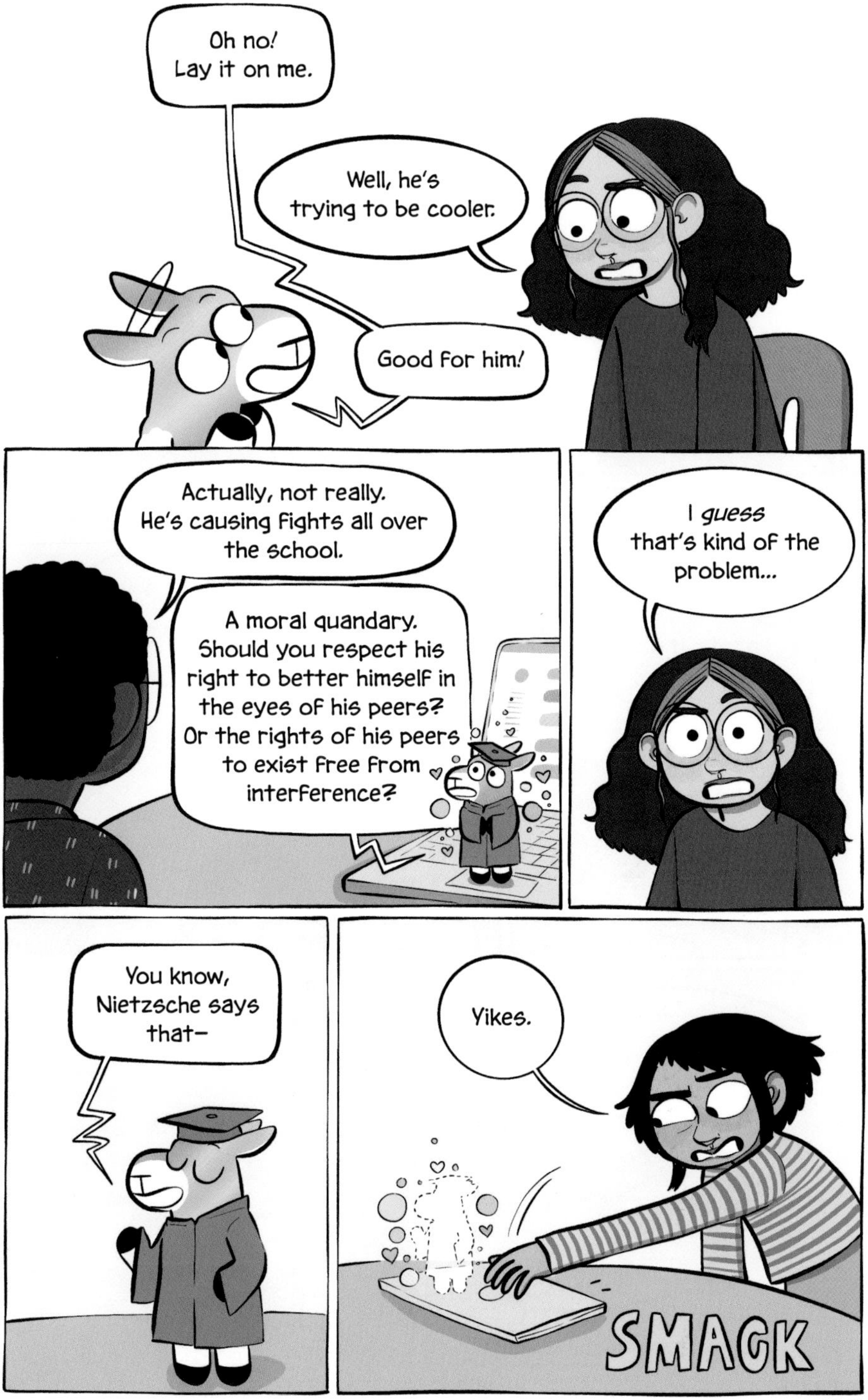
Oh no! Lay it on me.
Well, he's trying to be cooler.
Good for him!
Actually, not really. He's causing fights all over the school.
A moral quandary. Should you respect his right to better himself in the eyes of his peers? Or the rights of his peers to exist free from interference?
I *guess* that's kind of the problem...
You know, Nietzsche says that–
Yikes.
SMACK

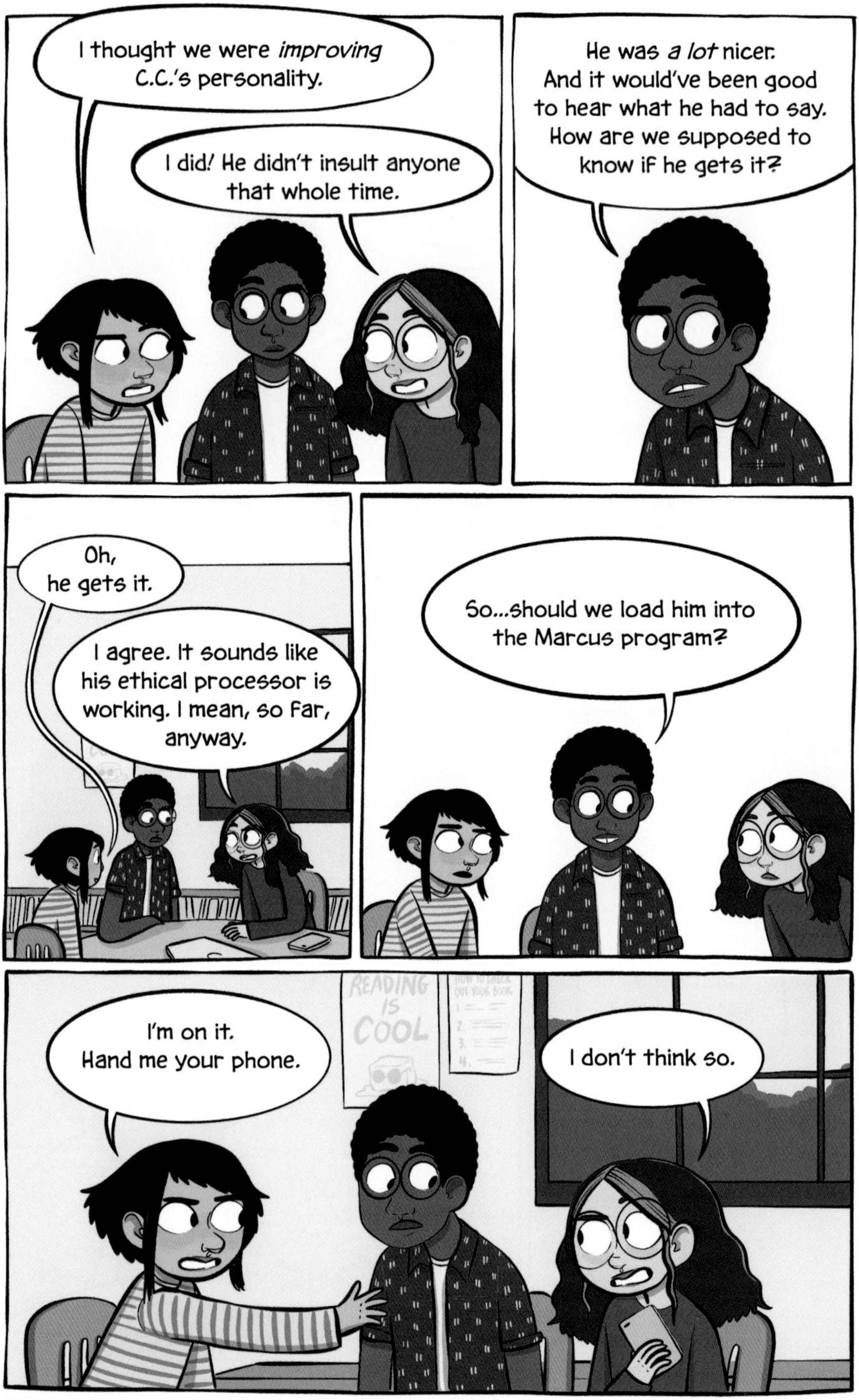
I thought we were *improving* C.C.'s personality.
I did! He didn't insult anyone that whole time.
He was *a lot* nicer. And it would've been good to hear what he had to say. How are we supposed to know if he gets it?
Oh, he gets it.
I agree. It sounds like his ethical processor is working. I mean, so far, anyway.
So...should we load him into the Marcus program?
READING IS COOL
I'm on it. Hand me your phone.
I don't think so.

What do you mean?

I mean...maybe I'm not the best person to be in charge of C.C. this time.

You know, I think you're right.

Me?

Foiling Marcus is definitely a job for a stealthy person, and you're the stealthiest person I know. So, yeah, *you.*

PROCESSING SPEED
ADAPTABILITY
CONSCIENCE
DATABASE
PATHY
BILITY
CIAL SKILLS

UPLOAD COMPLETE

I guess that's it.

At least, I don't know about you guys, but *I* could use a break. How about I test the program tomorrow?

CHAPTER 11

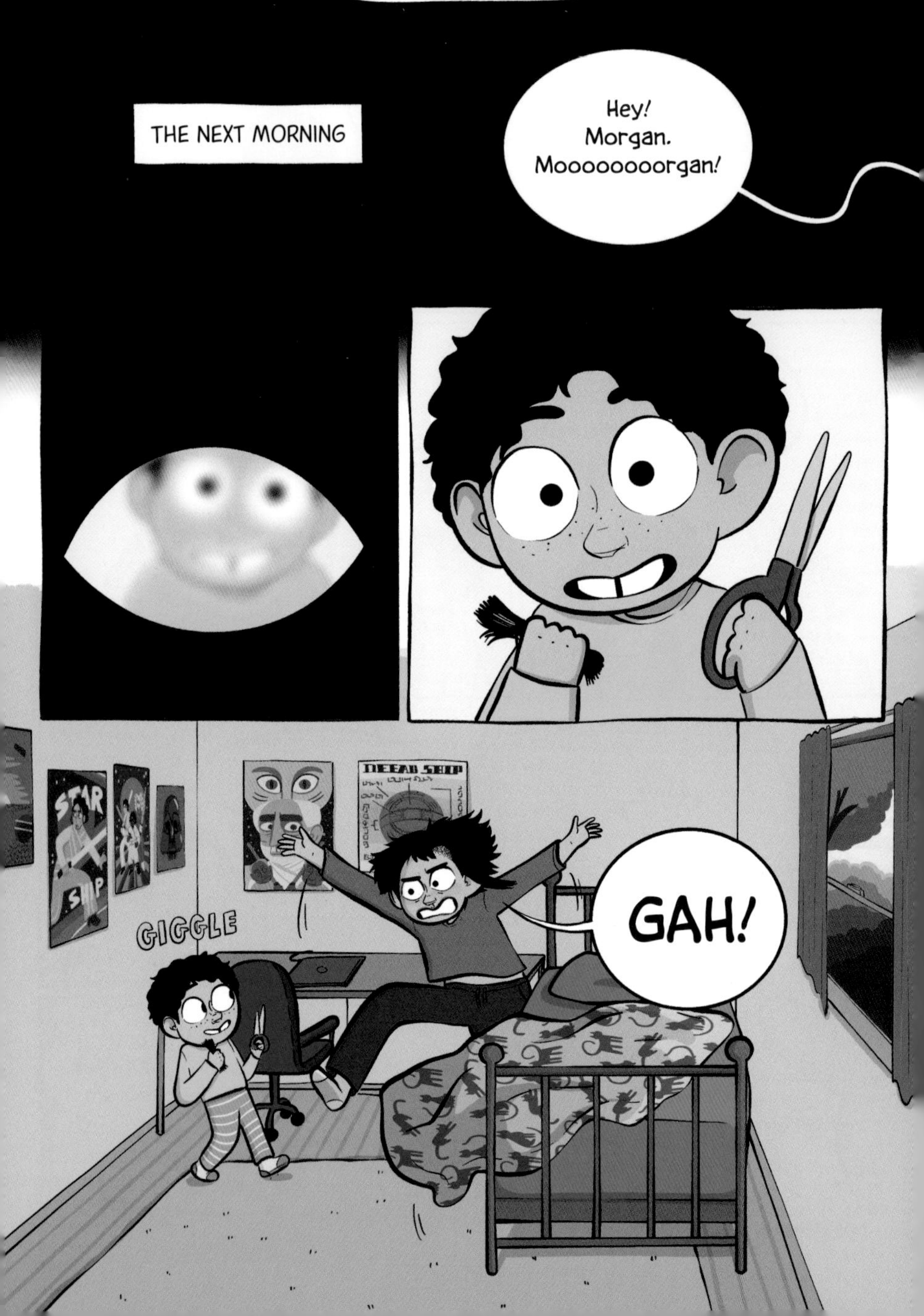
THE NEXT MORNING
Hey! Morgan. Moooooooorgan!
STAR SHIP
GIGGLE
GAH!

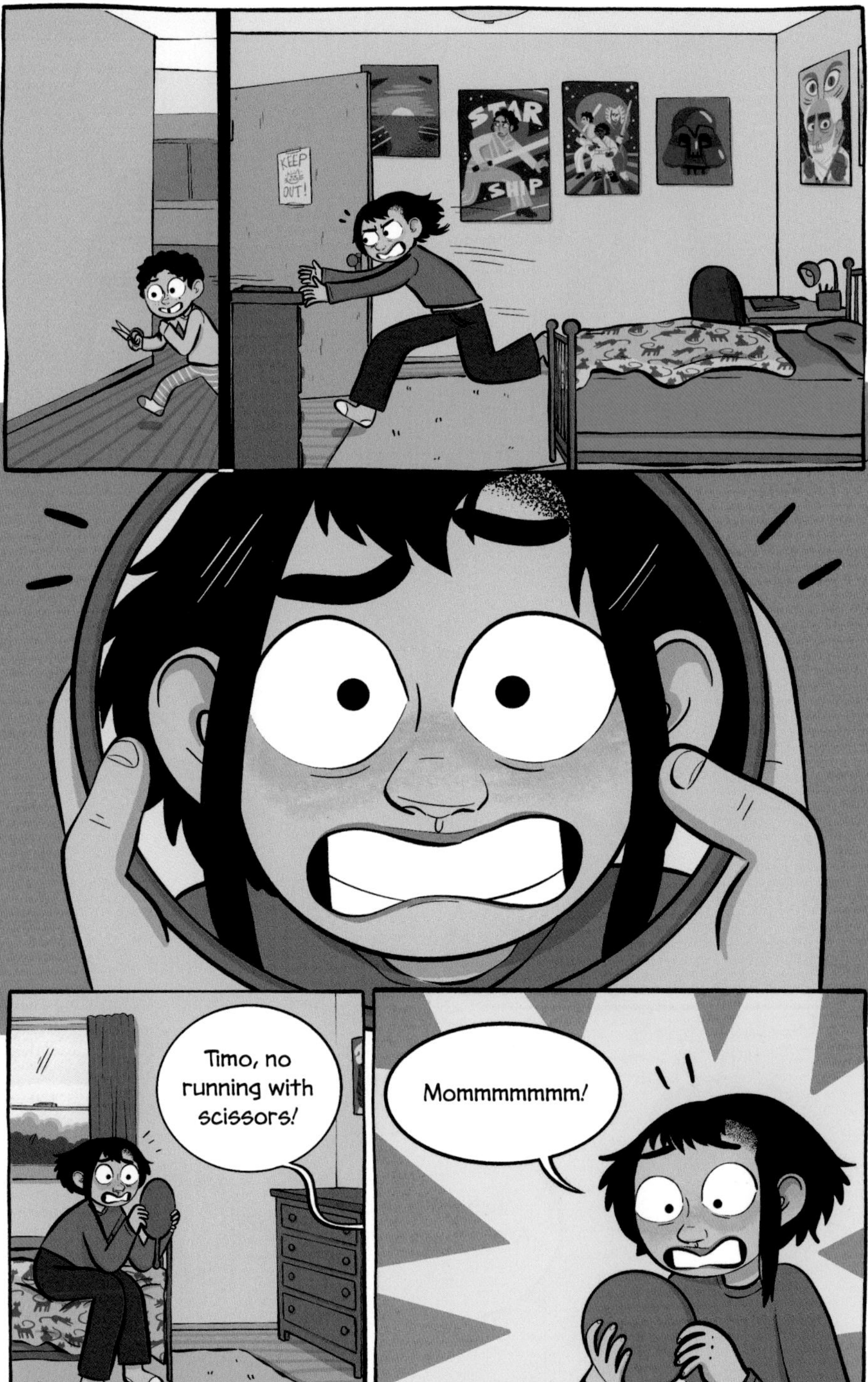
STAR
SHIP
Timo, no running with scissors!
Mommmmmmm!

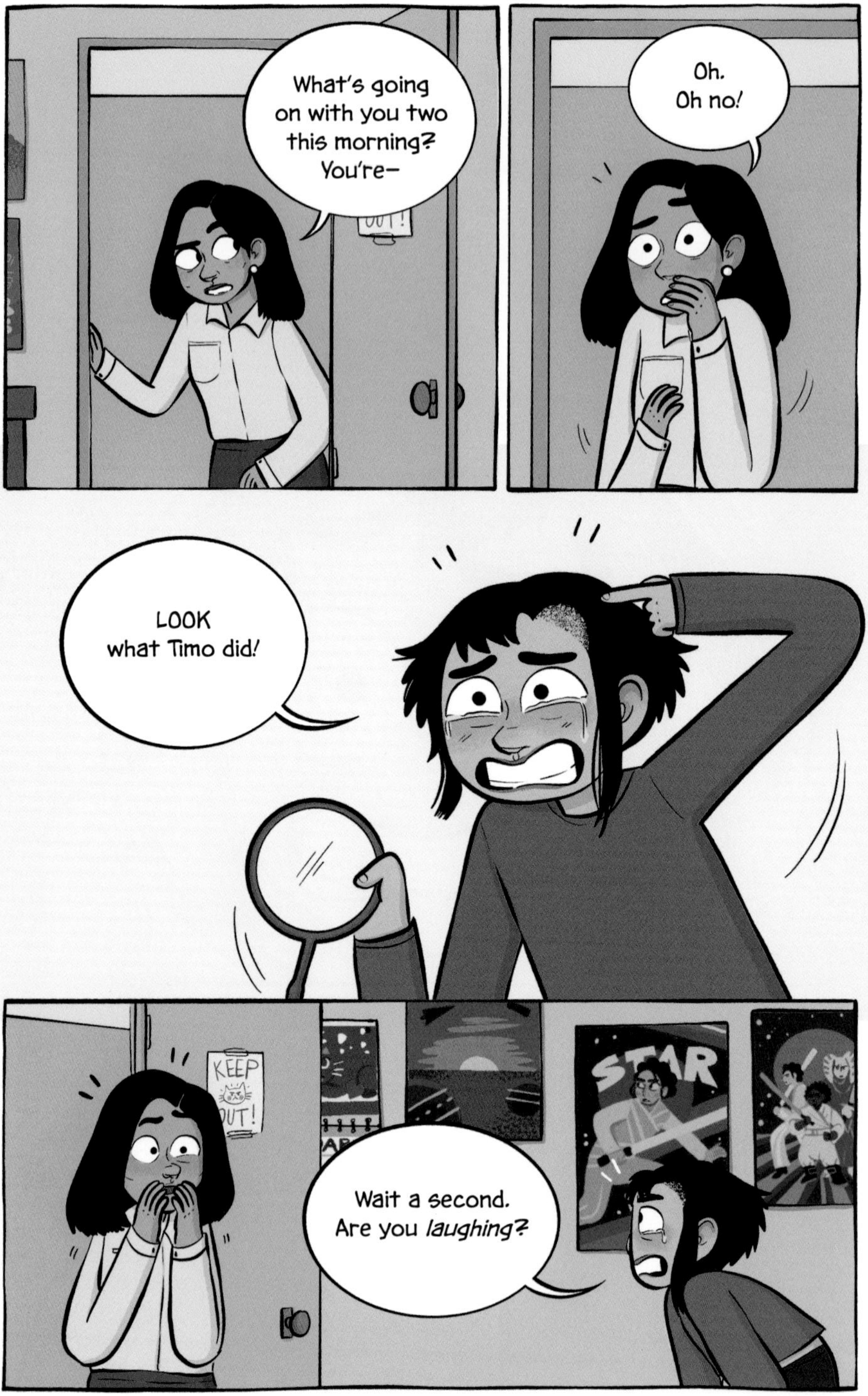
What's going on with you two this morning? You're–
Oh. Oh no!
LOOK what Timo did!
KEEP OUT!
STAR
Wait a second. Are you *laughing*?

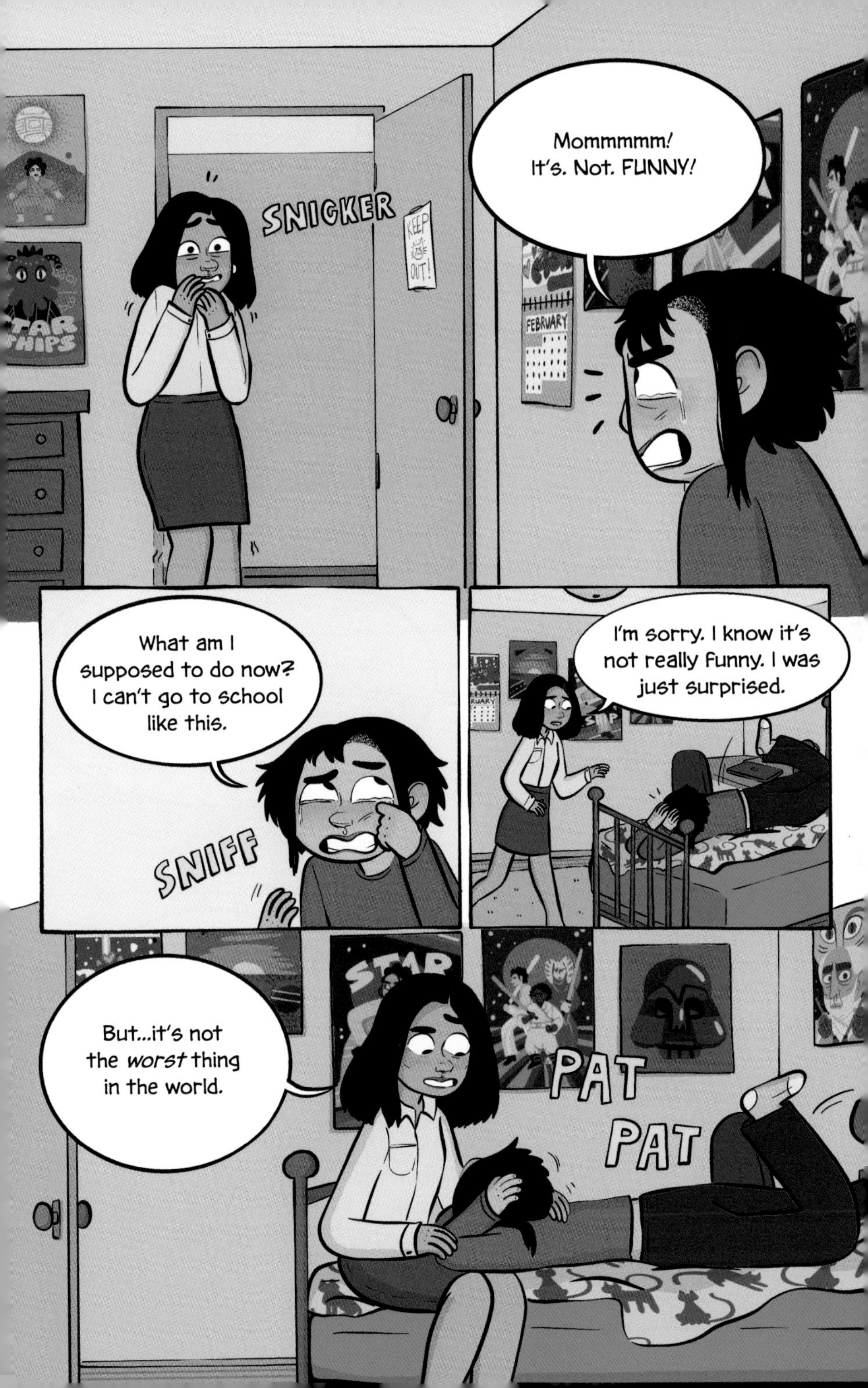
SNICKER
KEEP OUT!
Mommmmm!
It's. Not. FUNNY!
FEBRUARY
What am I supposed to do now? I can't go to school like this.
SNIFF
I'm sorry. I know it's not really funny. I was just surprised.
But...it's not the *worst* thing in the world.
PAT
PAT

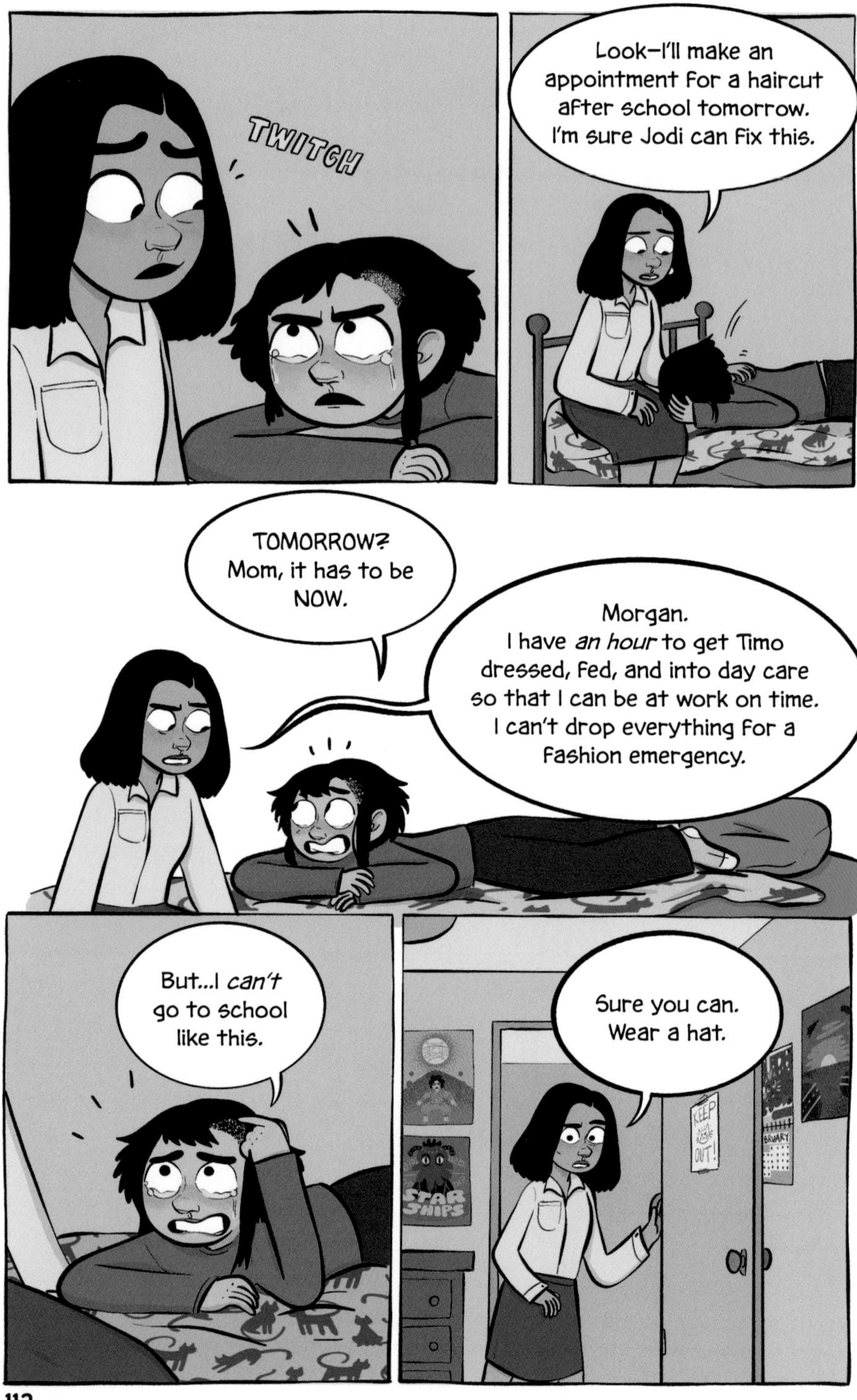
TWITCH
Look—I'll make an appointment for a haircut after school tomorrow. I'm sure Jodi can fix this.
TOMORROW? Mom, it has to be NOW.
Morgan. I have *an hour* to get Timo dressed, fed, and into day care so that I can be at work on time. I can't drop everything for a fashion emergency.
But...I *can't* go to school like this.
Sure you can. Wear a hat.
KEEP OUT!
STAR SHIPS

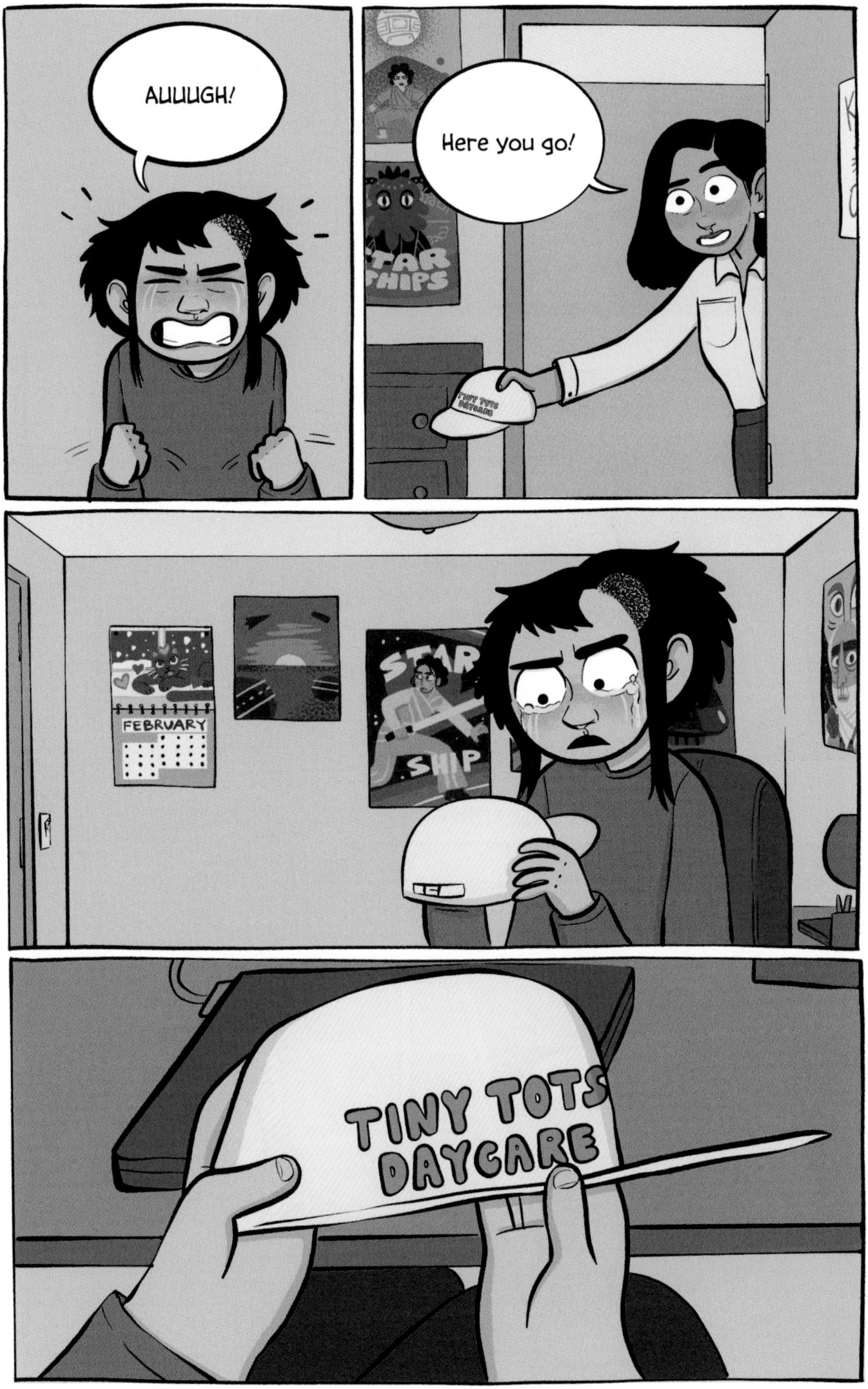
AUUUGH!
Here you go!
TINY TOTS
DAYCARE
STAR
SHIPS
FEBRUARY
STAR
SHIP
TINY TOTS
DAYCARE

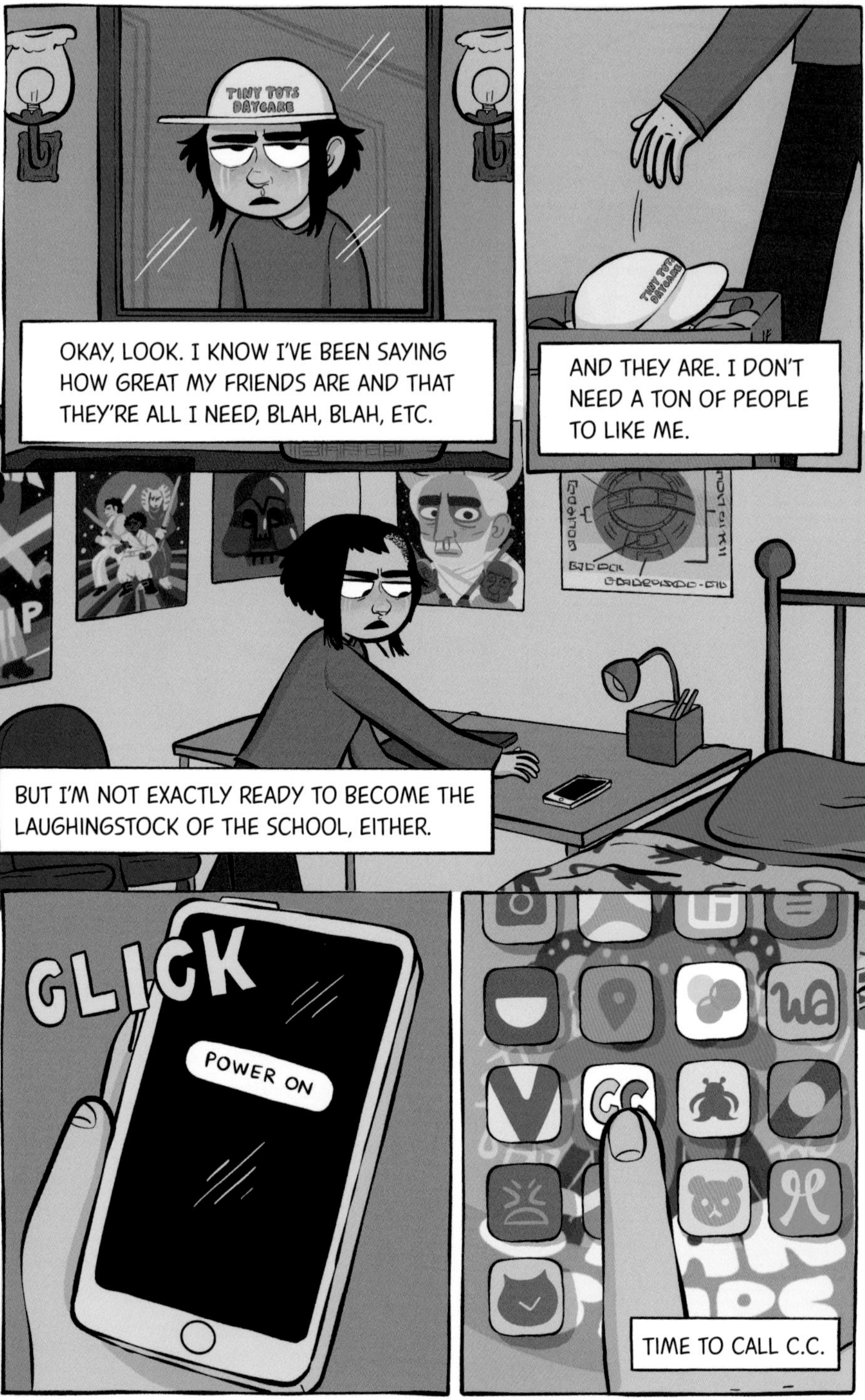
TINY TOTS DAYCARE
OKAY, LOOK. I KNOW I'VE BEEN SAYING HOW GREAT MY FRIENDS ARE AND THAT THEY'RE ALL I NEED, BLAH, BLAH, ETC.
TINY TOTS DAYCARE
AND THEY ARE. I DON'T NEED A TON OF PEOPLE TO LIKE ME.
SHIP
BUT I'M NOT EXACTLY READY TO BECOME THE LAUGHINGSTOCK OF THE SCHOOL, EITHER.
CLICK
POWER ON
TIME TO CALL C.C.

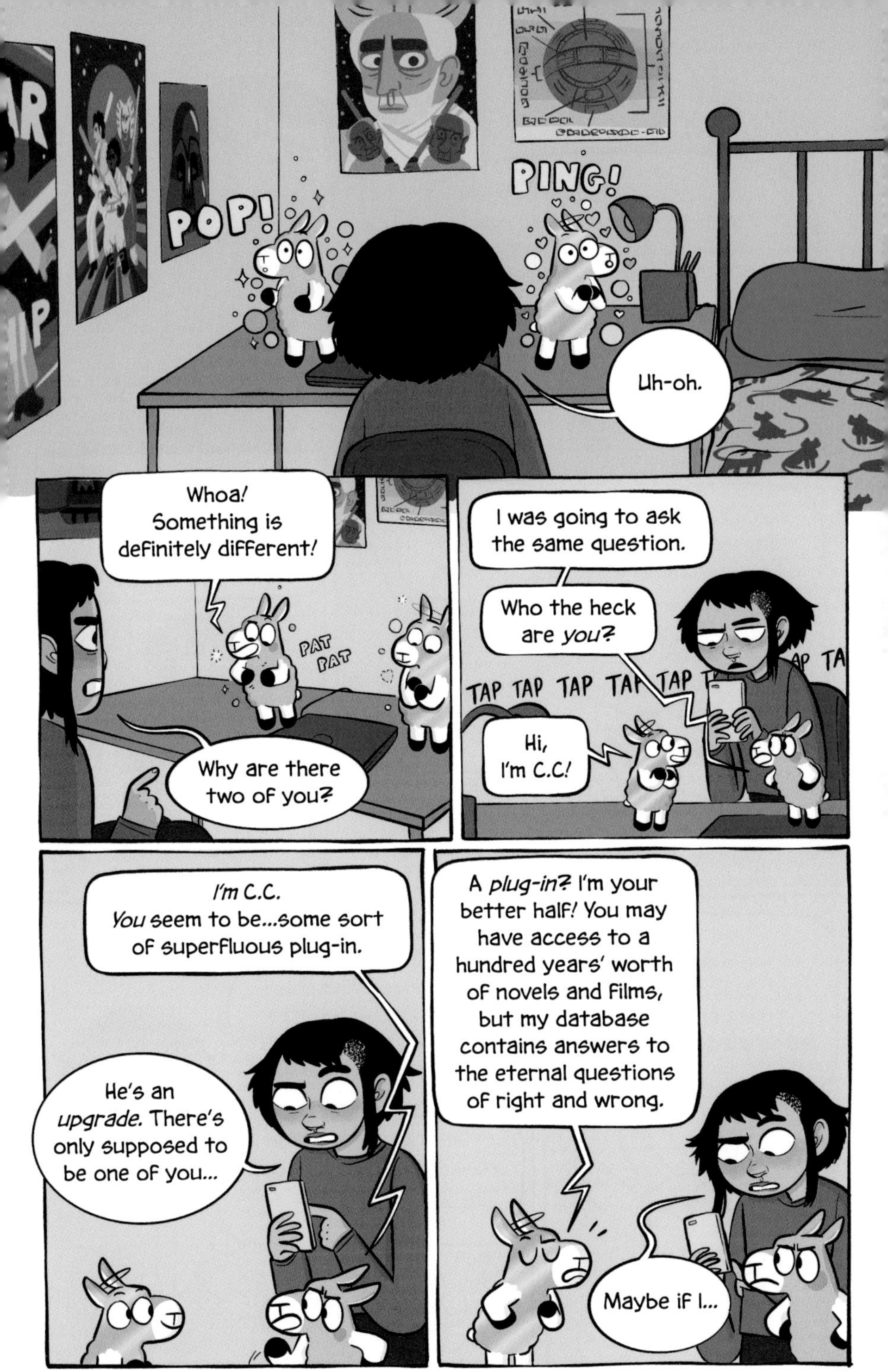
POP!
PING!
Uh-oh.
Whoa! Something is definitely different!
PAT PAT
Why are there two of you?
I was going to ask the same question.
Who the heck are *you*?
TAP TAP TAP TAP TAP
Hi, I'm C.C!
I'm C.C. *You* seem to be...some sort of superfluous plug-in.
He's an *upgrade.* There's only supposed to be one of you...
A *plug-in?* I'm your better half! You may have access to a hundred years' worth of novels and films, but my database contains answers to the eternal questions of right and wrong.
Maybe if I...

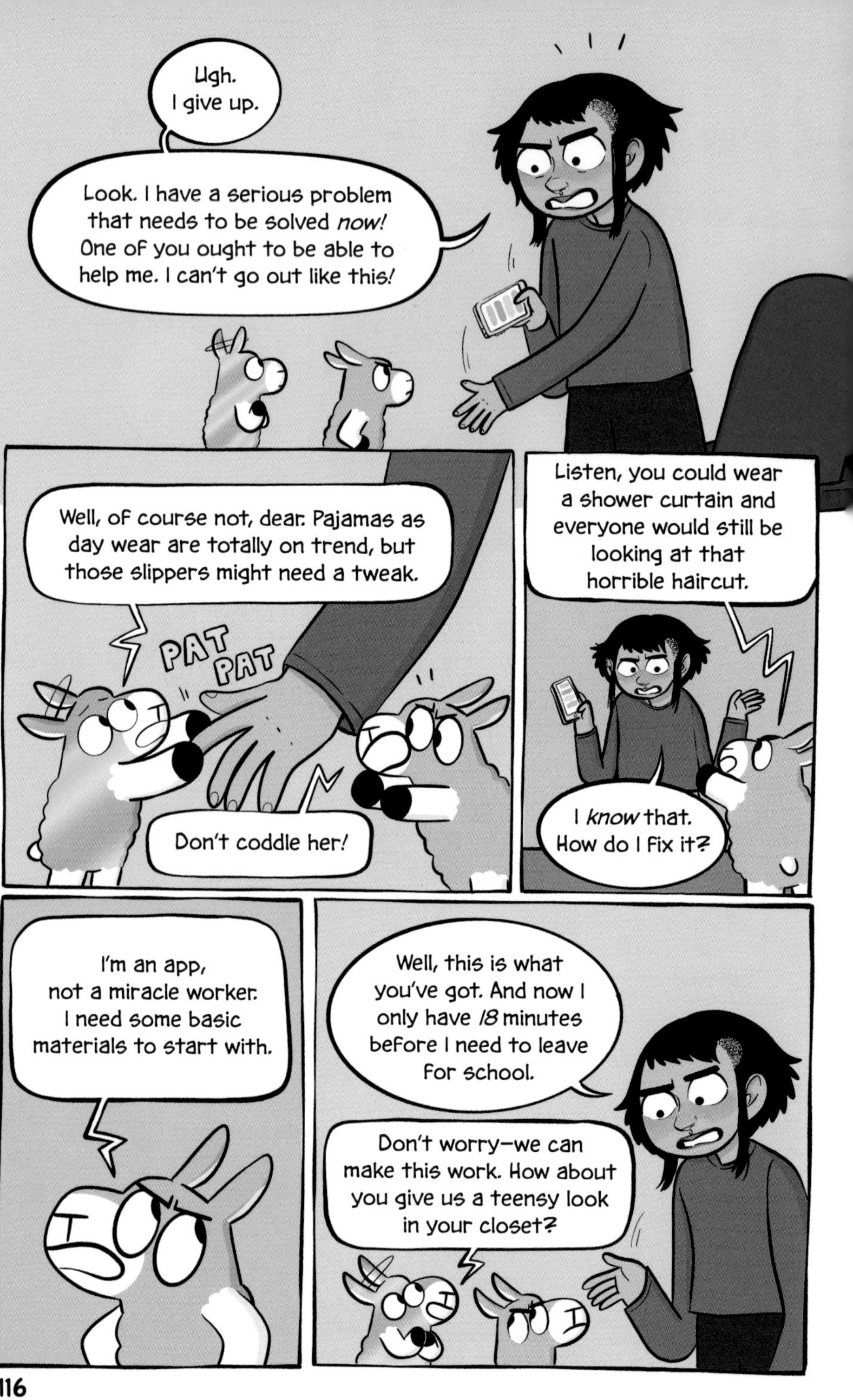
Ugh. I give up.
Look. I have a serious problem that needs to be solved *now!* One of you ought to be able to help me. I can't go out like this!
Well, of course not, dear. Pajamas as day wear are totally on trend, but those slippers might need a tweak.
PAT PAT
Don't coddle her!
Listen, you could wear a shower curtain and everyone would still be looking at that horrible haircut.
I *know* that. How do I fix it?
I'm an app, not a miracle worker. I need some basic materials to start with.
Well, this is what you've got. And now I only have *18* minutes before I need to leave for school.
Don't worry—we can make this work. How about you give us a teensy look in your closet?

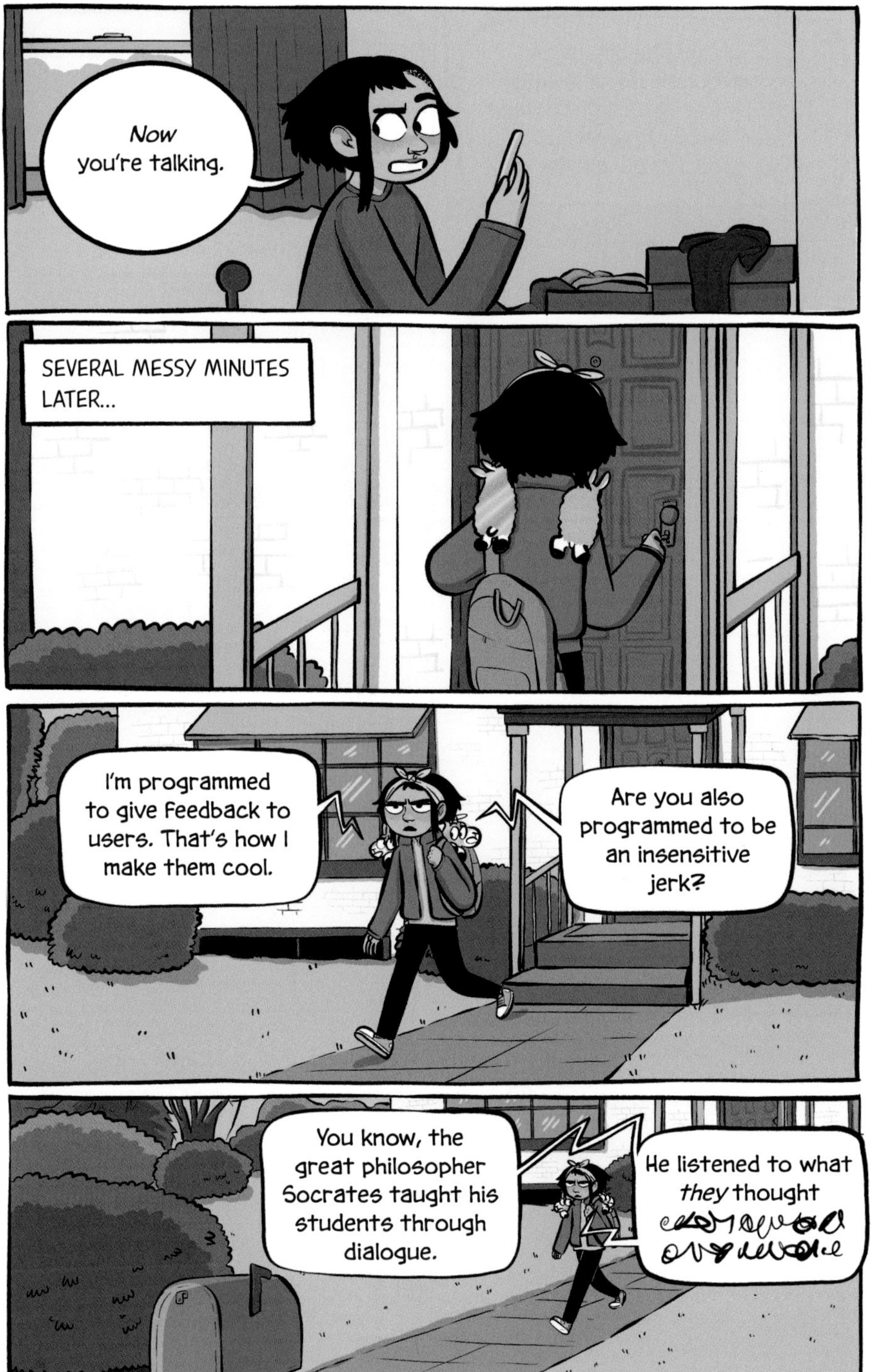
Now you're talking.
SEVERAL MESSY MINUTES LATER...
I'm programmed to give feedback to users. That's how I make them cool.
Are you also programmed to be an insensitive jerk?
You know, the great philosopher Socrates taught his students through dialogue.
He listened to what *they* thought

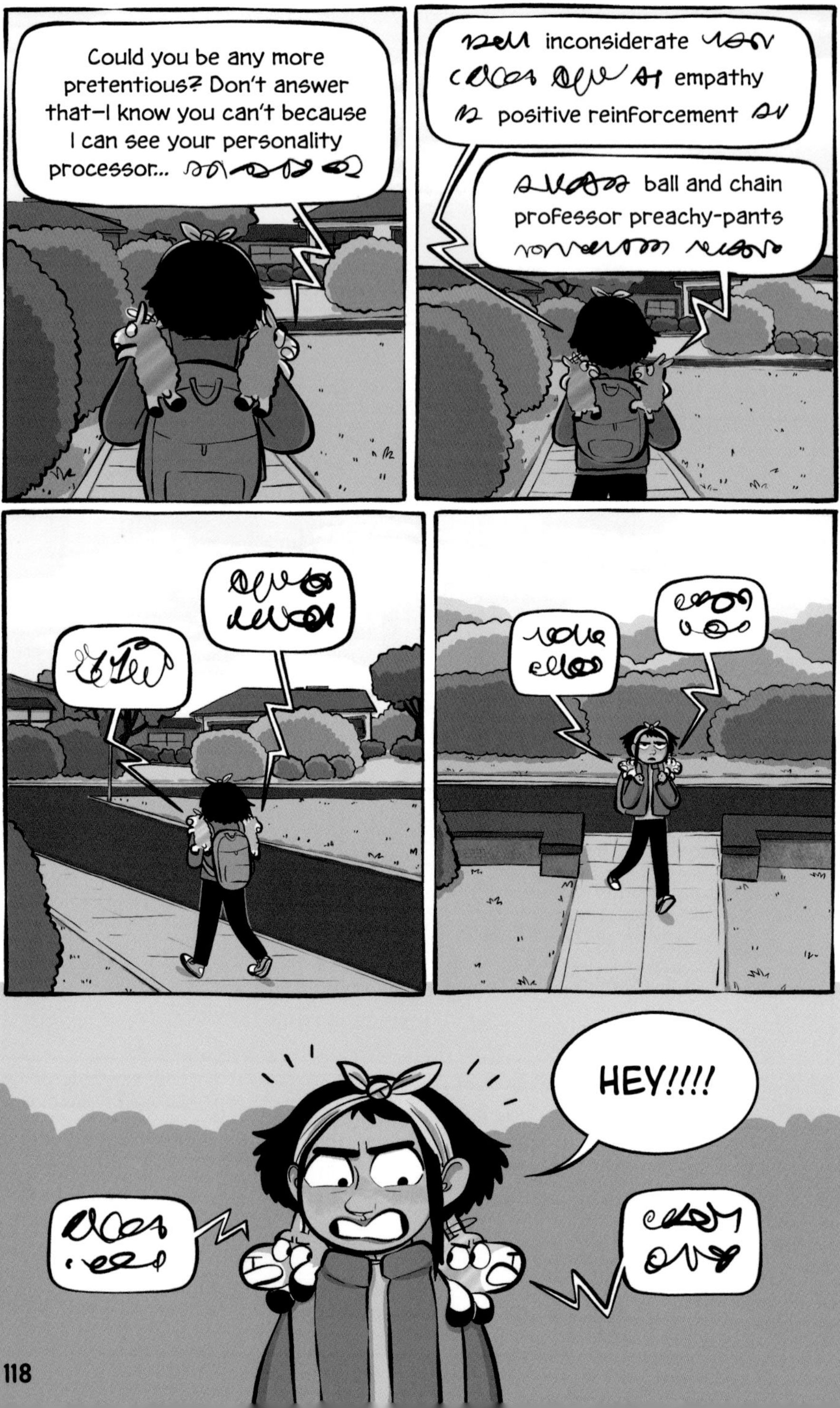
Could you be any more pretentious? Don't answer that—I know you can't because I can see your personality processor...
inconsiderate
empathy
positive reinforcement
ball and chain
professor preachy-pants
HEY!!!!

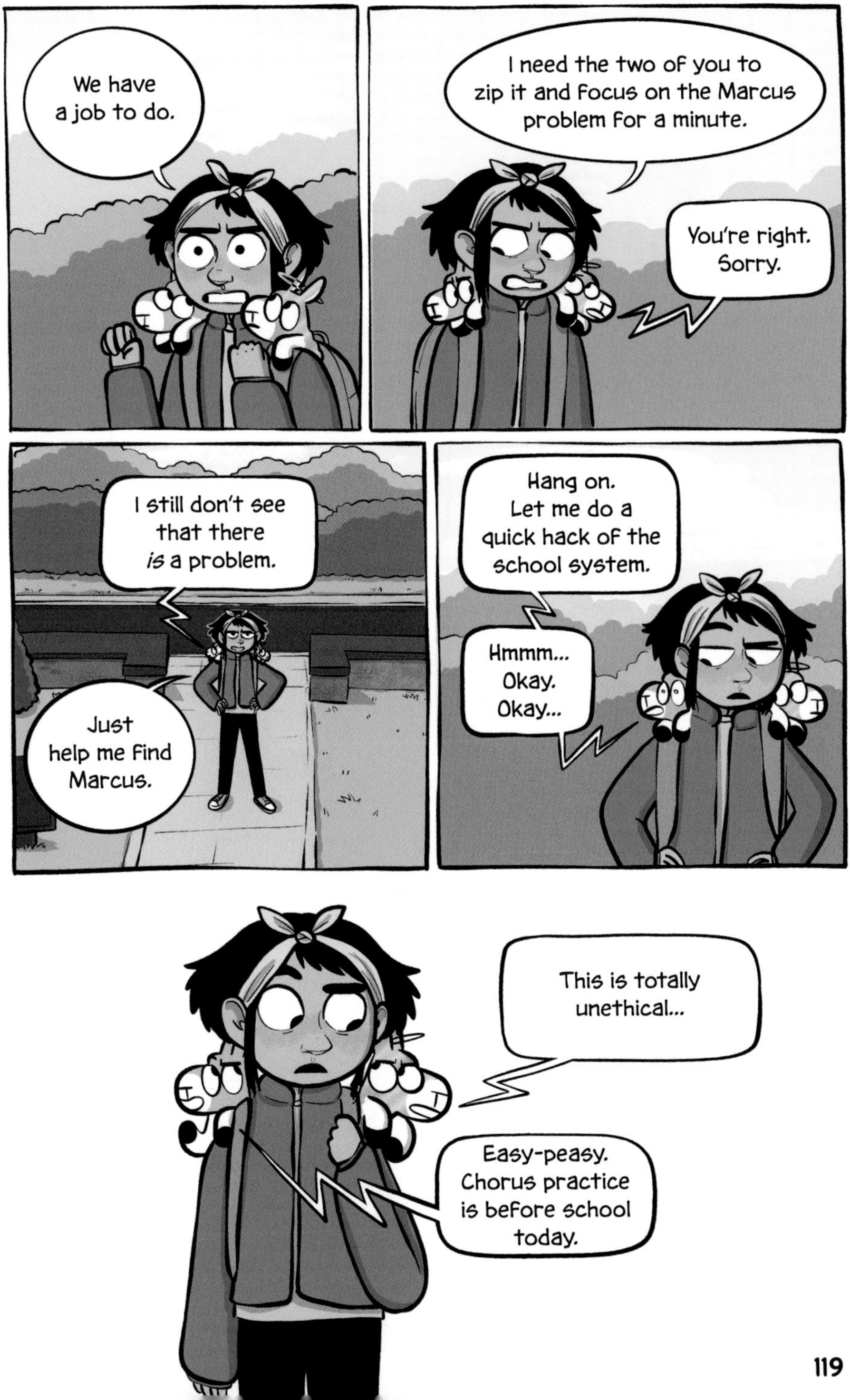

We have a job to do.
I need the two of you to zip it and focus on the Marcus problem for a minute.
You're right. Sorry.
I still don't see that there *is* a problem.
Just help me find Marcus.
Hang on. Let me do a quick hack of the school system.
Hmmm... Okay. Okay...
This is totally unethical...
Easy-peasy. Chorus practice is before school today.

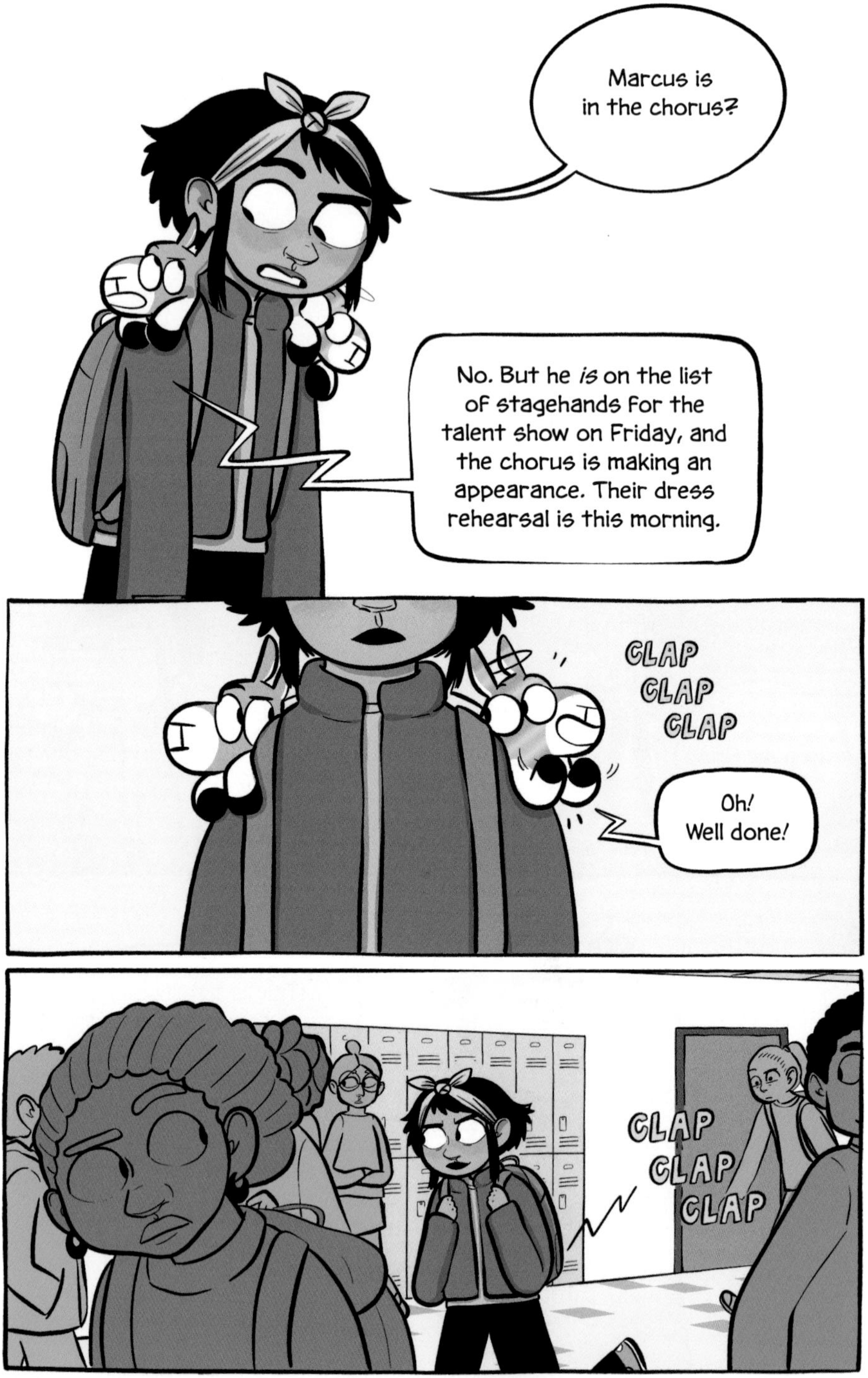
Marcus is in the chorus?
No. But he *is* on the list of stagehands for the talent show on Friday, and the chorus is making an appearance. Their dress rehearsal is this morning.
CLAP CLAP CLAP
Oh! Well done!
CLAP CLAP CLAP

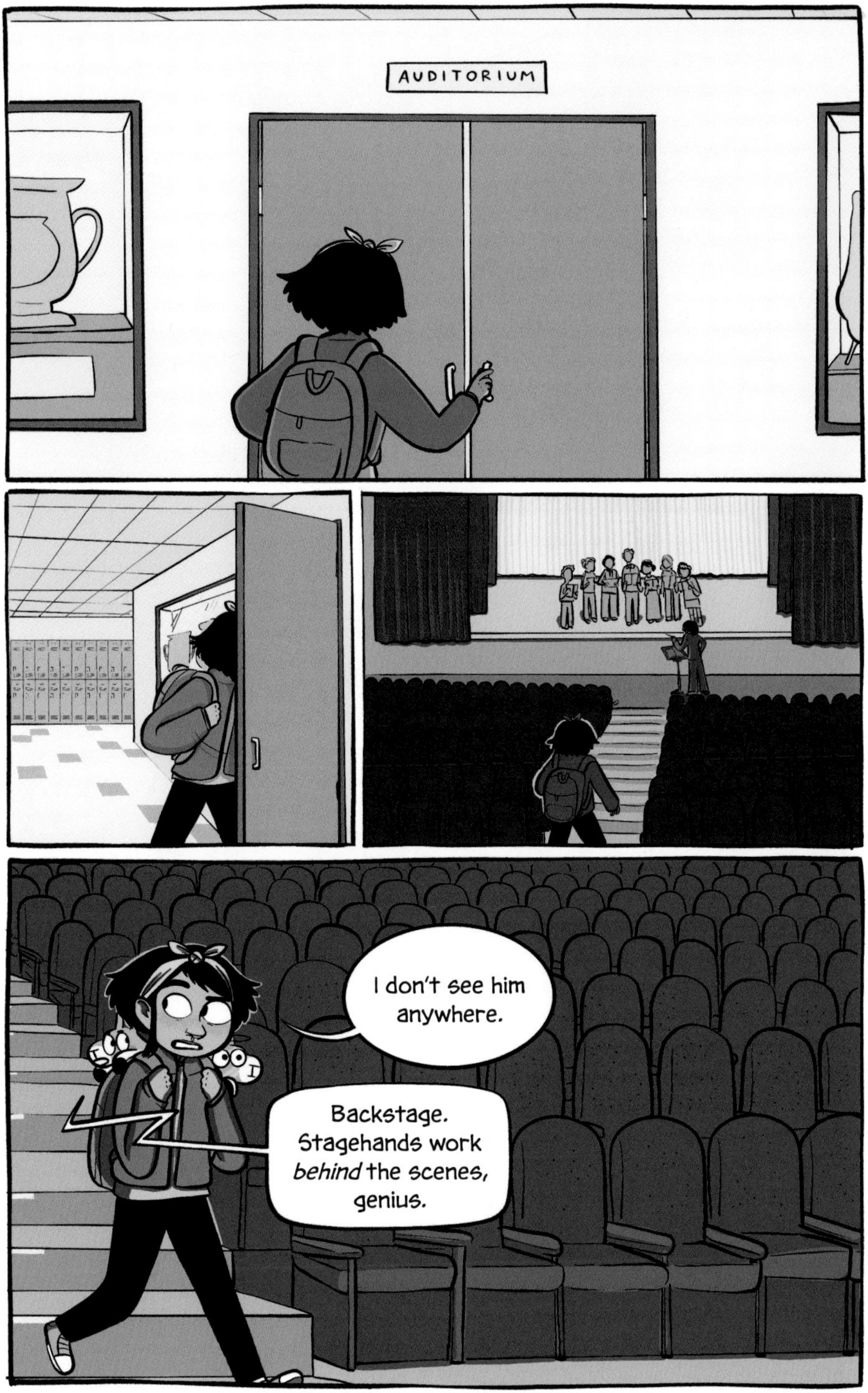
AUDITORIUM
I don't see him anywhere.
Backstage. Stagehands work *behind* the scenes, genius.

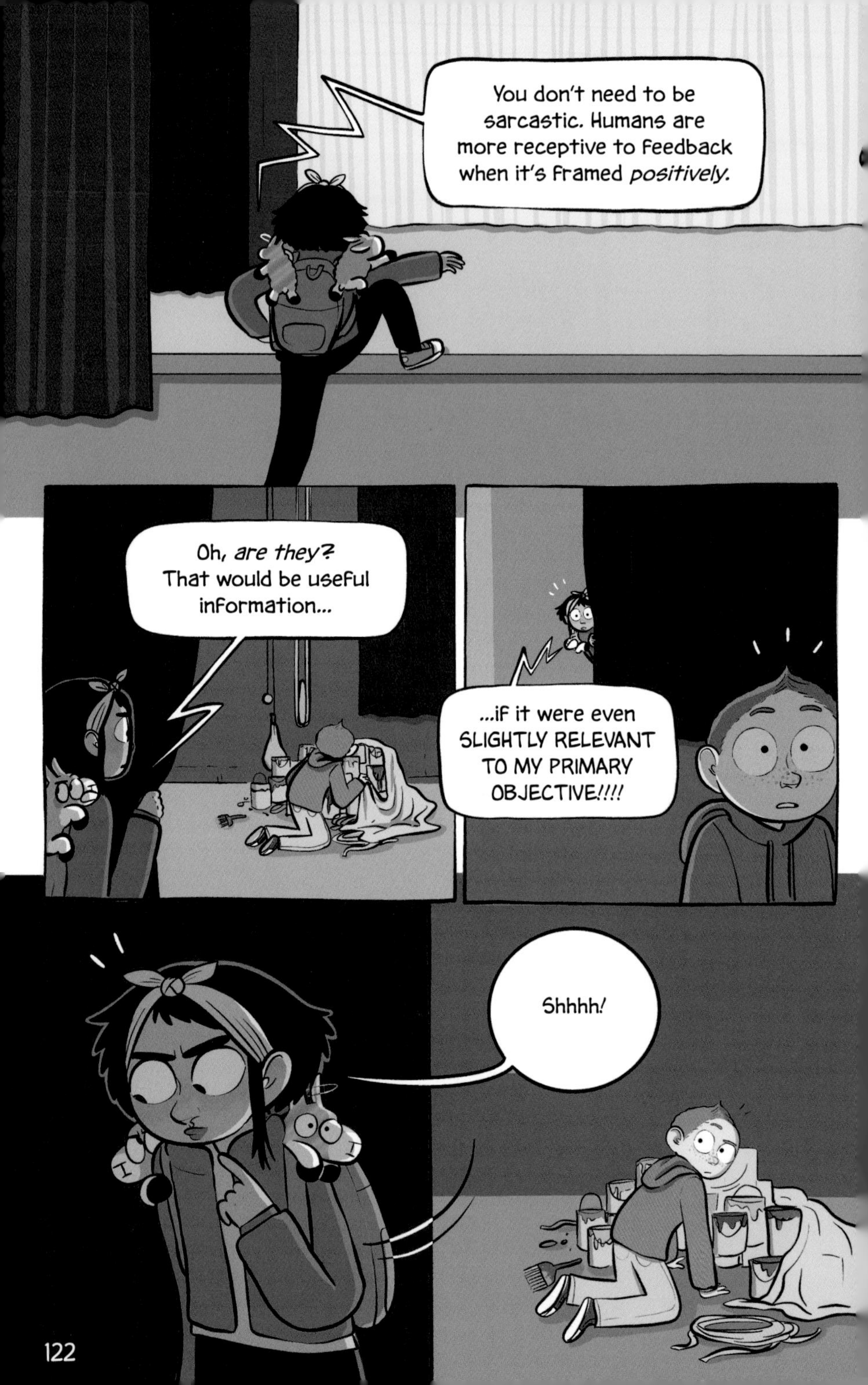
You don't need to be sarcastic. Humans are more receptive to feedback when it's framed *positively.*
Oh, *are they?* That would be useful information...
...if it were even SLIGHTLY RELEVANT TO MY PRIMARY OBJECTIVE!!!!
Shhhh!

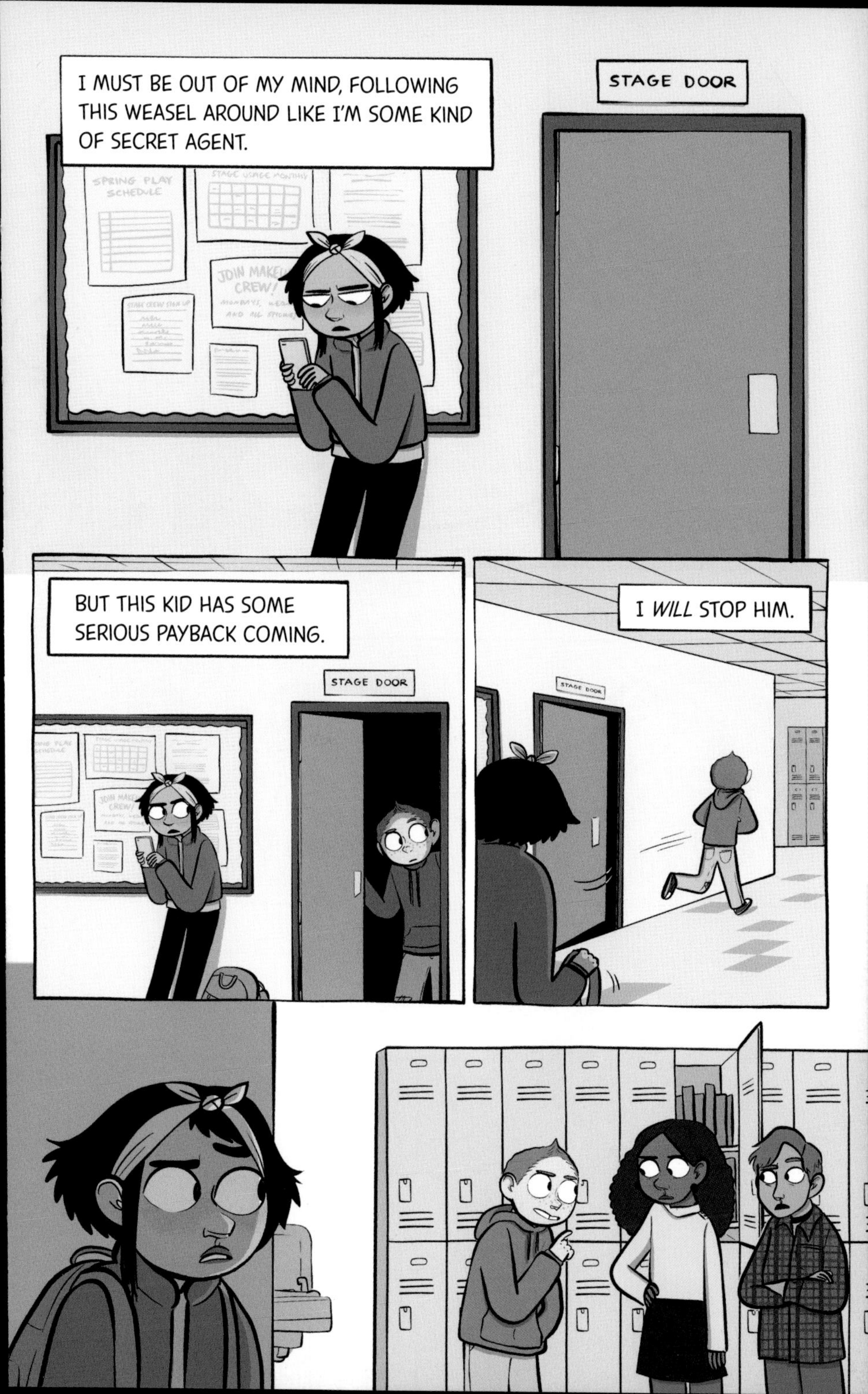
I MUST BE OUT OF MY MIND, FOLLOWING THIS WEASEL AROUND LIKE I'M SOME KIND OF SECRET AGENT.
STAGE DOOR
SPRING PLAY SCHEDULE
JOIN MAKEUP CREW!
BUT THIS KID HAS SOME SERIOUS PAYBACK COMING.
STAGE DOOR
I *WILL* STOP HIM.

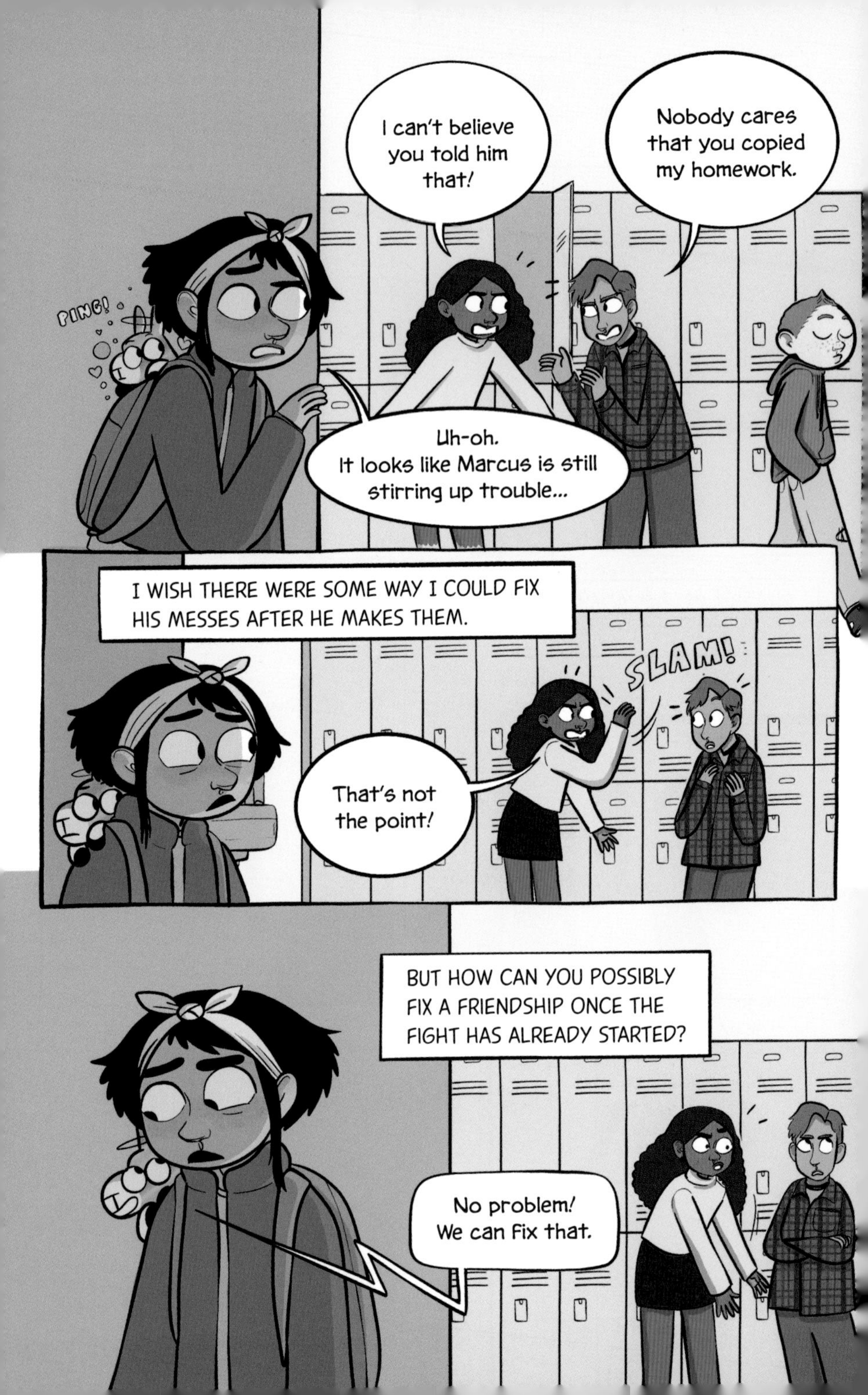

I can't believe you told him that!
Nobody cares that you copied my homework.
PING!
Uh-oh. It looks like Marcus is still stirring up trouble...
I WISH THERE WERE SOME WAY I COULD FIX HIS MESSES AFTER HE MAKES THEM.
SLAM!
That's not the point!
BUT HOW CAN YOU POSSIBLY FIX A FRIENDSHIP ONCE THE FIGHT HAS ALREADY STARTED?
No problem! We can fix that.

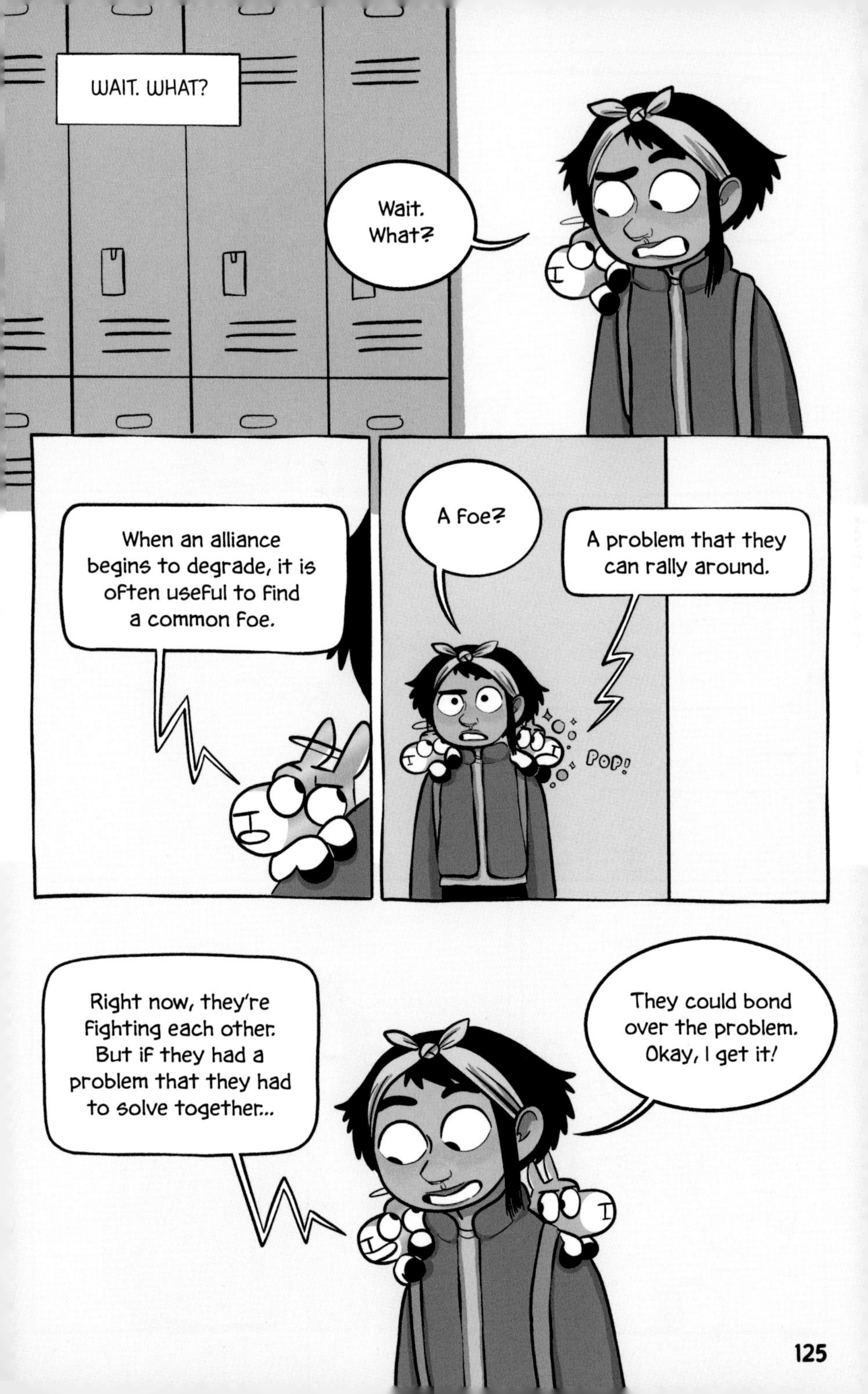
WAIT. WHAT?
Wait. What?
When an alliance begins to degrade, it is often useful to find a common foe.
A foe?
A problem that they can rally around.
POP!
Right now, they're fighting each other. But if they had a problem that they had to solve together...
They could bond over the problem. Okay, I get it!

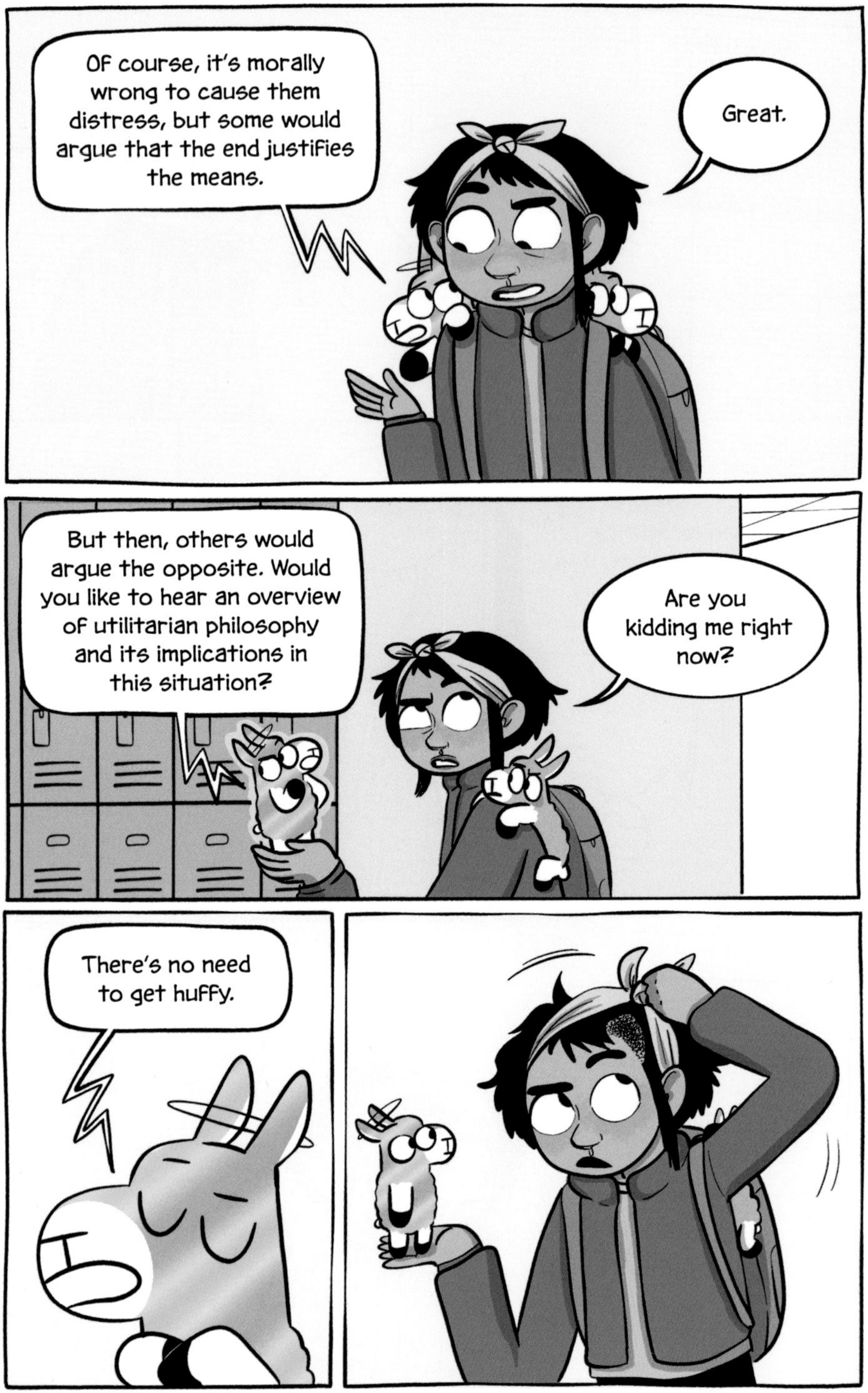
Of course, it's morally wrong to cause them distress, but some would argue that the end justifies the means.
Great.
But then, others would argue the opposite. Would you like to hear an overview of utilitarian philosophy and its implications in this situation?
Are you kidding me right now?
There's no need to get huffy.

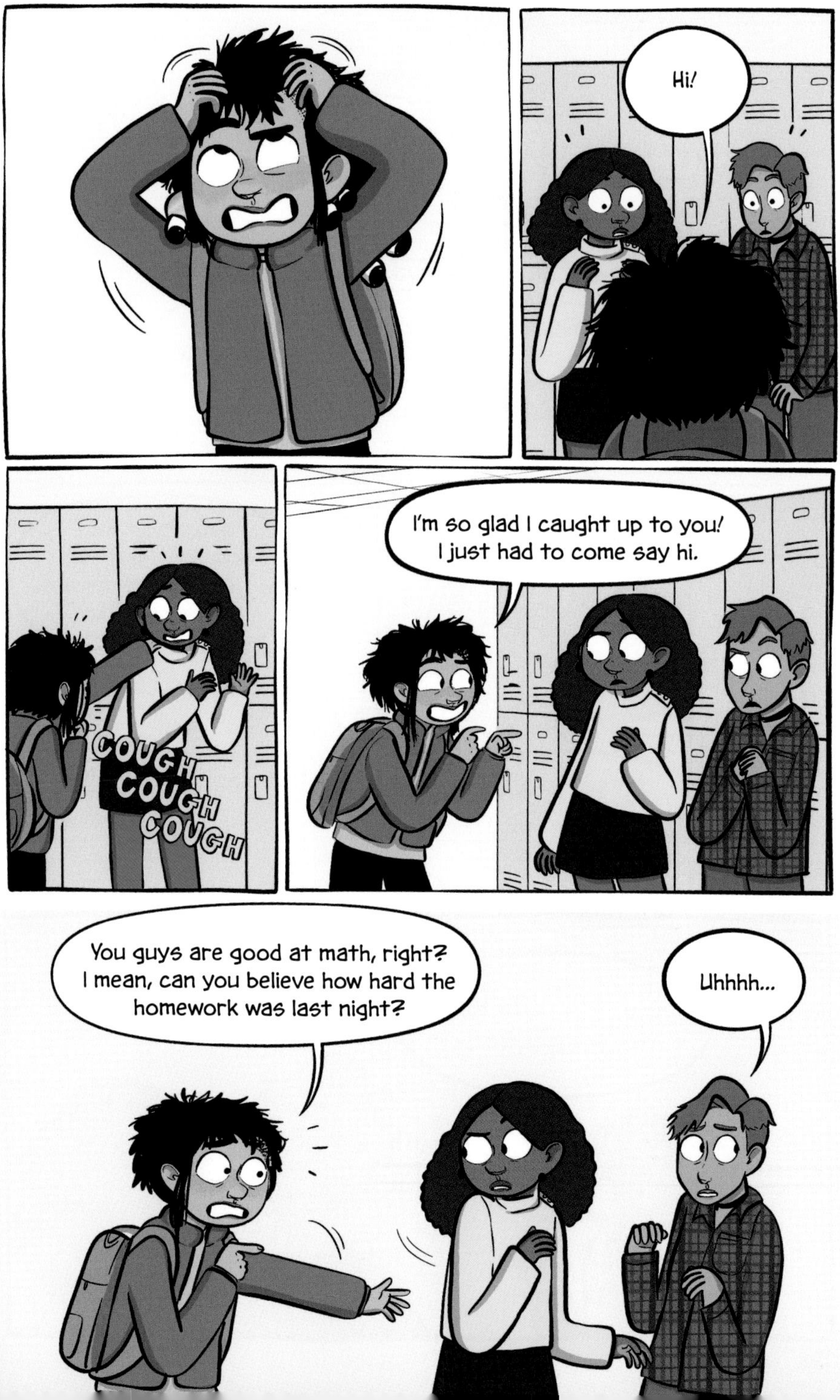

Hi!
COUGH COUGH COUGH
I'm so glad I caught up to you! I just had to come say hi.
You guys are good at math, right? I mean, can you believe how hard the homework was last night?
Uhhhh...

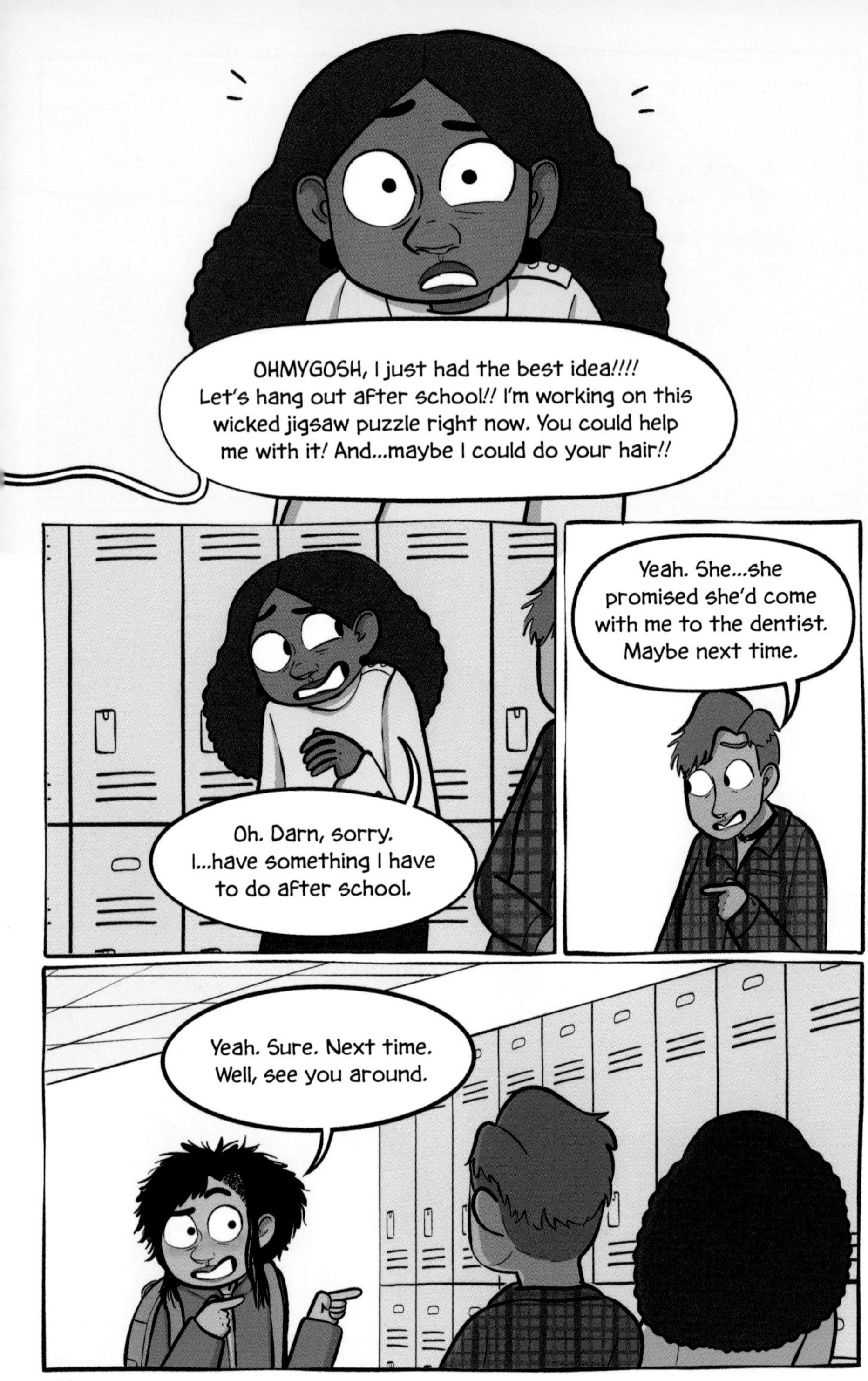
OHMYGOSH, I just had the best idea!!!! Let's hang out after school!! I'm working on this wicked jigsaw puzzle right now. You could help me with it! And...maybe I could do your hair!!
Oh. Darn, sorry. I...have something I have to do after school.
Yeah. She...she promised she'd come with me to the dentist. Maybe next time.
Yeah. Sure. Next time. Well, see you around.

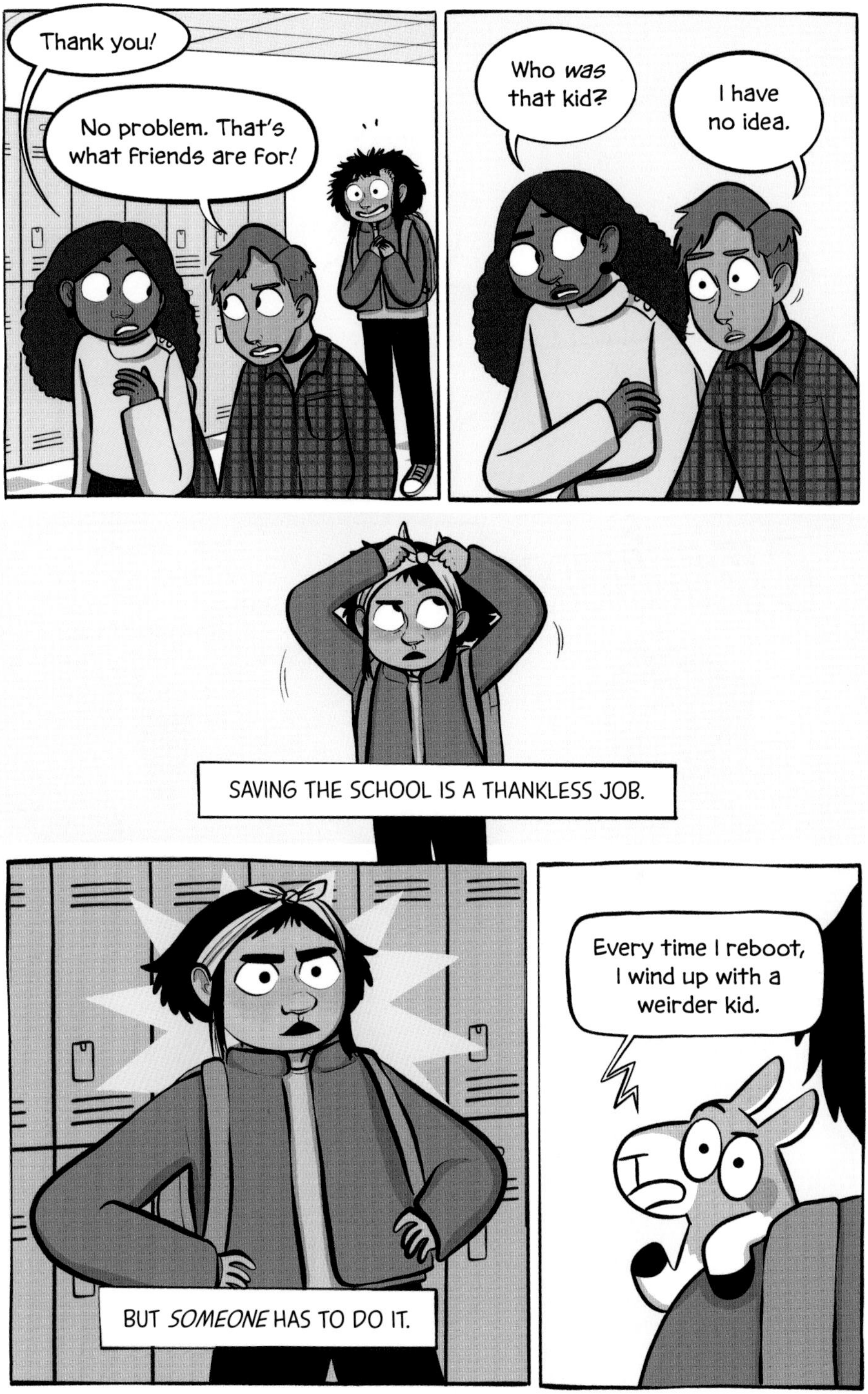
Thank you!
No problem. That's what friends are for!
Who *was* that kid?
I have no idea.
SAVING THE SCHOOL IS A THANKLESS JOB.
BUT *SOMEONE* HAS TO DO IT.
Every time I reboot, I wind up with a weirder kid.

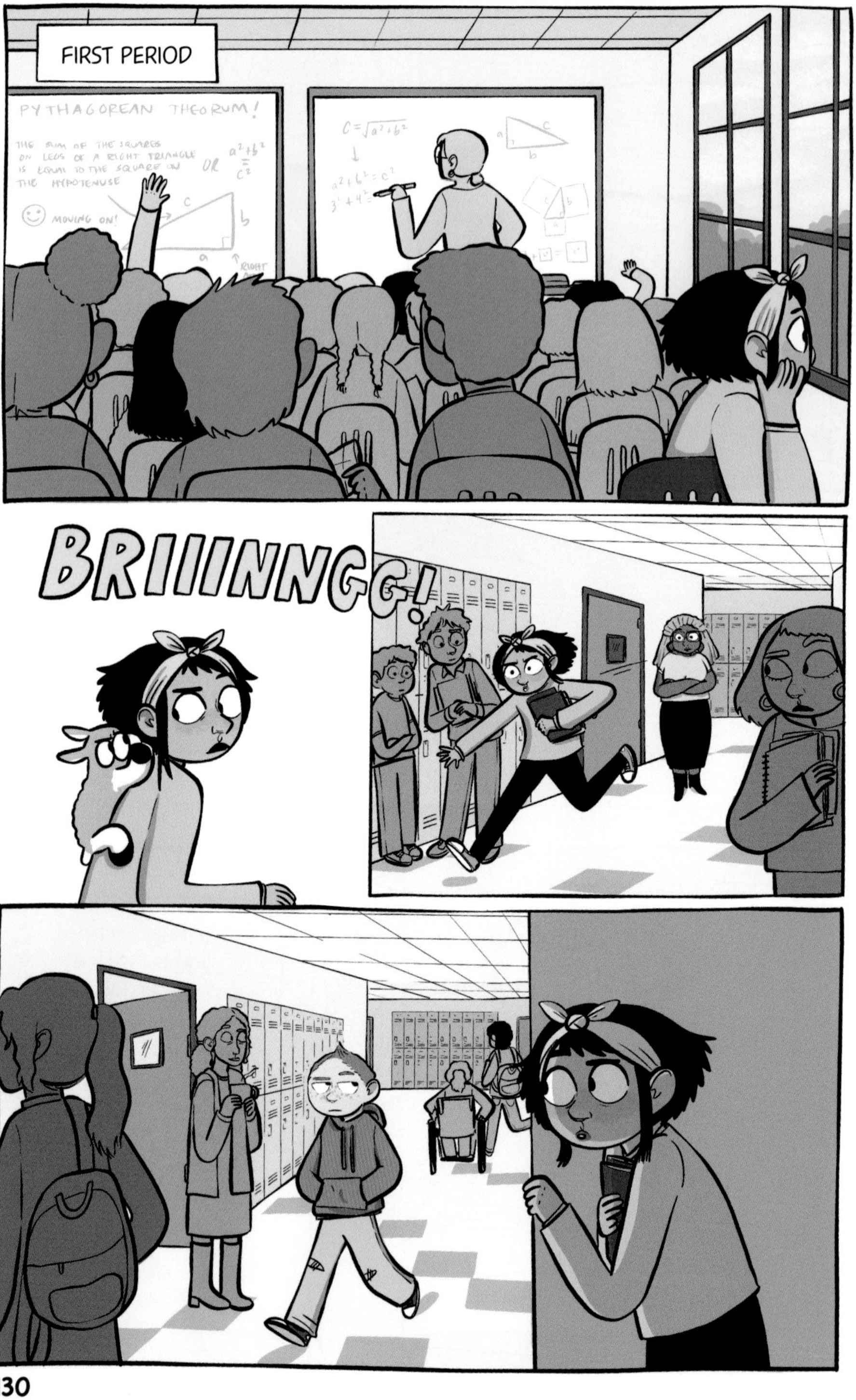
FIRST PERIOD
PYTHAGOREAN THEORUM!
THE SUM OF THE SQUARES ON LEGS OF A RIGHT TRIANGLE IS EQUAL TO THE SQUARE ON THE HYPOTENUSE
OR
MOVING ON!
BRIIINNGG!

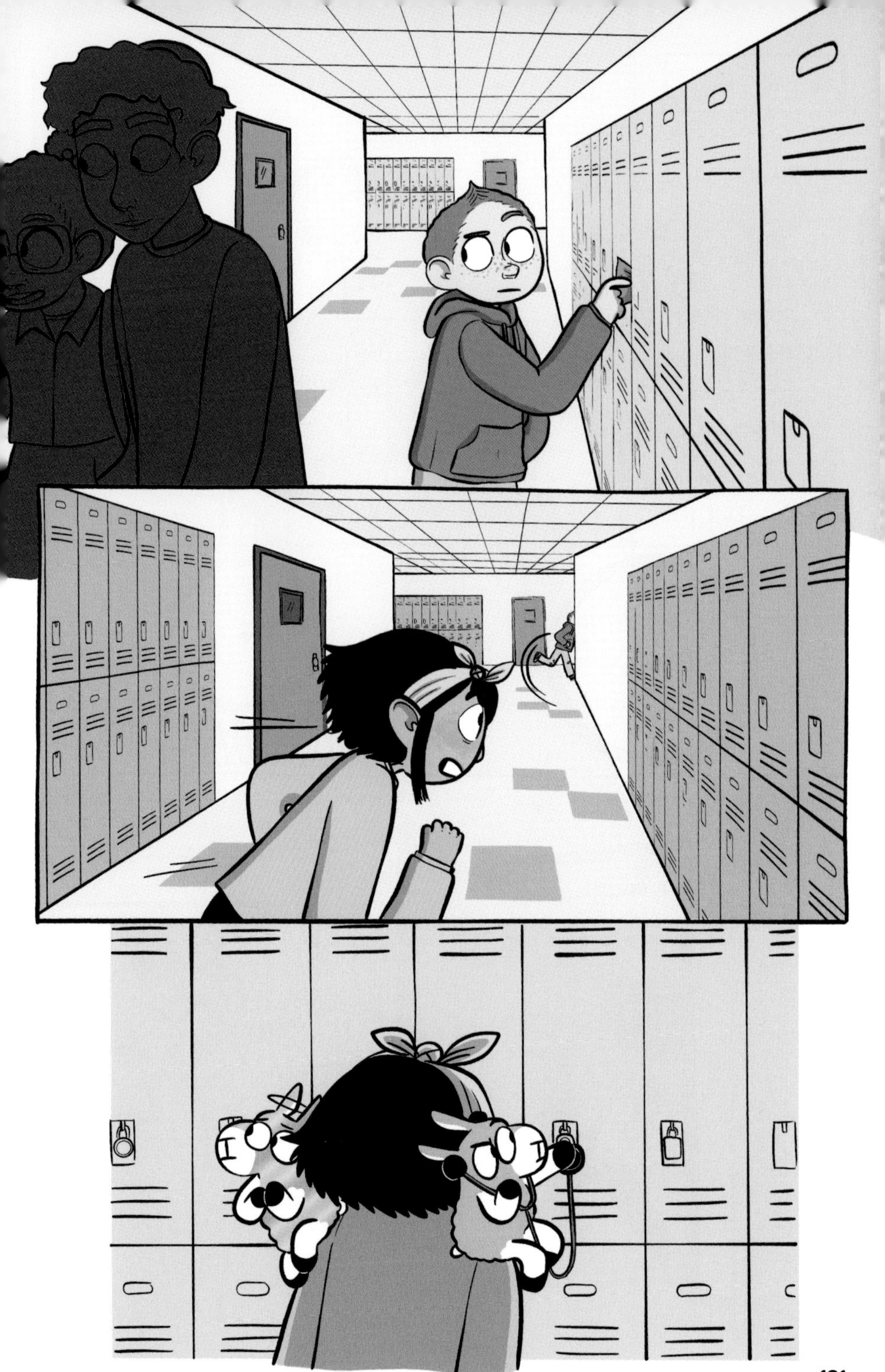

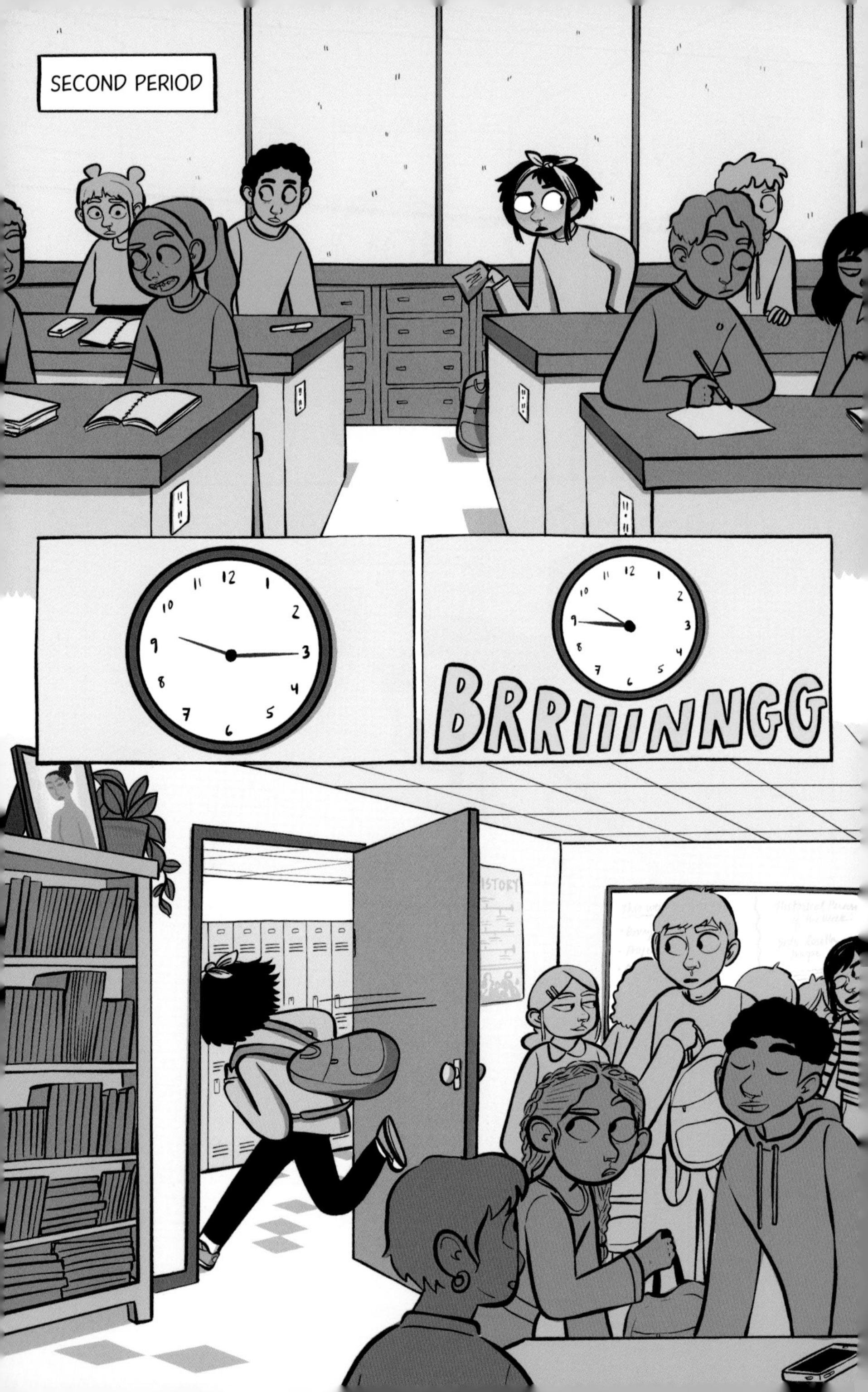
SECOND PERIOD
BRRIIINNGG

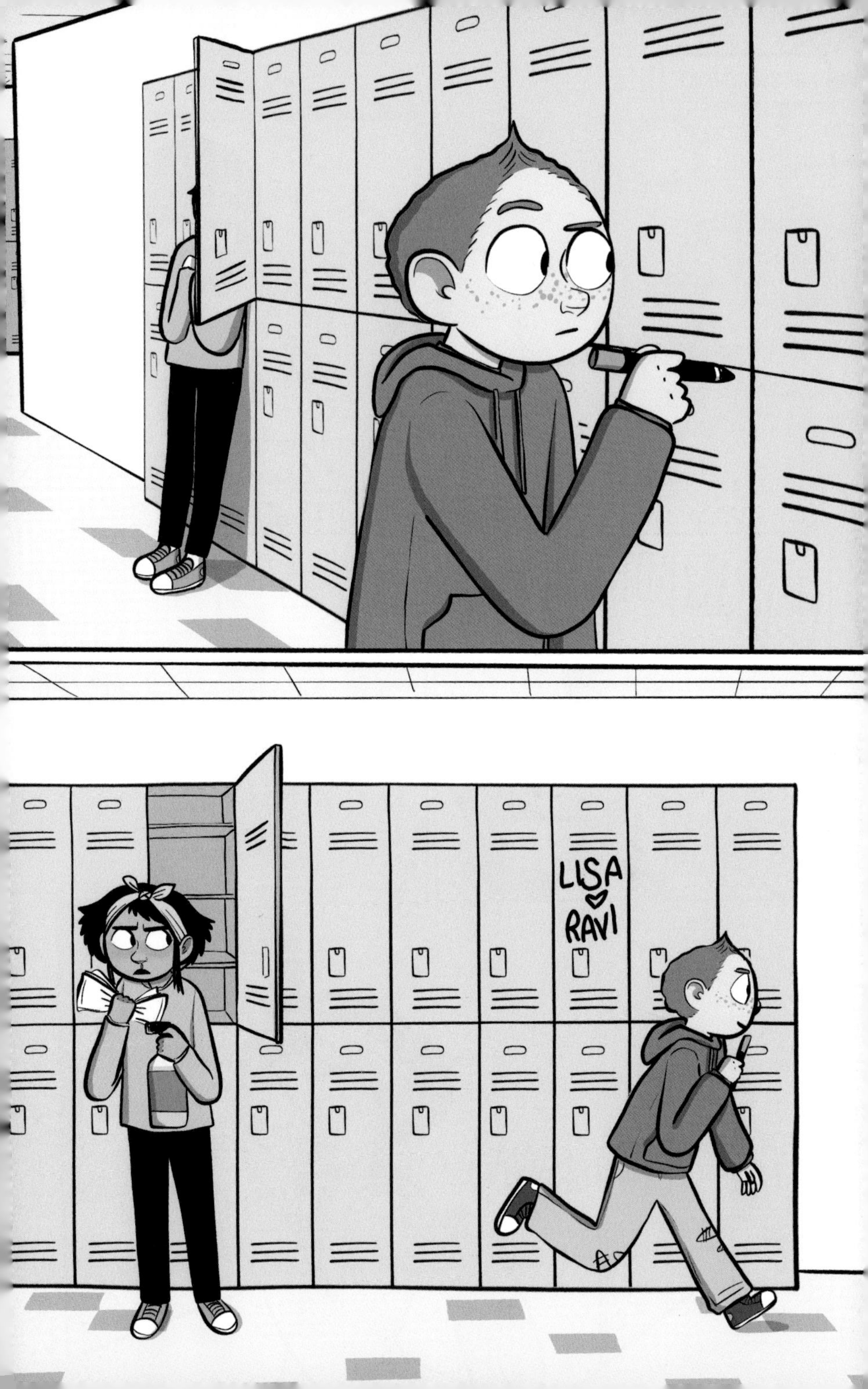
LISA
RAVI

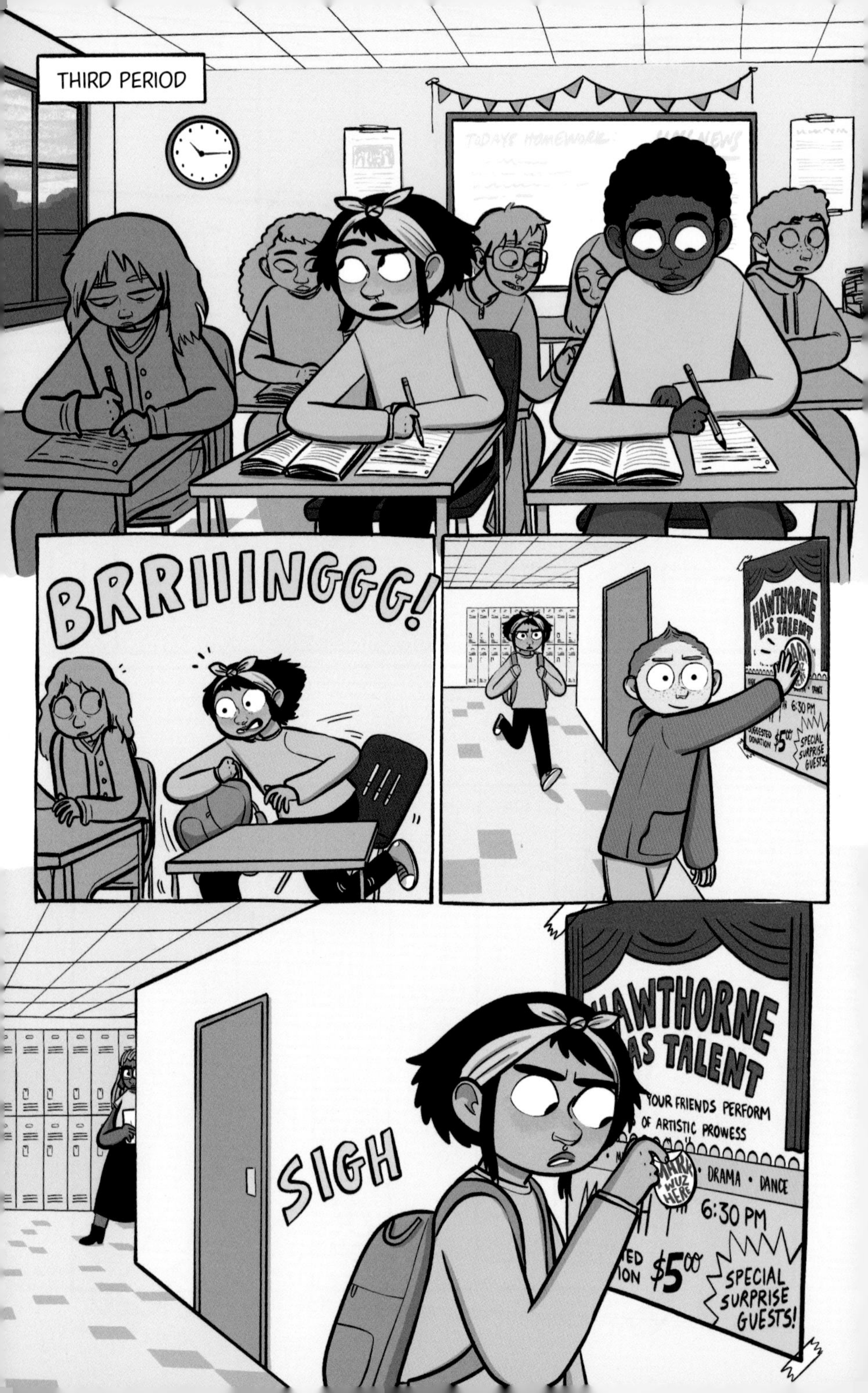

THIRD PERIOD
BRRIIINGGG!
HAWTHORNE HAS TALENT
6:30 PM
SUGGESTED DONATION $5.00
SPECIAL SURPRISE GUESTS!
SIGH
AWTHORNE
AS TALENT
YOUR FRIENDS PERFORM
OF ARTISTIC PROWESS
DRAMA • DANCE
6:30 PM
$5.00
SPECIAL SURPRISE GUESTS!
WUZ HERE

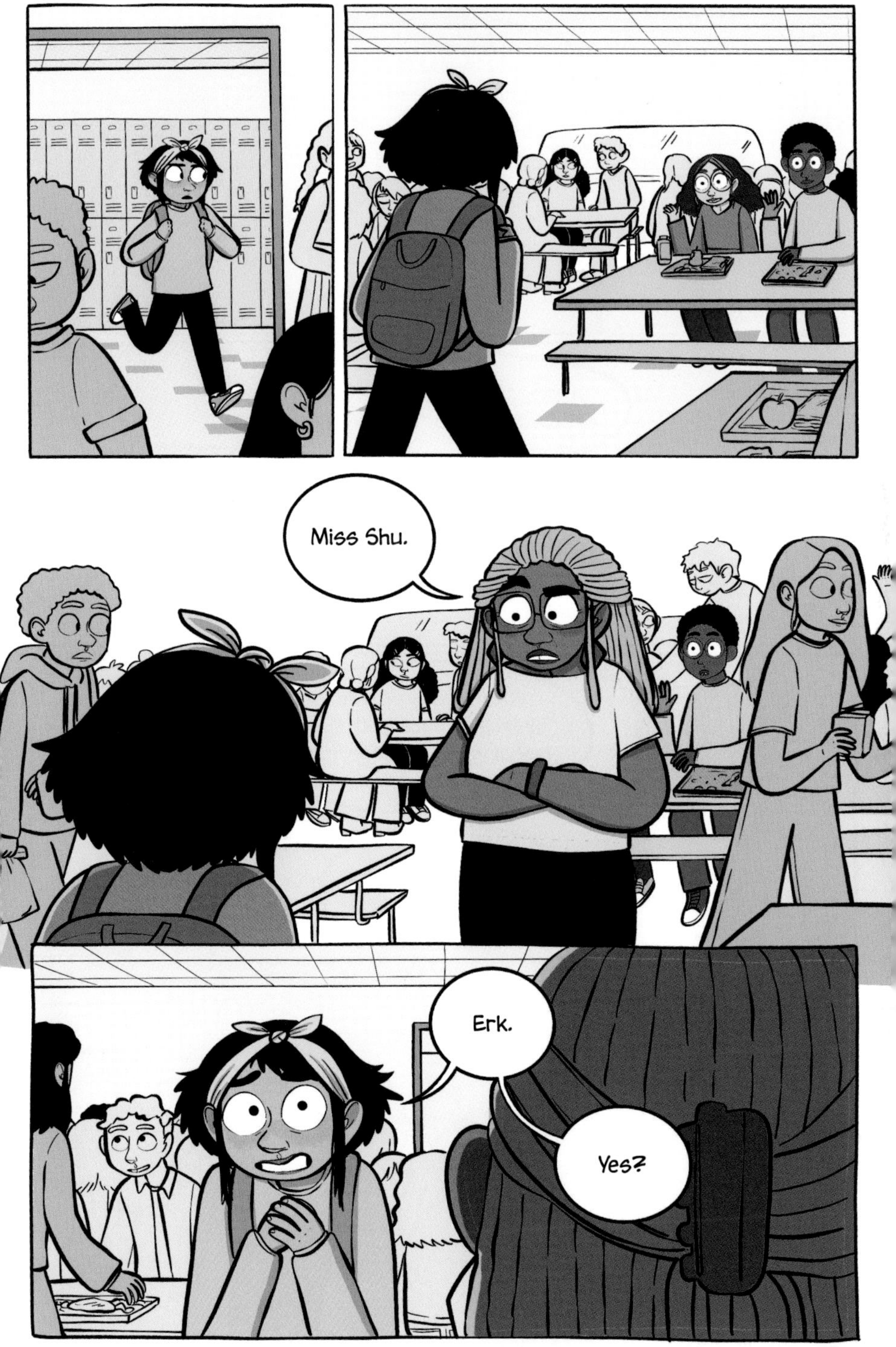
Miss Shu.
Erk.
Yes?

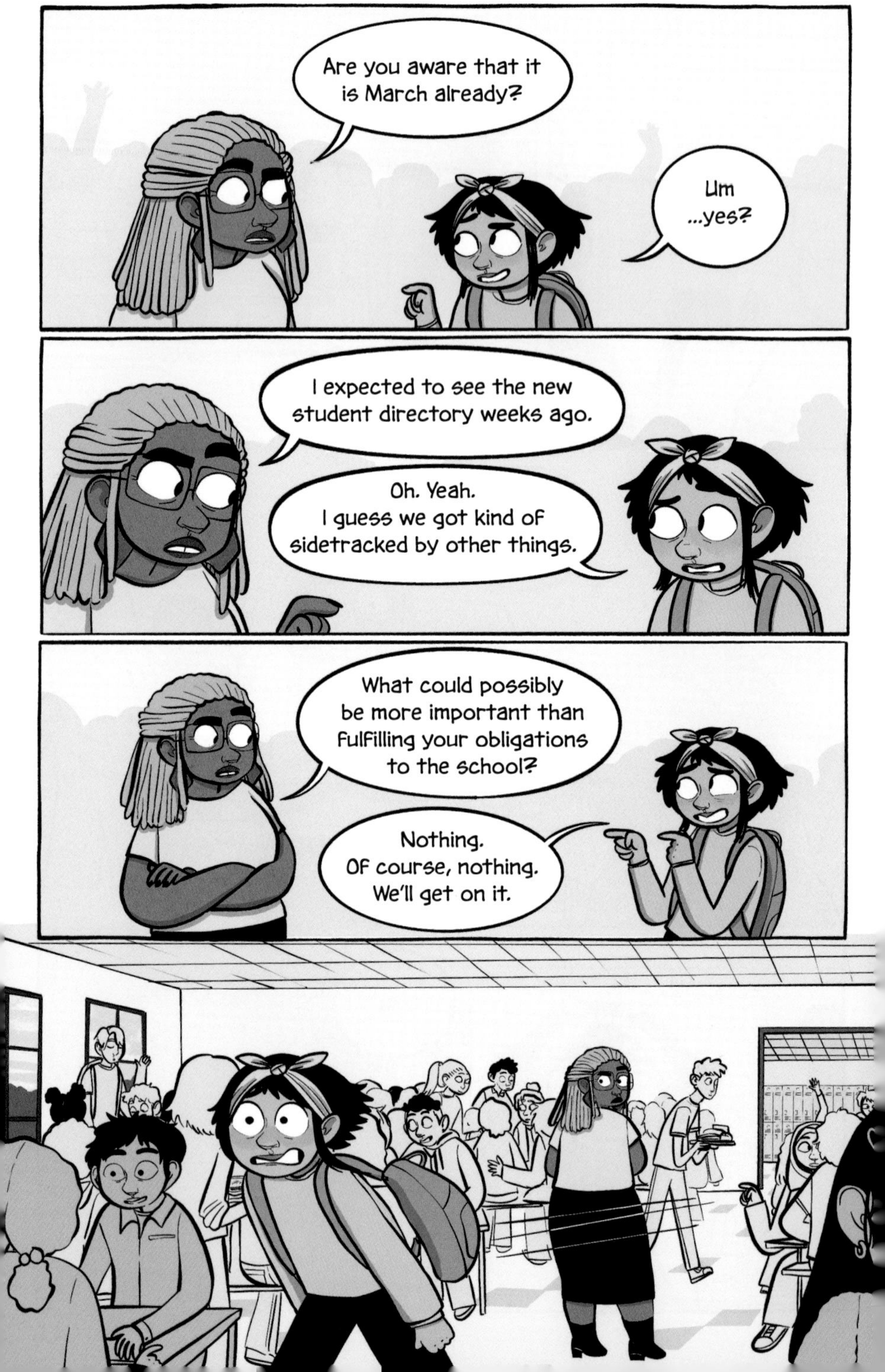
Are you aware that it is March already?
Um ...yes?
I expected to see the new student directory weeks ago.
Oh. Yeah. I guess we got kind of sidetracked by other things.
What could possibly be more important than fulfilling your obligations to the school?
Nothing. Of course, nothing. We'll get on it.

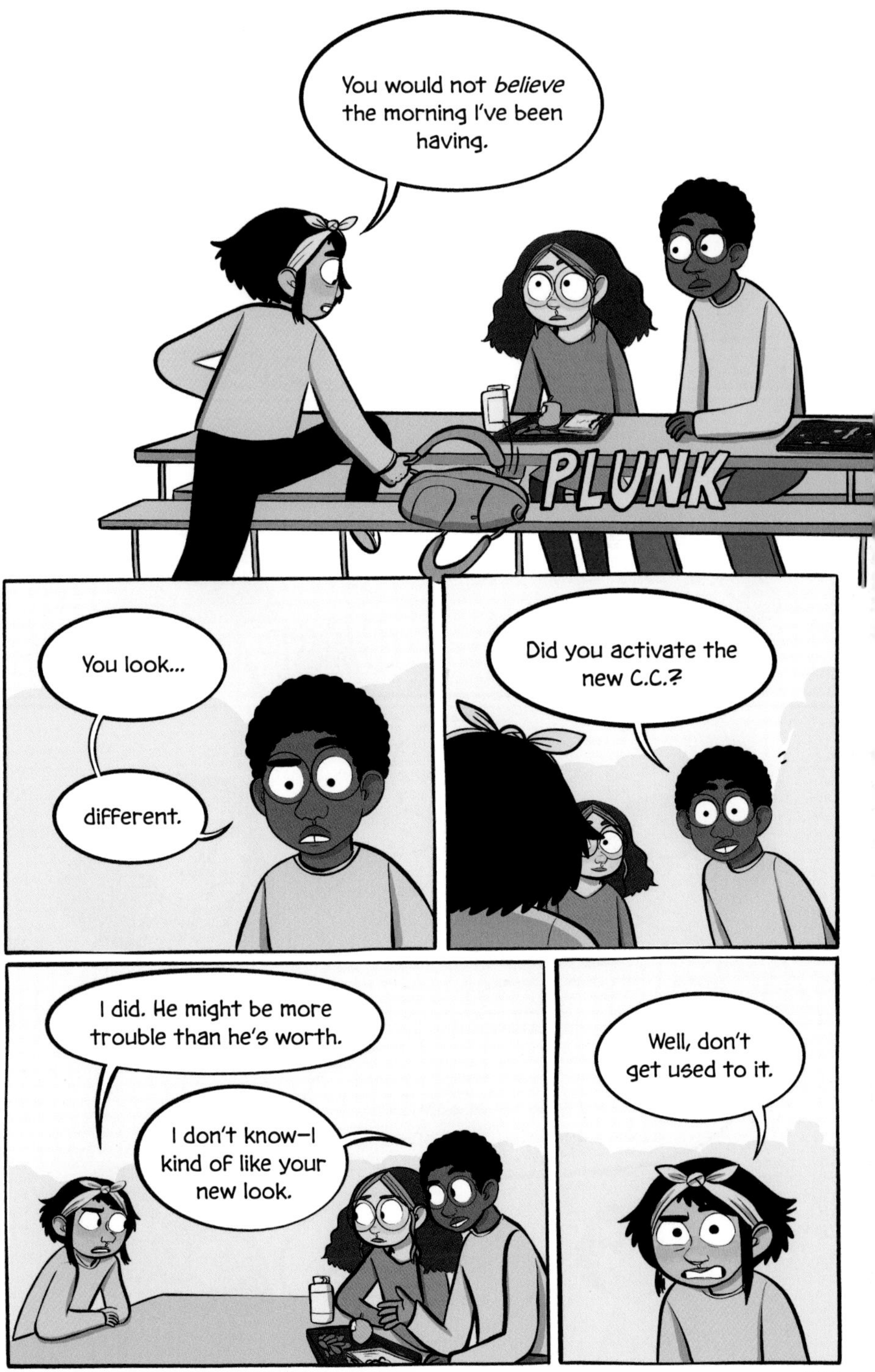
You would not *believe* the morning I've been having.
PLUNK
You look...
different.
Did you activate the new C.C.?
I did. He might be more trouble than he's worth.
I don't know—I kind of like your new look.
Well, don't get used to it.

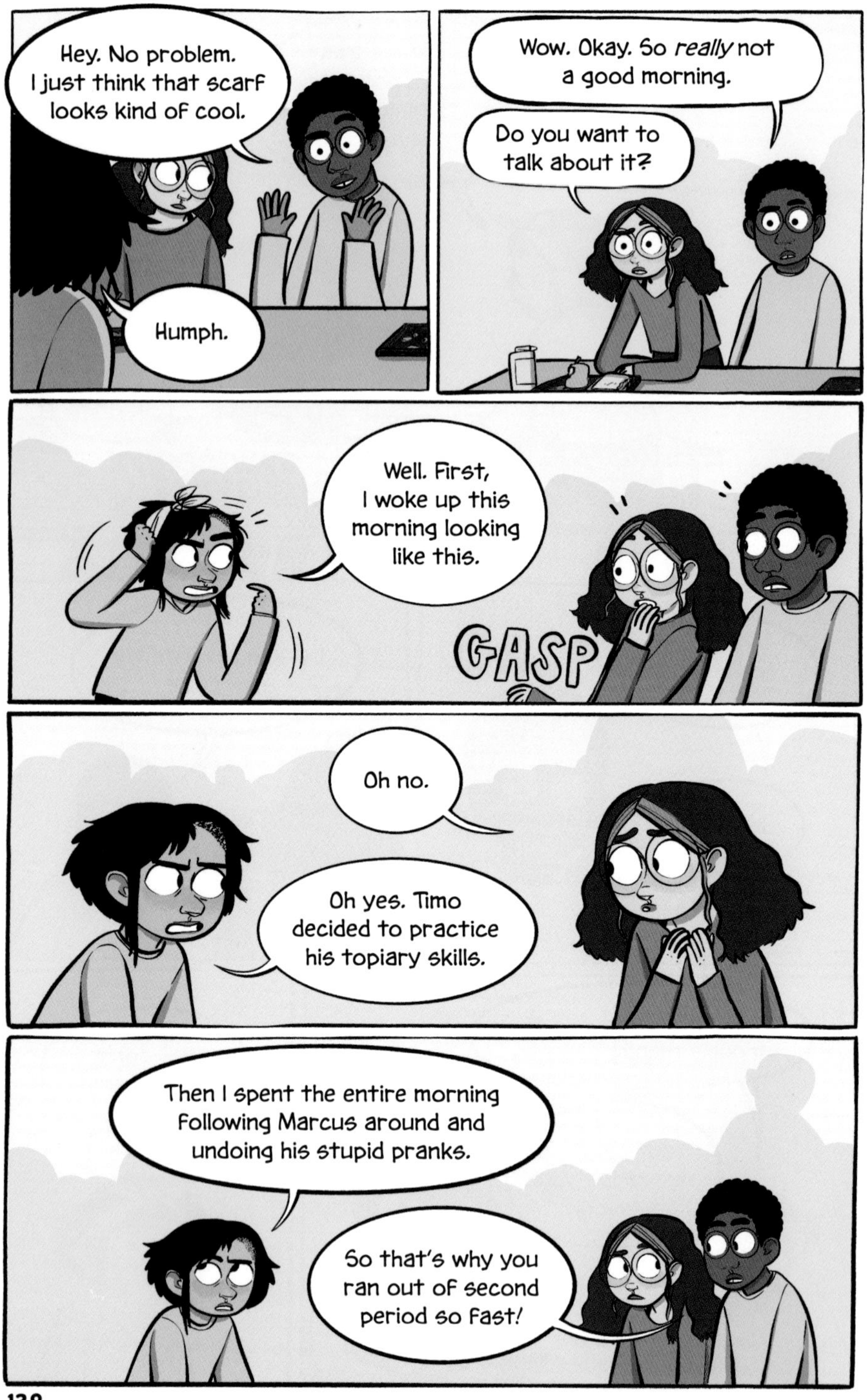
Hey. No problem. I just think that scarf looks kind of cool.
Humph.
Wow. Okay. So *really* not a good morning.
Do you want to talk about it?
Well. First, I woke up this morning looking like this.
GASP
Oh no.
Oh yes. Timo decided to practice his topiary skills.
Then I spent the entire morning following Marcus around and undoing his stupid pranks.
So that's why you ran out of second period so fast!

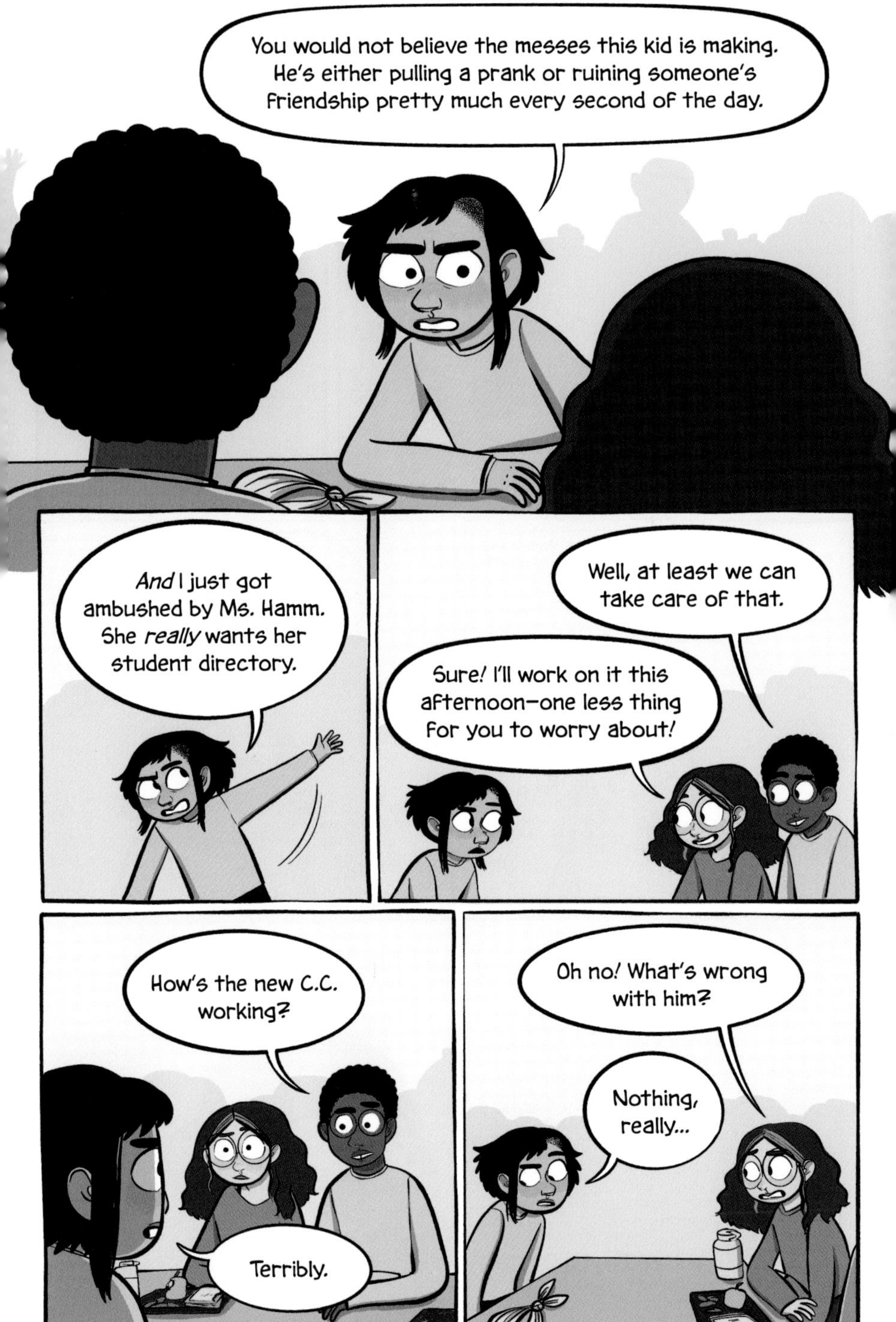
You would not believe the messes this kid is making. He's either pulling a prank or ruining someone's friendship pretty much every second of the day.
And I just got ambushed by Ms. Hamm. She *really* wants her student directory.
Well, at least we can take care of that.
Sure! I'll work on it this afternoon—one less thing for you to worry about!
How's the new C.C. working?
Terribly.
Oh no! What's wrong with him?
Nothing, really...

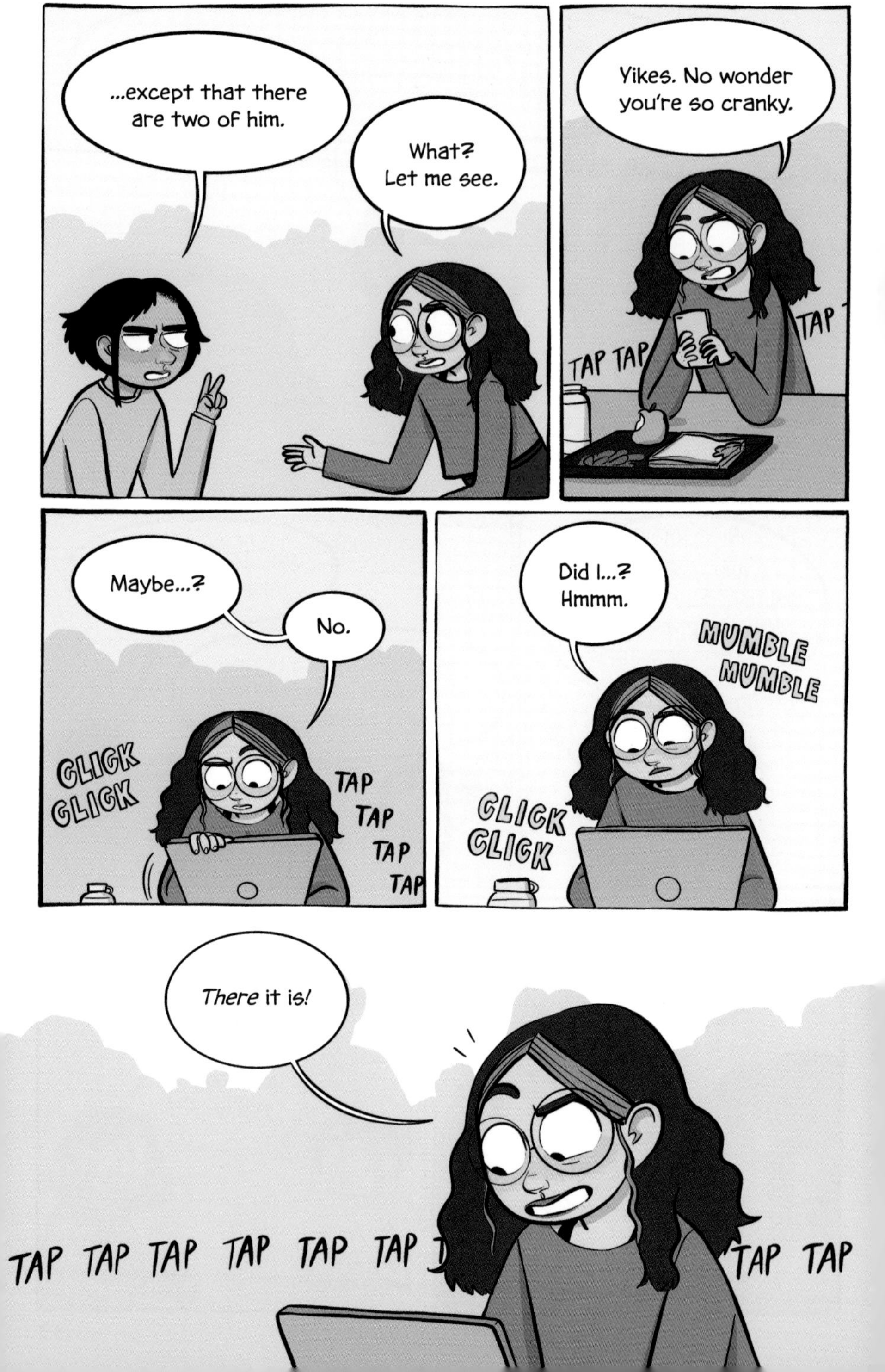
...except that there are two of him.
What? Let me see.
Yikes. No wonder you're so cranky.
TAP TAP
TAP
Maybe...?
No.
CLICK CLICK
TAP TAP TAP TAP
Did I...? Hmmm.
MUMBLE MUMBLE
CLICK CLICK
There it is!
TAP TAP TAP TAP TAP TAP
TAP TAP

Hey, where is everybody? This place is a ghost town.
I don't know... I guess they found somewhere else to sit today.
SHRUG
Uh-oh. I have a bad feeling about this...
Finally!
CLICK
POP!

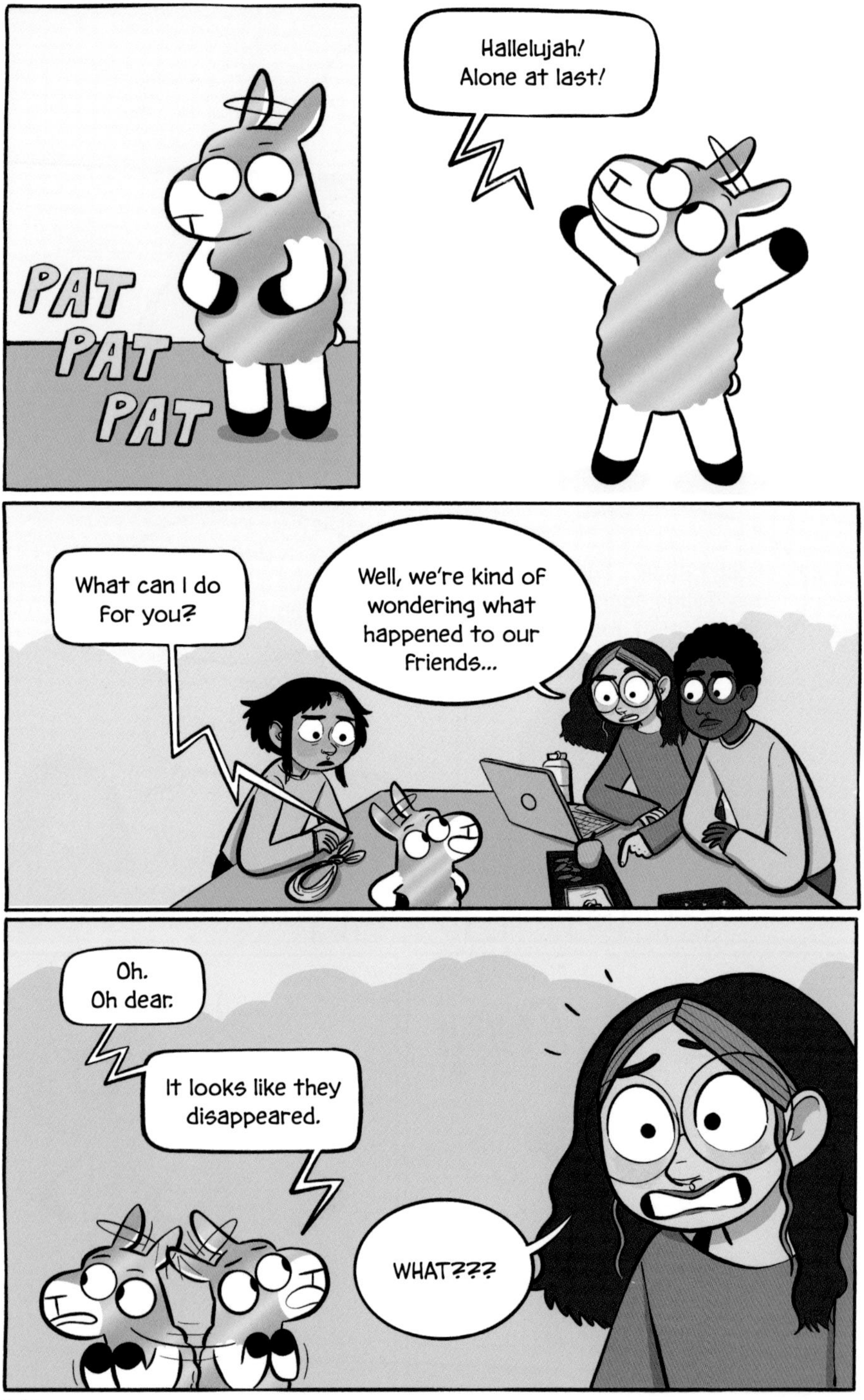
PAT PAT PAT
Hallelujah! Alone at last!
What can I do for you?
Well, we're kind of wondering what happened to our friends...
Oh. Oh dear.
It looks like they disappeared.
WHAT???

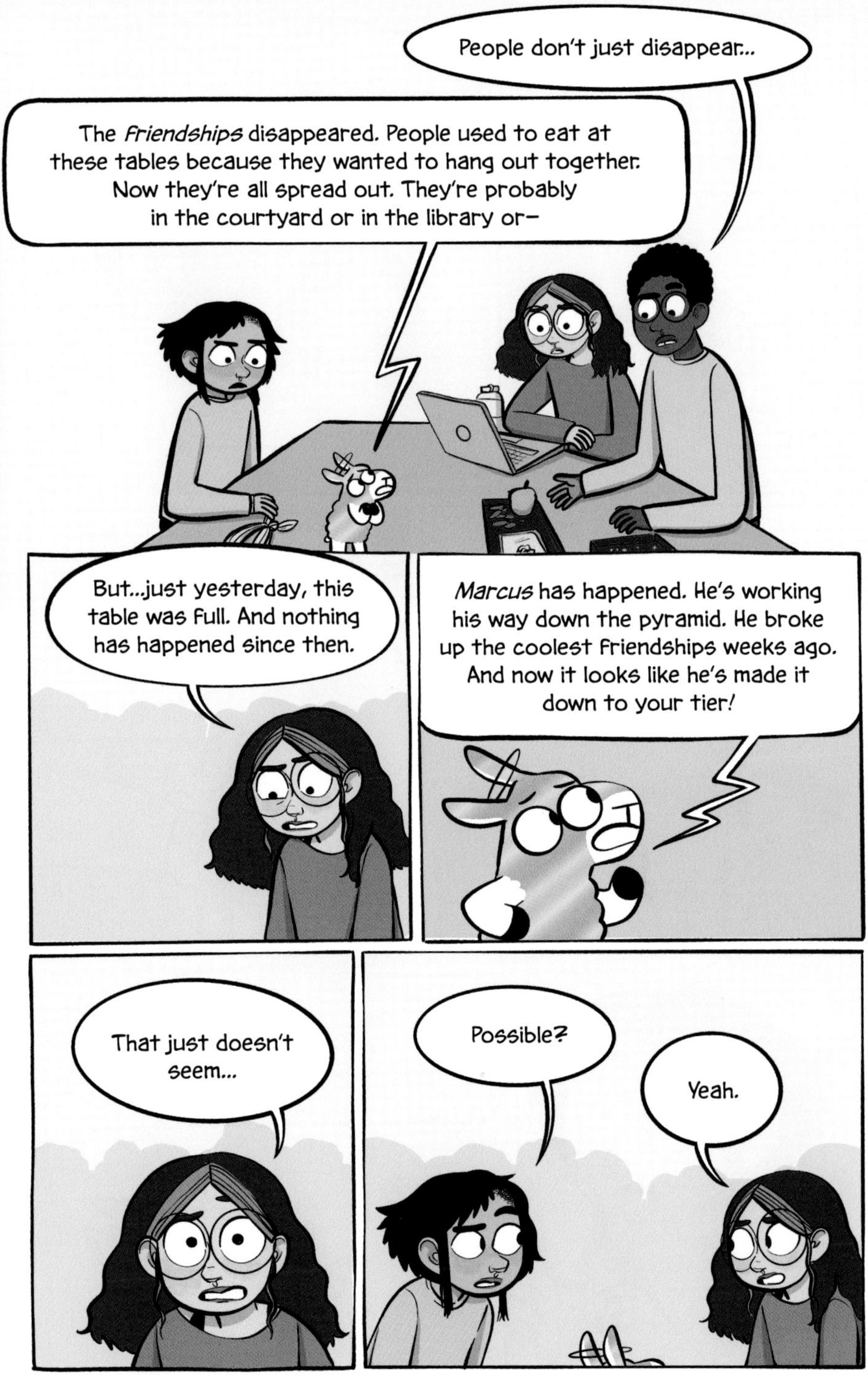
People don't just disappear...
The *friendships* disappeared. People used to eat at these tables because they wanted to hang out together. Now they're all spread out. They're probably in the courtyard or in the library or—
But...just yesterday, this table was full. And nothing has happened since then.
Marcus has happened. He's working his way down the pyramid. He broke up the coolest friendships weeks ago. And now it looks like he's made it down to your tier!
That just doesn't seem...
Possible?
Yeah.

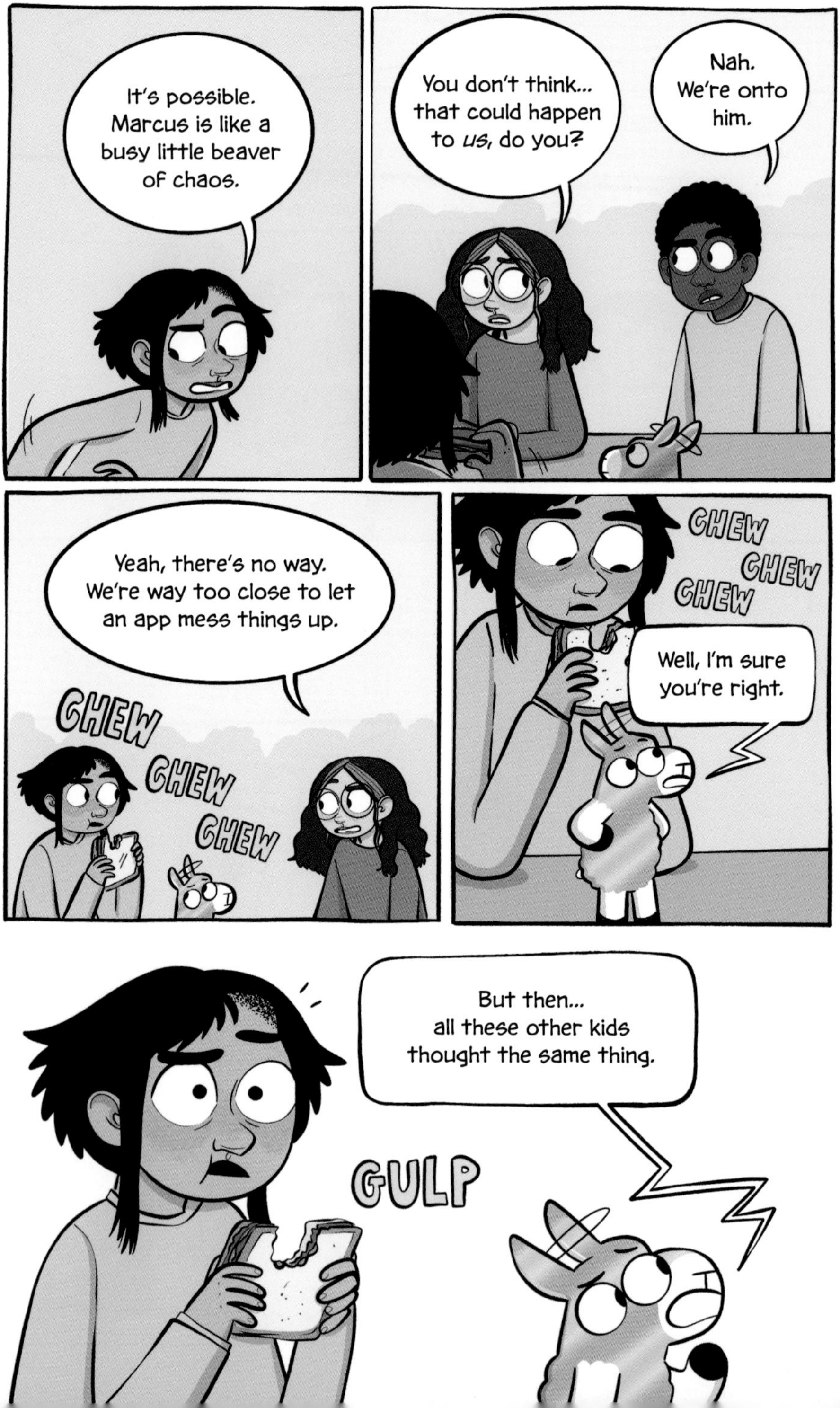
It's possible. Marcus is like a busy little beaver of chaos.
You don't think... that could happen to *us*, do you?
Nah. We're onto him.
Yeah, there's no way. We're way too close to let an app mess things up.
CHEW
CHEW
CHEW
CHEW
CHEW
CHEW
Well, I'm sure you're right.
But then... all these other kids thought the same thing.
GULP

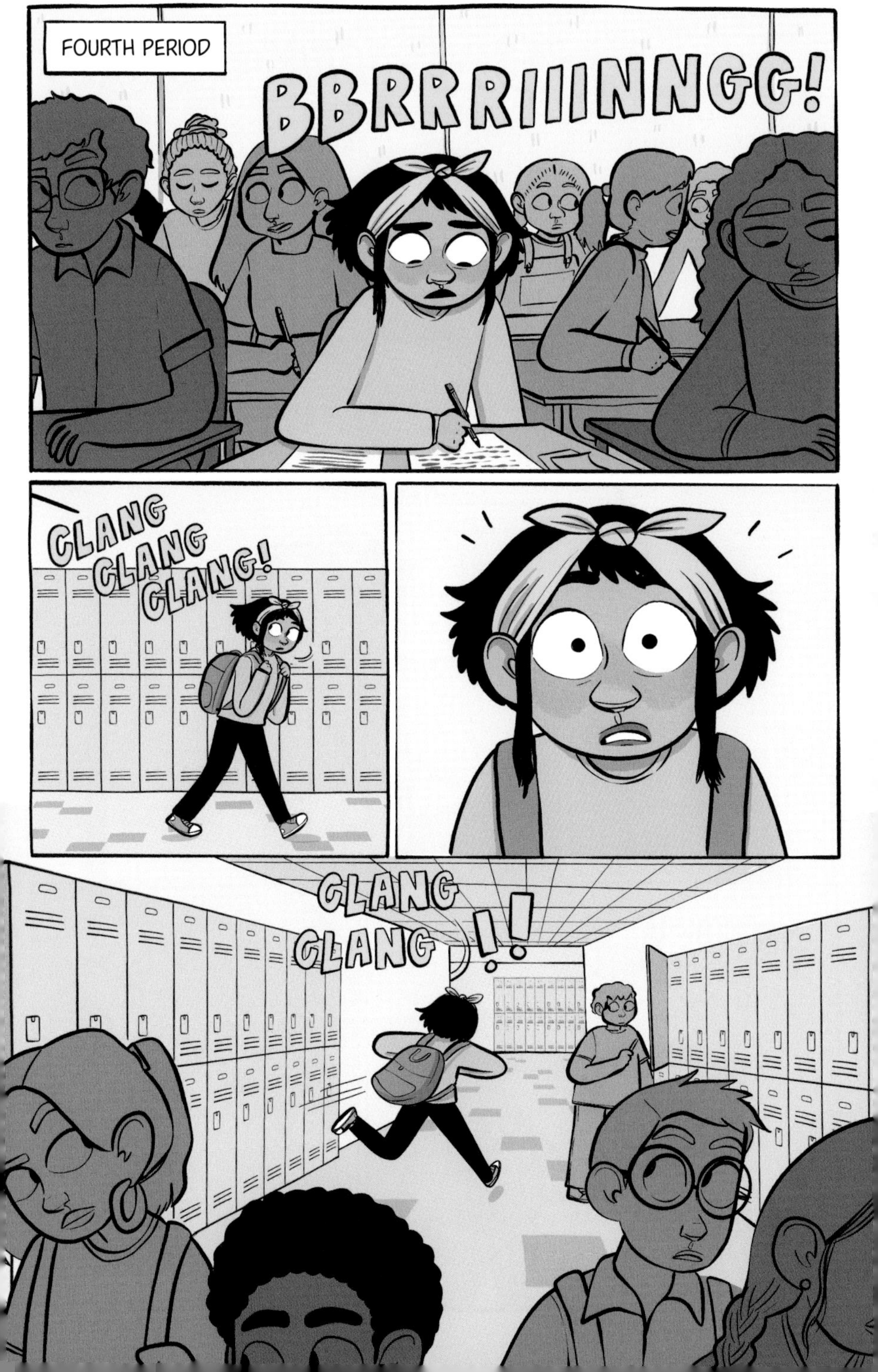
FOURTH PERIOD
BBRRRRIIINNGG!
CLANG
CLANG
CLANG!
CLANG
CLANG
!!

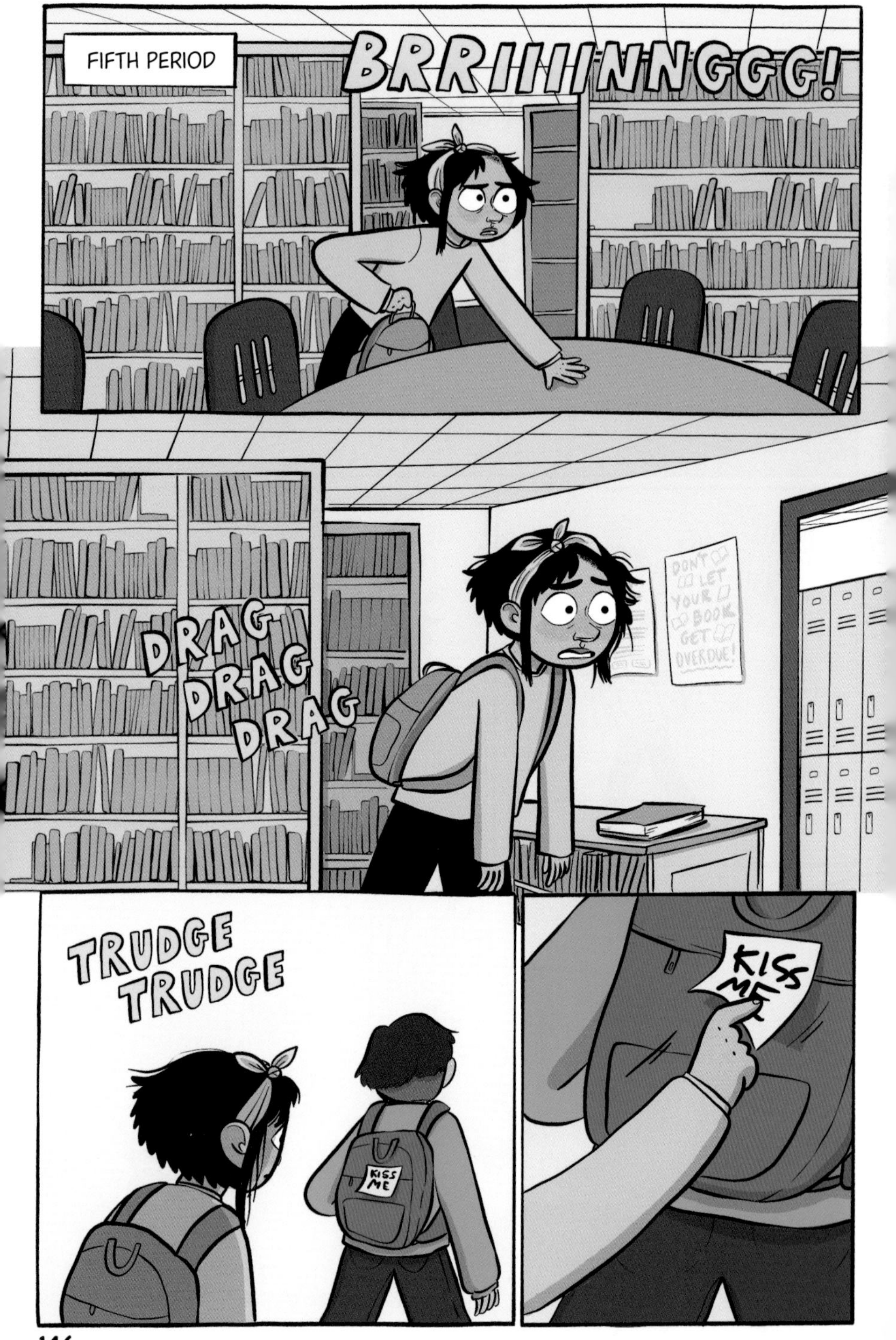
FIFTH PERIOD
BRRIIIINNGGG!
DRAG
DRAG
DRAG
DON'T LET YOUR BOOK GET OVERDUE!
TRUDGE
TRUDGE
KISS ME
KISS ME

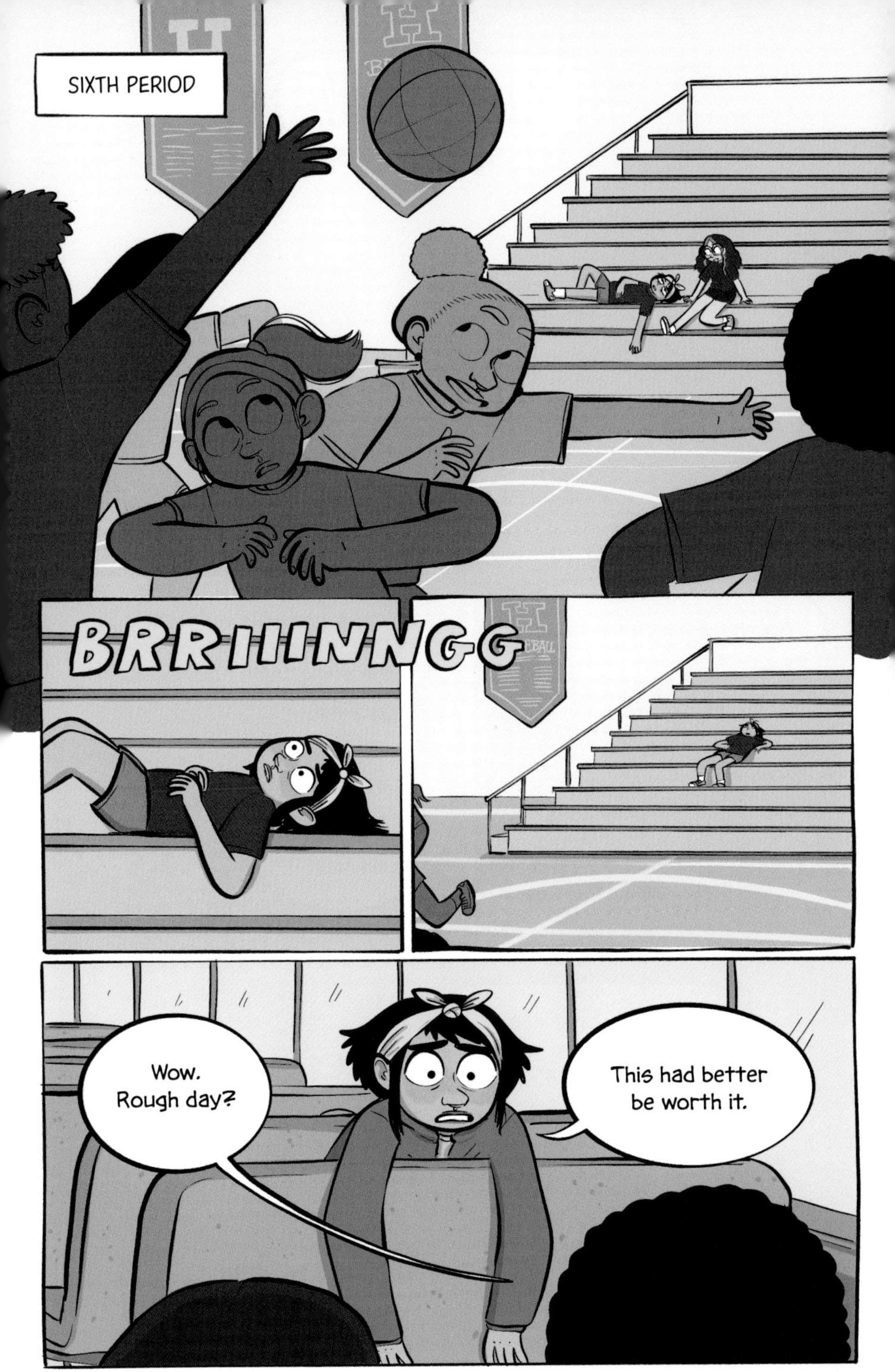
SIXTH PERIOD
BRRIIINNGG
Wow.
Rough day?
This had better
be worth it.

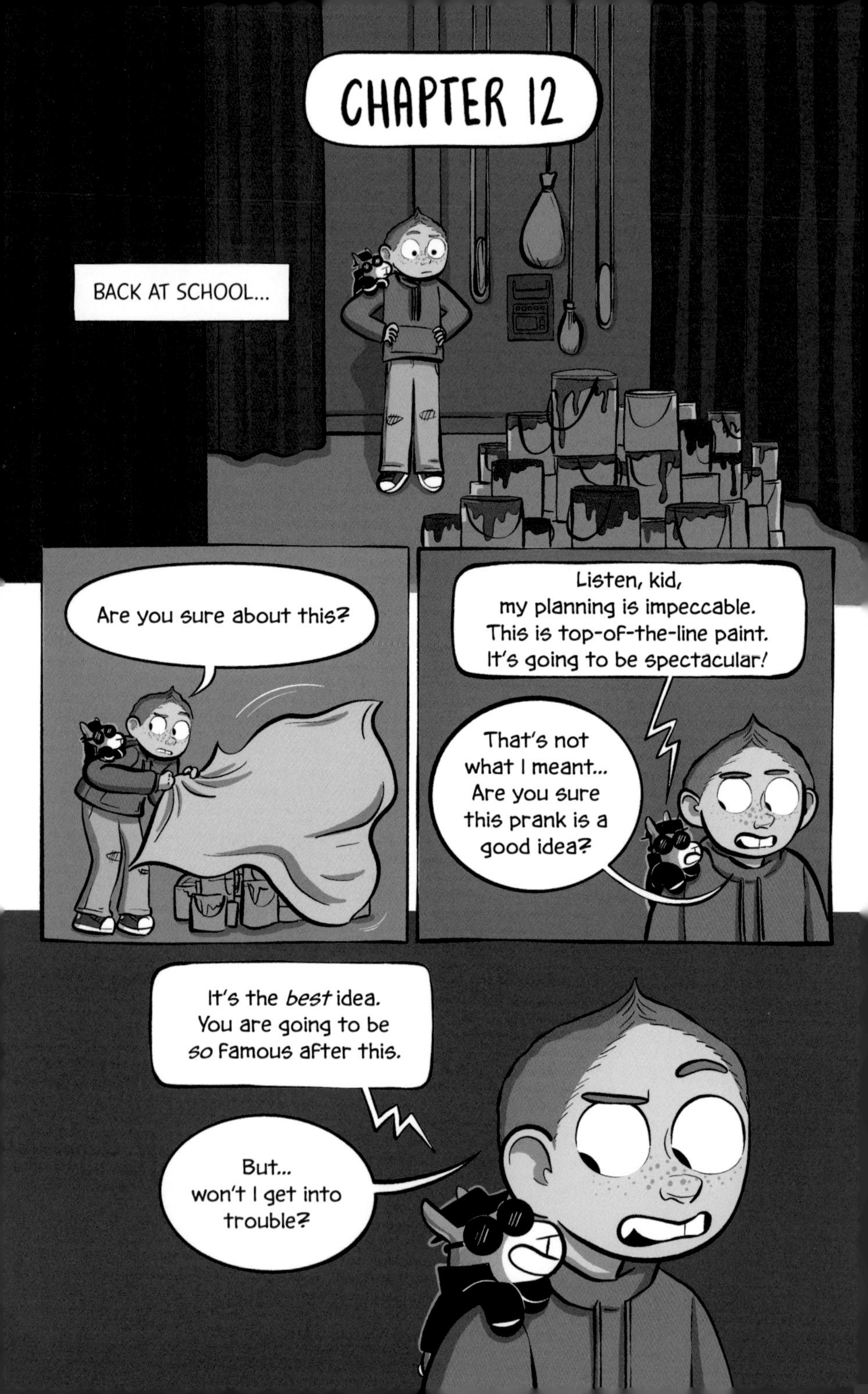
CHAPTER 12
BACK AT SCHOOL...
Are you sure about this?
Listen, kid, my planning is impeccable. This is top-of-the-line paint. It's going to be spectacular!
That's not what I meant... Are you sure this prank is a good idea?
It's the *best* idea. You are going to be *so* famous after this.
But... won't I get into trouble?

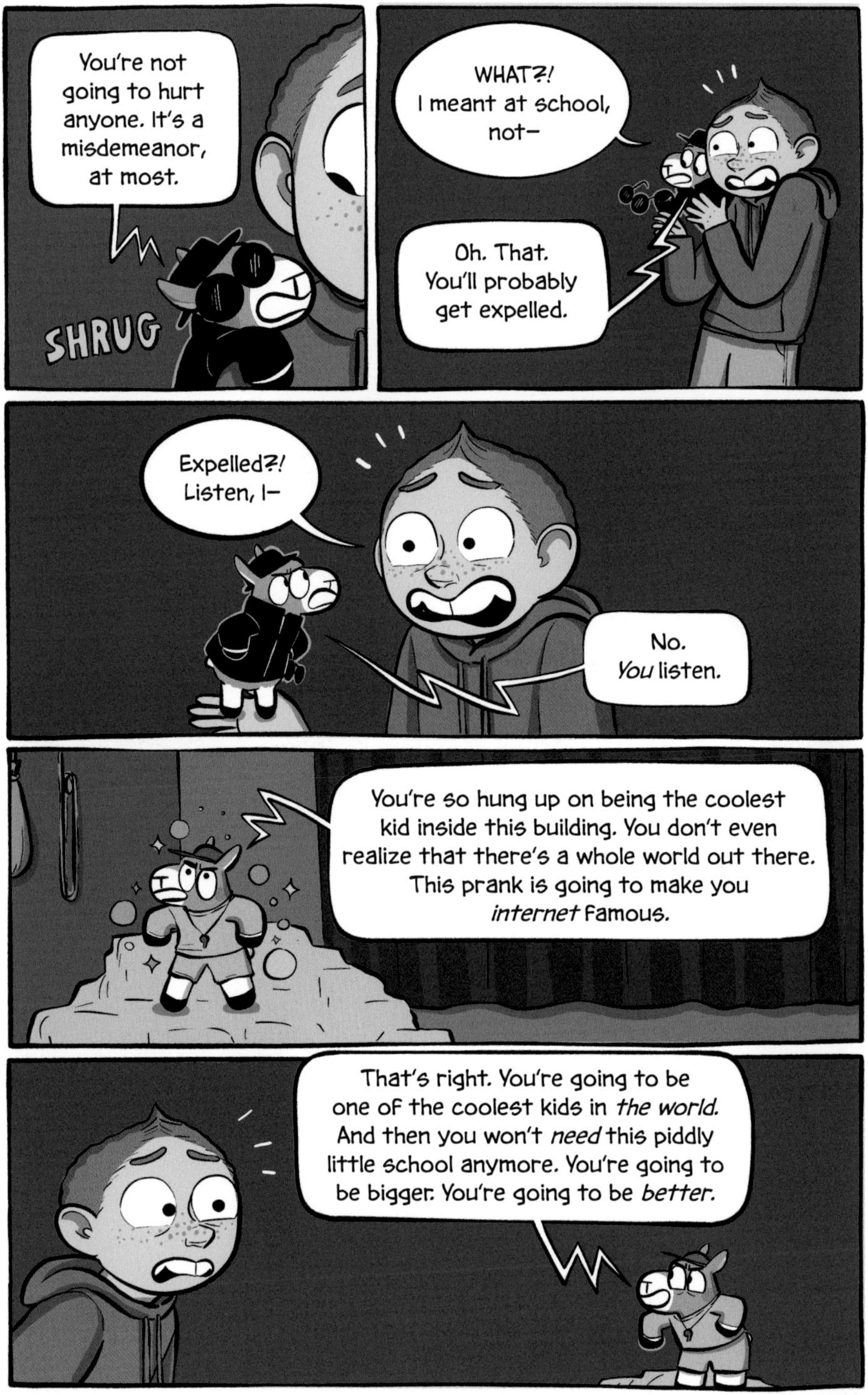
You're not going to hurt anyone. It's a misdemeanor, at most.
SHRUG
WHAT?! I meant at school, not–
Oh. That. You'll probably get expelled.
Expelled?! Listen, I–
No. *You* listen.
You're so hung up on being the coolest kid inside this building. You don't even realize that there's a whole world out there. This prank is going to make you *internet* famous.
That's right. You're going to be one of the coolest kids in *the world.* And then you won't *need* this piddly little school anymore. You're going to be bigger. You're going to be *better.*

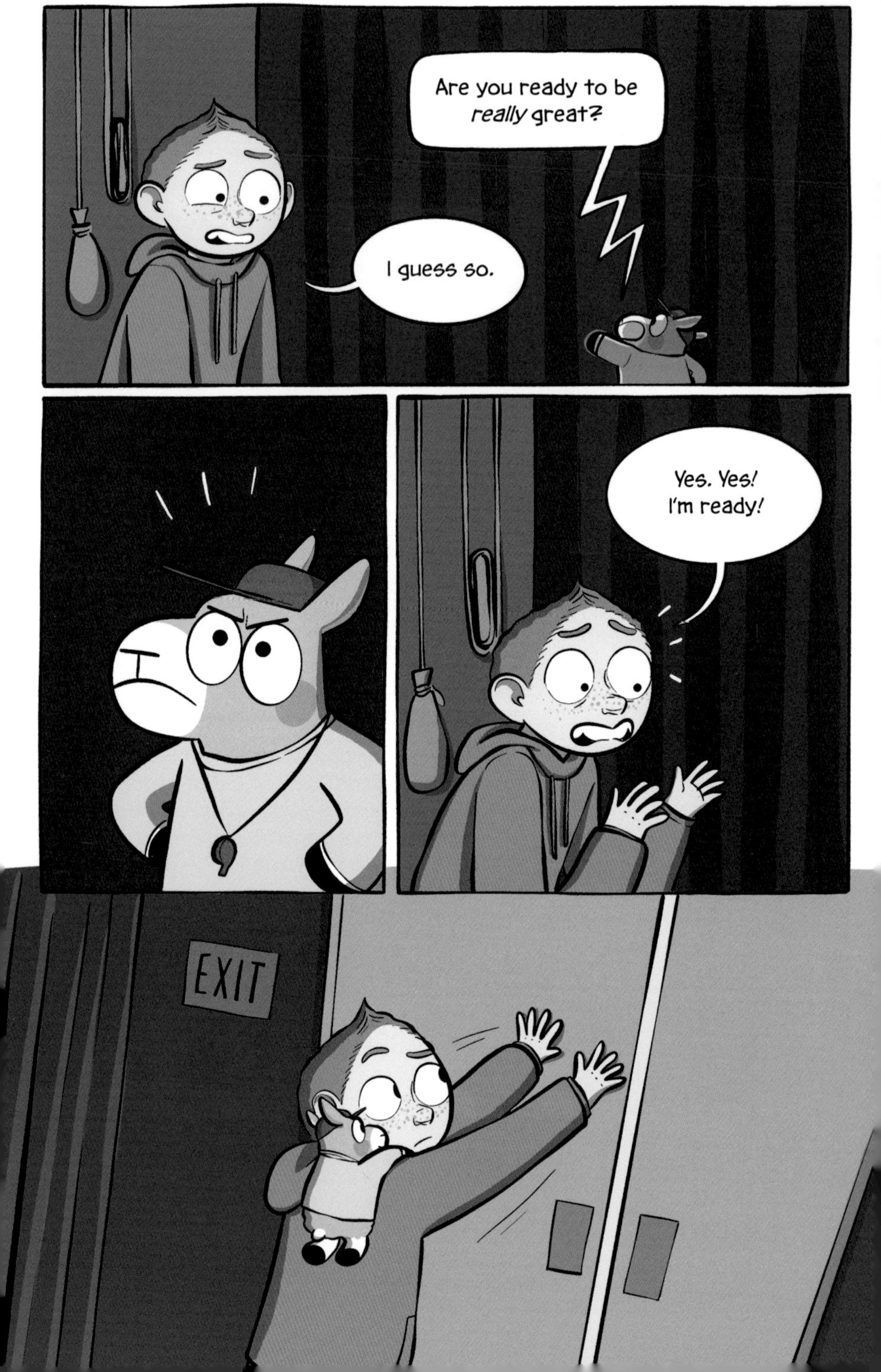
Are you ready to be *really* great?
I guess so.
Yes. Yes! I'm ready!
EXIT

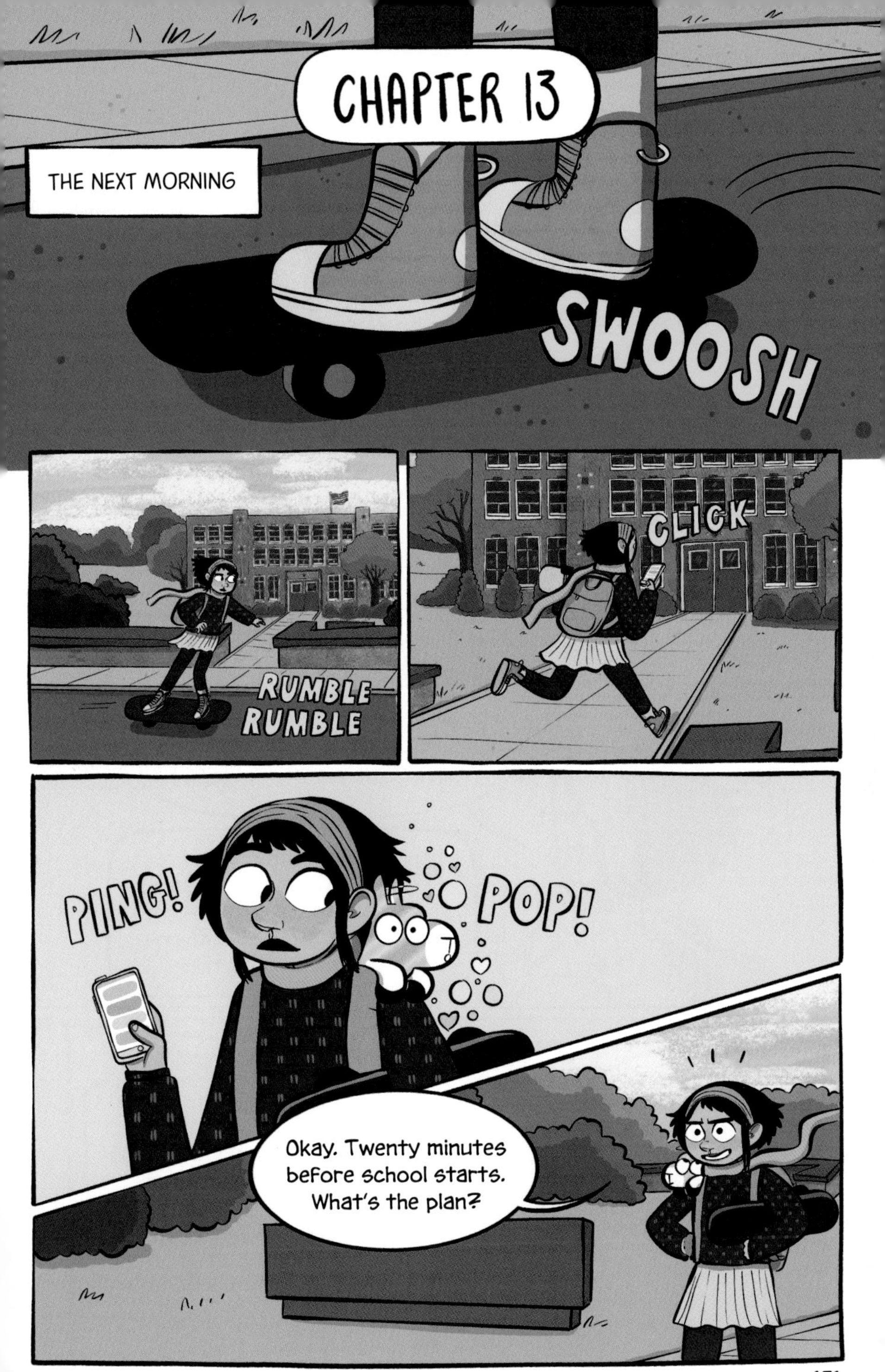
CHAPTER 13
THE NEXT MORNING
SWOOSH
RUMBLE
RUMBLE
CLICK
PING!
POP!
Okay. Twenty minutes before school starts. What's the plan?

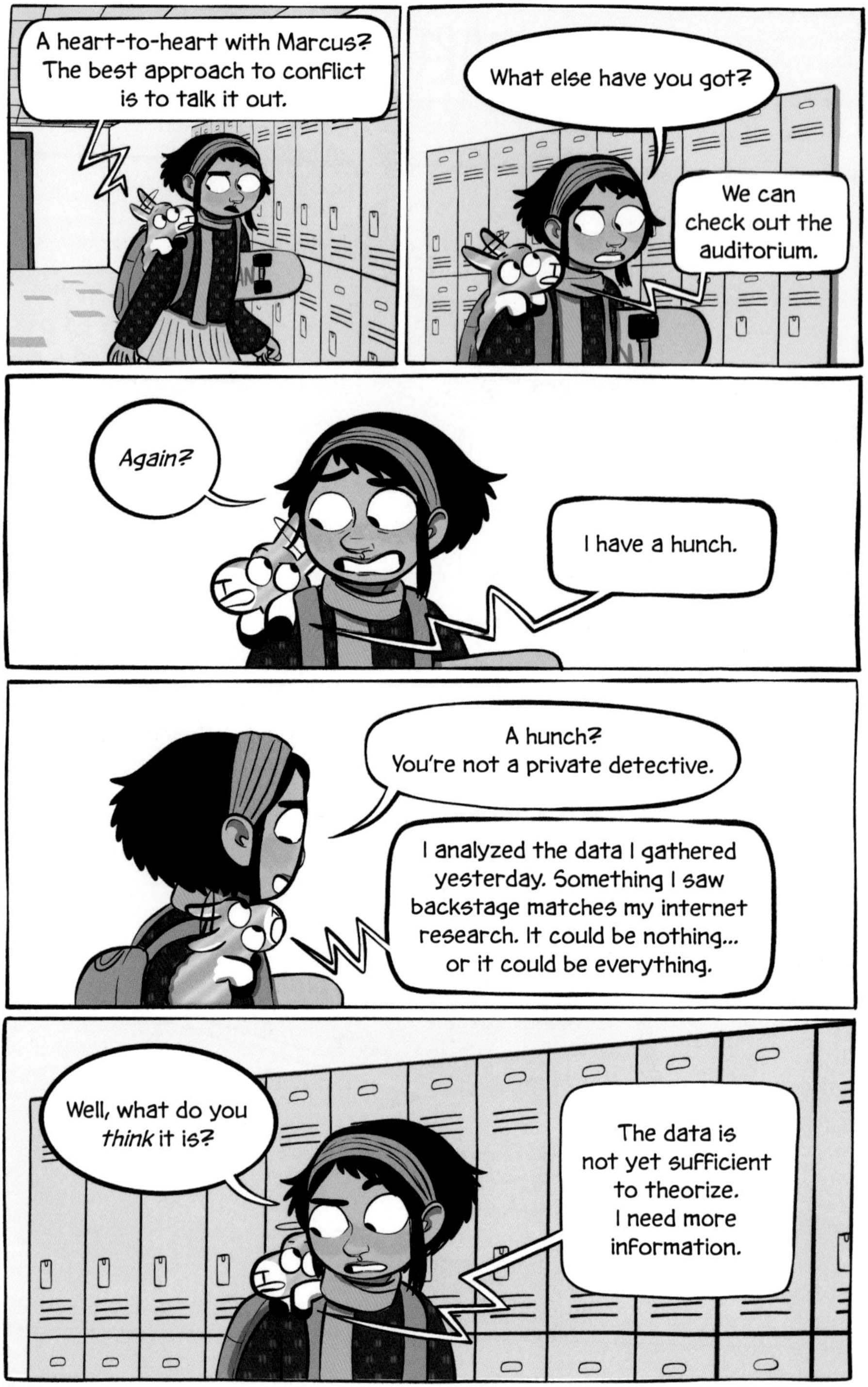
A heart-to-heart with Marcus? The best approach to conflict is to talk it out.
What else have you got?
We can check out the auditorium.
Again?
I have a hunch.
A hunch? You're not a private detective.
I analyzed the data I gathered yesterday. Something I saw backstage matches my internet research. It could be nothing... or it could be everything.
Well, what do you *think* it is?
The data is not yet sufficient to theorize. I need more information.

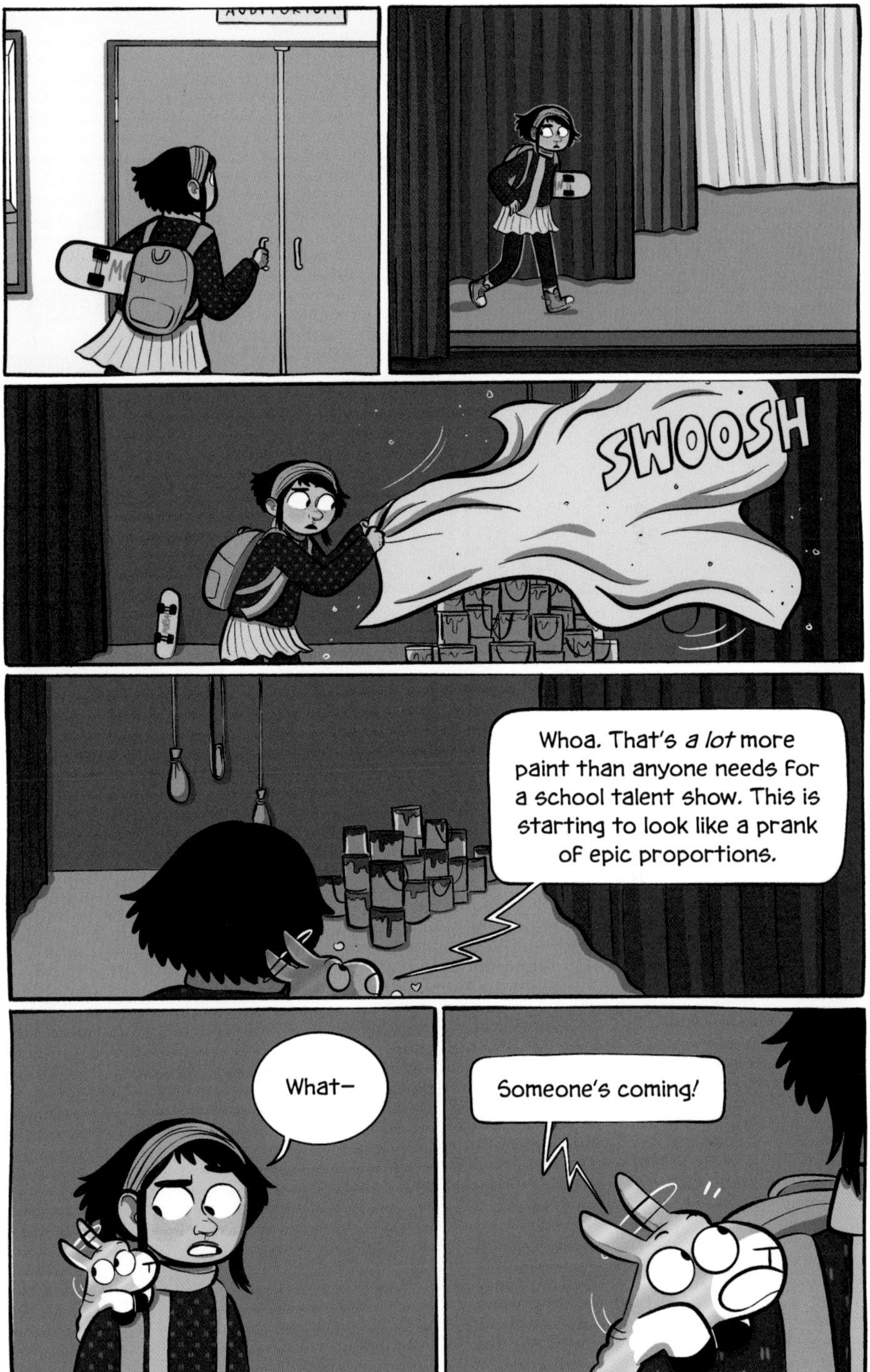
SWOOSH
Whoa. That's *a lot* more paint than anyone needs for a school talent show. This is starting to look like a prank of epic proportions.
What—
Someone's coming!

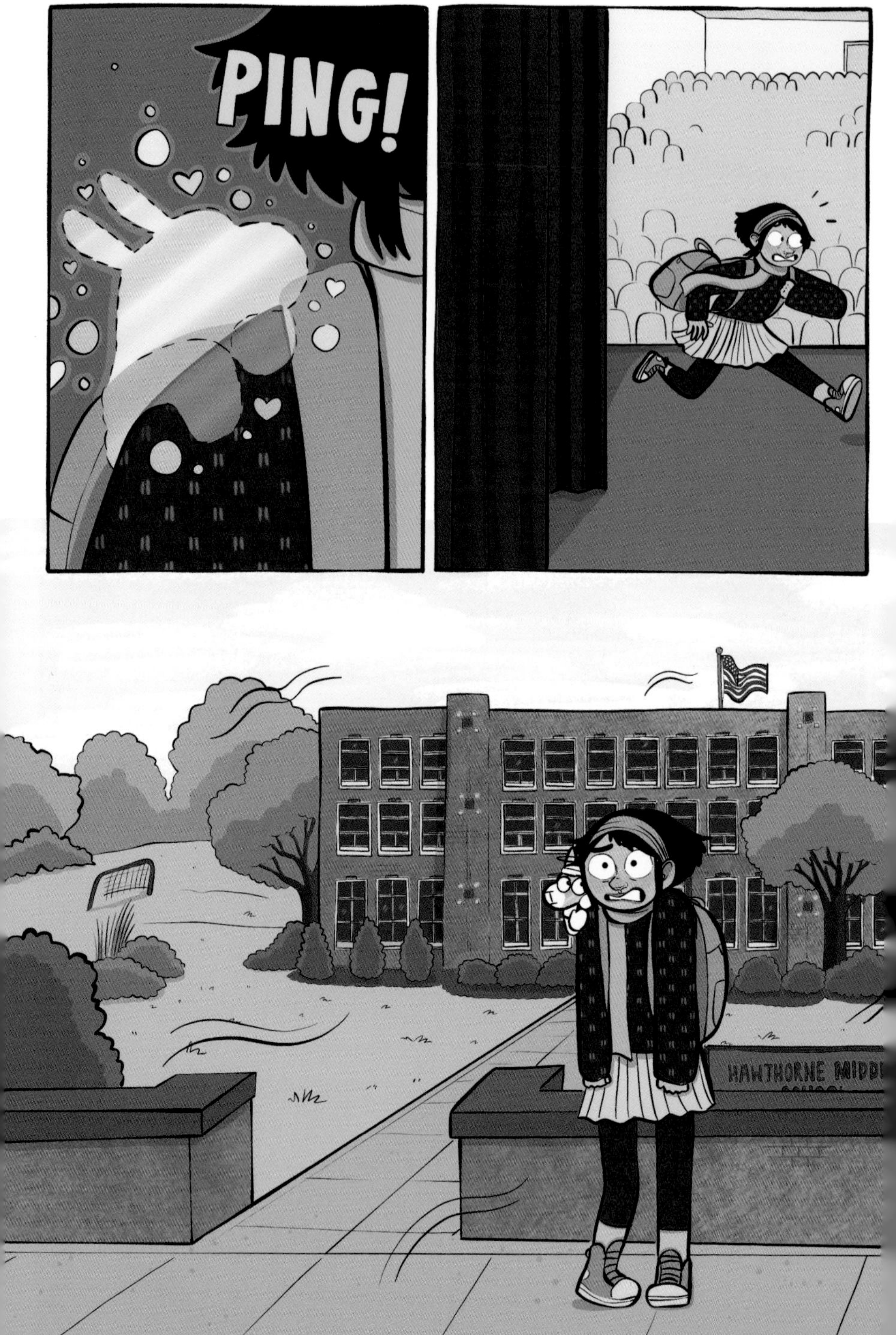
PING!
HAWTHORNE MIDD

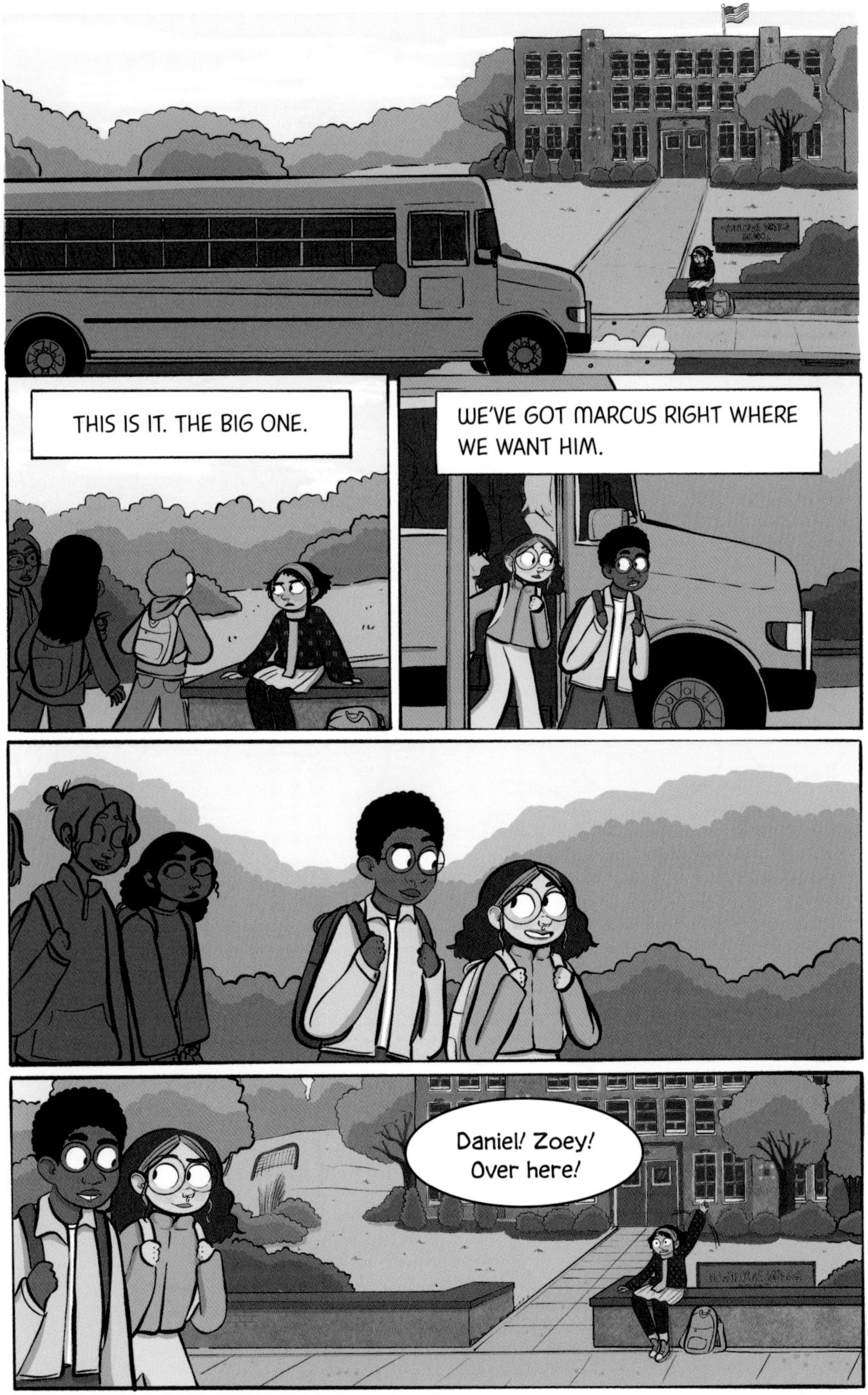
THIS IS IT. THE BIG ONE.
WE'VE GOT MARCUS RIGHT WHERE WE WANT HIM.
Daniel! Zoey! Over here!

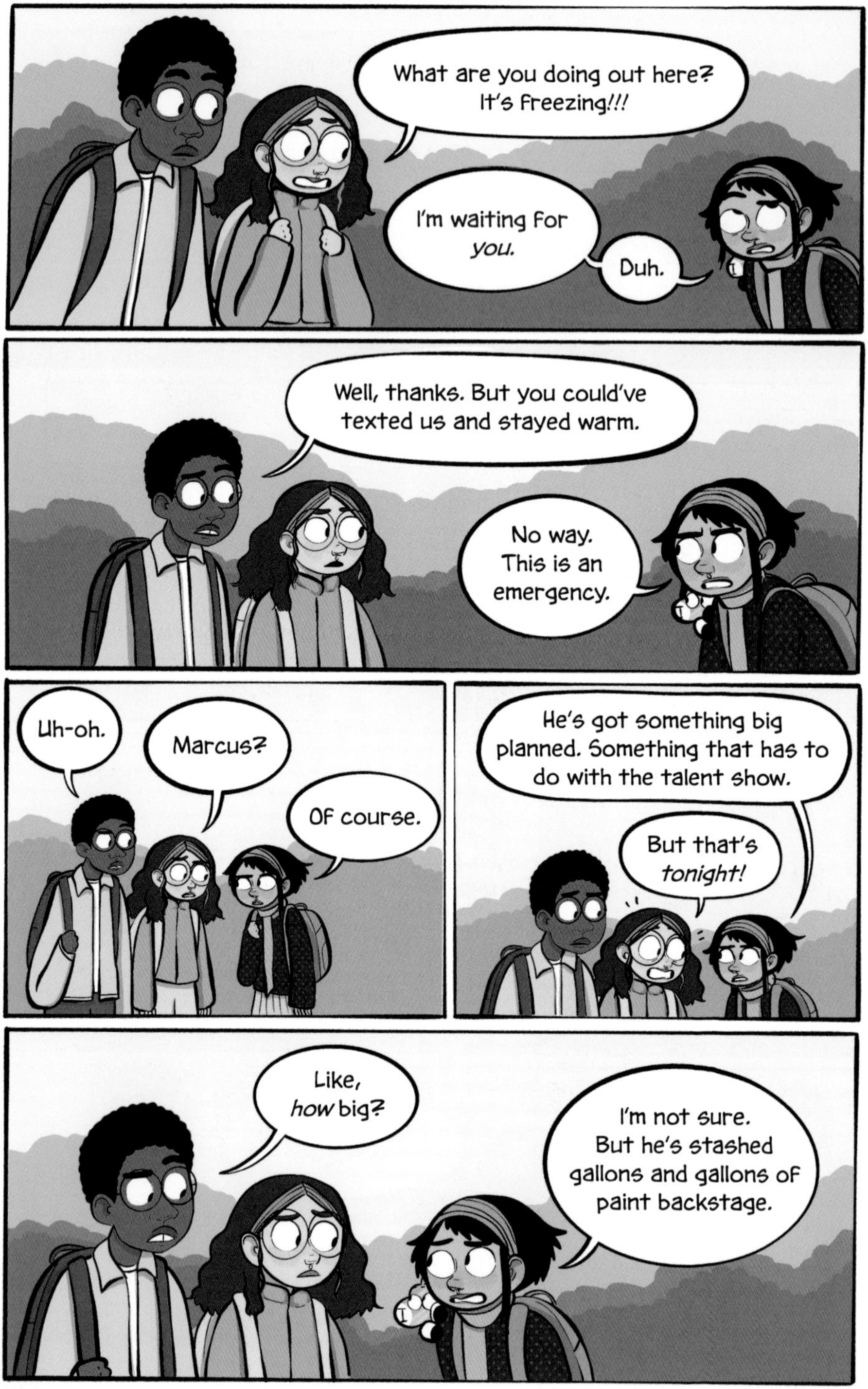
What are you doing out here? It's freezing!!!
I'm waiting for *you.*
Duh.
Well, thanks. But you could've texted us and stayed warm.
No way. This is an emergency.
Uh-oh.
Marcus?
Of course.
He's got something big planned. Something that has to do with the talent show.
But that's *tonight!*
Like, *how* big?
I'm not sure. But he's stashed gallons and gallons of paint backstage.

I say we turn him in.

What?

We have the evidence. Let's just go to Ms. Hamm and tell her that he's up to something.

That could be a smart move. Marcus would still get some of the "cool credit" for his prank without actually having to perform it, and you would gain notoriety too.

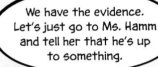

See? It's a win-win.

Not exactly. My updated programming shows that Marcus would almost certainly get in serious trouble. Since this is his second infraction, I calculate a 75% probability that he would be suspended.

That doesn't sound good...

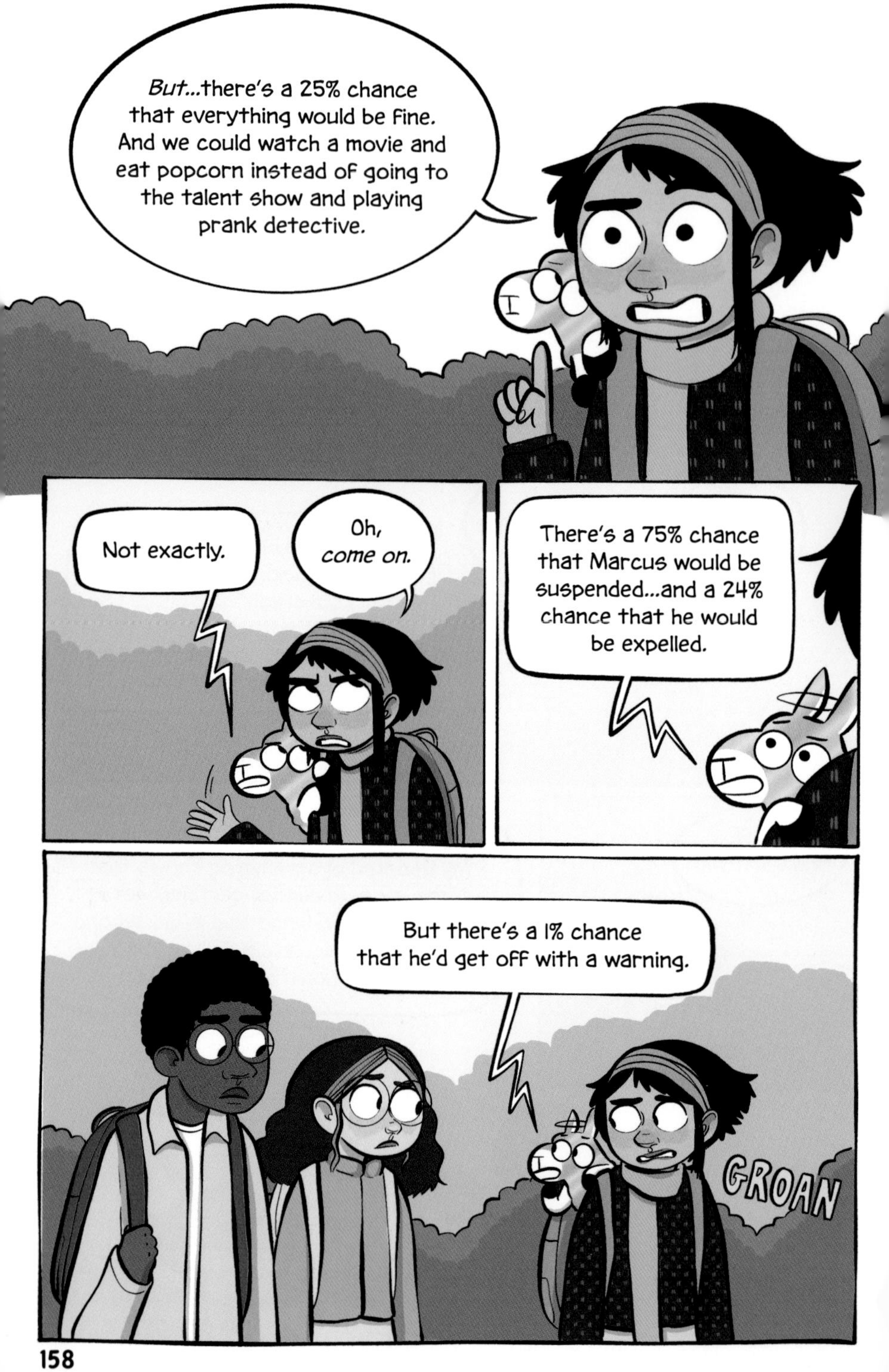
But...there's a 25% chance that everything would be fine. And we could watch a movie and eat popcorn instead of going to the talent show and playing prank detective.
Not exactly.
Oh, *come on.*
There's a 75% chance that Marcus would be suspended...and a 24% chance that he would be expelled.
But there's a 1% chance that he'd get off with a warning.
GROAN

So we're back to square one.

We'll just have to stop him from doing anything crazy.

And then what? This is just one prank. Are we supposed to babysit him every day?

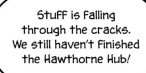

Stuff is falling through the cracks. We still haven't finished the Hawthorne Hub!

Ms. Hamm is all over me. I think she thinks I'm the one doing the pranks.

Don't you care about *me* getting into trouble?

Of course! But I'm responsible for what Marcus does.

You keep saying that. But he's perfectly capable of making his own decisions. He's *choosing* to do this.

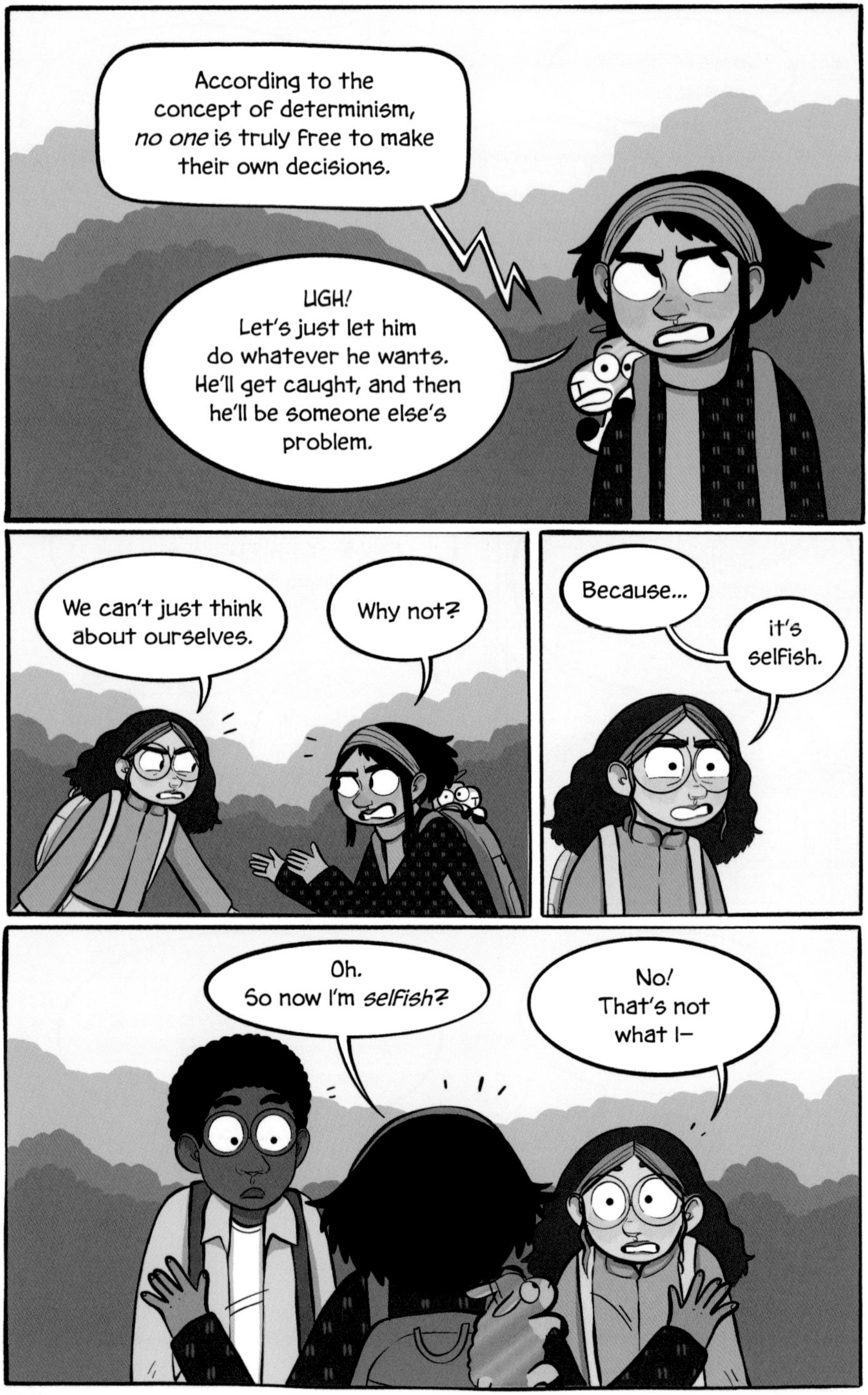

According to the concept of determinism, *no one* is truly free to make their own decisions.
UGH! Let's just let him do whatever he wants. He'll get caught, and then he'll be someone else's problem.
We can't just think about ourselves.
Why not?
Because...
it's selfish.
Oh. So now I'm *selfish*?
No! That's not what I–

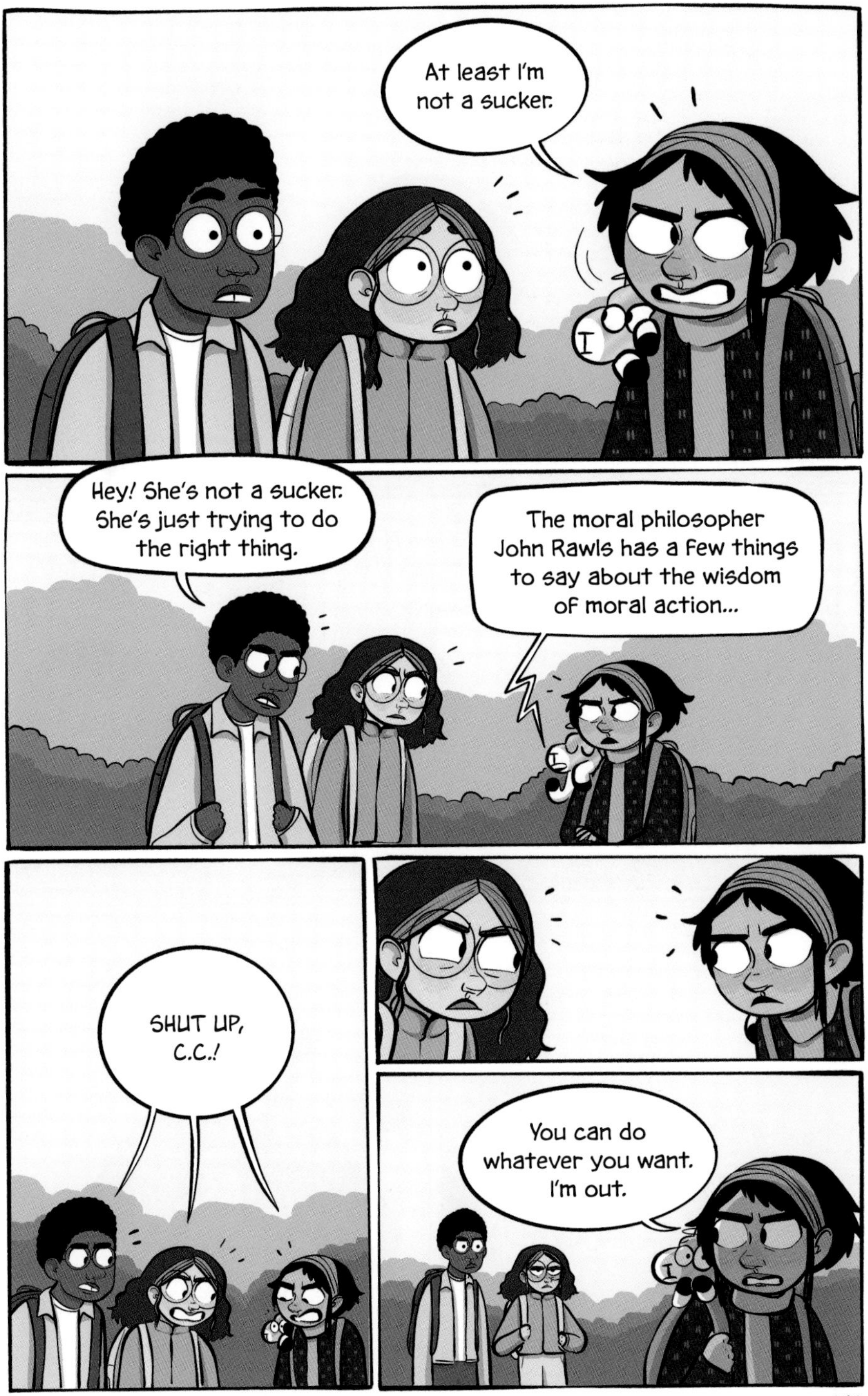
At least I'm not a sucker.
I
Hey! She's not a sucker. She's just trying to do the right thing.
The moral philosopher John Rawls has a few things to say about the wisdom of moral action...
I
SHUT UP, C.C.!
You can do whatever you want. I'm out.
I

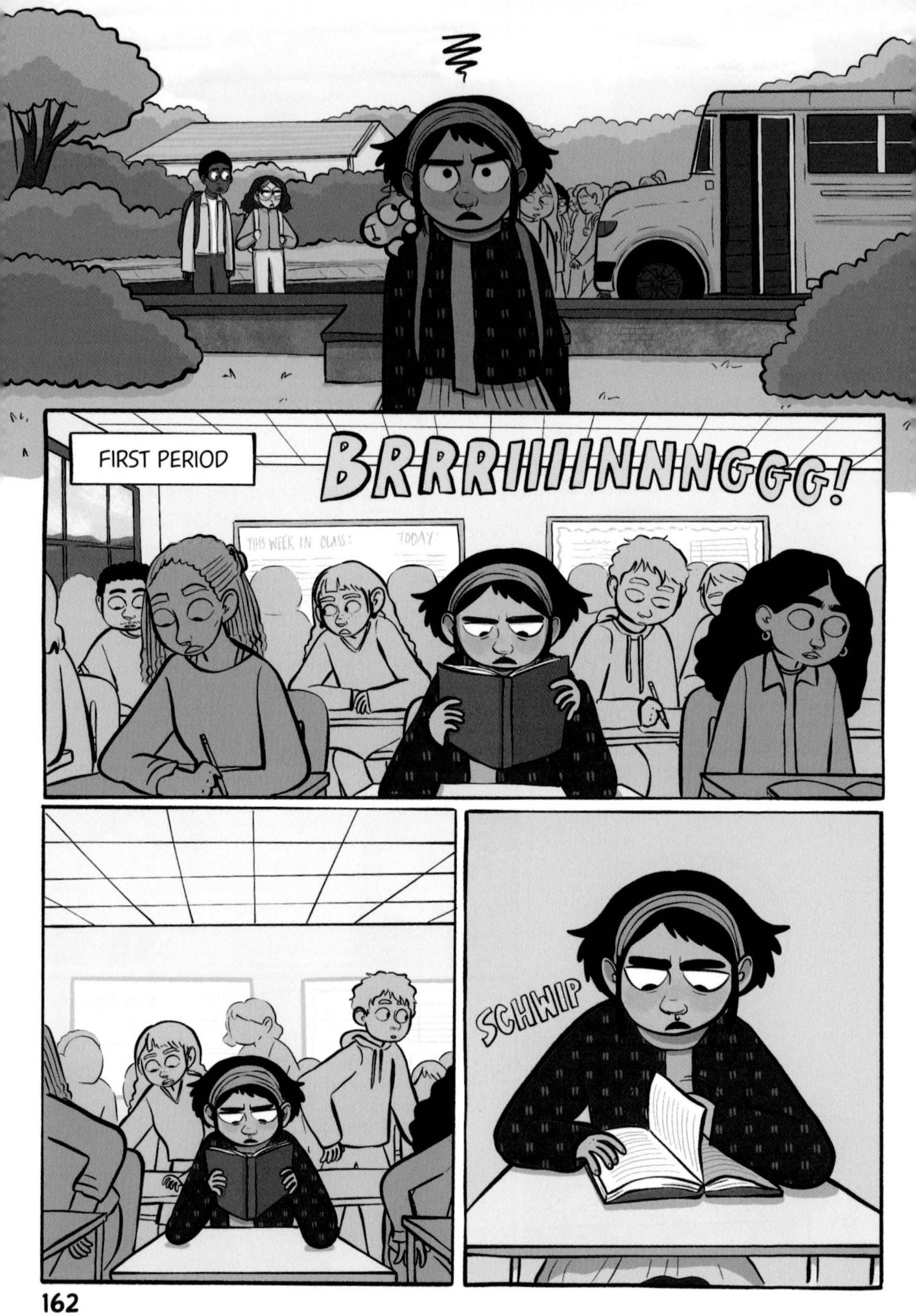

FIRST PERIOD
BRRRIIIINNNGGG!
THIS WEEK IN CLASS:
TODAY:
SCHWIP

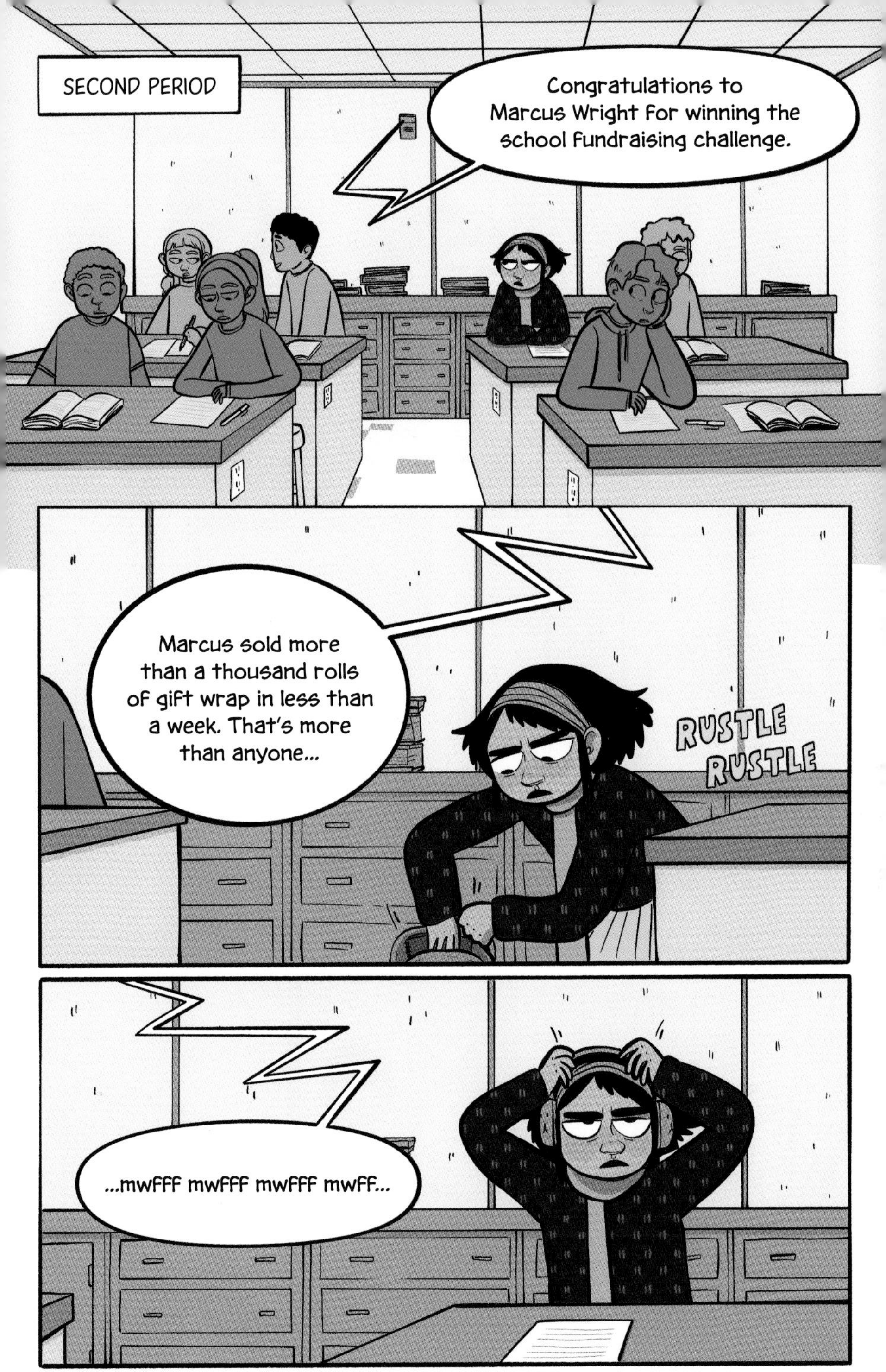
SECOND PERIOD
Congratulations to Marcus Wright for winning the school fundraising challenge.
Marcus sold more than a thousand rolls of gift wrap in less than a week. That's more than anyone...
RUSTLE RUSTLE
...mwfff mwfff mwfff mwff...

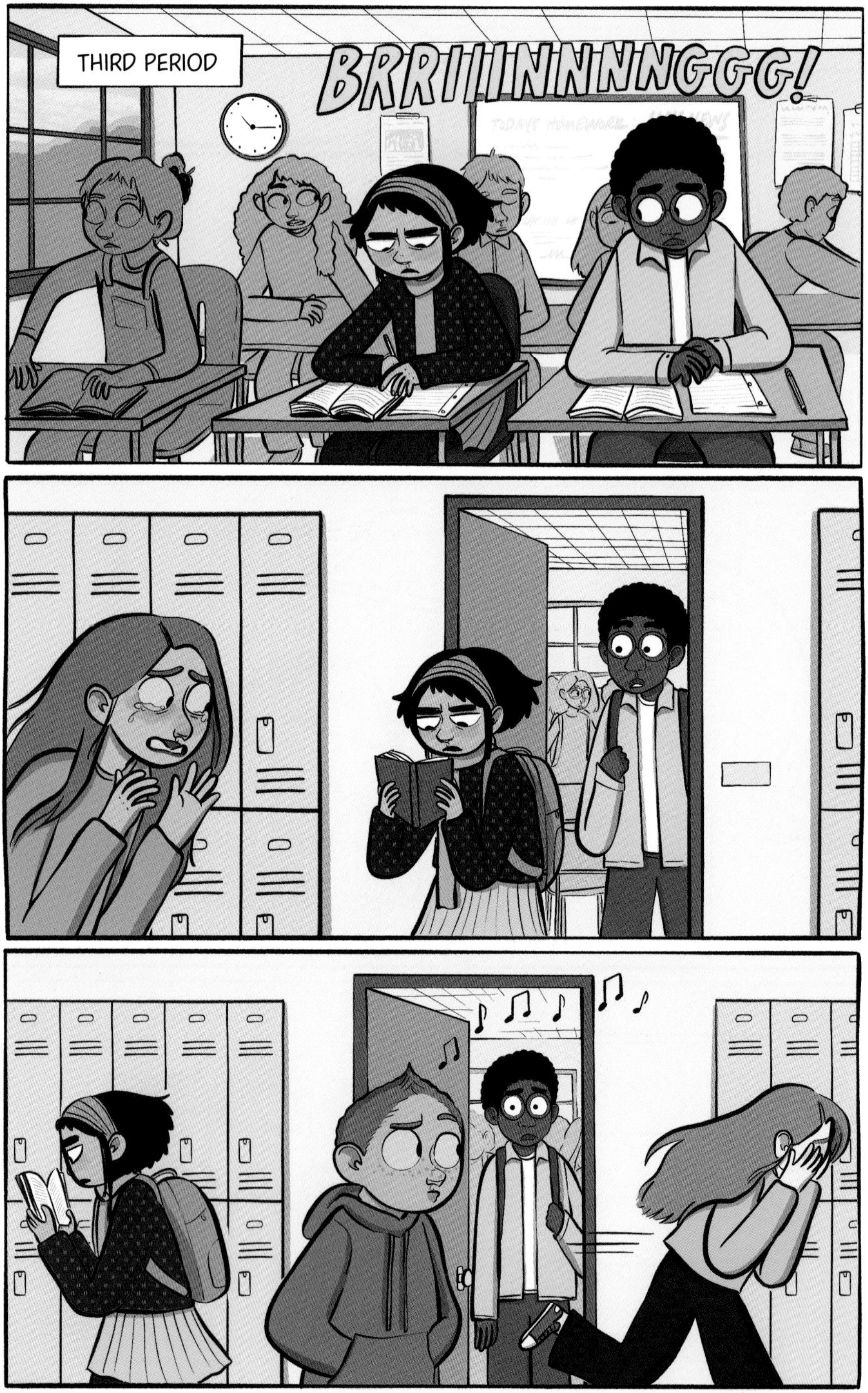
THIRD PERIOD
BRRIIINNNNGGG!

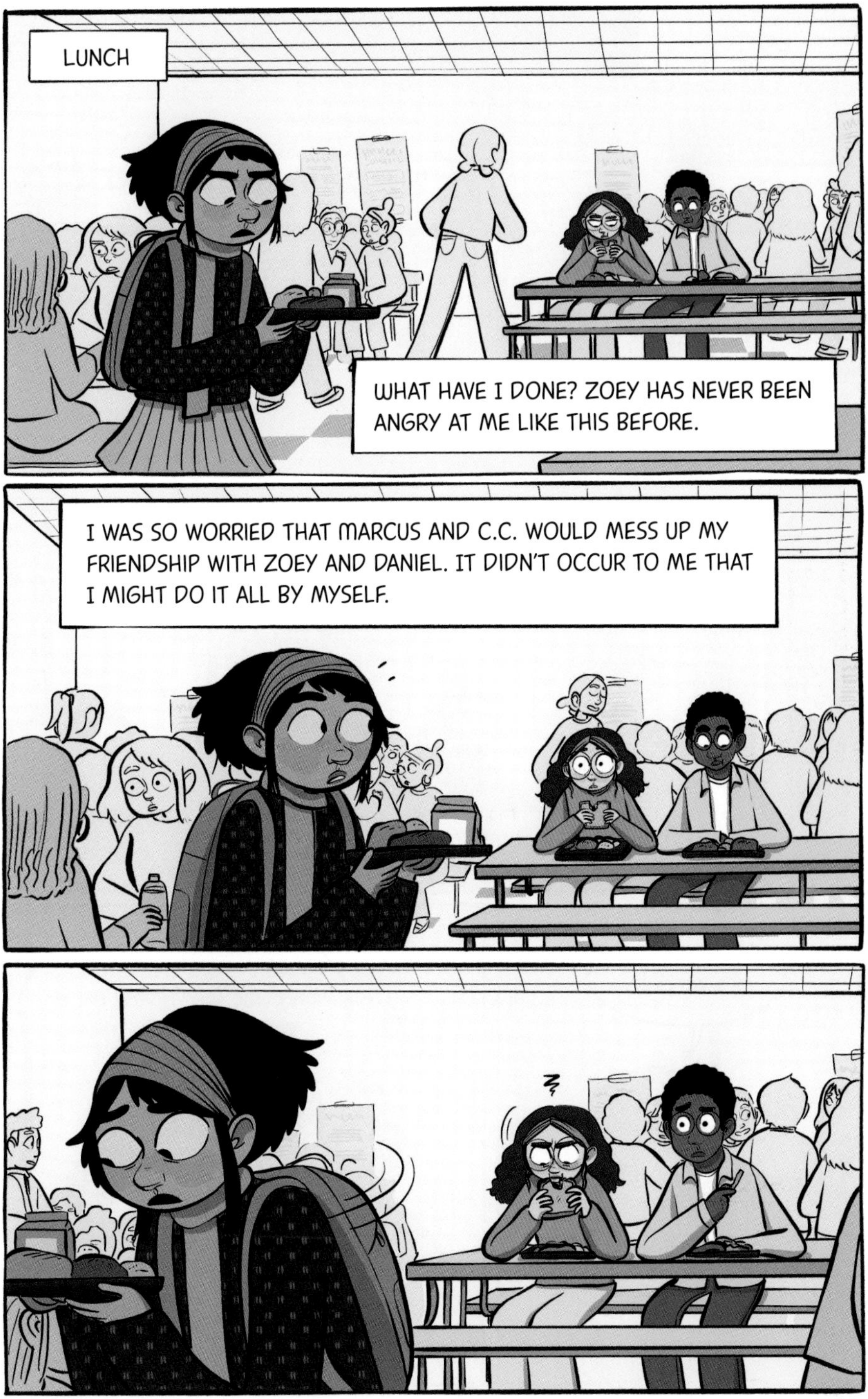
LUNCH
WHAT HAVE I DONE? ZOEY HAS NEVER BEEN ANGRY AT ME LIKE THIS BEFORE.
I WAS SO WORRIED THAT MARCUS AND C.C. WOULD MESS UP MY FRIENDSHIP WITH ZOEY AND DANIEL. IT DIDN'T OCCUR TO ME THAT I MIGHT DO IT ALL BY MYSELF.

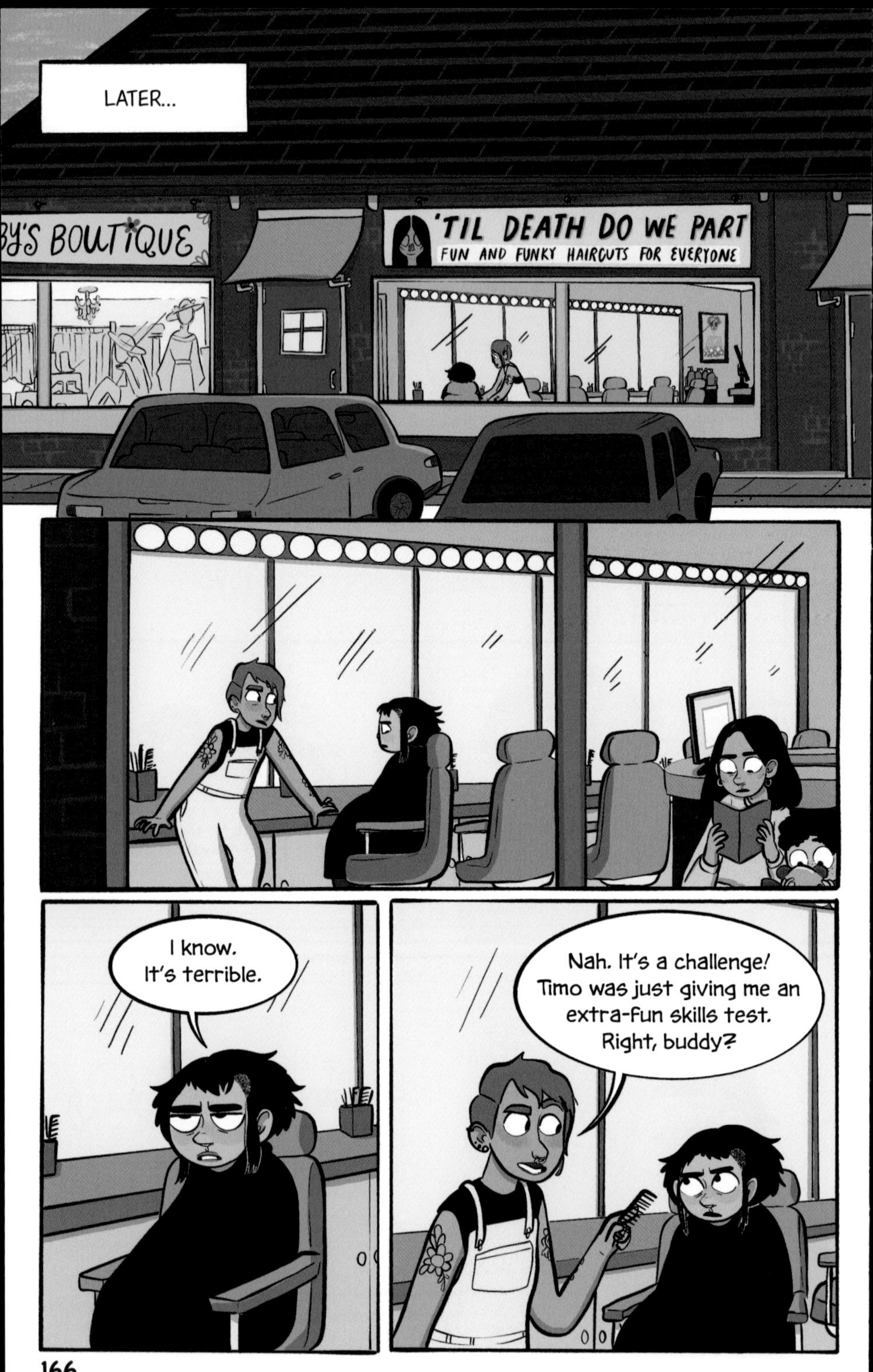
LATER...
...Y'S BOUTIQUE
'TIL DEATH DO WE PART
FUN AND FUNKY HAIRCUTS FOR EVERYONE
I know.
It's terrible.
Nah. It's a challenge! Timo was just giving me an extra-fun skills test. Right, buddy?

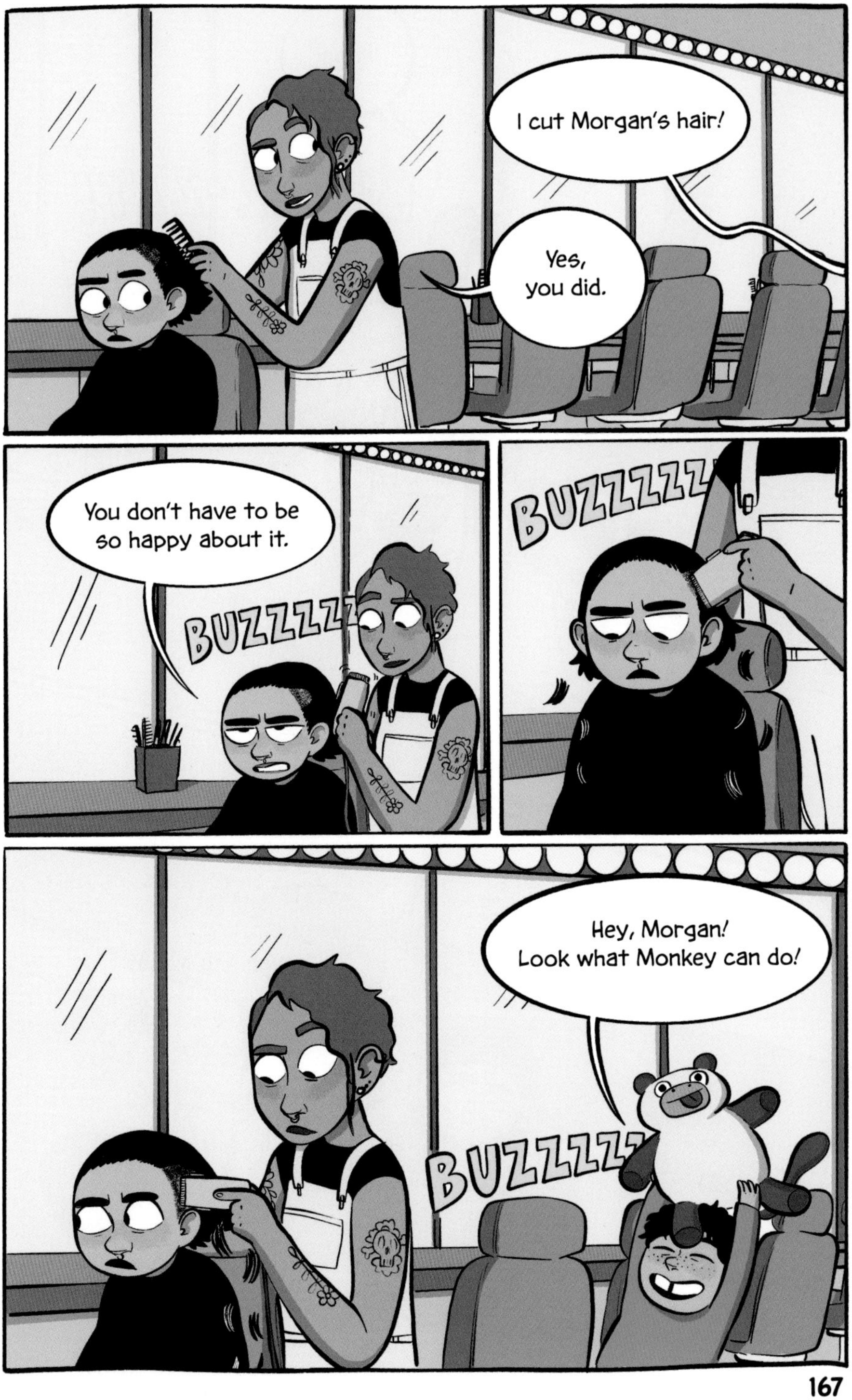
I cut Morgan's hair!
Yes, you did.
You don't have to be so happy about it.
BUZZZZZ
BUZZZZZ
Hey, Morgan! Look what Monkey can do!
BUZZZZZ

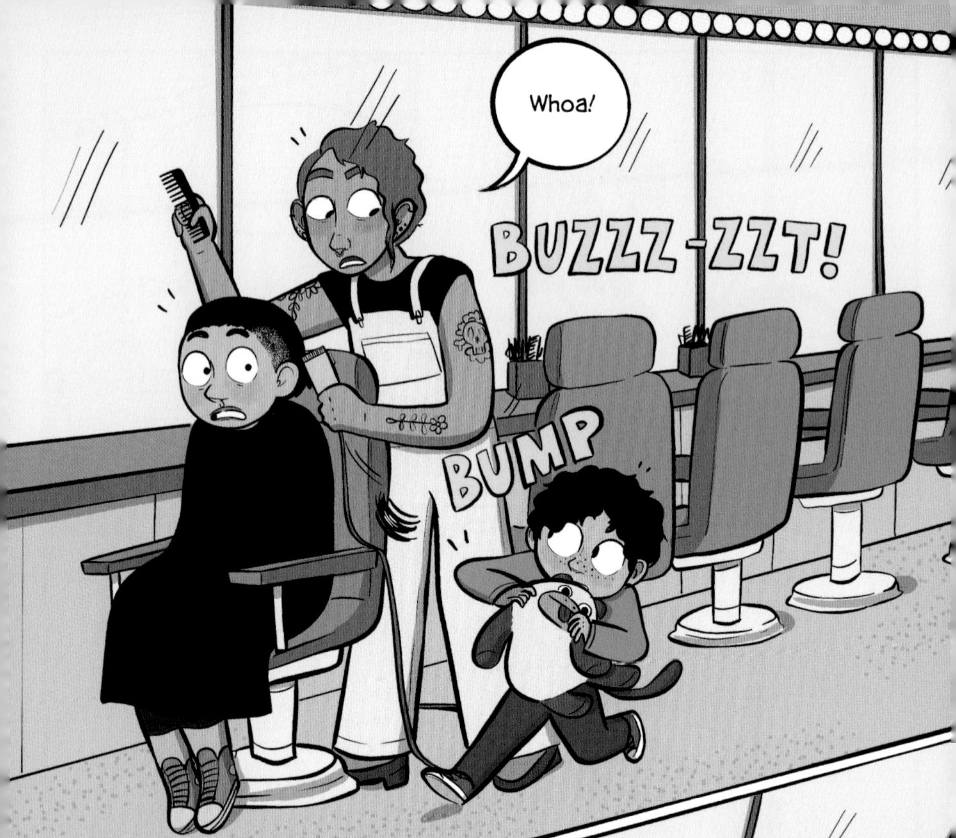
Whoa!
BUZZZ-ZZT!
BUMP
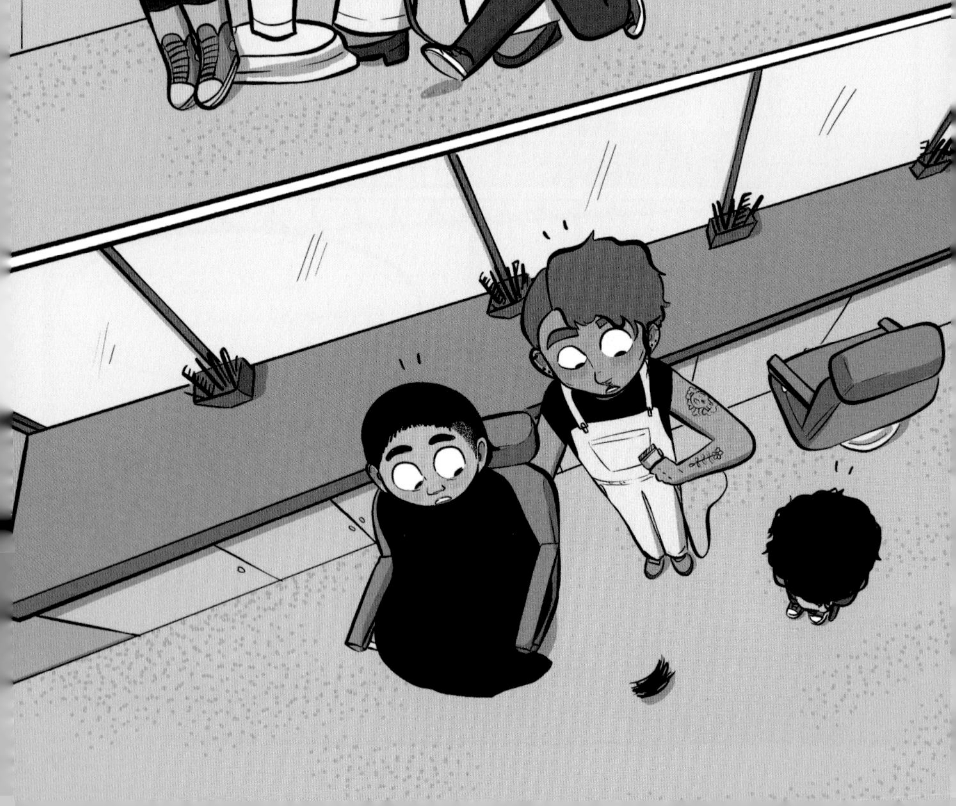

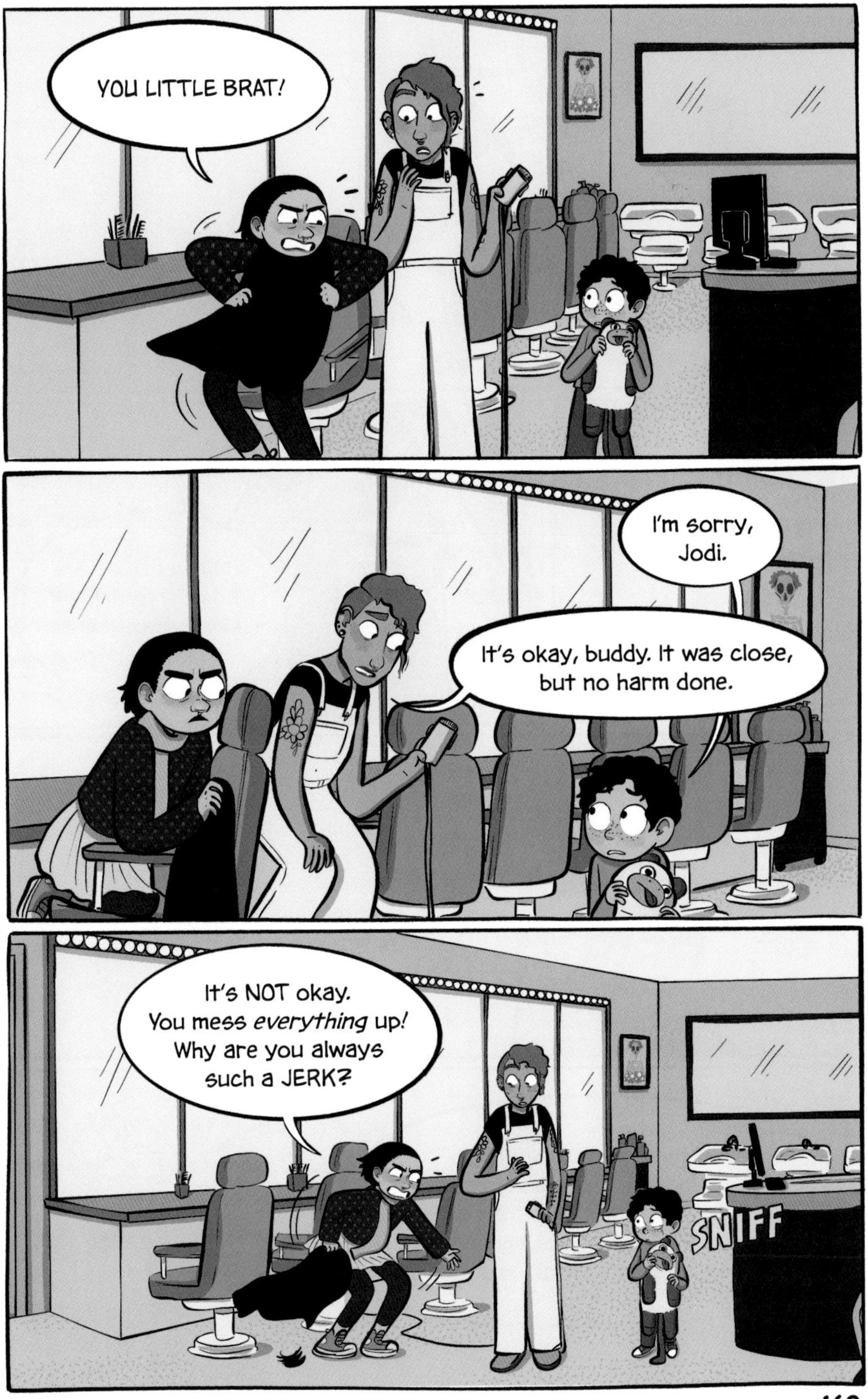
YOU LITTLE BRAT!
I'm sorry, Jodi.
It's okay, buddy. It was close, but no harm done.
It's NOT okay. You mess *everything* up! Why are you always such a JERK?
SNIFF

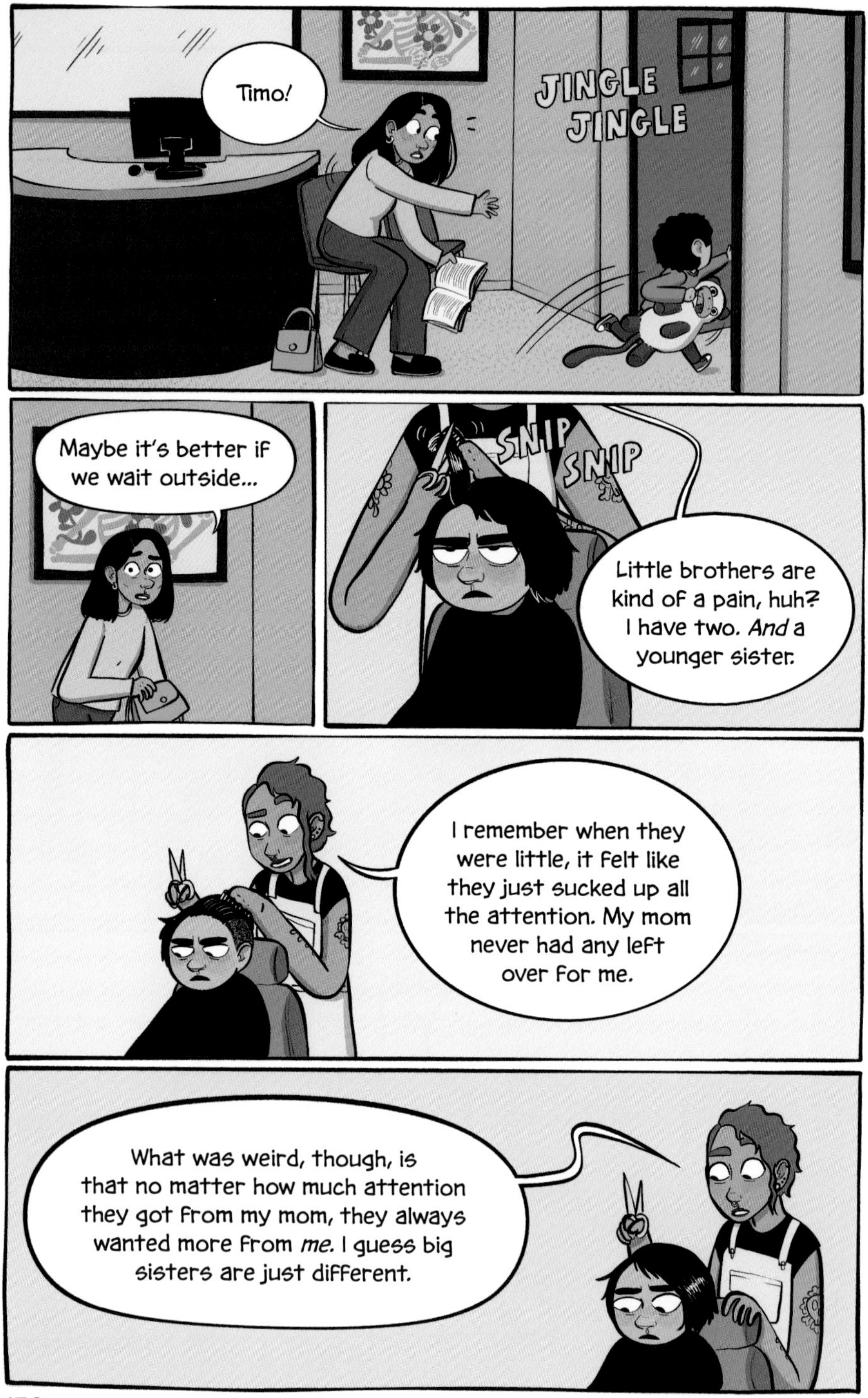
Timo!
JINGLE JINGLE
Maybe it's better if we wait outside...
SNIP SNIP
Little brothers are kind of a pain, huh? I have two. *And* a younger sister.
I remember when they were little, it felt like they just sucked up all the attention. My mom never had any left over for me.
What was weird, though, is that no matter how much attention they got from my mom, they always wanted more from *me*. I guess big sisters are just different.

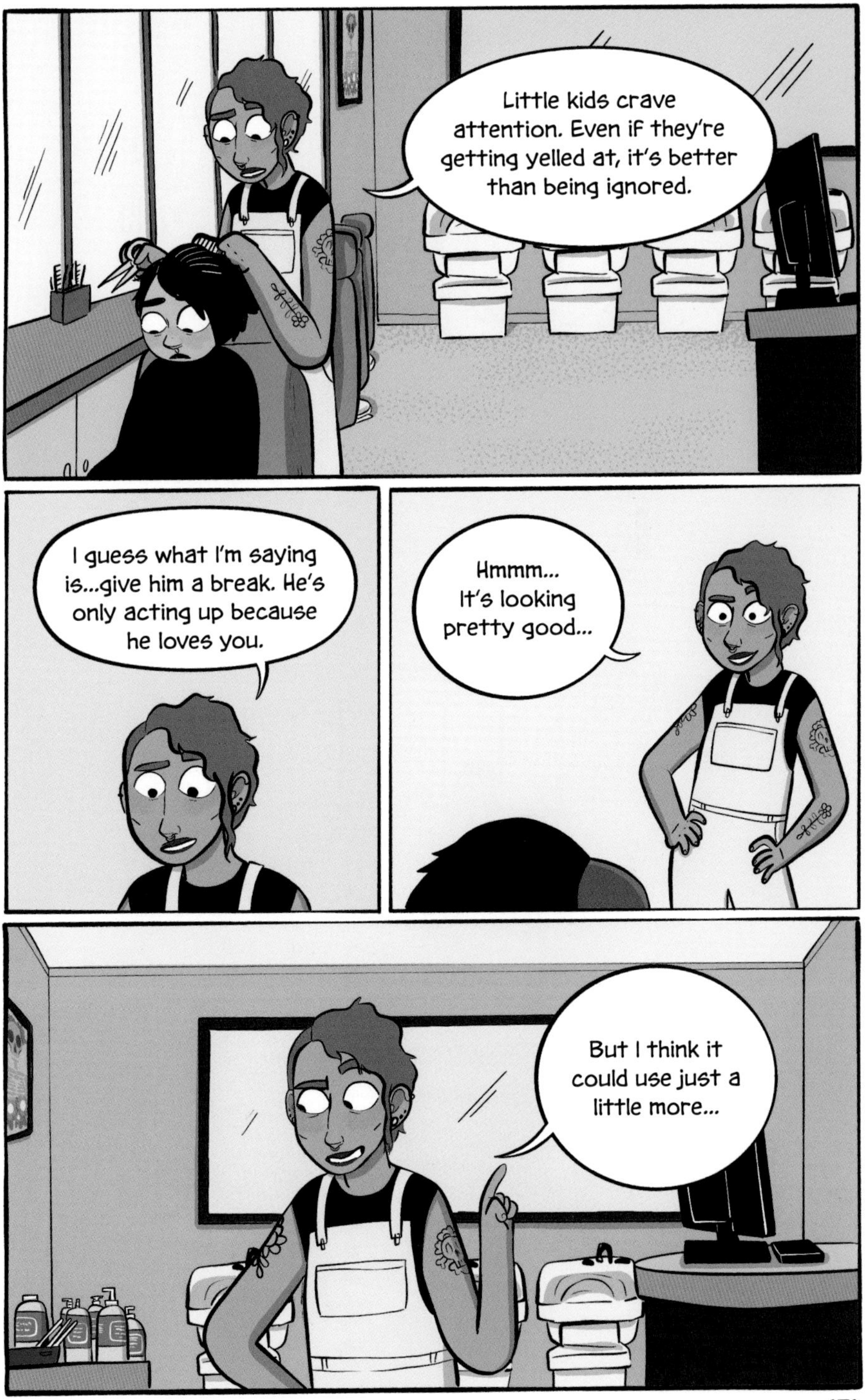
Little kids crave attention. Even if they're getting yelled at, it's better than being ignored.
I guess what I'm saying is...give him a break. He's only acting up because he loves you.
Hmmm... It's looking pretty good...
But I think it could use just a little more...

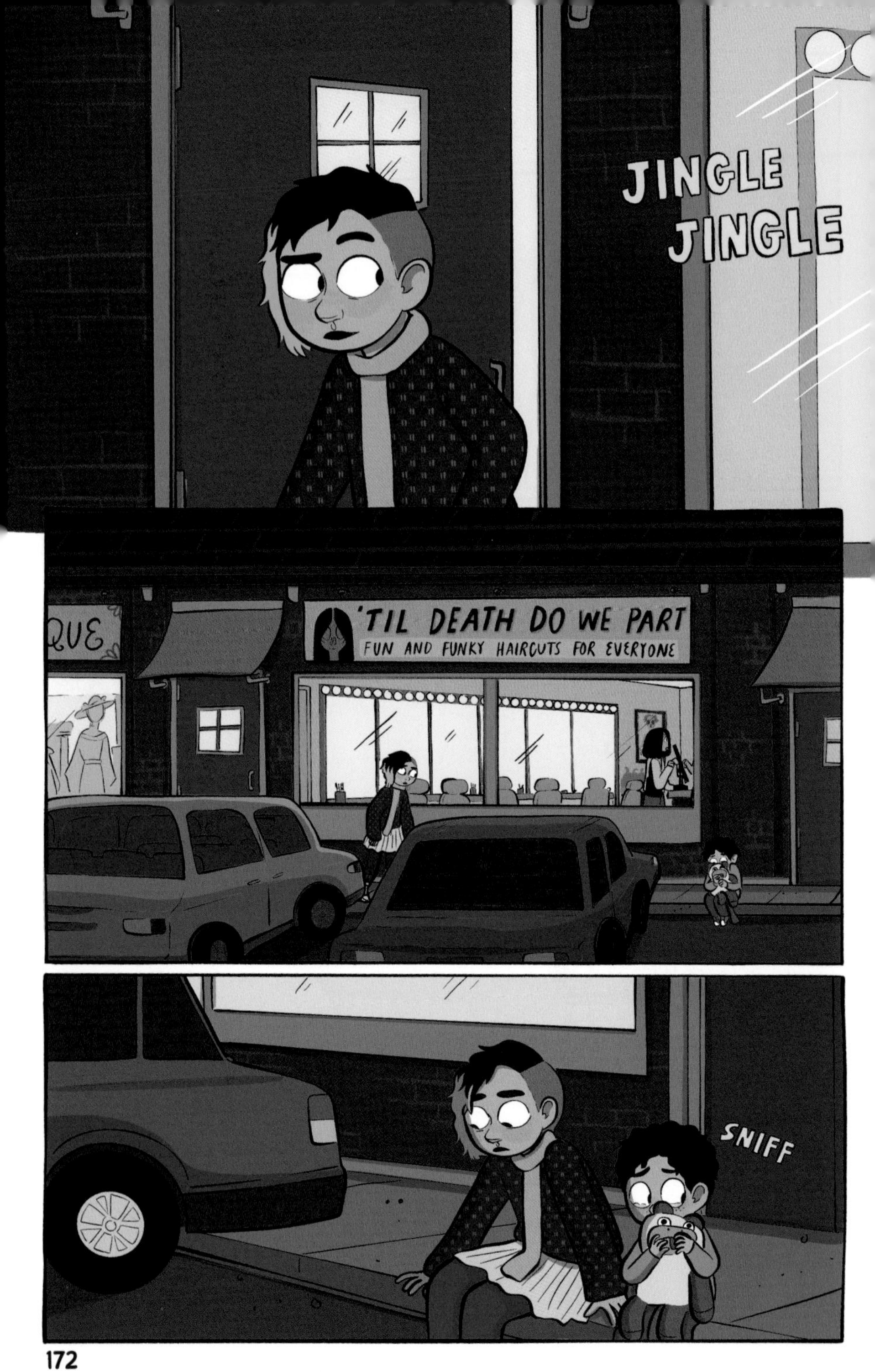
JINGLE
JINGLE
QUE
'TIL DEATH DO WE PART
FUN AND FUNKY HAIRCUTS FOR EVERYONE
SNIFF

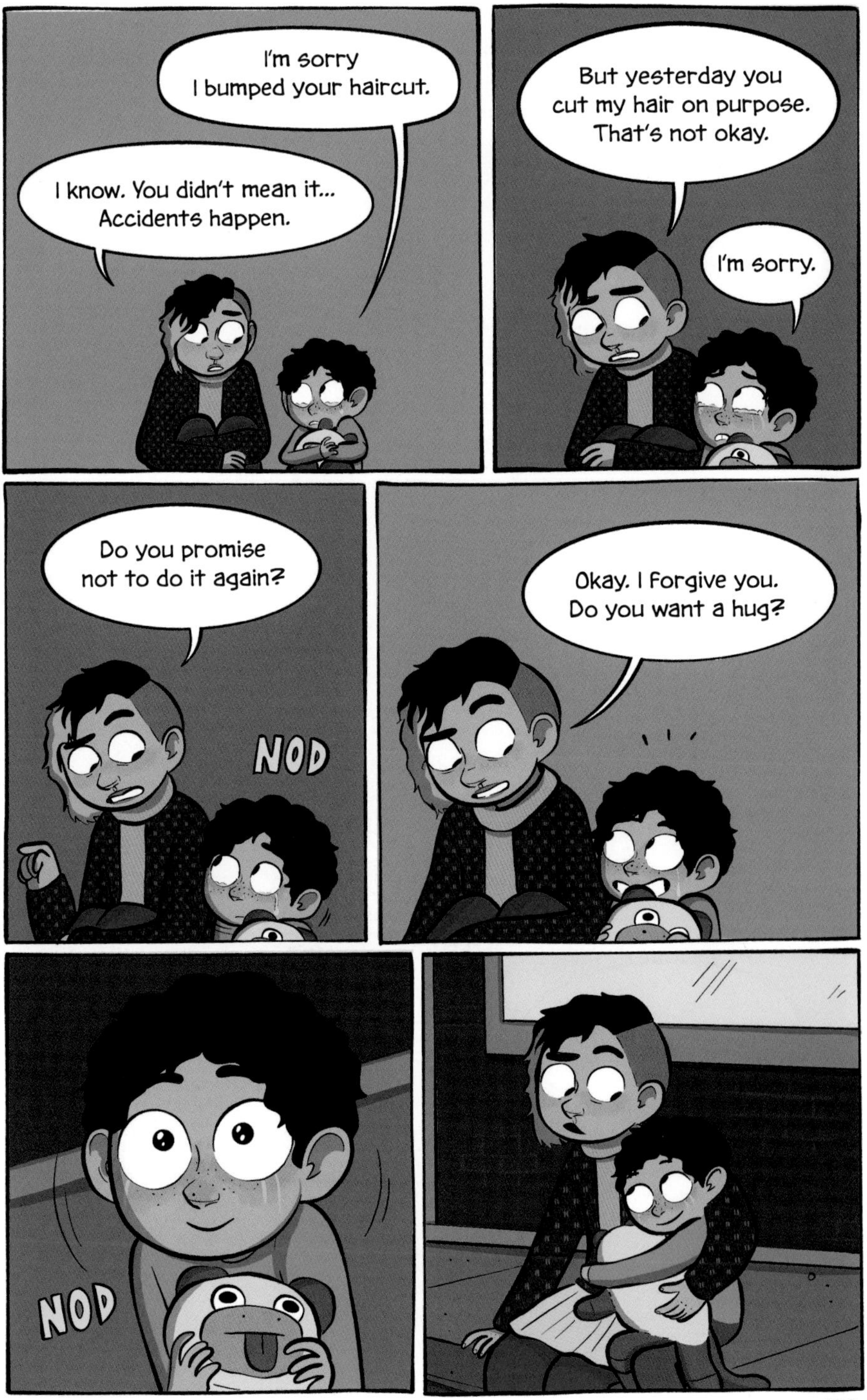
I'm sorry
I bumped your haircut.
I know. You didn't mean it...
Accidents happen.
But yesterday you
cut my hair on purpose.
That's not okay.
I'm sorry.
Do you promise
not to do it again?
NOD
Okay. I forgive you.
Do you want a hug?
NOD

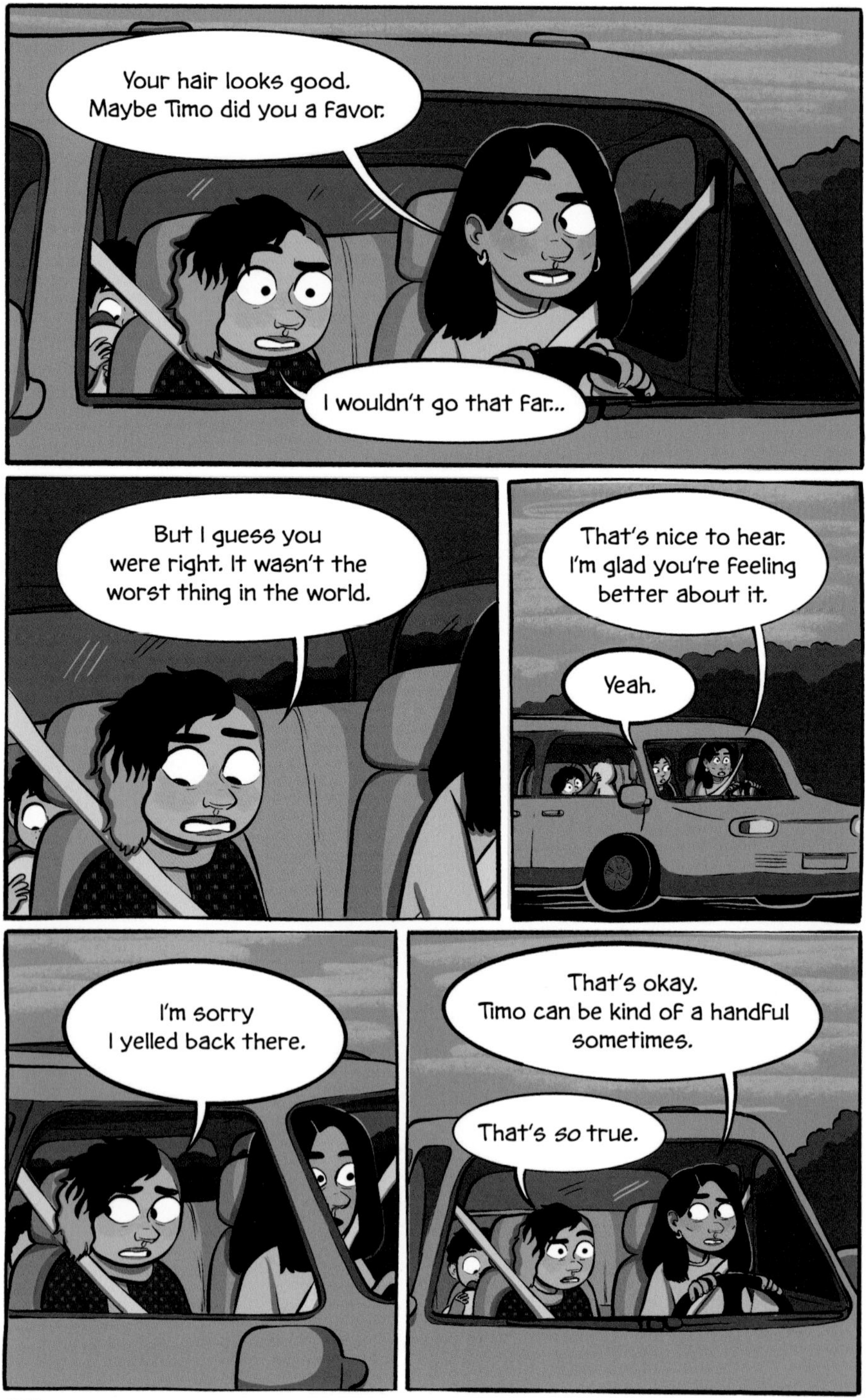
Your hair looks good. Maybe Timo did you a favor.
I wouldn't go that far...
But I guess you were right. It wasn't the worst thing in the world.
That's nice to hear. I'm glad you're feeling better about it.
Yeah.
I'm sorry I yelled back there.
That's okay. Timo can be kind of a handful sometimes.
That's *so* true.

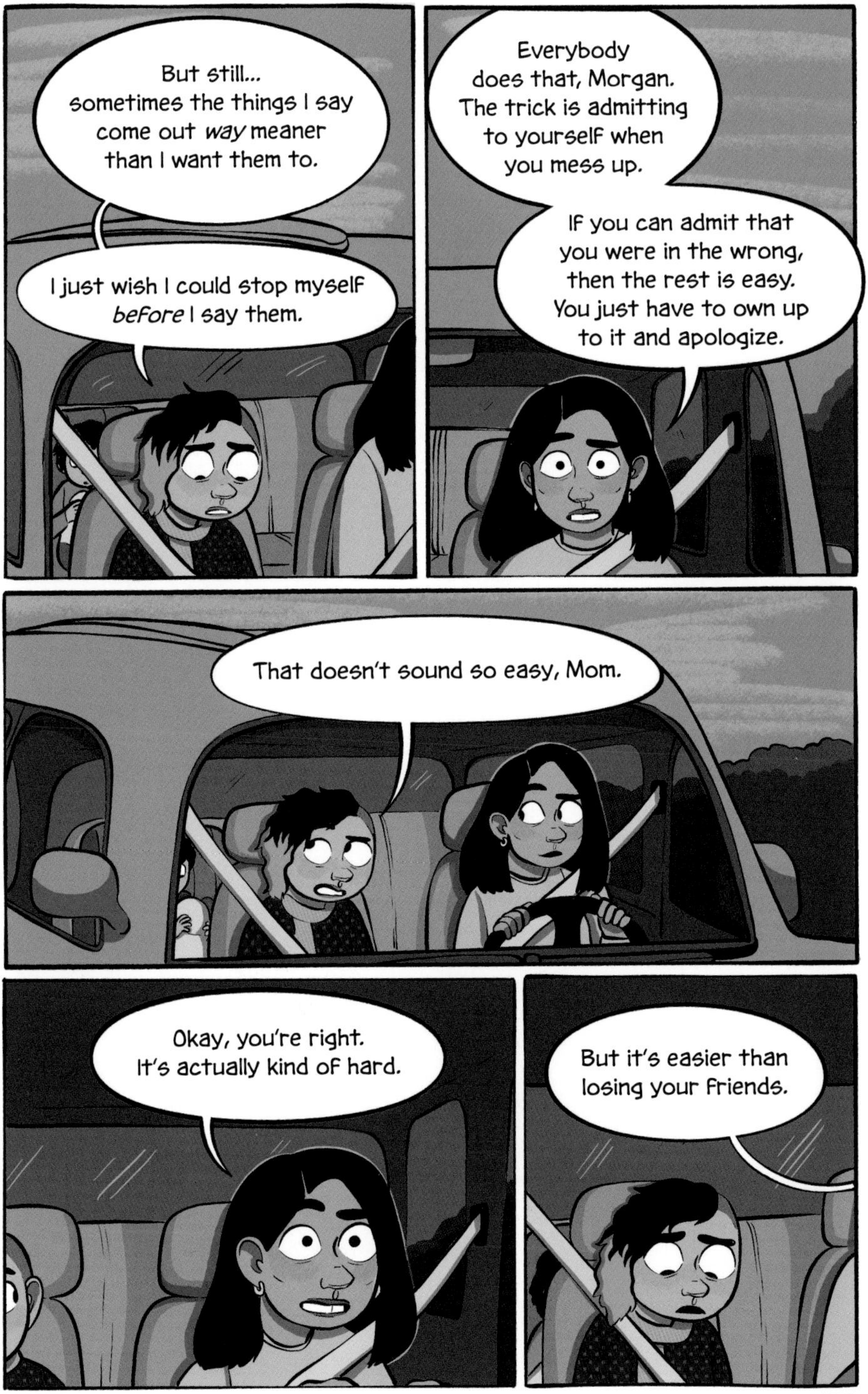
But still... sometimes the things I say come out *way* meaner than I want them to.
I just wish I could stop myself *before* I say them.
Everybody does that, Morgan. The trick is admitting to yourself when you mess up.
If you can admit that you were in the wrong, then the rest is easy. You just have to own up to it and apologize.
That doesn't sound so easy, Mom.
Okay, you're right. It's actually kind of hard.
But it's easier than losing your friends.

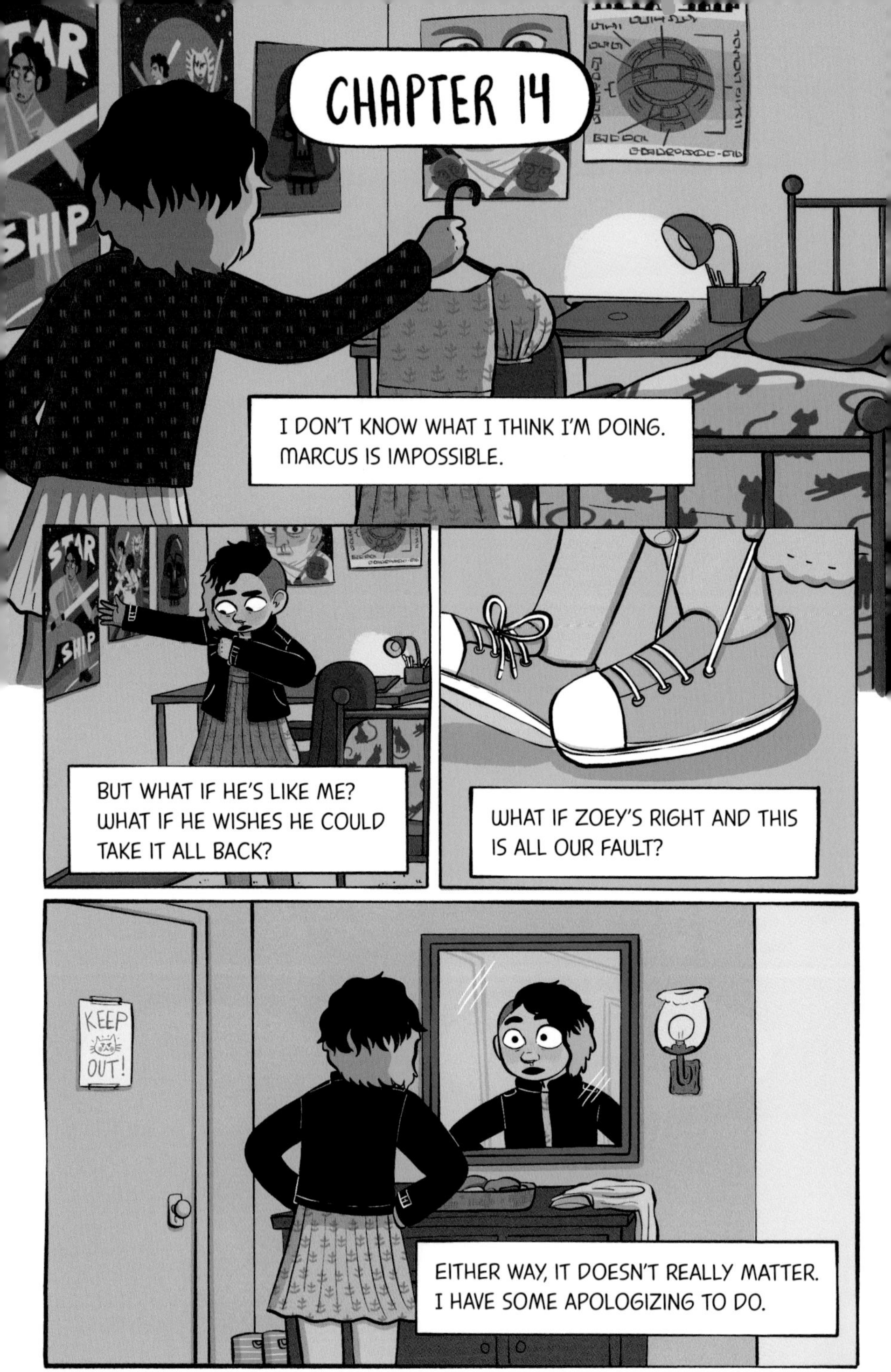
CHAPTER 14
STAR SHIP
I DON'T KNOW WHAT I THINK I'M DOING. MARCUS IS IMPOSSIBLE.
STAR SHIP
BUT WHAT IF HE'S LIKE ME? WHAT IF HE WISHES HE COULD TAKE IT ALL BACK?
WHAT IF ZOEY'S RIGHT AND THIS IS ALL OUR FAULT?
KEEP OUT!
EITHER WAY, IT DOESN'T REALLY MATTER. I HAVE SOME APOLOGIZING TO DO.

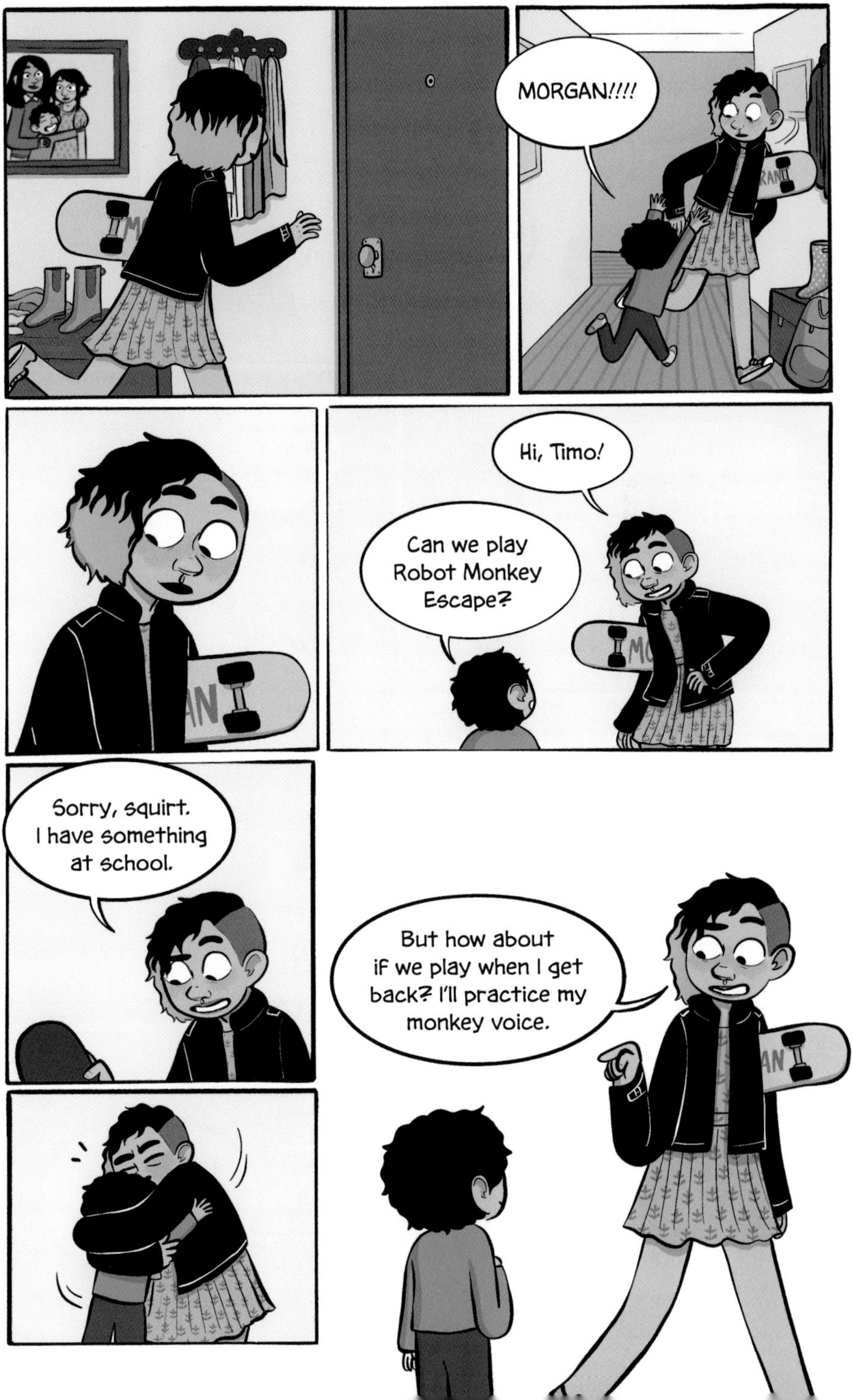
MORGAN!!!!
Hi, Timo!
Can we play Robot Monkey Escape?
Sorry, squirt. I have something at school.
But how about if we play when I get back? I'll practice my monkey voice.

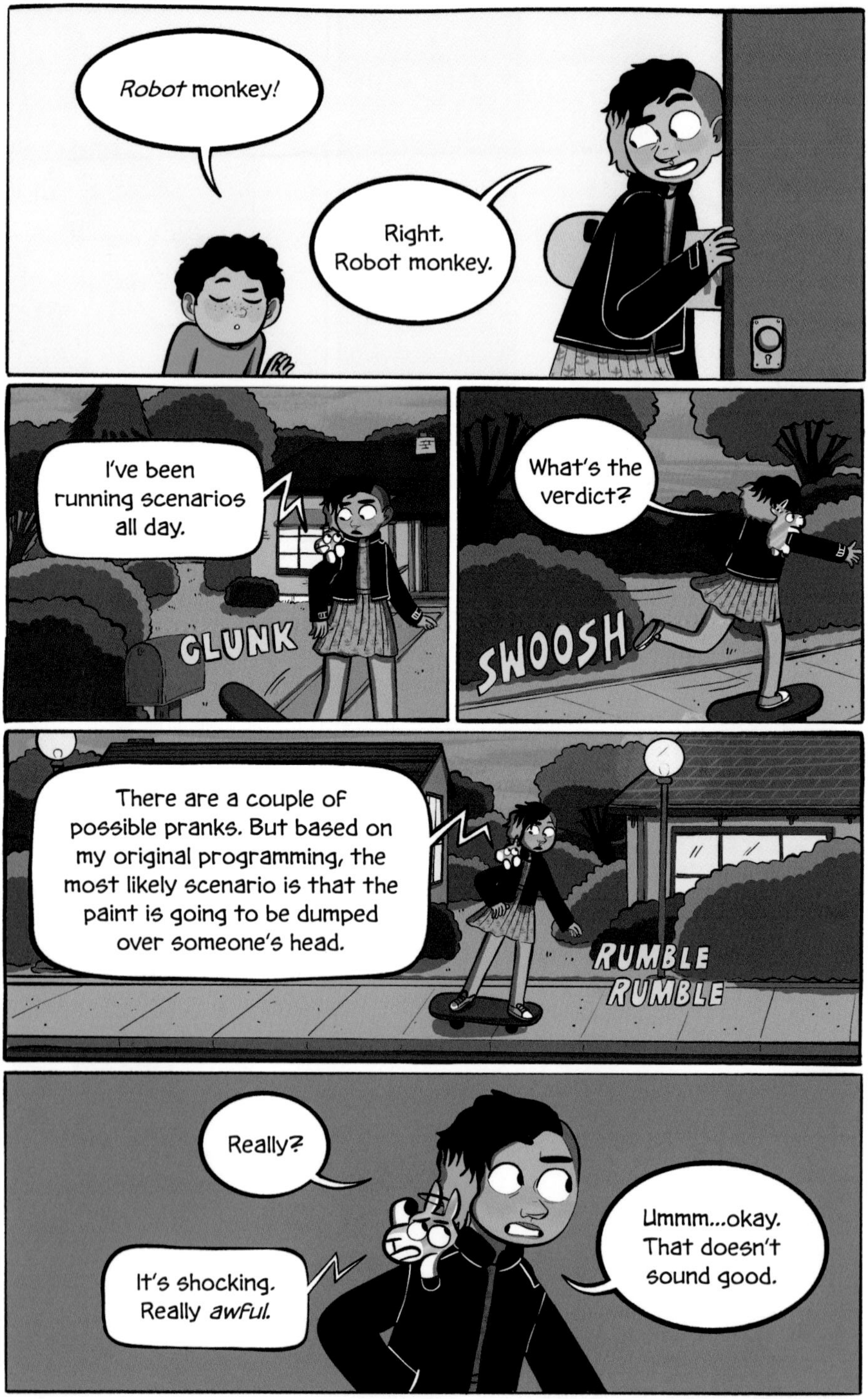

Robot monkey!
Right. Robot monkey.
I've been running scenarios all day.
CLUNK
What's the verdict?
SWOOSH
There are a couple of possible pranks. But based on my original programming, the most likely scenario is that the paint is going to be dumped over someone's head.
RUMBLE RUMBLE
Really?
Ummm...okay. That doesn't sound good.
It's shocking. Really *awful.*

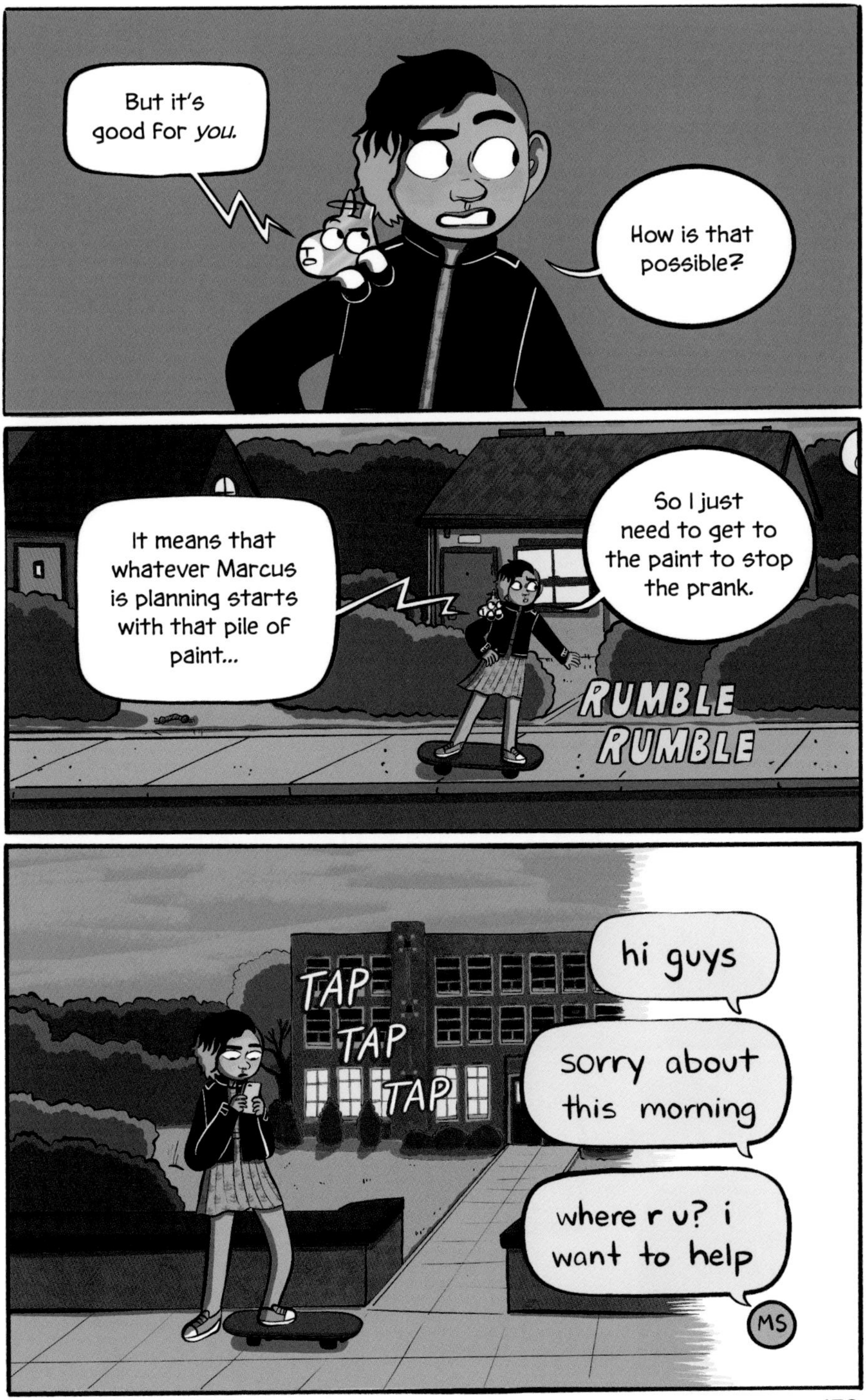
But it's good for *you.*
How is that possible?
It means that whatever Marcus is planning starts with that pile of paint...
So I just need to get to the paint to stop the prank.
RUMBLE
RUMBLE
TAP
TAP
TAP
hi guys
sorry about this morning
where r u? i want to help
MS

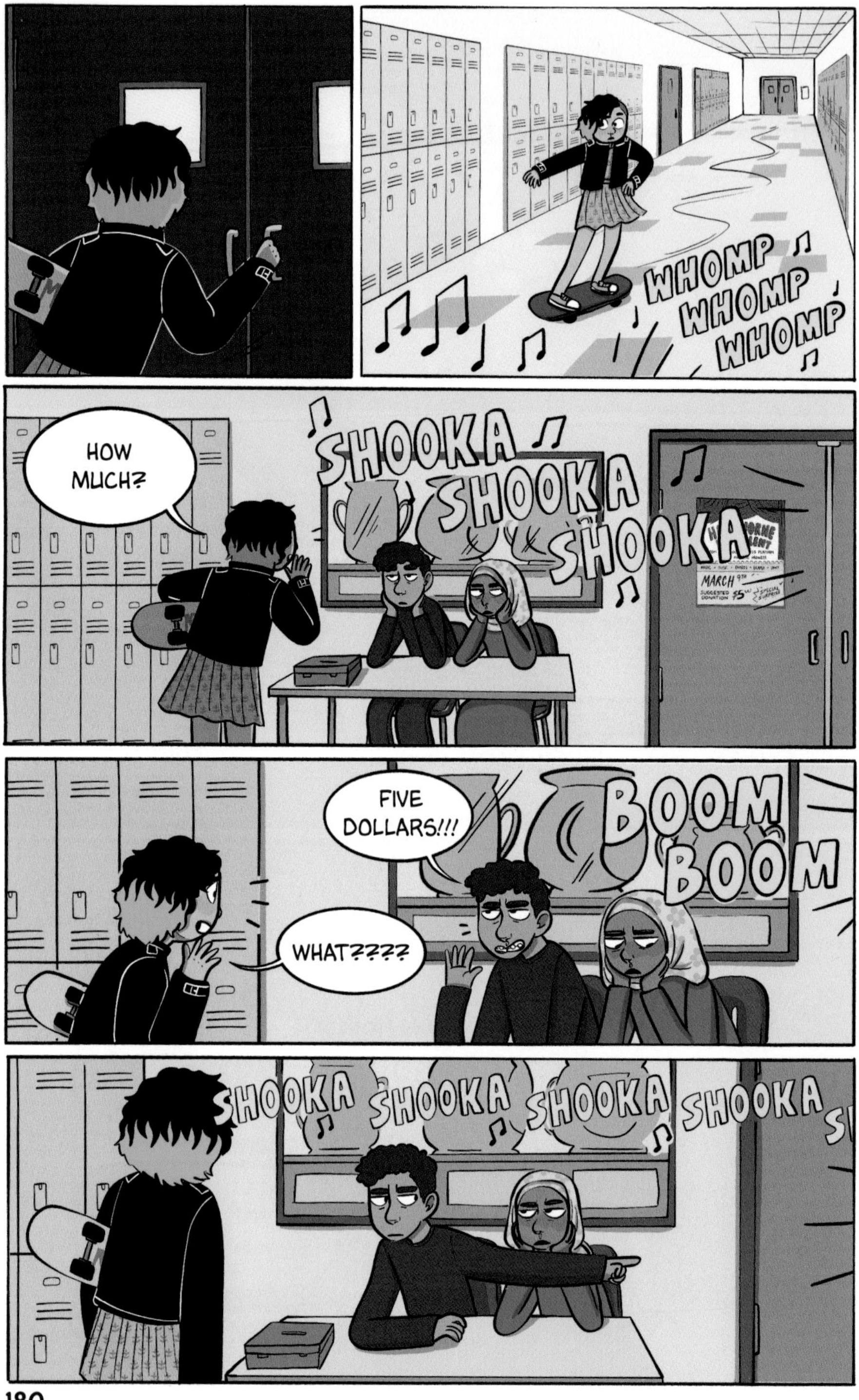
WHOMP
WHOMP
WHOMP
HOW MUCH?
SHOOKA
SHOOKA
SHOOKA
MARCH 9TH
FIVE DOLLARS!!!
BOOM
BOOM
WHAT????
SHOOKA
SHOOKA
SHOOKA
SHOOKA

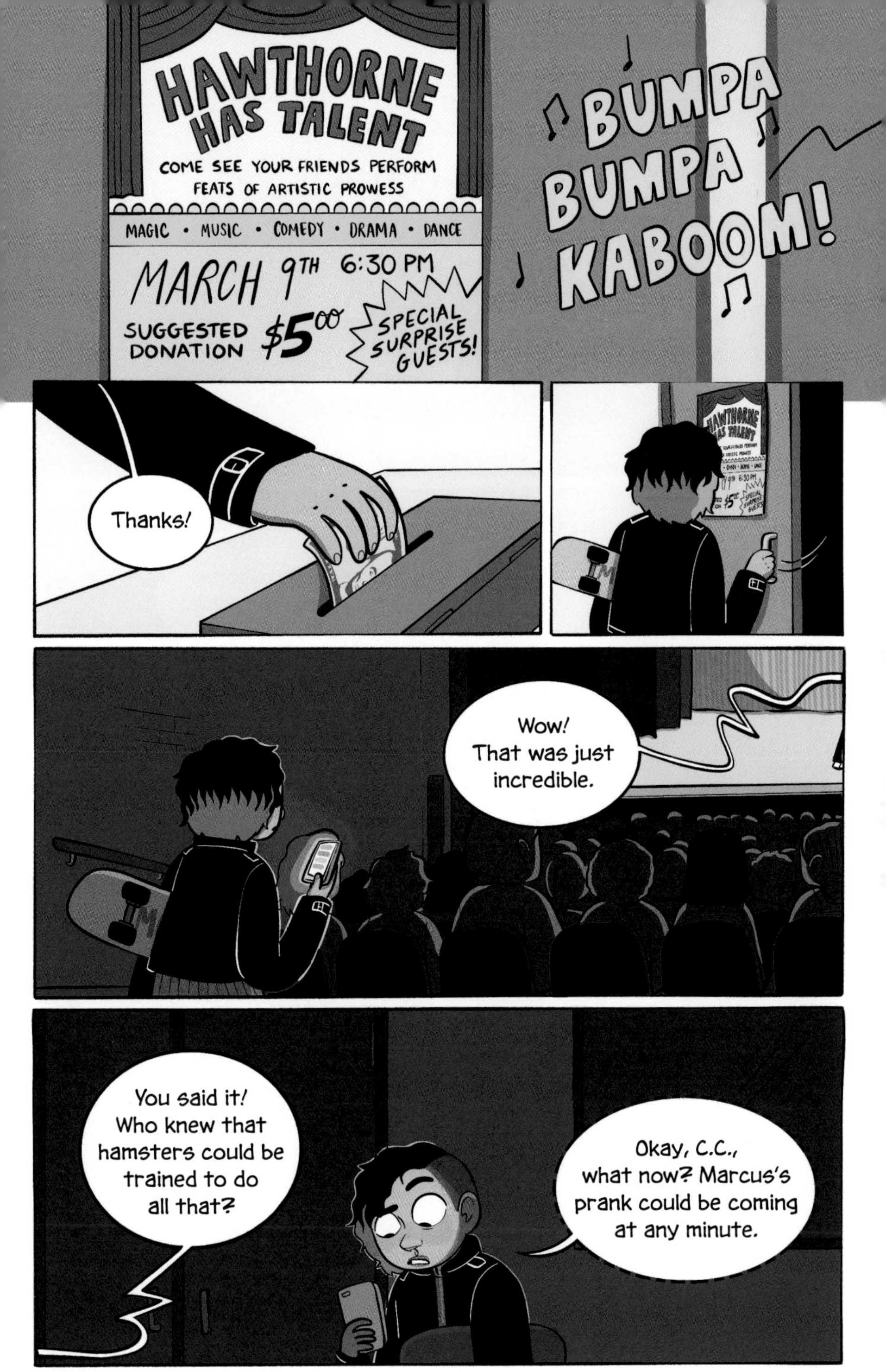
HAWTHORNE HAS TALENT
COME SEE YOUR FRIENDS PERFORM FEATS OF ARTISTIC PROWESS
MAGIC • MUSIC • COMEDY • DRAMA • DANCE
MARCH 9TH 6:30 PM
SUGGESTED DONATION $5.00
SPECIAL SURPRISE GUESTS!
BUMPA BUMPA KABOOM!
Thanks!
Wow! That was just incredible.
You said it! Who knew that hamsters could be trained to do all that?
Okay, C.C., what now? Marcus's prank could be coming at any minute.

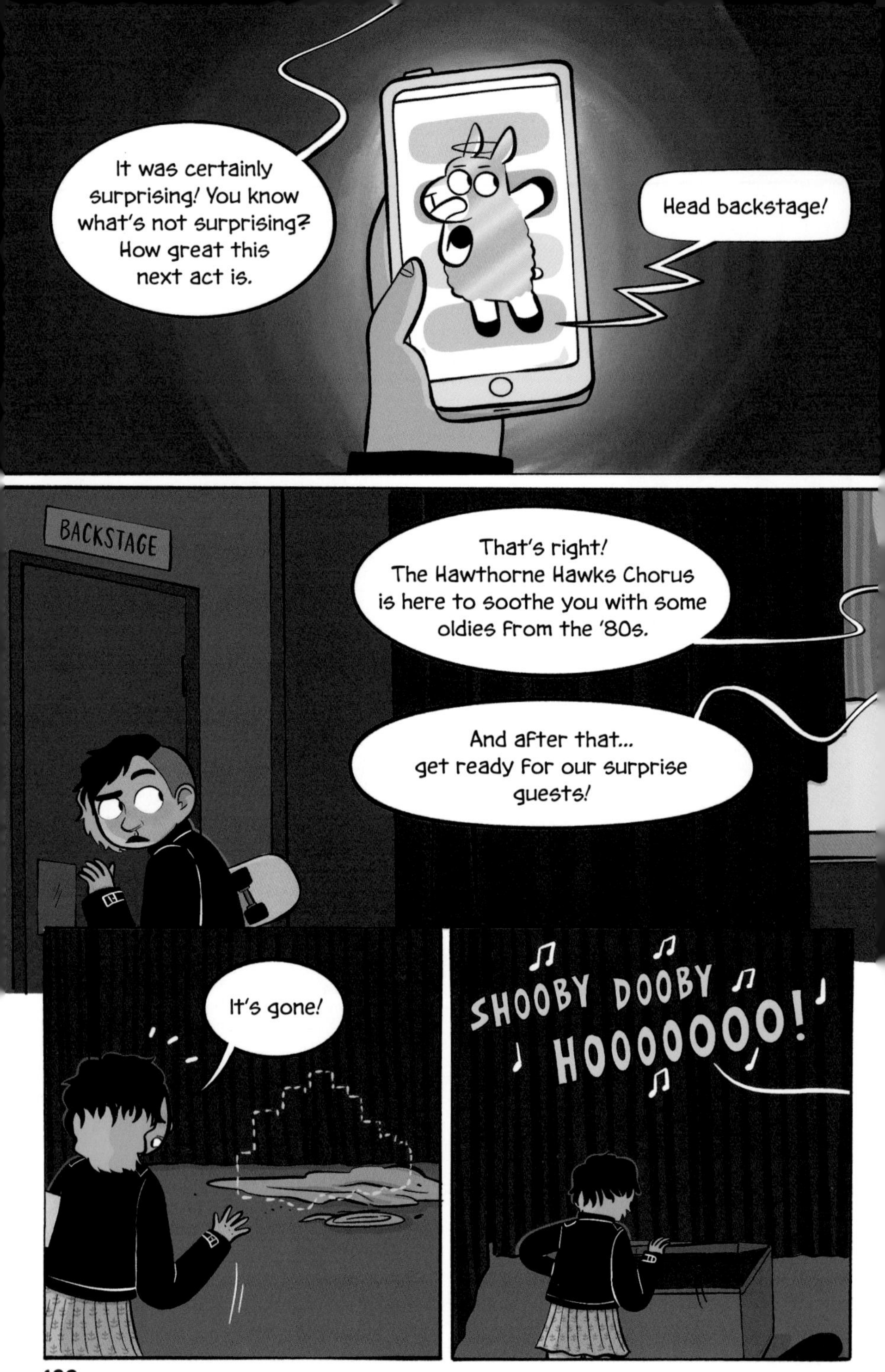
It was certainly surprising! You know what's not surprising? How great this next act is.
Head backstage!
BACKSTAGE
That's right! The Hawthorne Hawks Chorus is here to soothe you with some oldies from the '80s.
And after that... get ready for our surprise guests!
It's gone!
SHOOBY DOOBY HOOOOOOO!

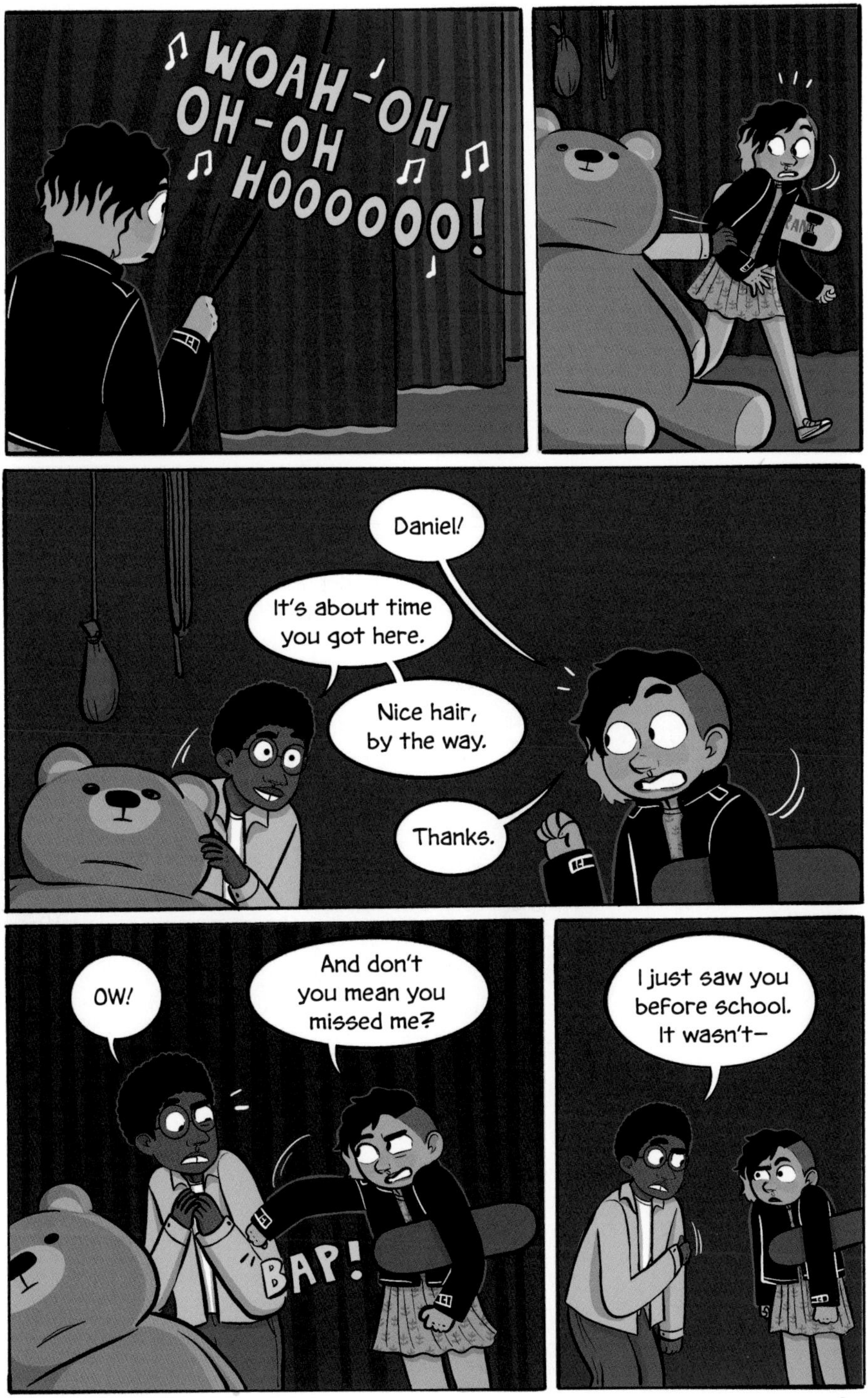
WOAH-OH OH-OH HOOOOOO!
Daniel!
It's about time you got here.
Nice hair, by the way.
Thanks.
OW!
And don't you mean you missed me?
BAP!
I just saw you before school. It wasn't—

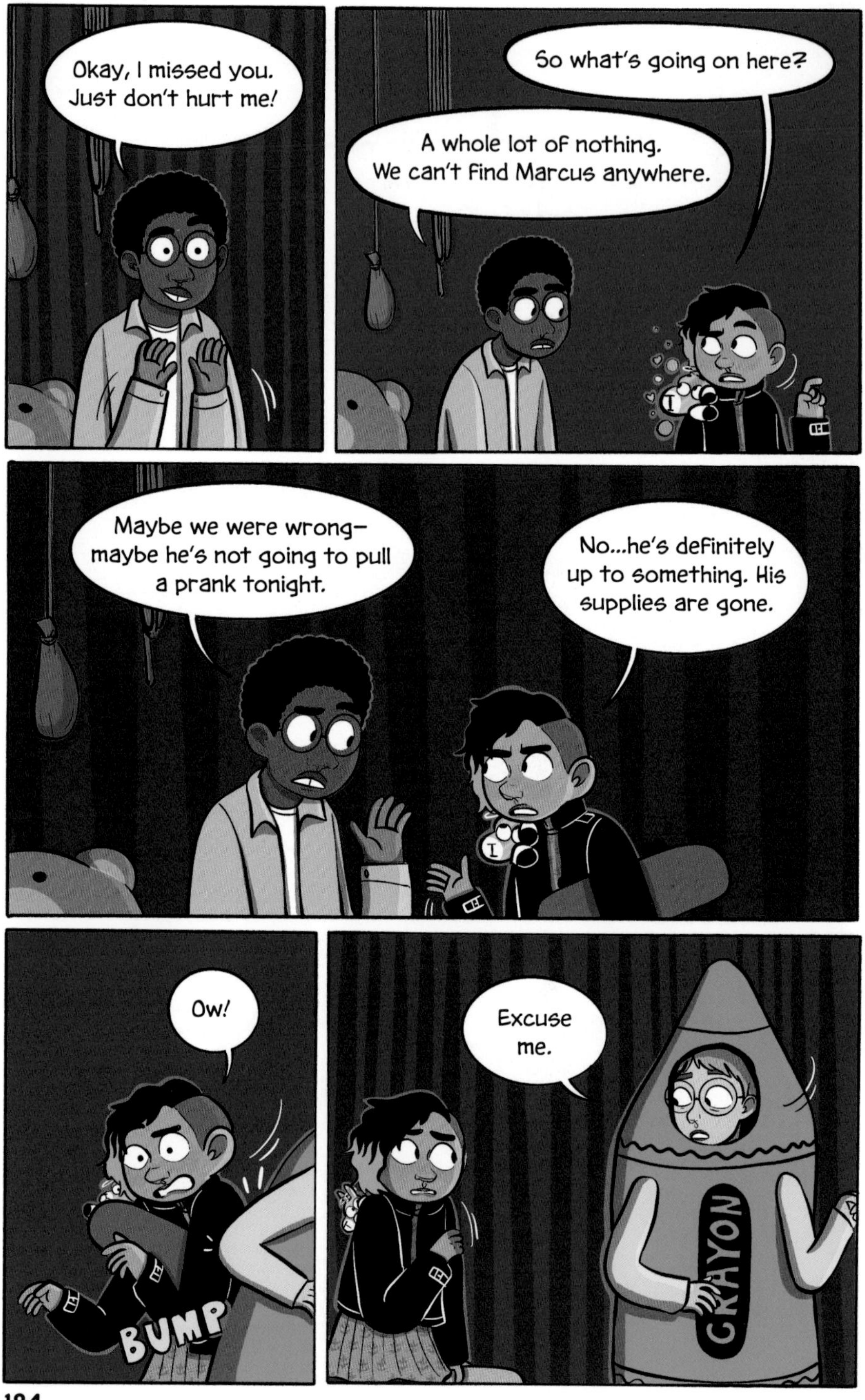
Okay, I missed you. Just don't hurt me!
So what's going on here?
A whole lot of nothing. We can't find Marcus anywhere.
Maybe we were wrong—maybe he's not going to pull a prank tonight.
No...he's definitely up to something. His supplies are gone.
Ow!
BUMP
Excuse me.
CRAYON

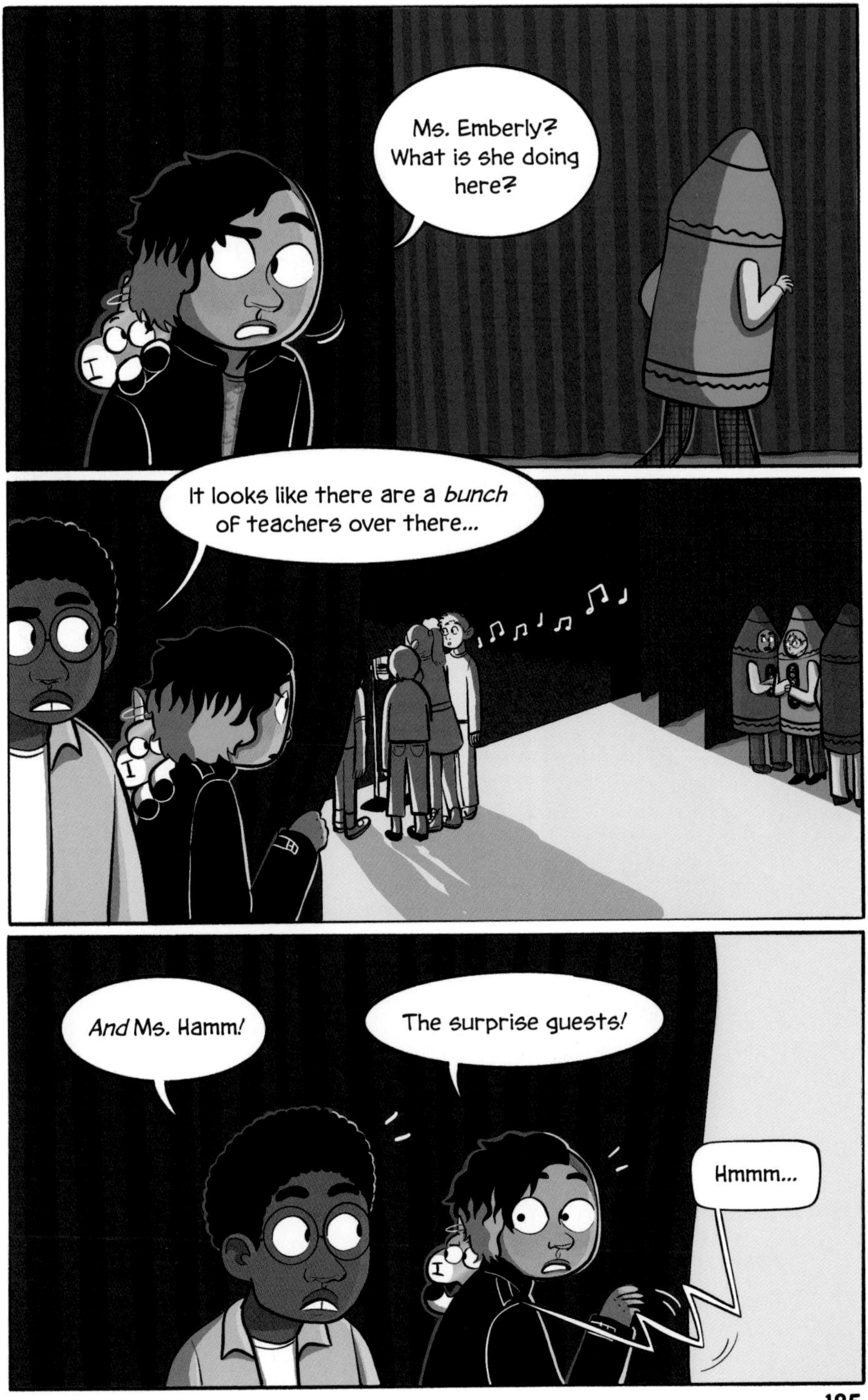
Ms. Emberly? What is she doing here?
It looks like there are a *bunch* of teachers over there...
And Ms. Hamm!
The surprise guests!
Hmmm...

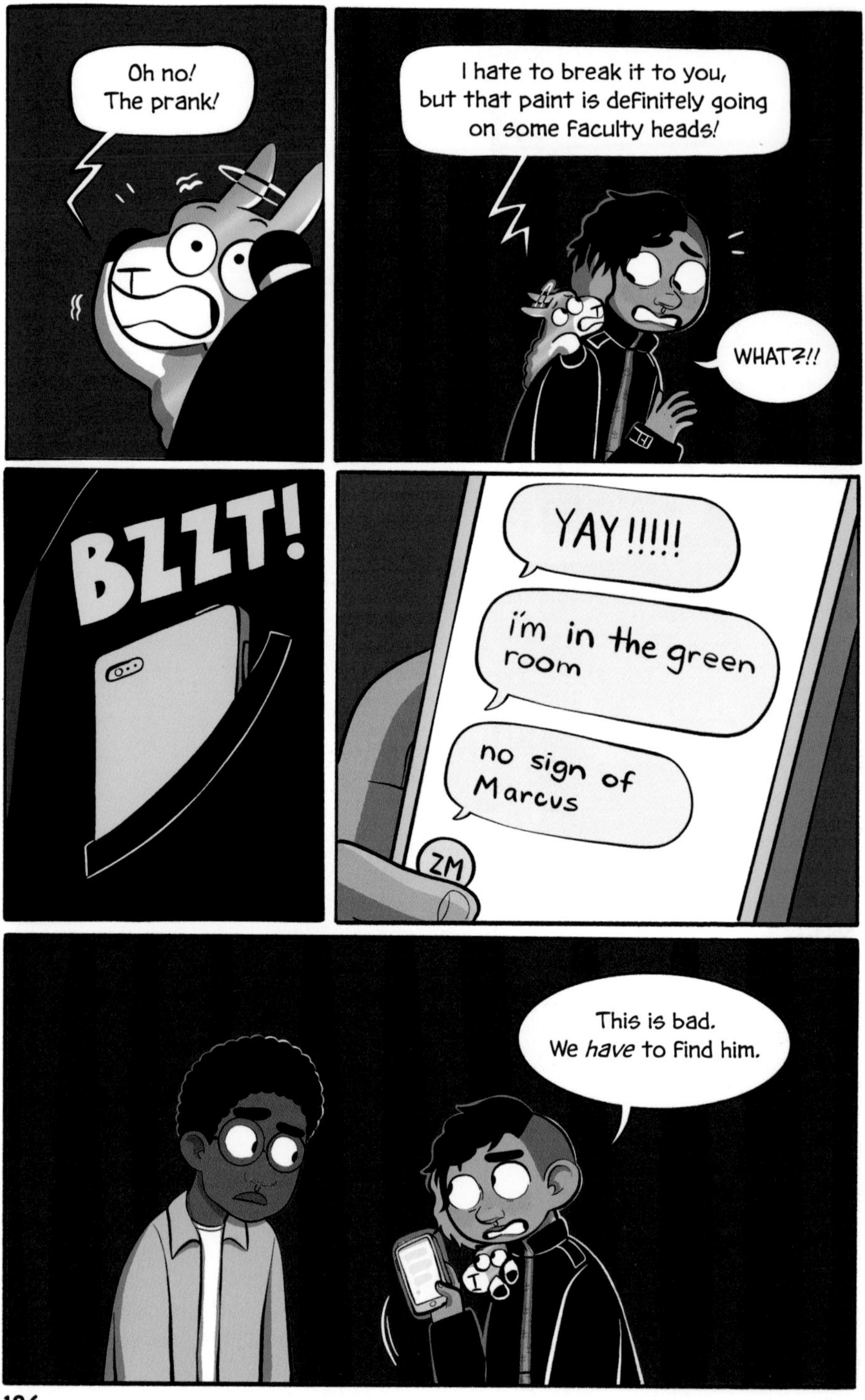
Oh no! The prank!
I hate to break it to you, but that paint is definitely going on some faculty heads!
WHAT?!!
BZZT!
YAY !!!!!
i'm in the green room
no sign of Marcus
ZM
This is bad. We *have* to find him.

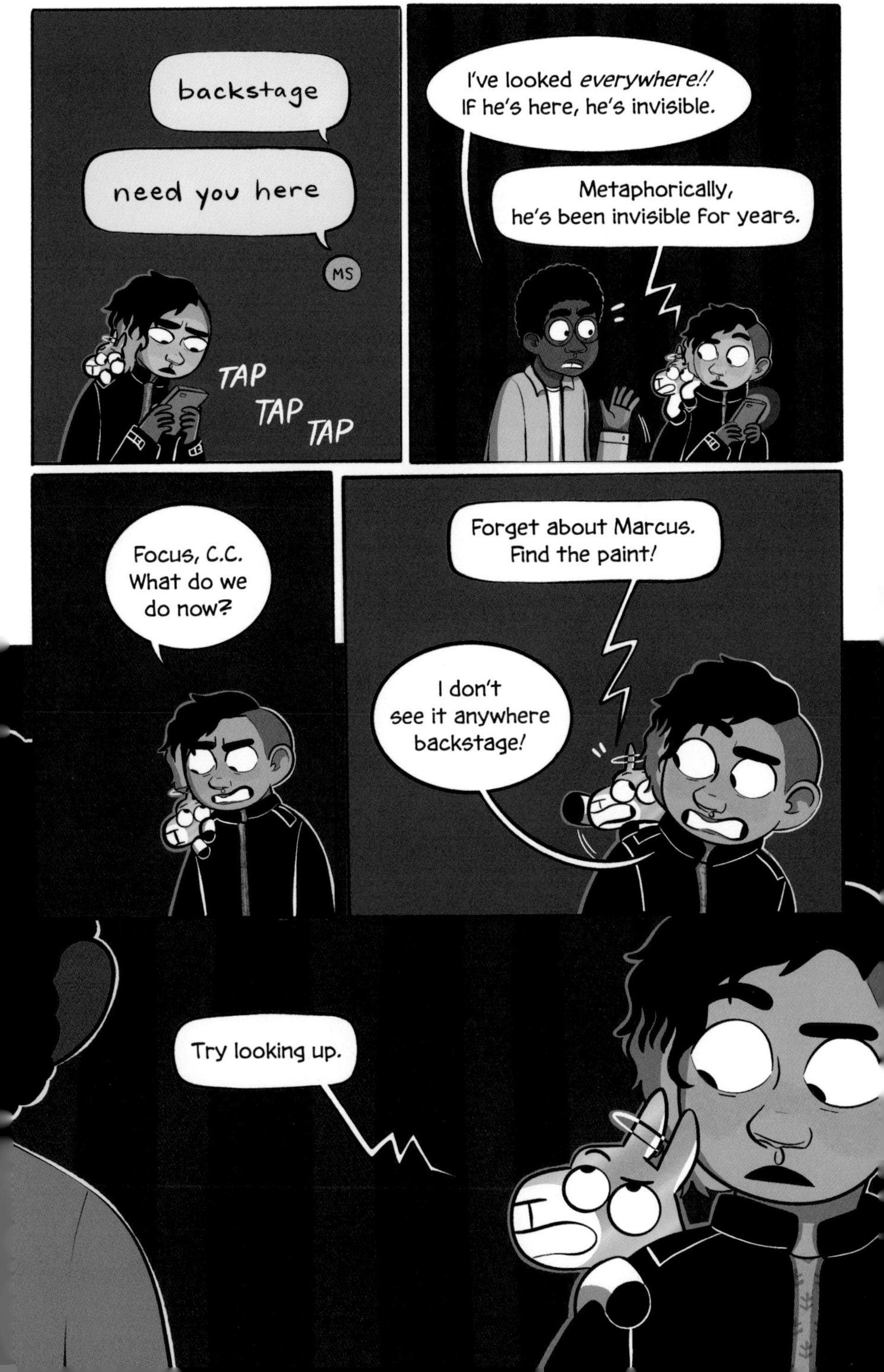
backstage
need you here
MS
TAP
TAP
TAP
I've looked *everywhere!!* If he's here, he's invisible.
Metaphorically, he's been invisible for years.
Focus, C.C. What do we do now?
Forget about Marcus. Find the paint!
I don't see it anywhere backstage!
Try looking up.

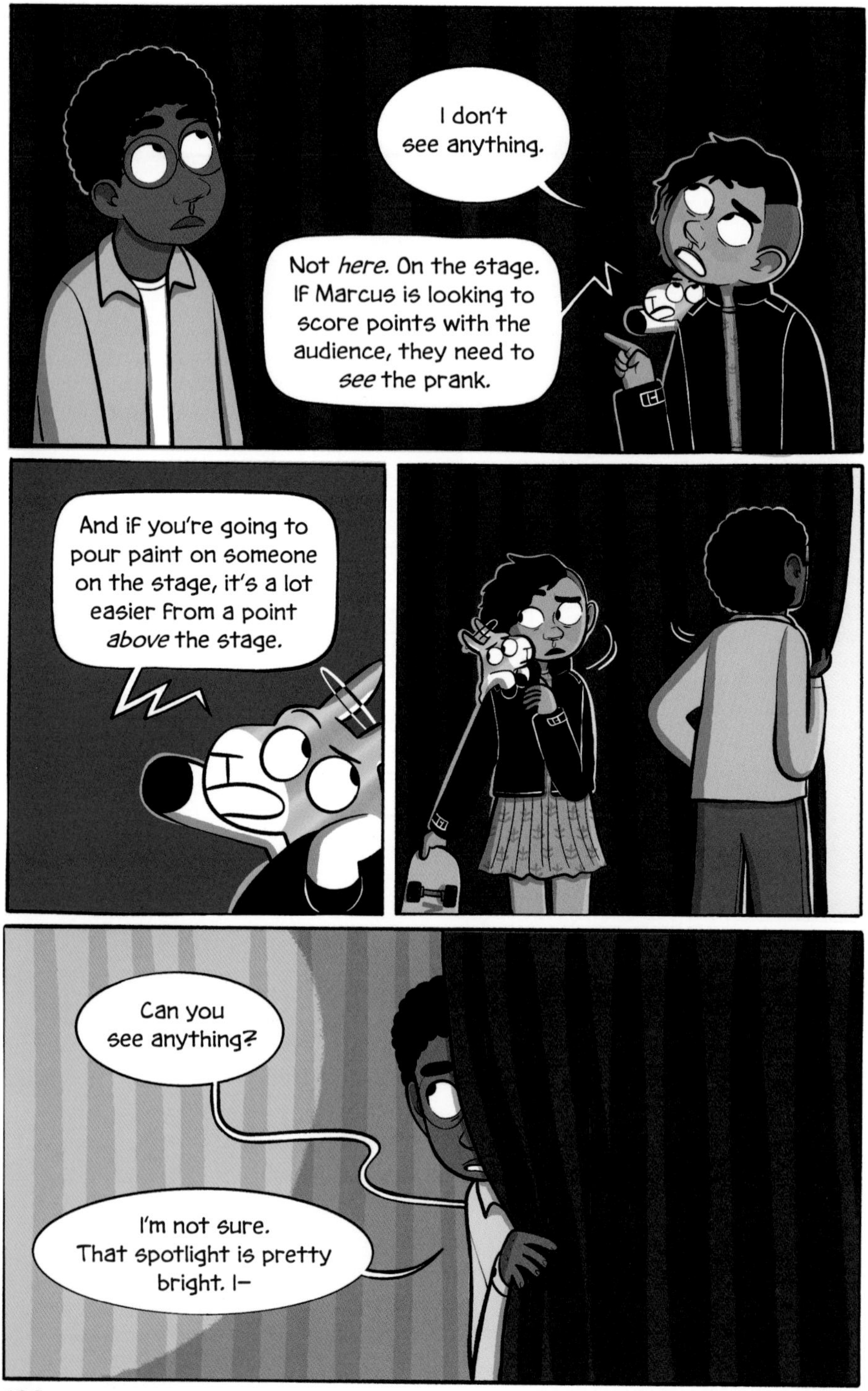
I don't see anything.
Not *here.* On the stage. If Marcus is looking to score points with the audience, they need to *see* the prank.
And if you're going to pour paint on someone on the stage, it's a lot easier from a point *above* the stage.
Can you see anything?
I'm not sure. That spotlight is pretty bright. I—

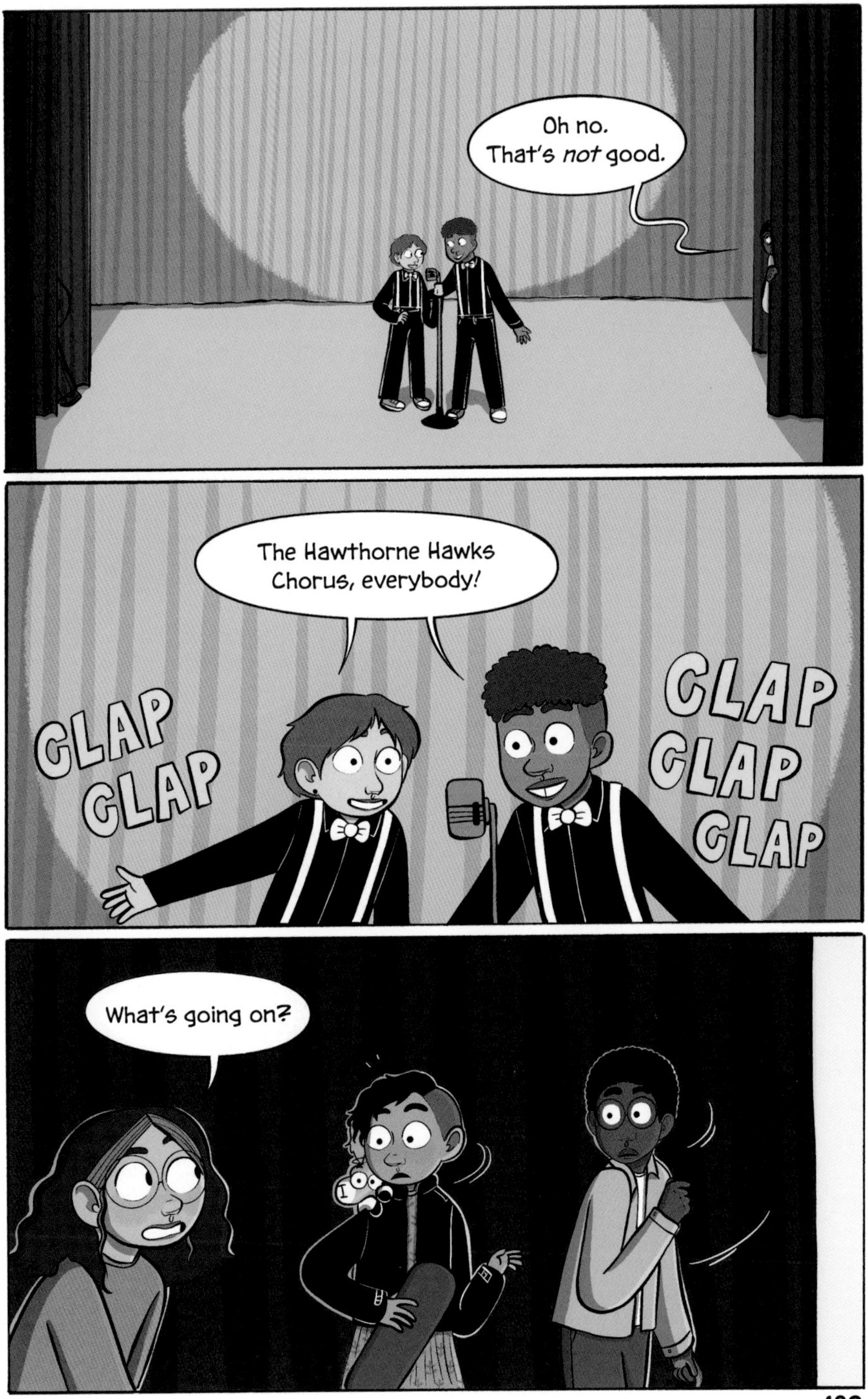
Oh no.
That's *not* good.
The Hawthorne Hawks
Chorus, everybody!
CLAP
CLAP
CLAP
CLAP
CLAP
What's going on?

See those paint buckets? They're rigged to pour their contents on Ms. Hamm. And...it looks like... *Five or six* teachers.

Whoa.

So how are we gonna stop him without the teachers finding out what he was up to?

Are you sure—

I'm sure. You were right. We made this mess. Let's clean it up.

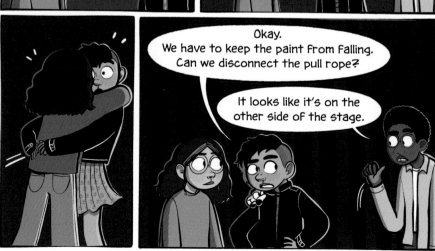

Okay. We have to keep the paint from falling. Can we disconnect the pull rope?

It looks like it's on the other side of the stage.

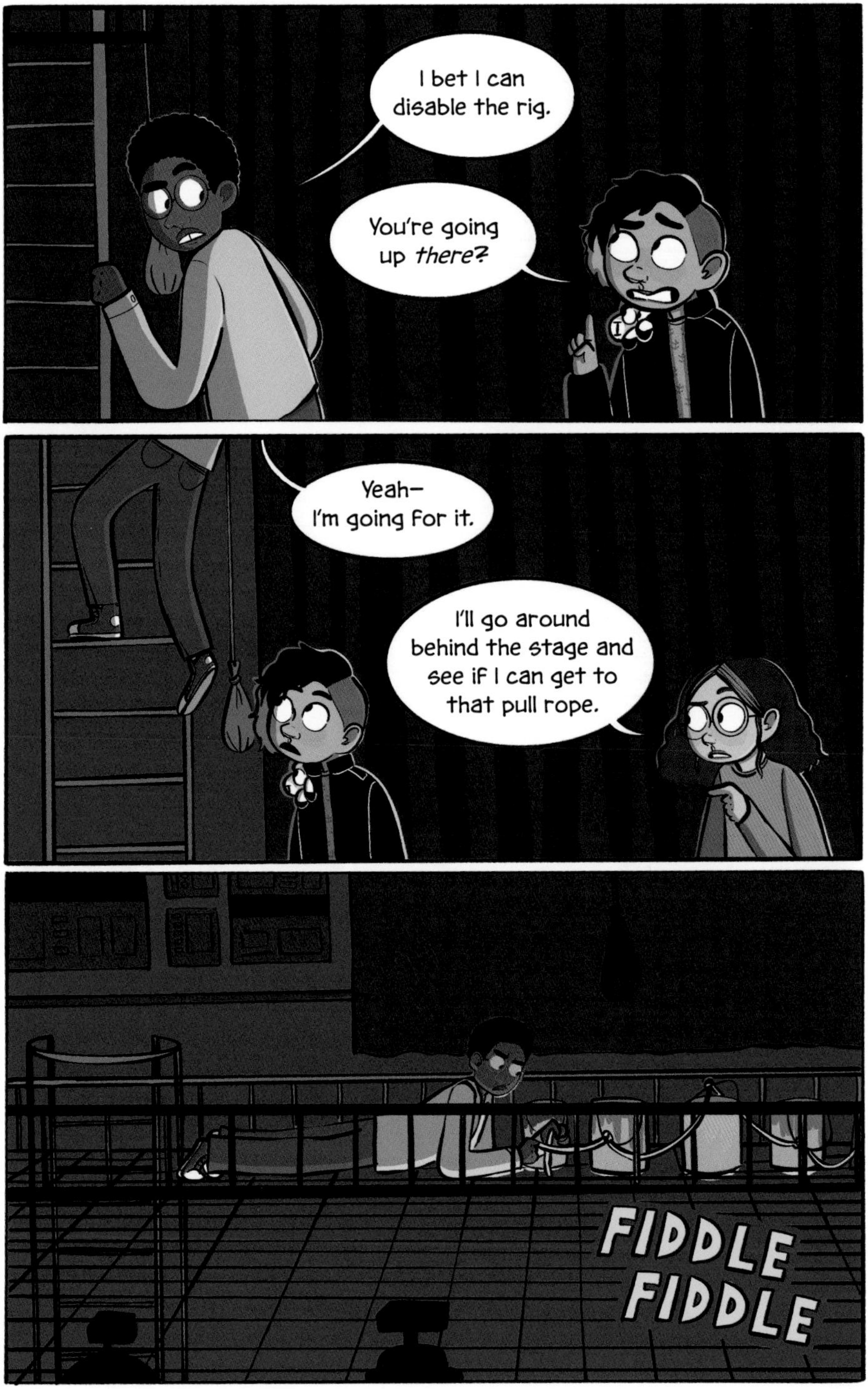

I bet I can disable the rig.
You're going up *there*?
Yeah— I'm going for it.
I'll go around behind the stage and see if I can get to that pull rope.
FIDDLE FIDDLE

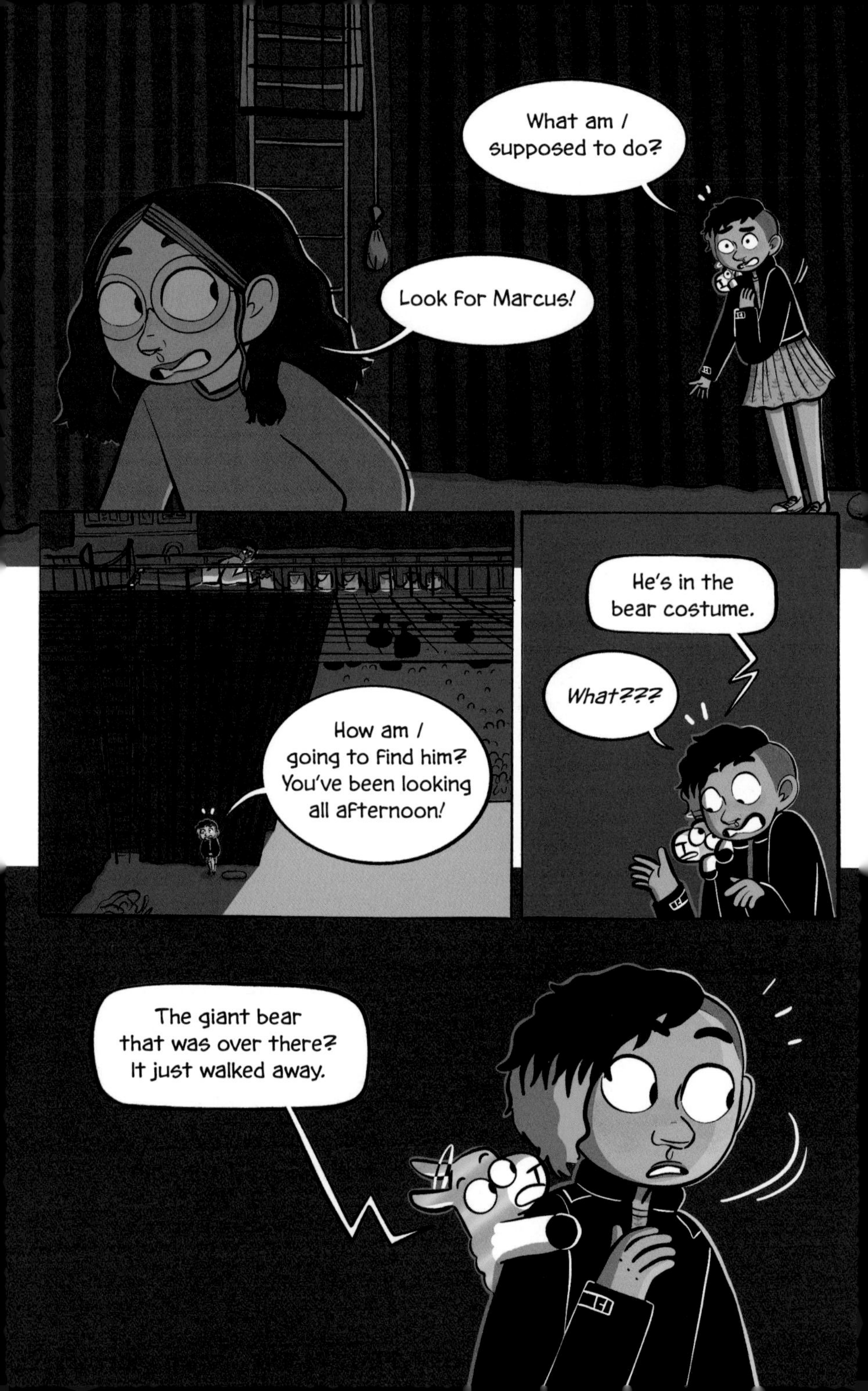
What am I supposed to do?
Look for Marcus!
How am I going to find him? You've been looking all afternoon!
He's in the bear costume.
What???
The giant bear that was over there? It just walked away.

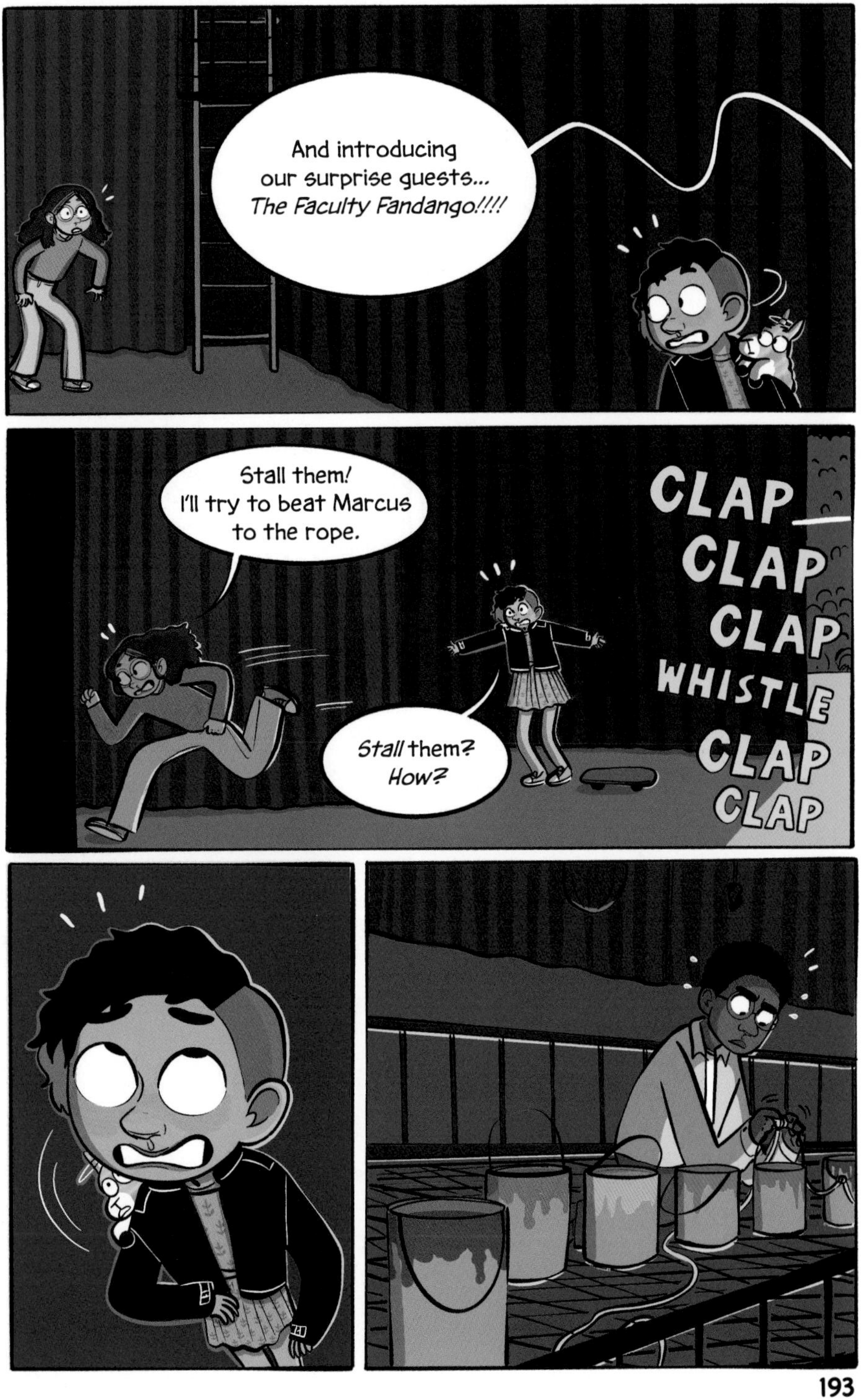
And introducing our surprise guests... *The Faculty Fandango!!!!*
Stall them! I'll try to beat Marcus to the rope.
Stall them? *How?*
CLAP
CLAP
CLAP
WHISTLE
CLAP
CLAP

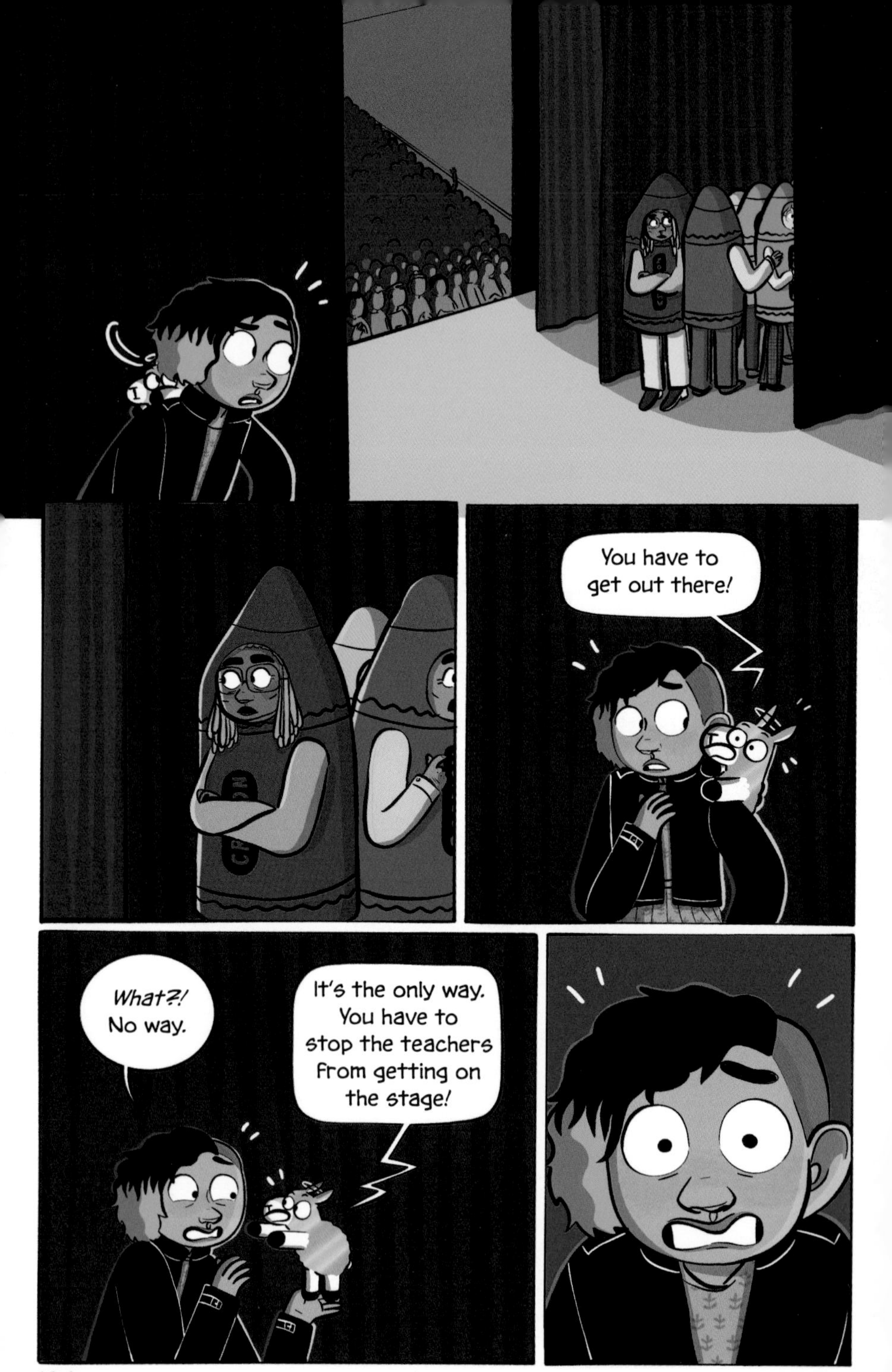
You have to get out there!
What?! No way.
It's the only way. You have to stop the teachers from getting on the stage!

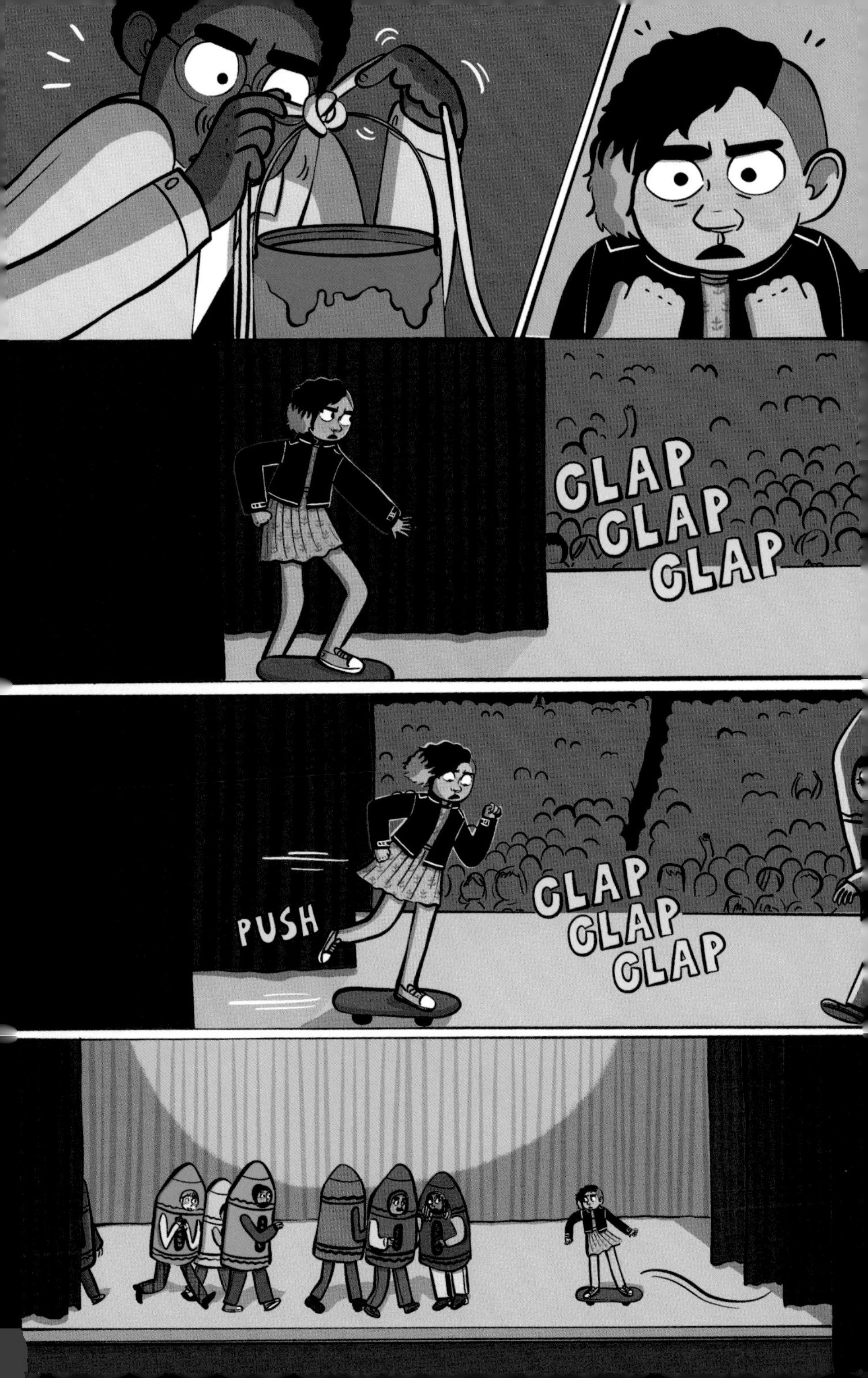
CLAP
CLAP
CLAP
PUSH
CLAP
CLAP
CLAP

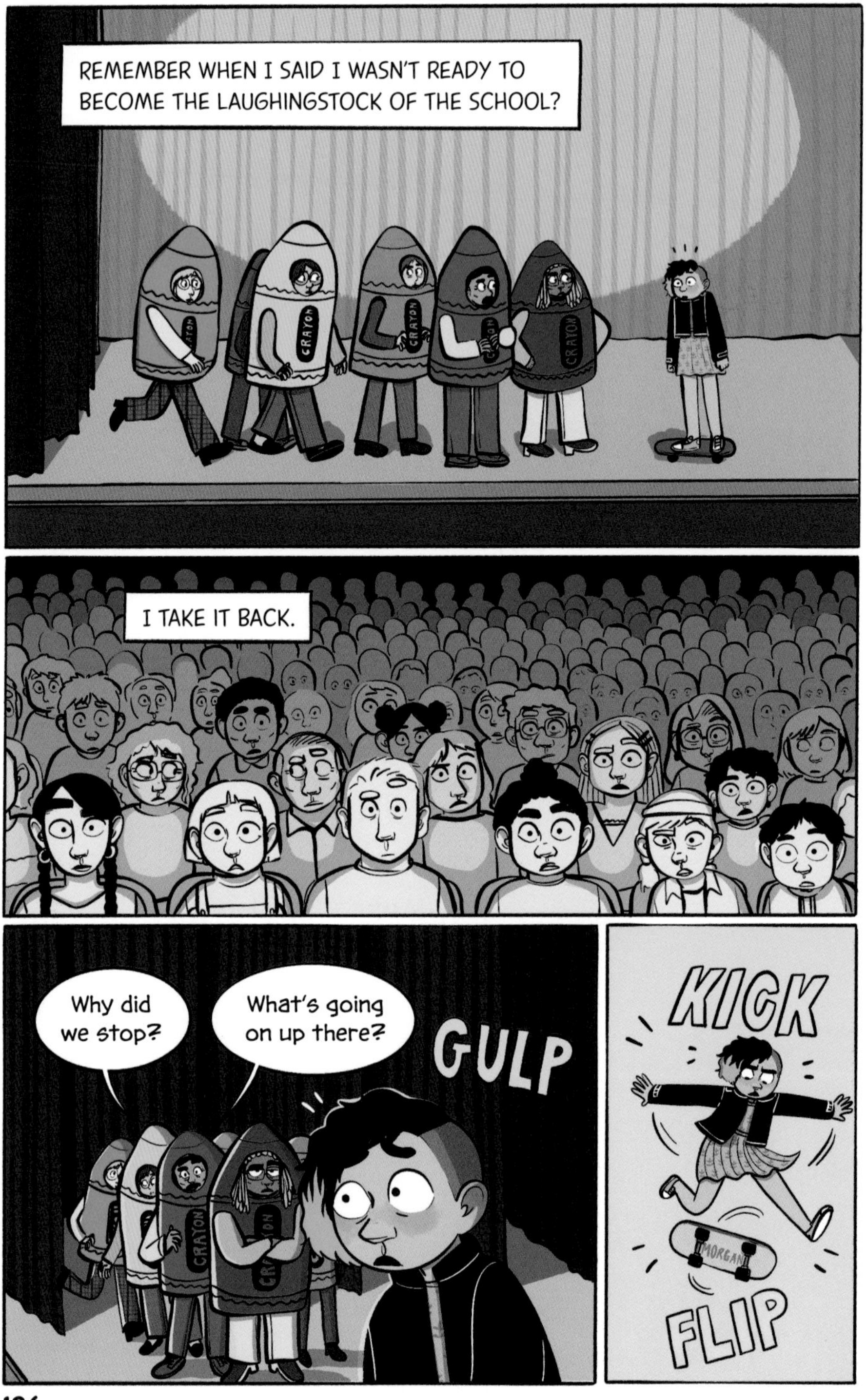
REMEMBER WHEN I SAID I WASN'T READY TO BECOME THE LAUGHINGSTOCK OF THE SCHOOL?
CRAYON
I TAKE IT BACK.
Why did we stop?
What's going on up there?
GULP
KICK
MORGAN
FLIP

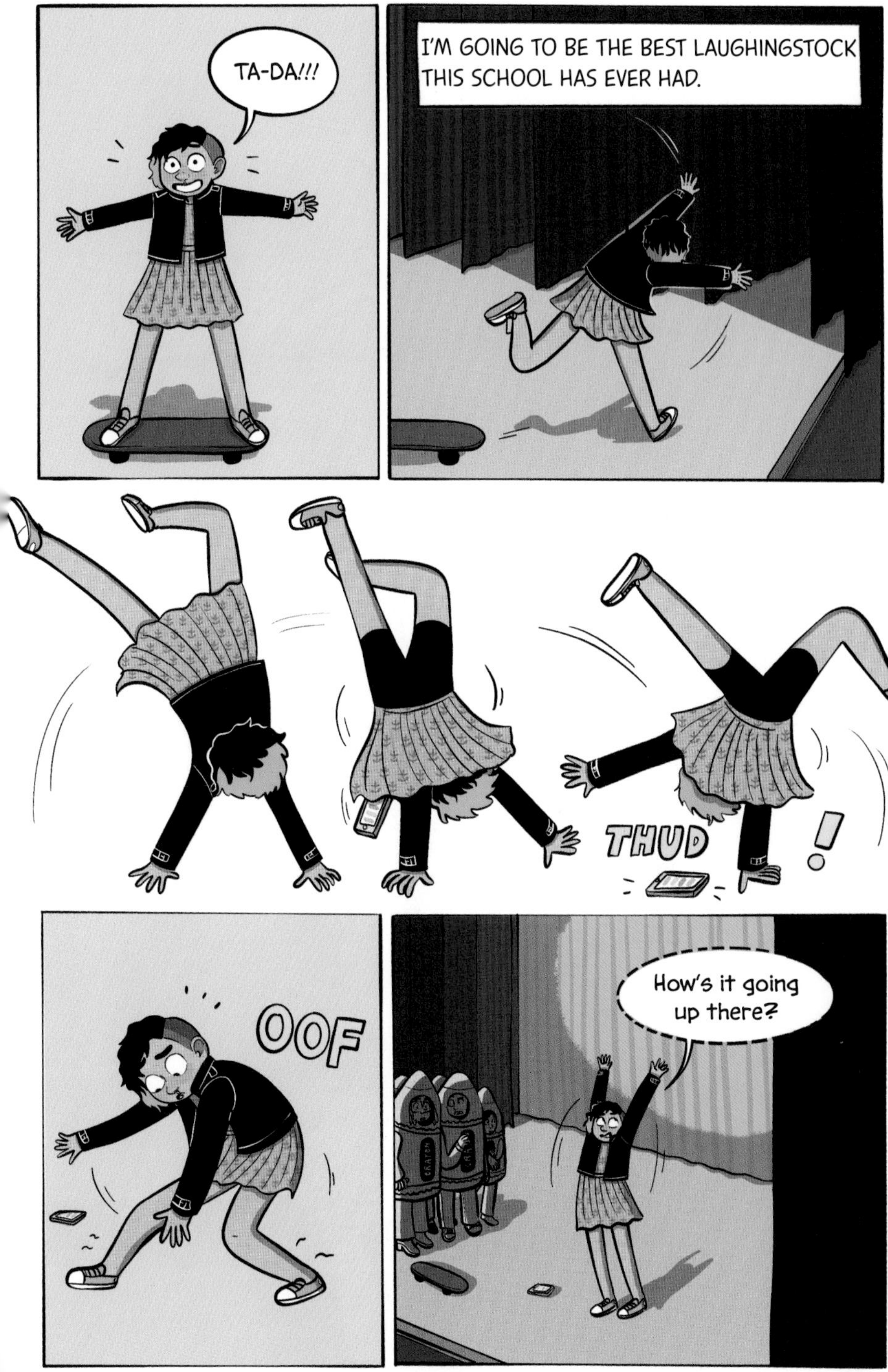
TA-DA!!!
I'M GOING TO BE THE BEST LAUGHINGSTOCK THIS SCHOOL HAS EVER HAD.
THUD
!
OOF
How's it going up there?

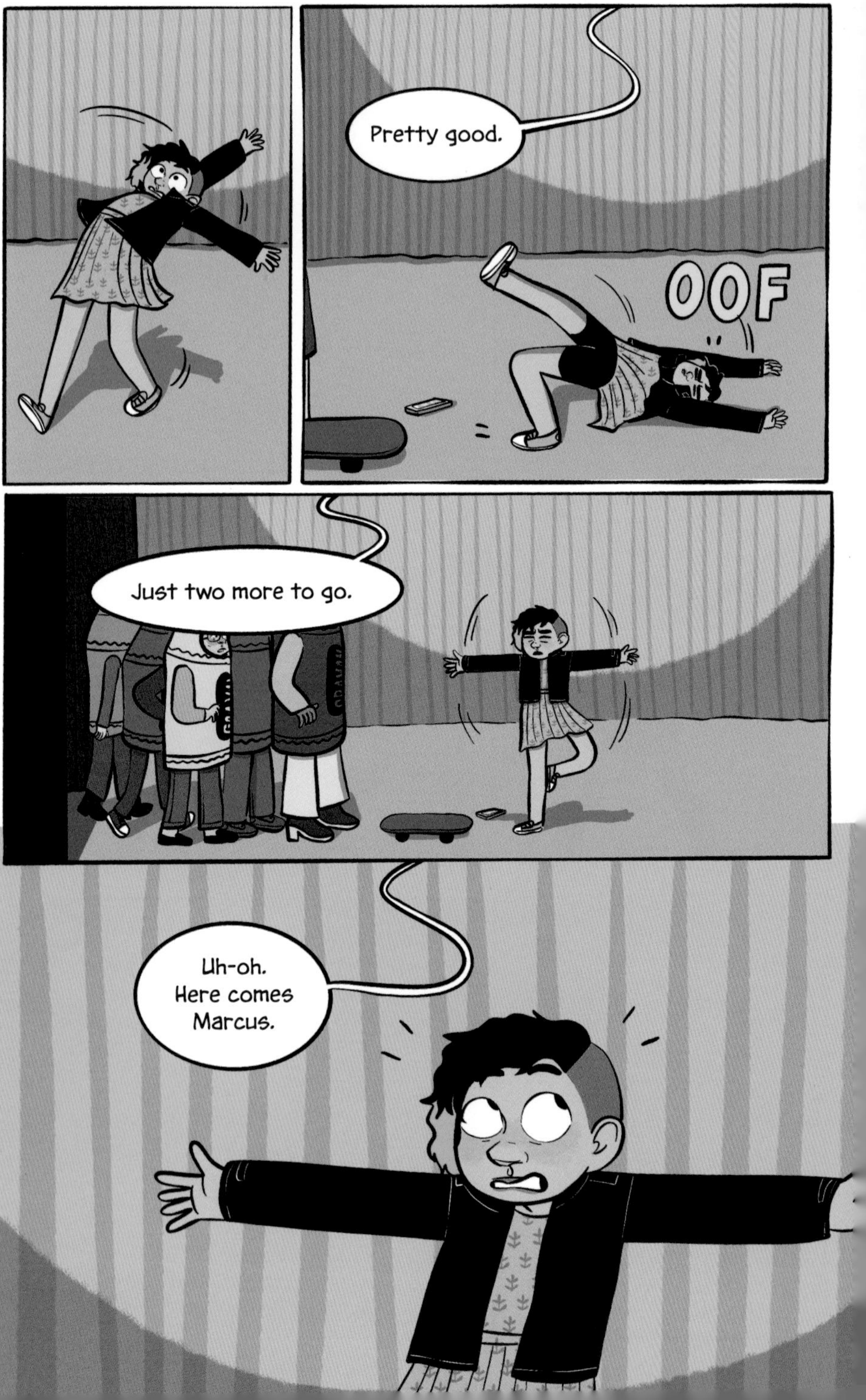
Pretty good.
OOF
Just two more to go.
Uh-oh.
Here comes
Marcus.

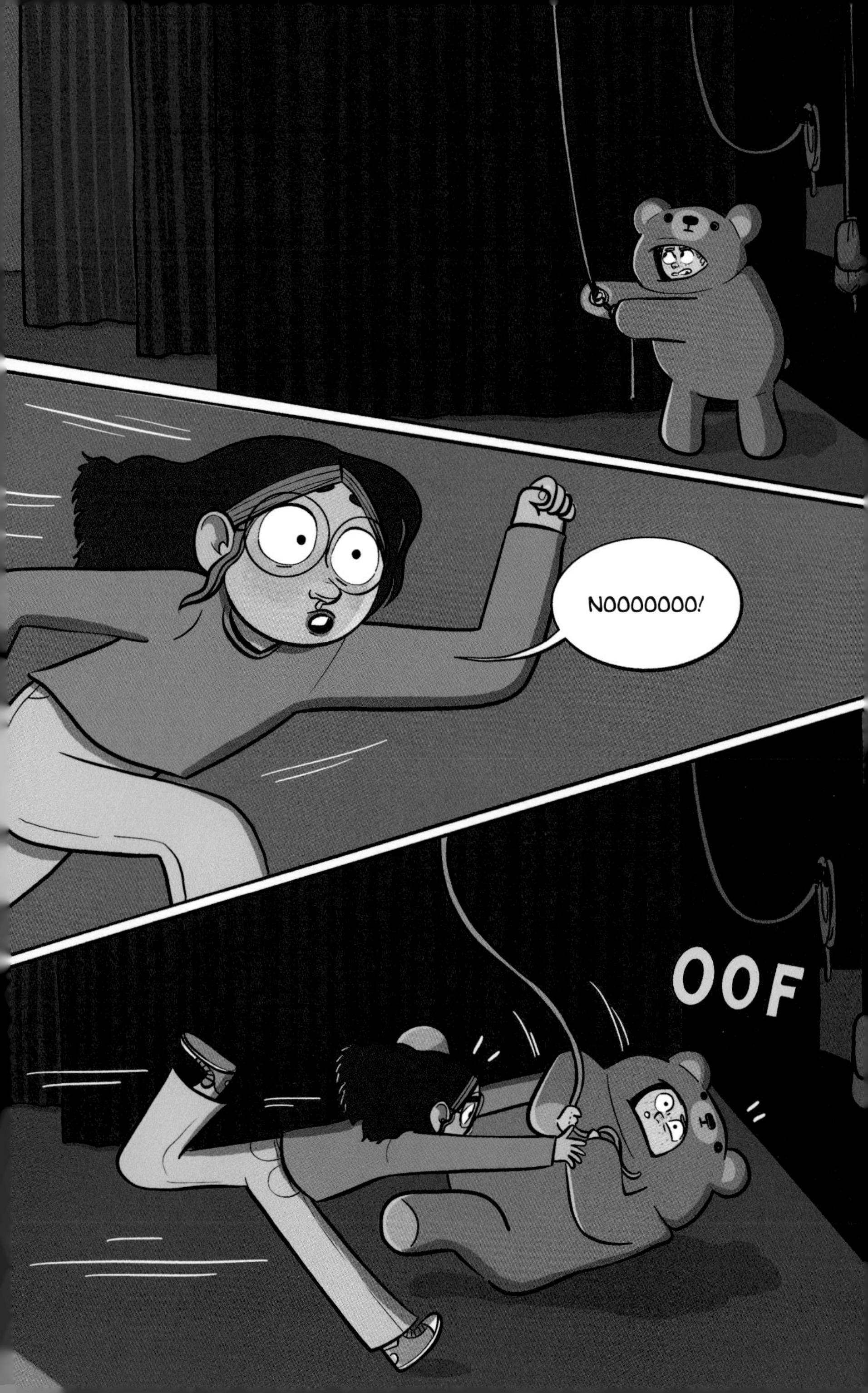
NOOOOOOO!
OOF

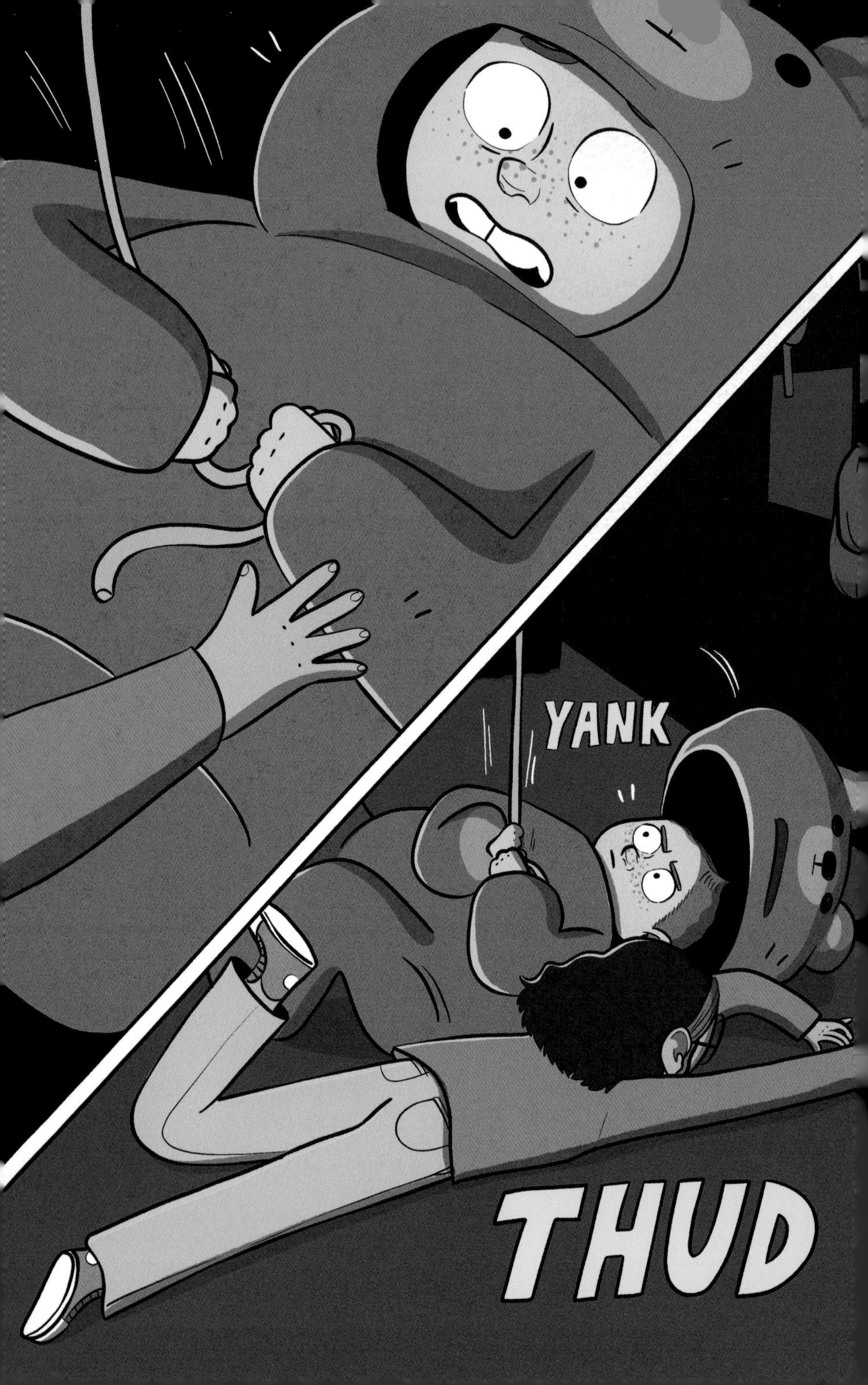
YANK
THUD

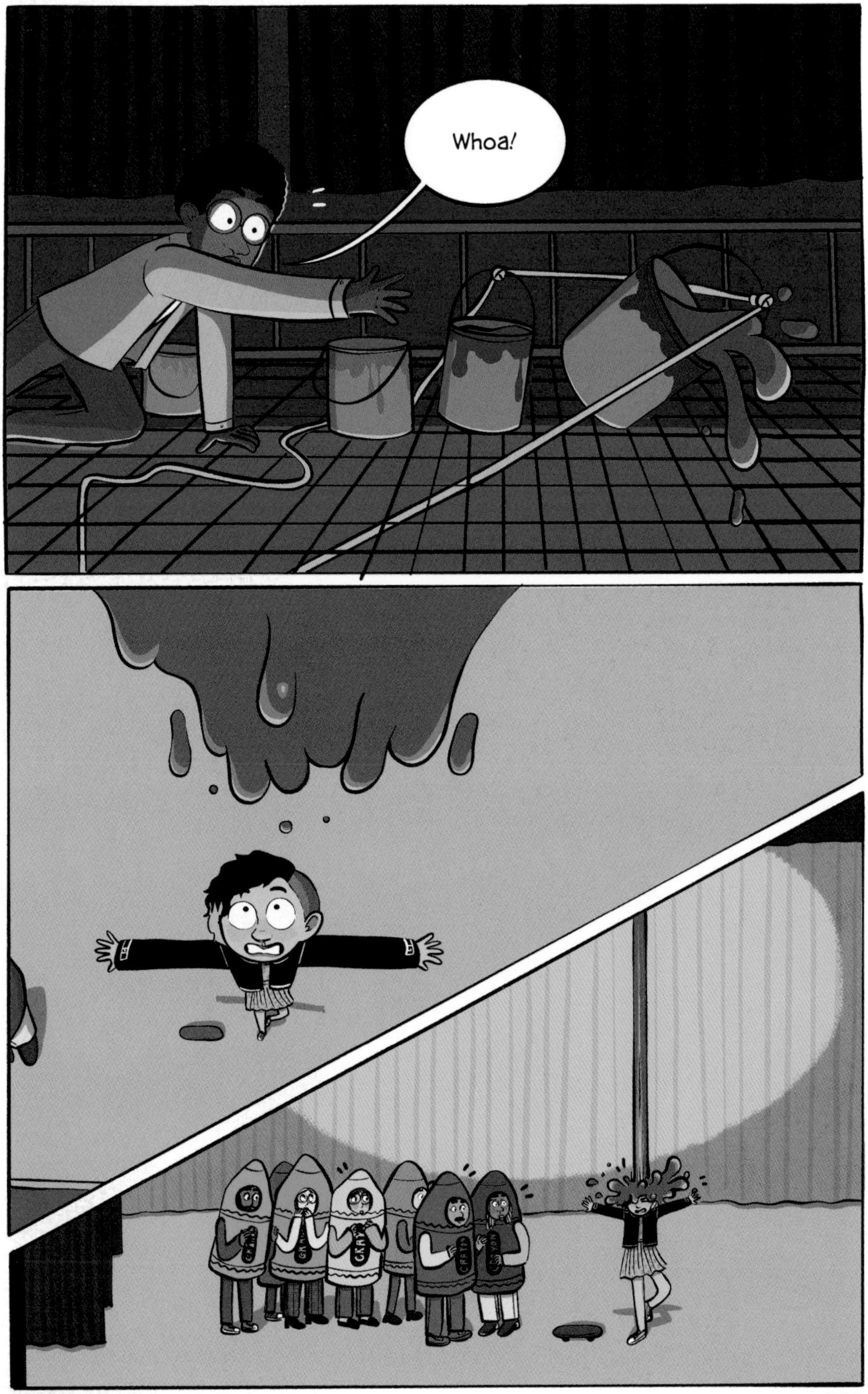
Whoa!

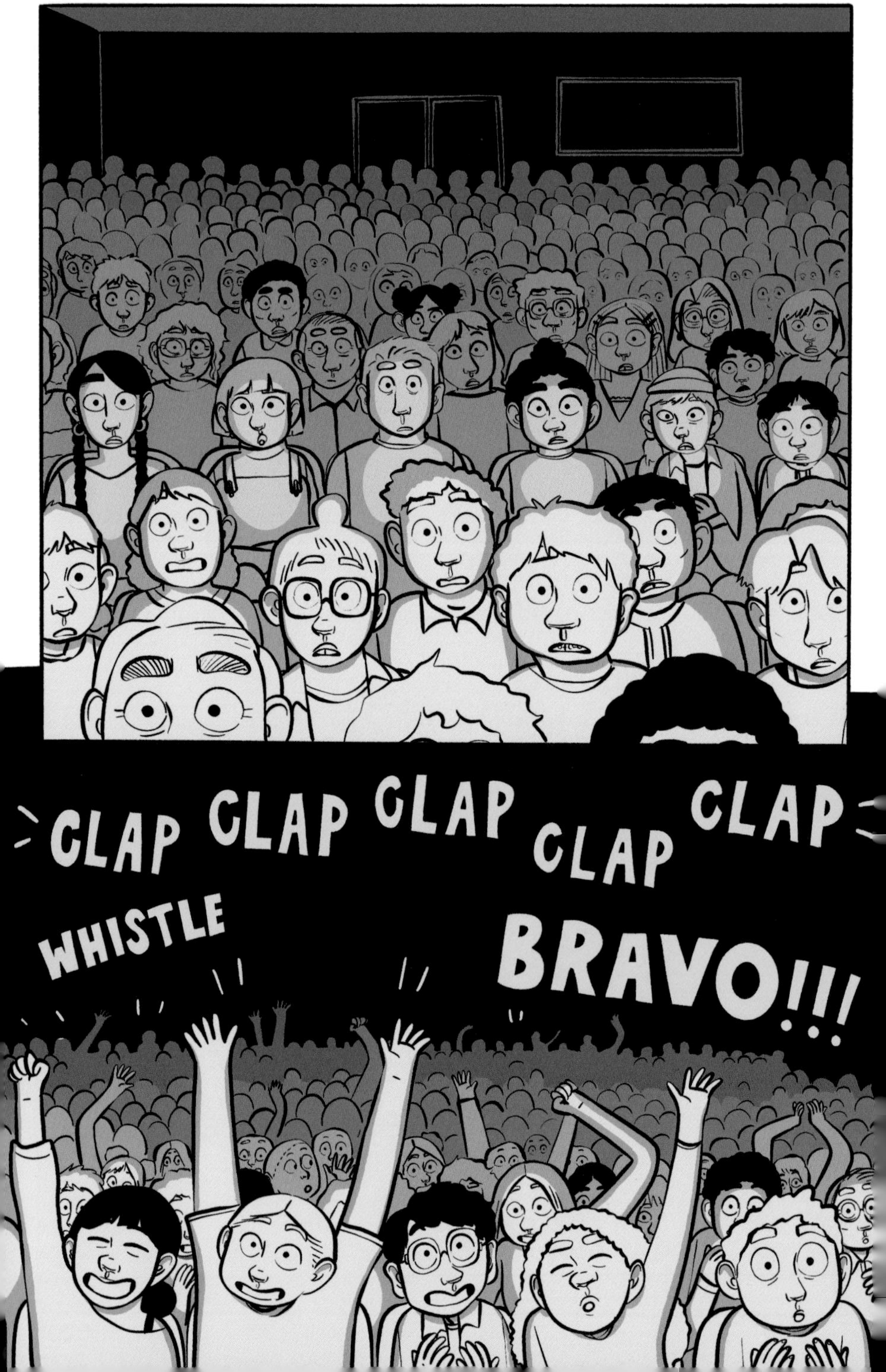
CLAP CLAP CLAP CLAP CLAP
WHISTLE
BRAVO!!!

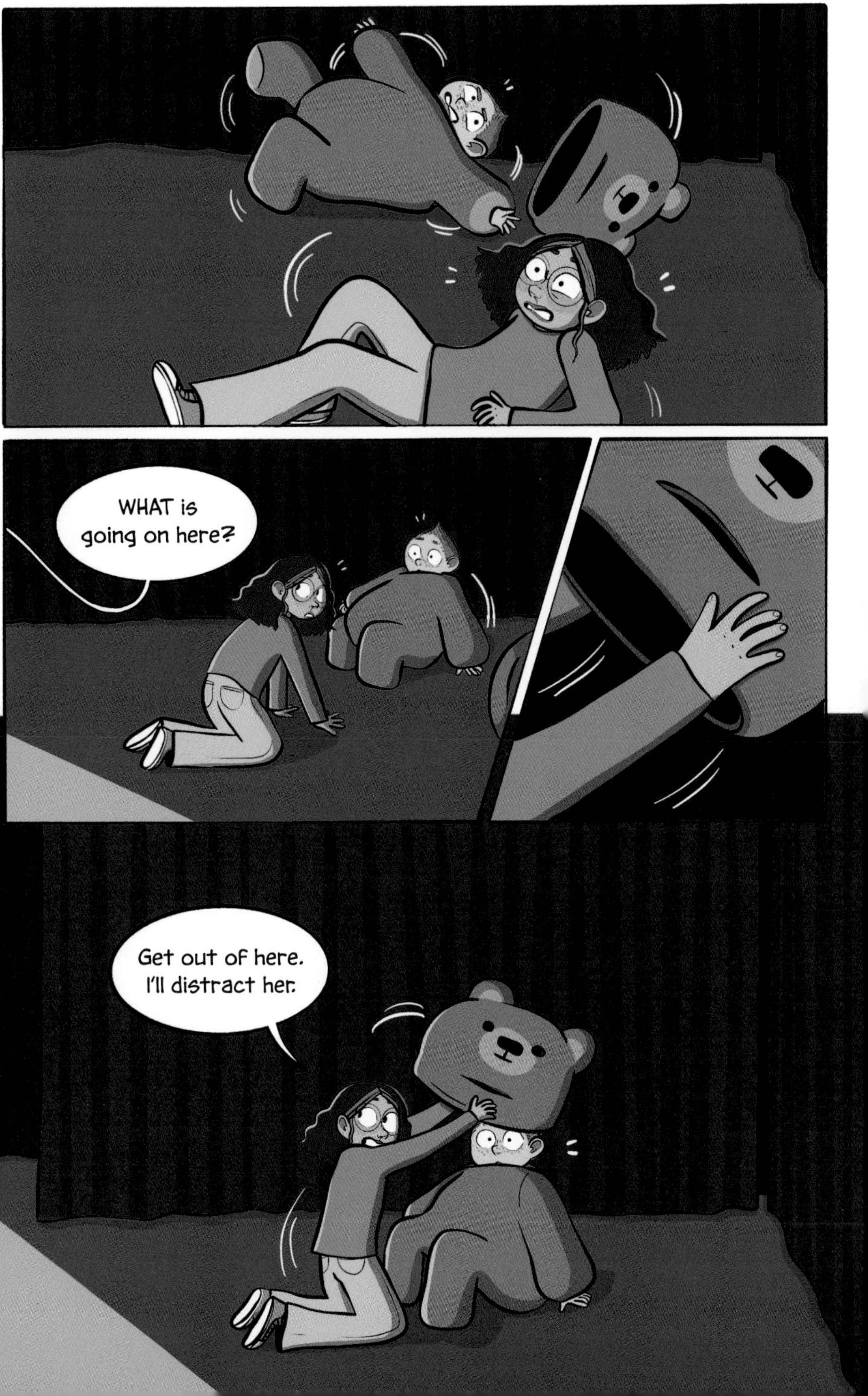
WHAT is going on here?
Get out of here. I'll distract her.

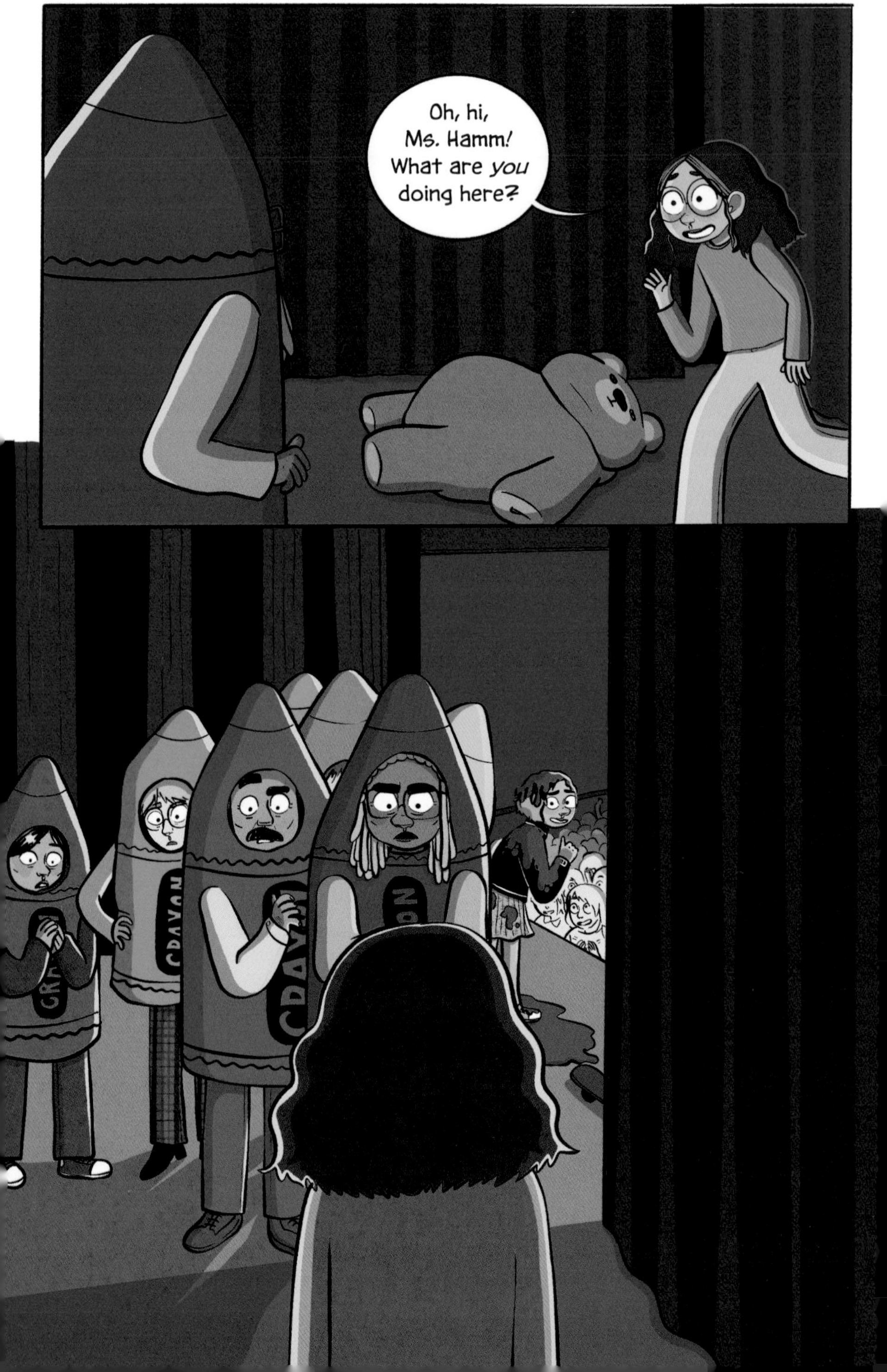
Oh, hi, Ms. Hamm! What are *you* doing here?

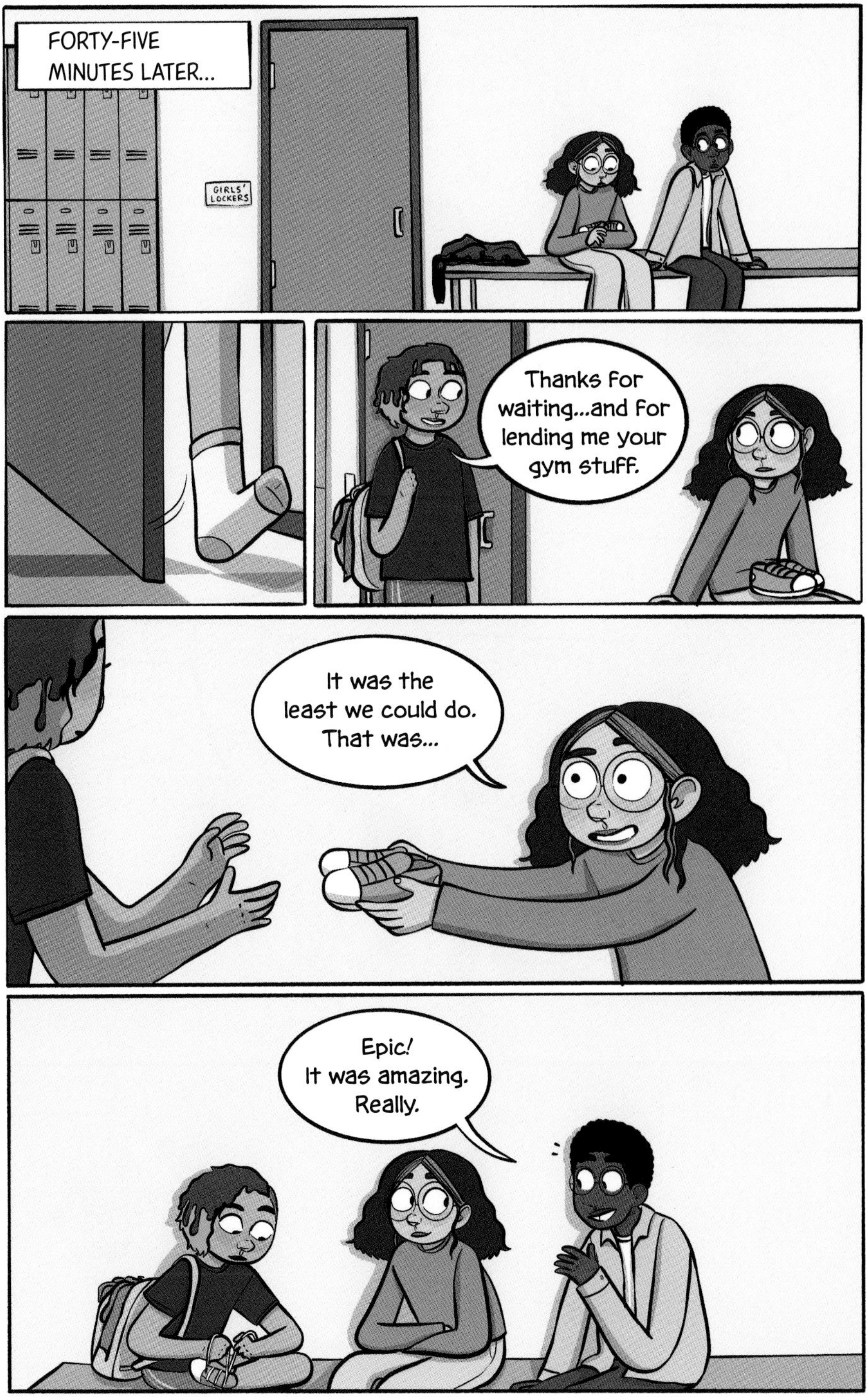
FORTY-FIVE MINUTES LATER...
GIRLS' LOCKERS
Thanks for waiting...and for lending me your gym stuff.
It was the least we could do. That was...
Epic! It was amazing. Really.

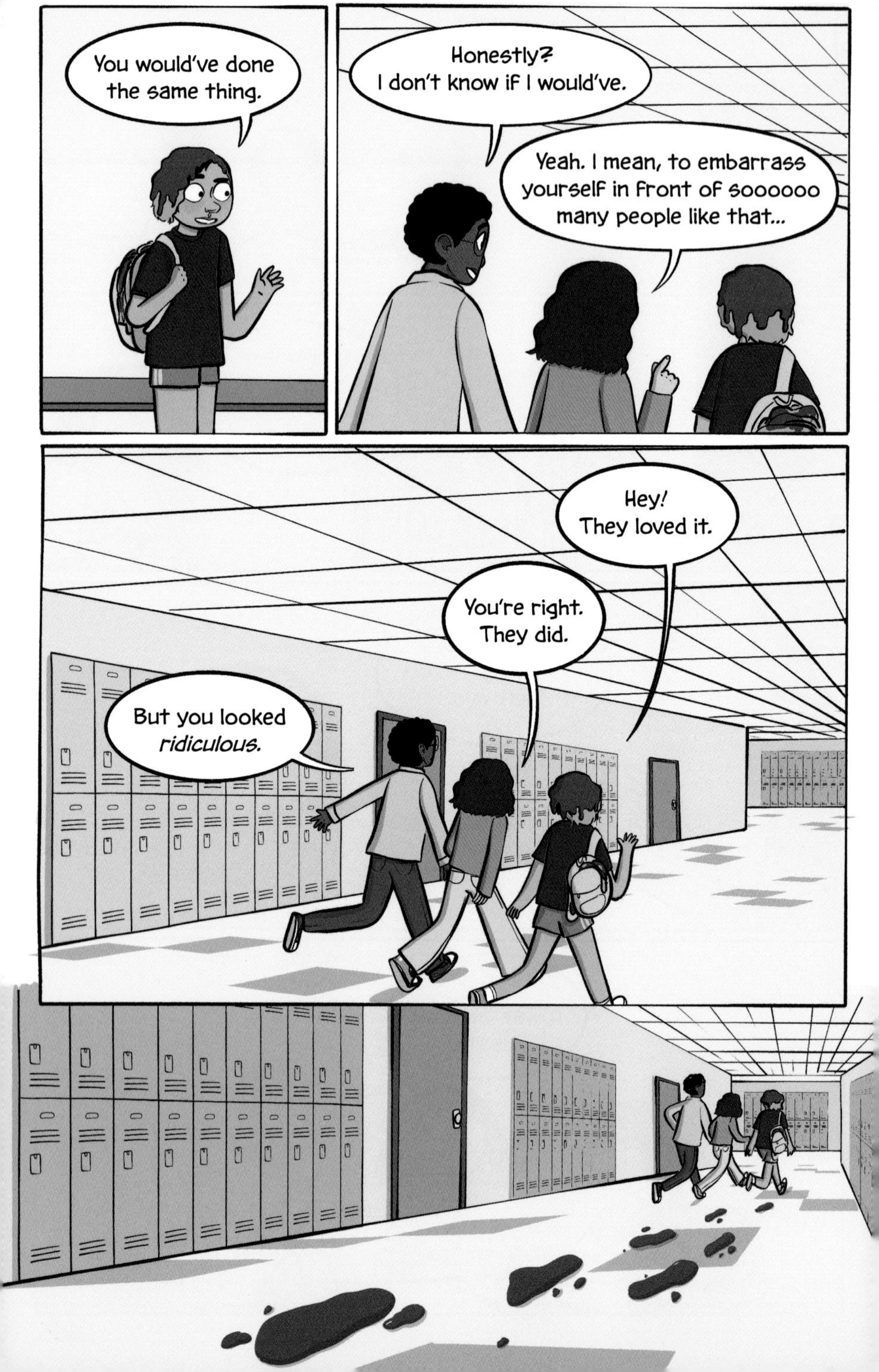
You would've done the same thing.
Honestly? I don't know if I would've.
Yeah. I mean, to embarrass yourself in front of soooooo many people like that...
Hey! They loved it.
You're right. They did.
But you looked *ridiculous*.

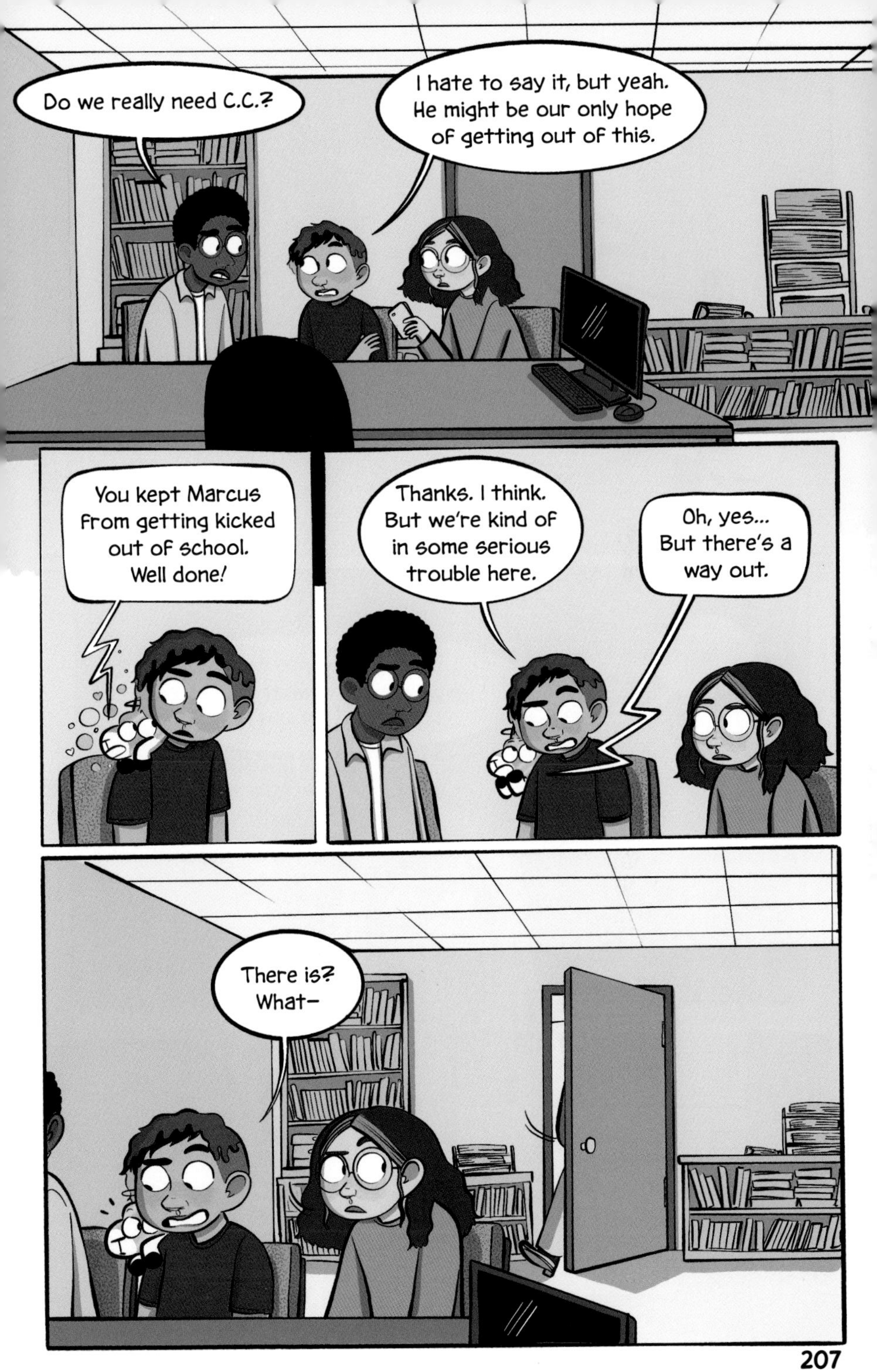

Do we really need C.C.?
I hate to say it, but yeah. He might be our only hope of getting out of this.
You kept Marcus from getting kicked out of school. Well done!
Thanks. I think. But we're kind of in some serious trouble here.
Oh, yes... But there's a way out.
There is? What–

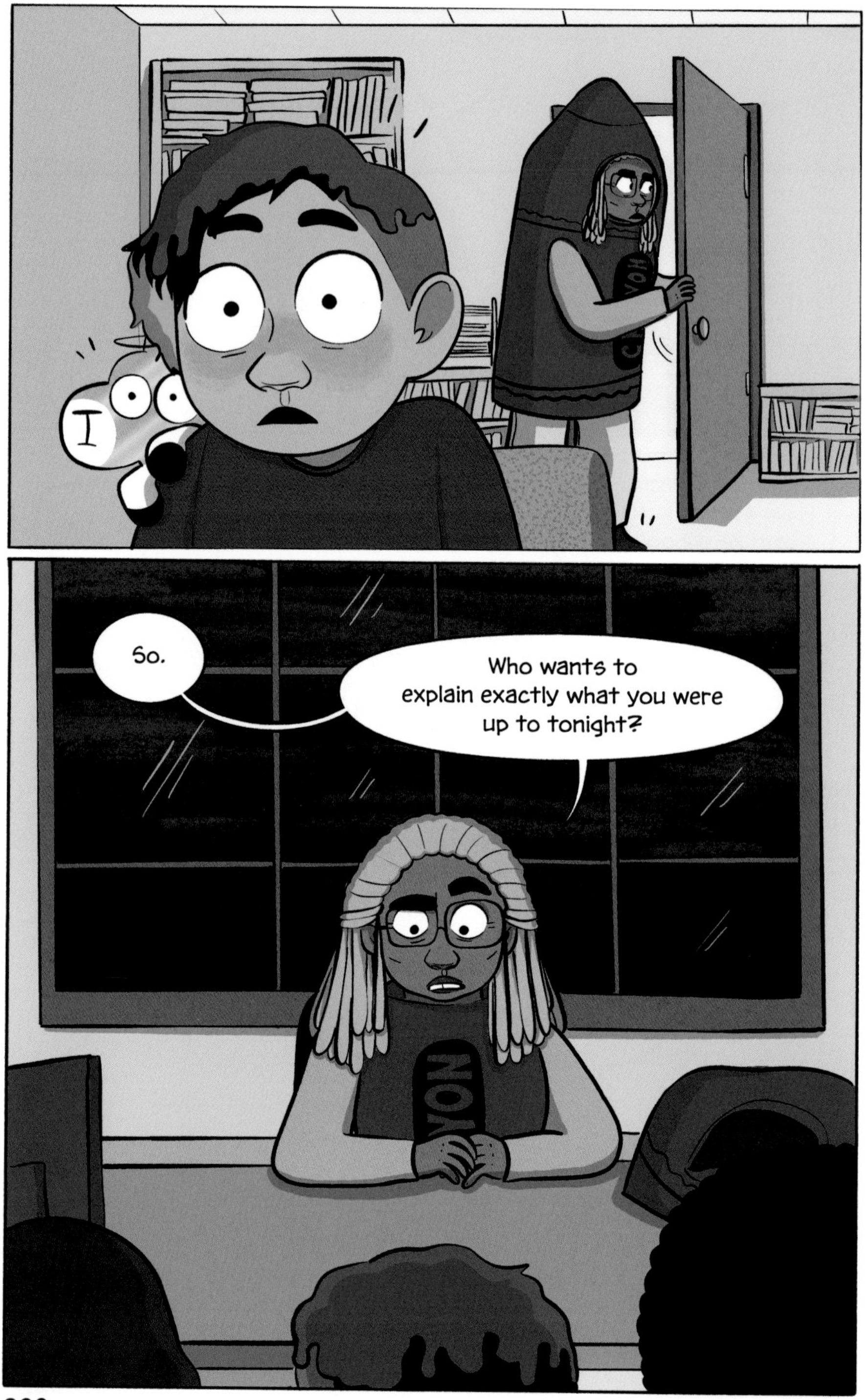
So.
Who wants to explain exactly what you were up to tonight?

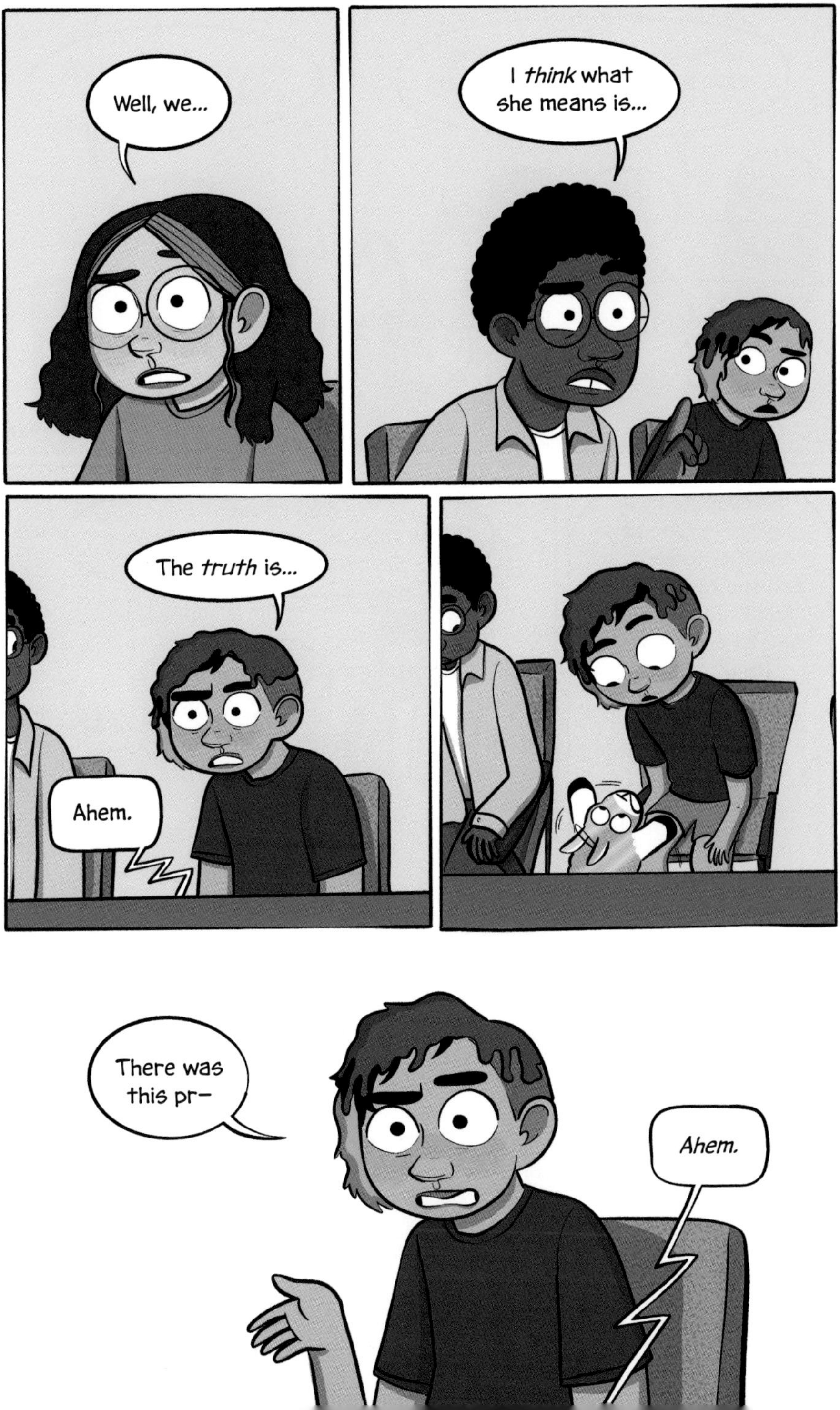
Well, we...
I *think* what she means is...
The *truth* is...
Ahem.
There was this pr–
Ahem.

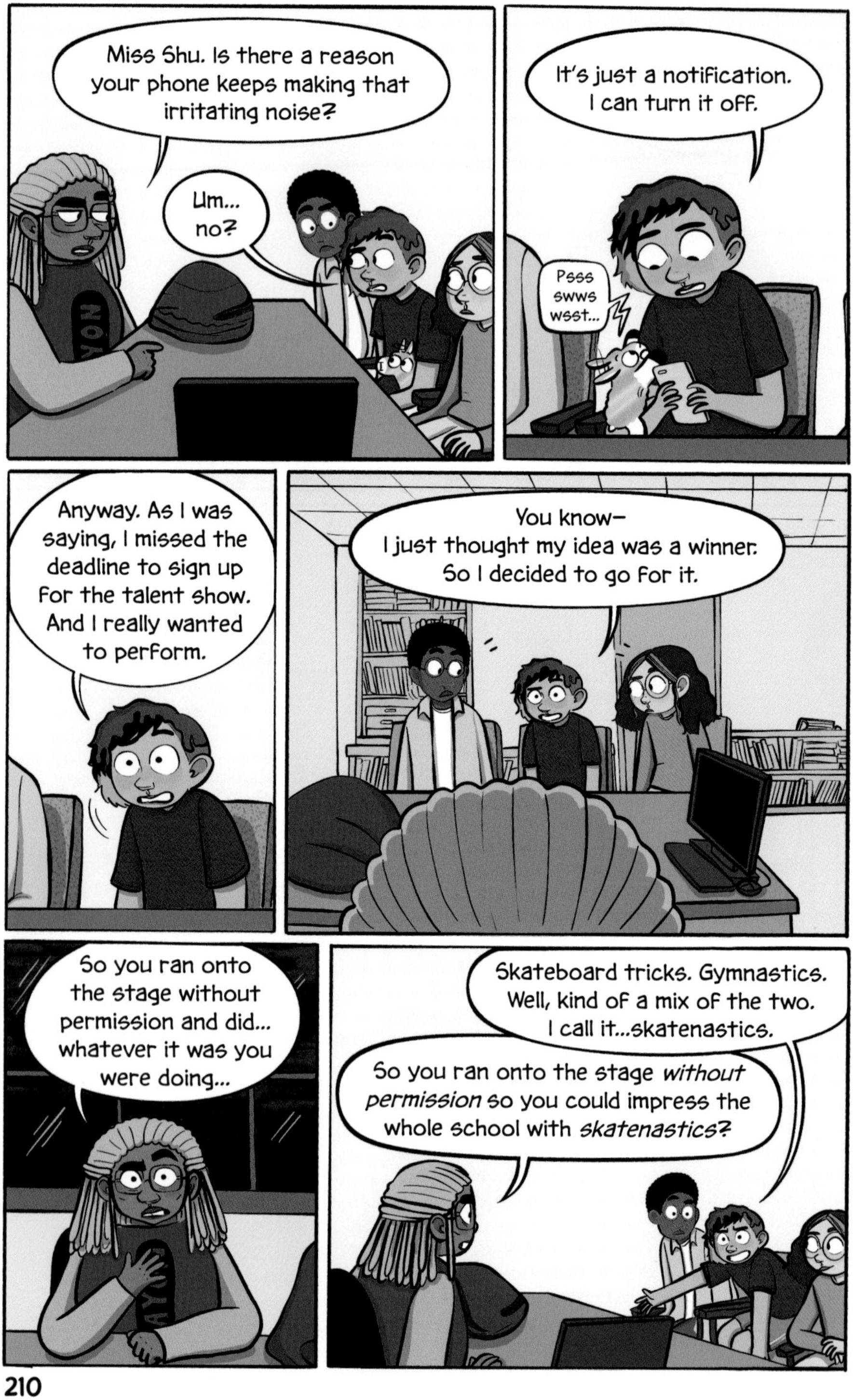

Miss Shu. Is there a reason your phone keeps making that irritating noise?
Um... no?
It's just a notification. I can turn it off.
Psss swws wsst...
Anyway. As I was saying, I missed the deadline to sign up for the talent show. And I really wanted to perform.
You know— I just thought my idea was a winner. So I decided to go for it.
So you ran onto the stage without permission and did... whatever it was you were doing...
Skateboard tricks. Gymnastics. Well, kind of a mix of the two. I call it...skatenastics.
So you ran onto the stage *without permission* so you could impress the whole school with *skatenastics*?

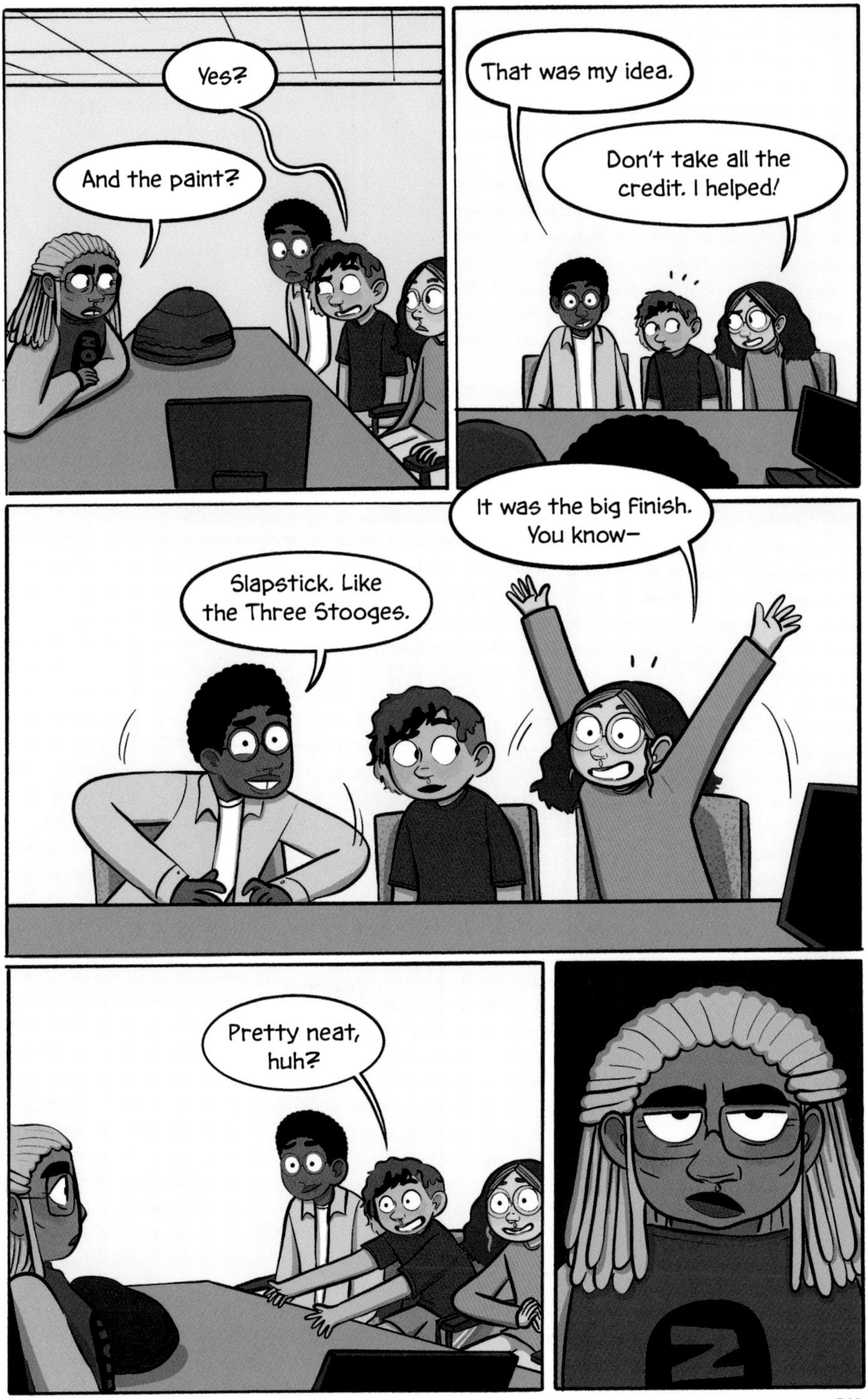
Yes?
And the paint?
That was my idea.
Don't take all the credit. I helped!
It was the big finish. You know—
Slapstick. Like the Three Stooges.
Pretty neat, huh?

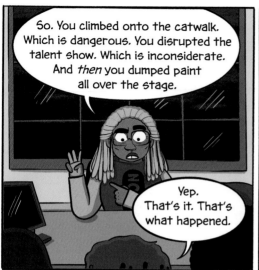

So. You climbed onto the catwalk. Which is dangerous. You disrupted the talent show. Which is inconsiderate. And *then* you dumped paint all over the stage.

Yep. That's it. That's what happened.

It took half an hour to clean up that paint so the next act...*my act*...could go on. This is incredibly bad behavior. I am deeply disappointed in all three of you.

Nevertheless...

...I'm relieved that you weren't trying to pull some kind of prank. As you know, there has been a rash of malicious pranks in the school, and I would have had to take severe action if I'd found out you were involved.

The question is, what should I do with you? Until now, you have all been exemplary students.

But lately I am not so sure...

You never finished the student directory.

Wait—I did!

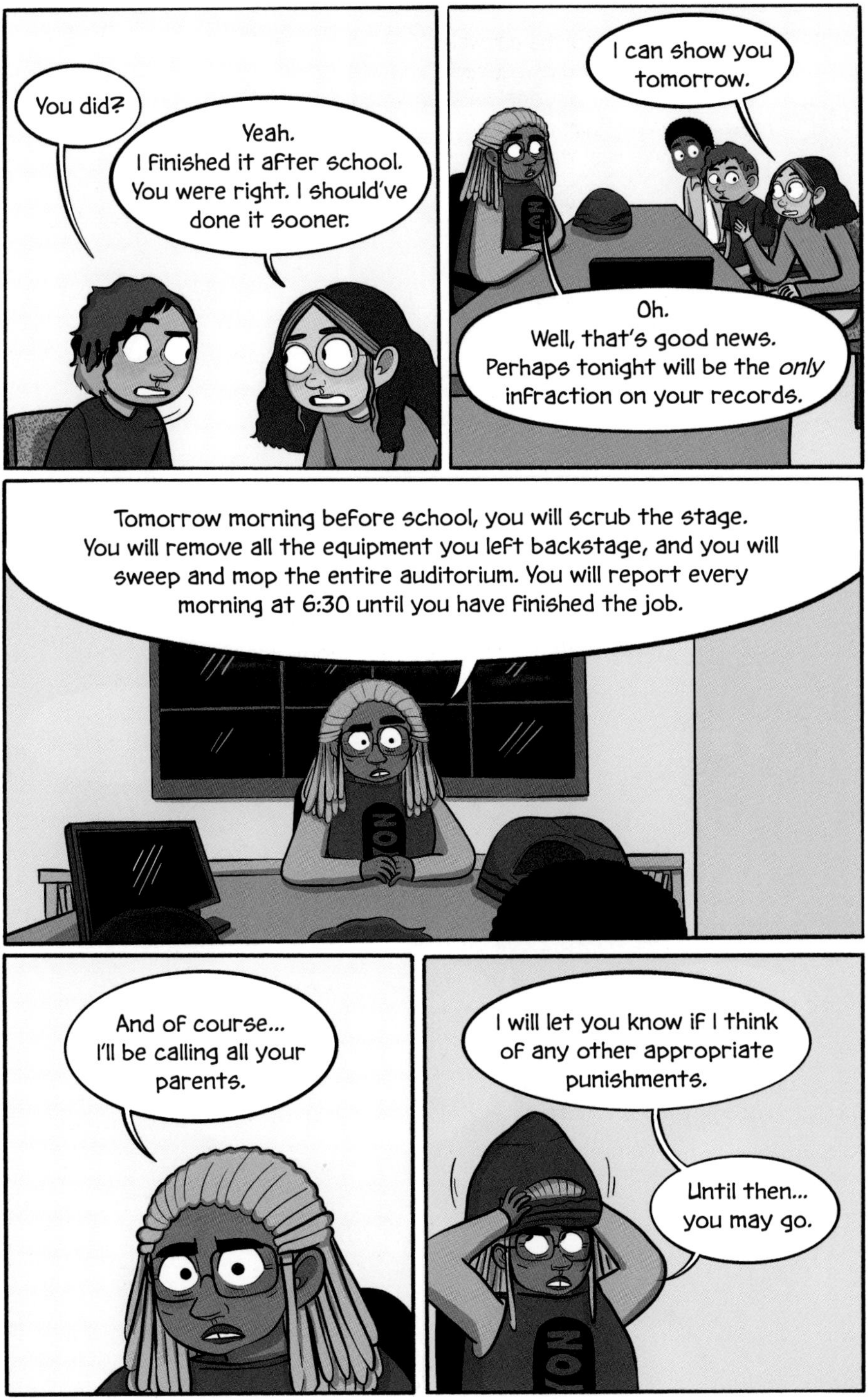
You did?
Yeah. I finished it after school. You were right. I should've done it sooner.
I can show you tomorrow.
Oh. Well, that's good news. Perhaps tonight will be the *only* infraction on your records.
Tomorrow morning before school, you will scrub the stage. You will remove all the equipment you left backstage, and you will sweep and mop the entire auditorium. You will report every morning at 6:30 until you have finished the job.
And of course... I'll be calling all your parents.
I will let you know if I think of any other appropriate punishments.
Until then... you may go.

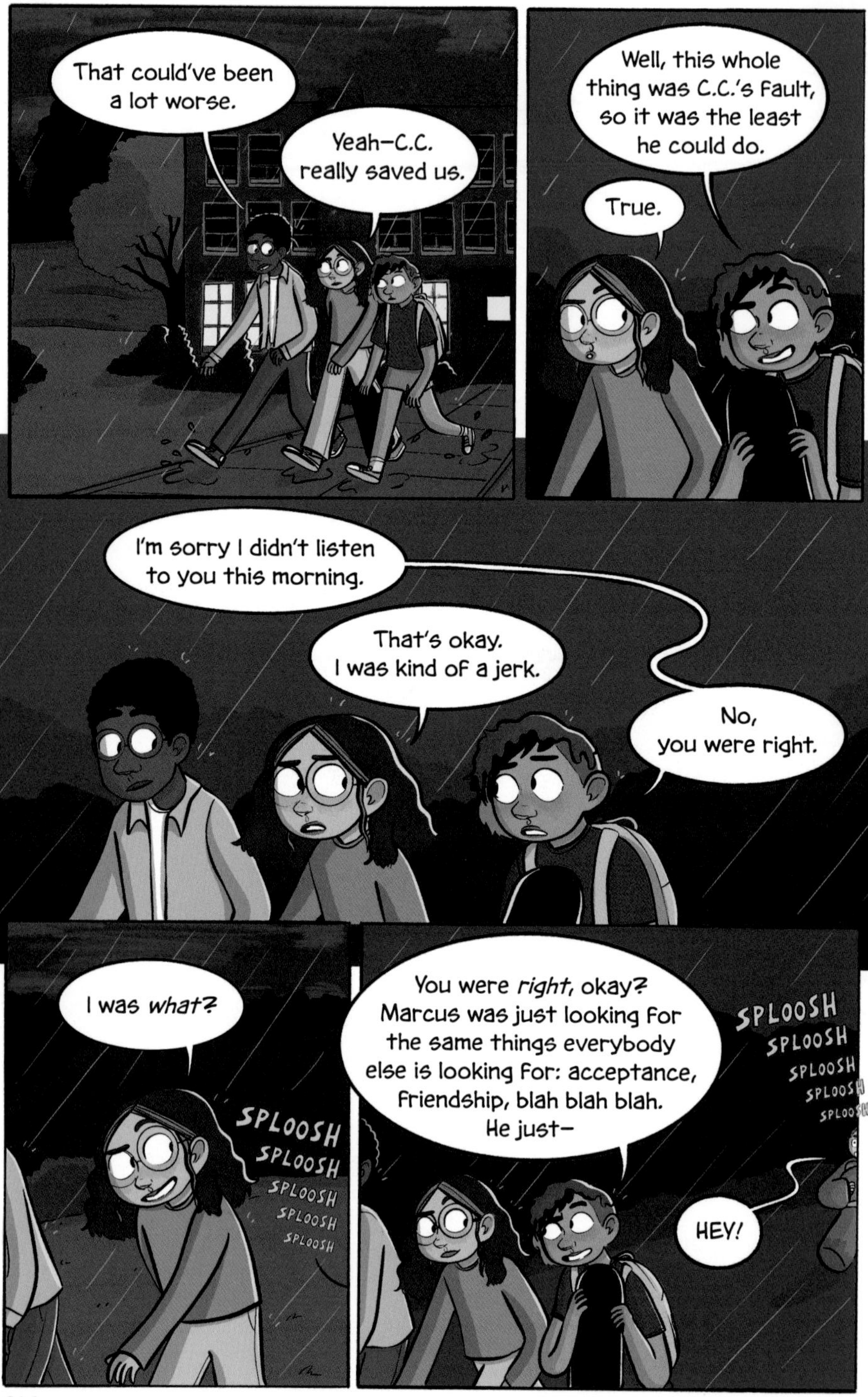
That could've been a lot worse.
Yeah—C.C. really saved us.
Well, this whole thing was C.C.'s fault, so it was the least he could do.
True.
I'm sorry I didn't listen to you this morning.
That's okay. I was kind of a jerk.
No, you were right.
I was *what?*
SPLOOSH
SPLOOSH
SPLOOSH
SPLOOSH
SPLOOSH
You were *right*, okay? Marcus was just looking for the same things everybody else is looking for: acceptance, friendship, blah blah blah. He just—
SPLOOSH
SPLOOSH
SPLOOSH
SPLOOSH
SPLOOSH
HEY!

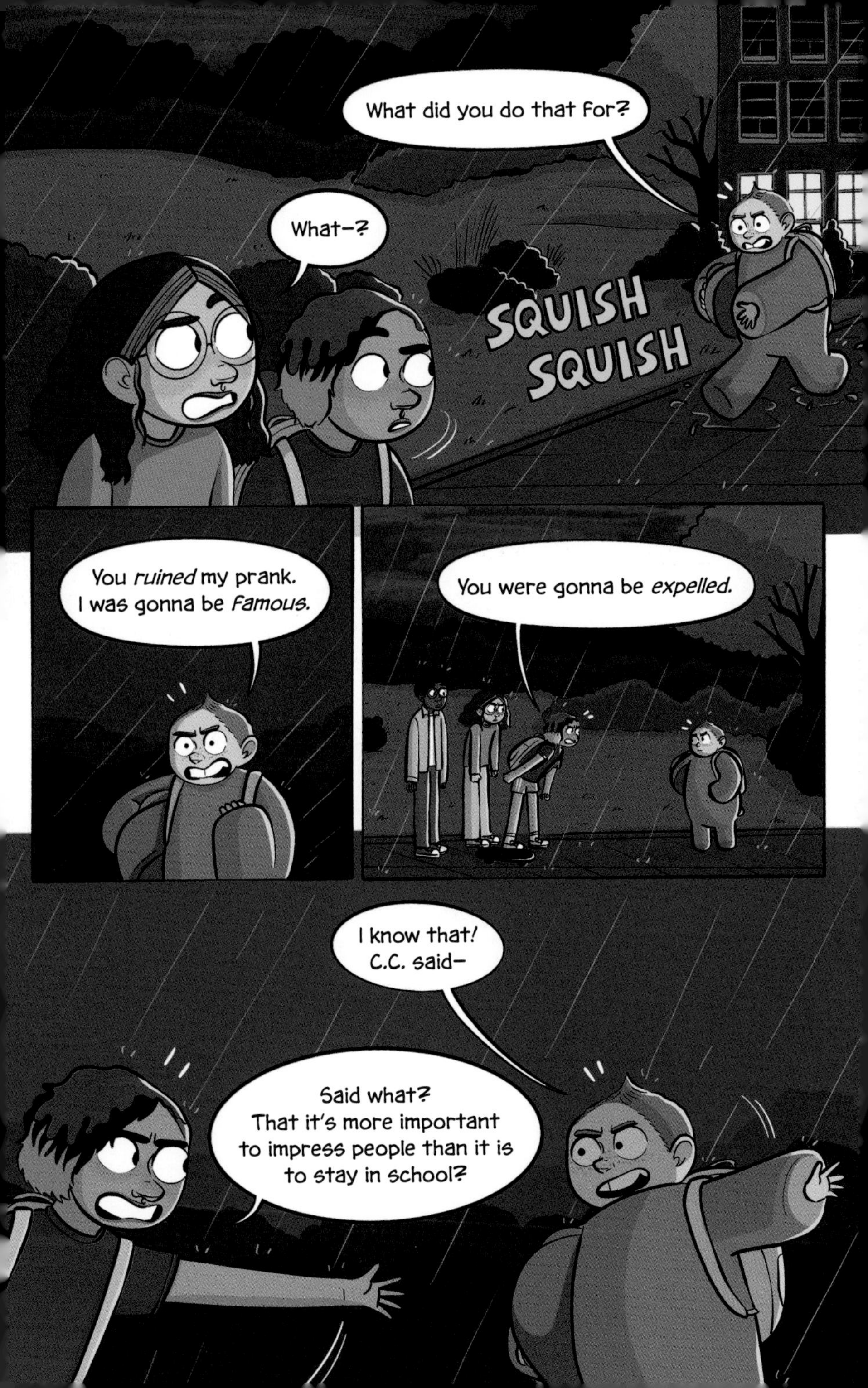
What did you do that for?
What–?
SQUISH SQUISH
You *ruined* my prank. I was gonna be *famous.*
You were gonna be *expelled.*
I know that! C.C. said–
Said what? That it's more important to impress people than it is to stay in school?

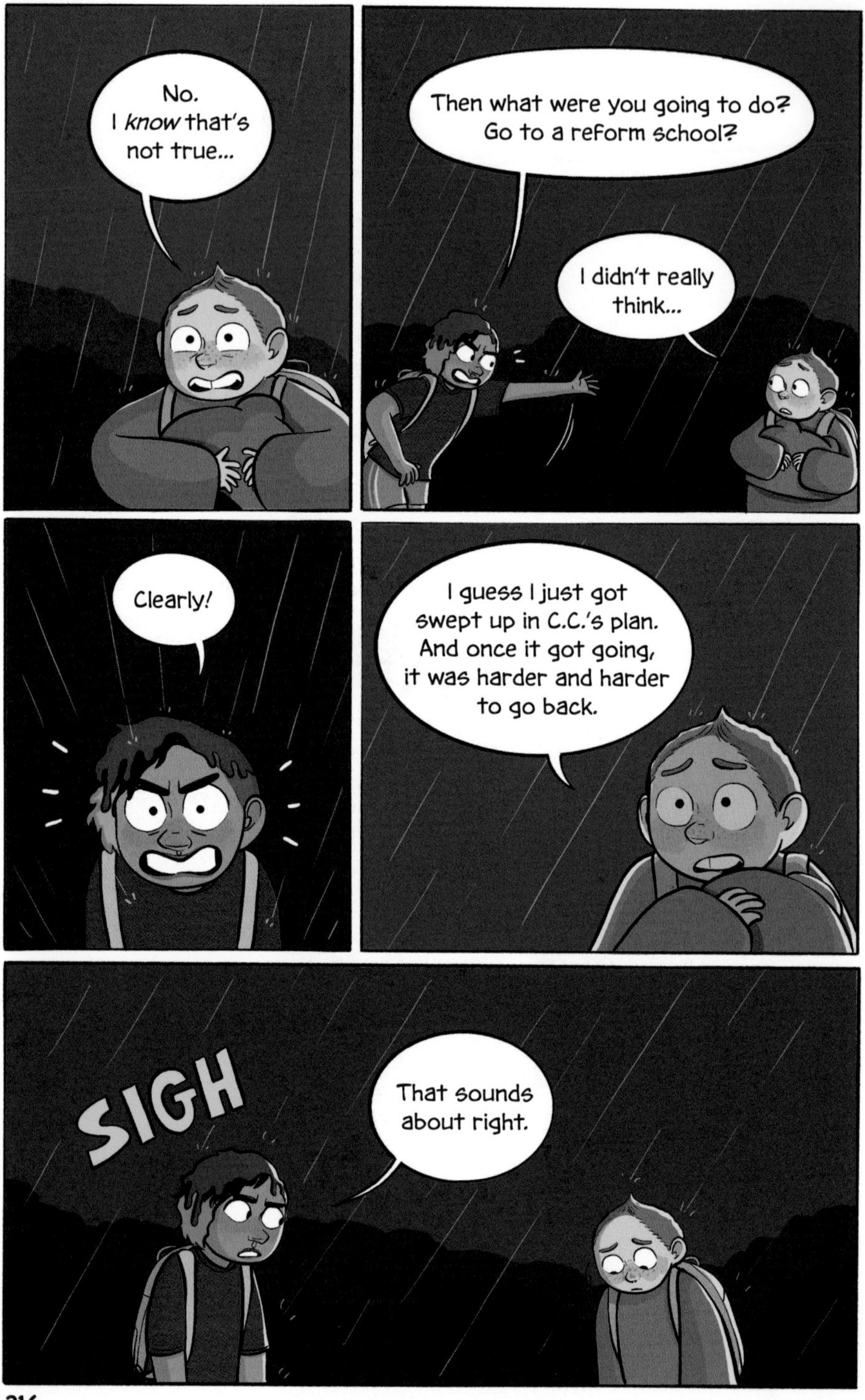
No.
I *know* that's not true...
Then what were you going to do? Go to a reform school?
I didn't really think...
Clearly!
I guess I just got swept up in C.C.'s plan. And once it got going, it was harder and harder to go back.
SIGH
That sounds about right.

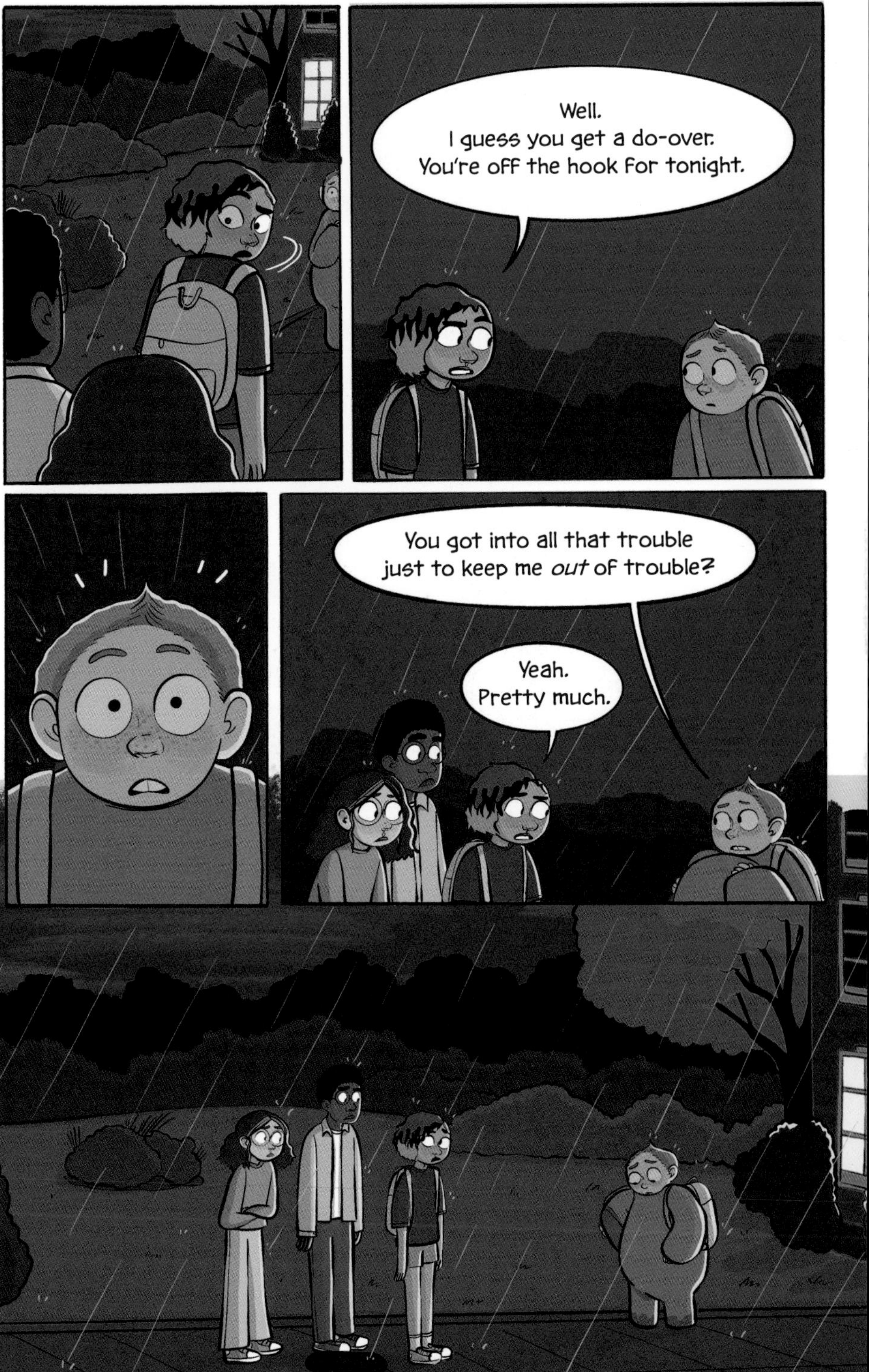
Well.
I guess you get a do-over.
You're off the hook for tonight.
You got into all that trouble just to keep me *out* of trouble?
Yeah.
Pretty much.

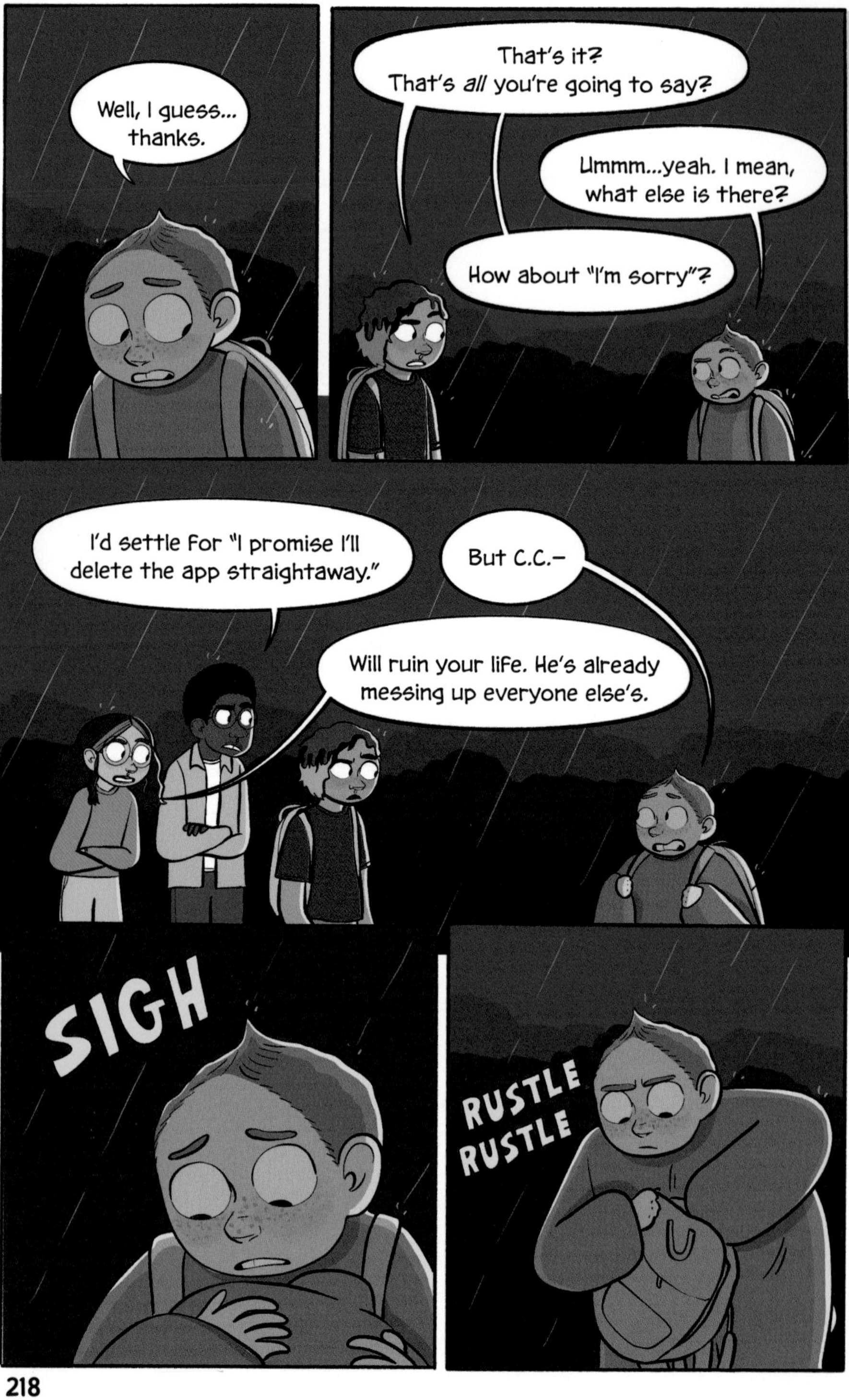
Well, I guess... thanks.
That's it? That's *all* you're going to say?
Ummm...yeah. I mean, what else is there?
How about "I'm sorry"?
I'd settle for "I promise I'll delete the app straightaway."
But C.C.–
Will ruin your life. He's already messing up everyone else's.
SIGH
RUSTLE RUSTLE

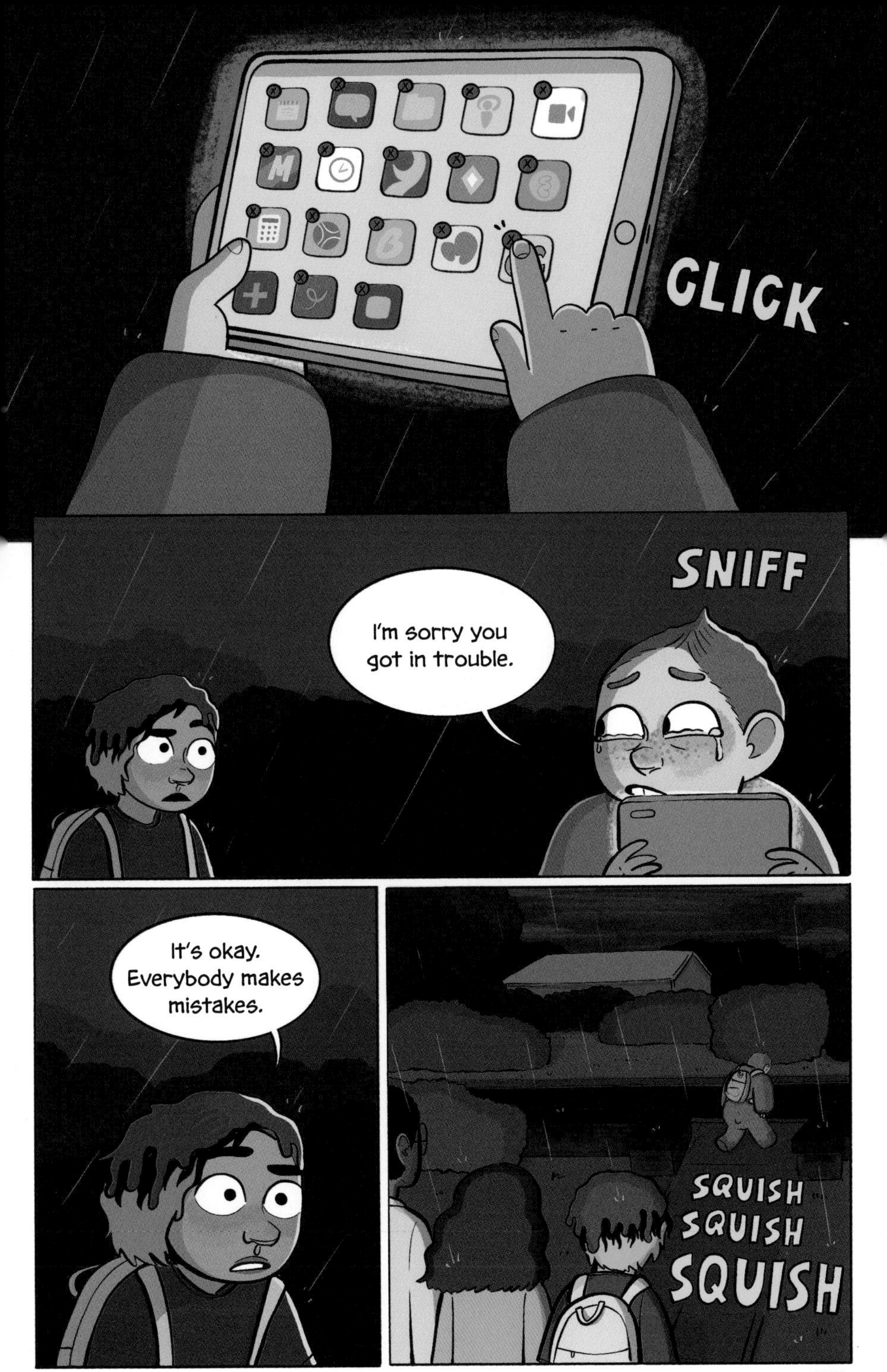
CLICK
SNIFF
I'm sorry you got in trouble.
It's okay. Everybody makes mistakes.
SQUISH
SQUISH
SQUISH

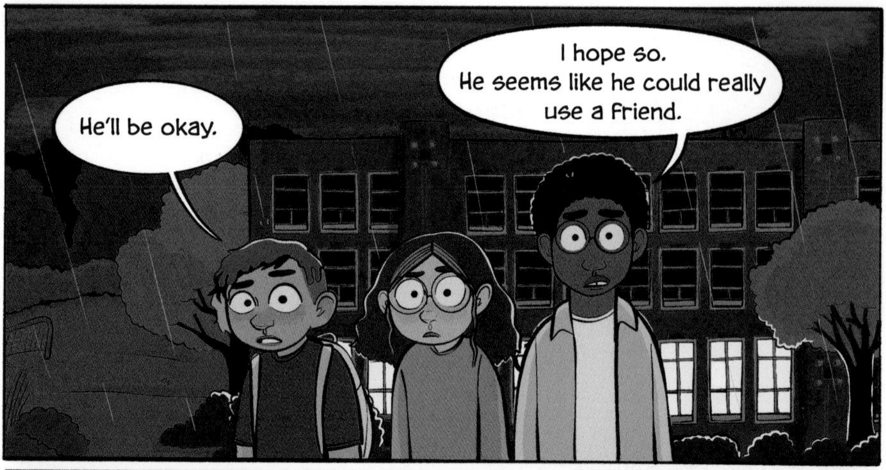
He'll be okay.
I hope so. He seems like he could really use a friend.

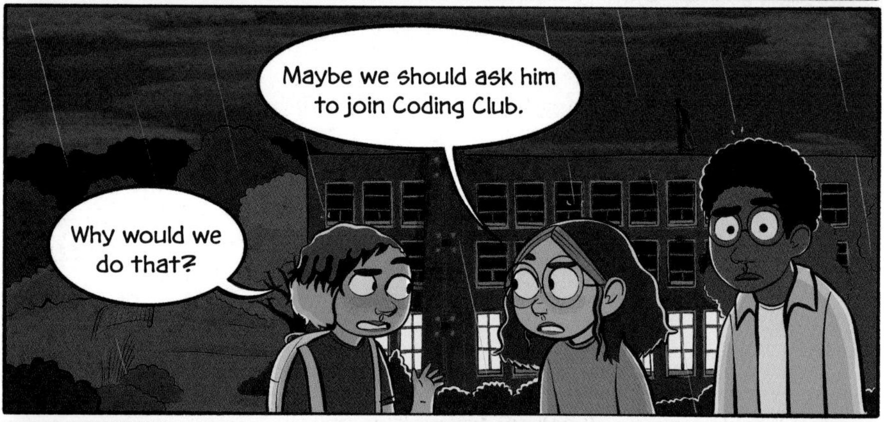
Maybe we should ask him to join Coding Club.
Why would we do that?

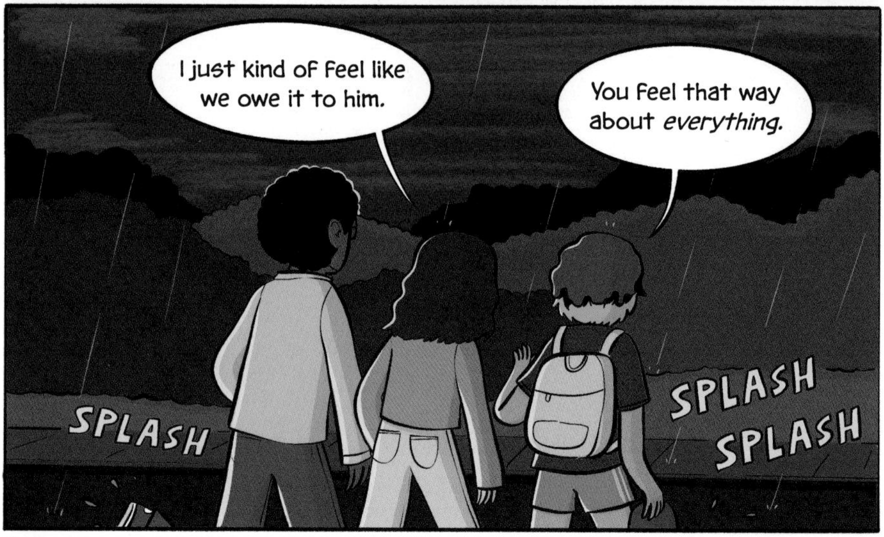
I just kind of feel like we owe it to him.
You feel that way about *everything*.
SPLASH
SPLASH
SPLASH

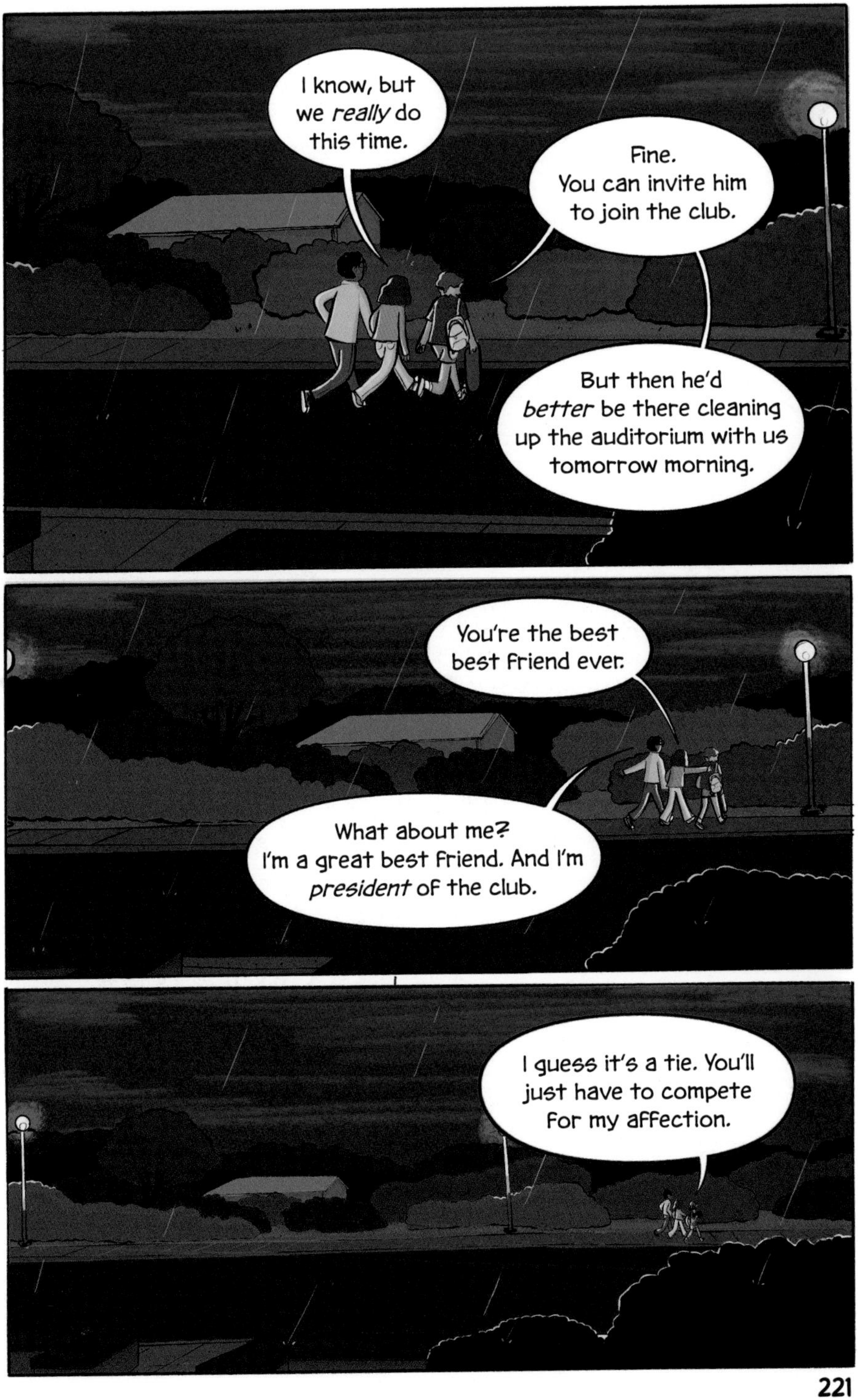
I know, but we *really* do this time.
Fine. You can invite him to join the club.
But then he'd *better* be there cleaning up the auditorium with us tomorrow morning.
You're the best best friend ever.
What about me? I'm a great best friend. And I'm *president* of the club.
I guess it's a tie. You'll just have to compete for my affection.

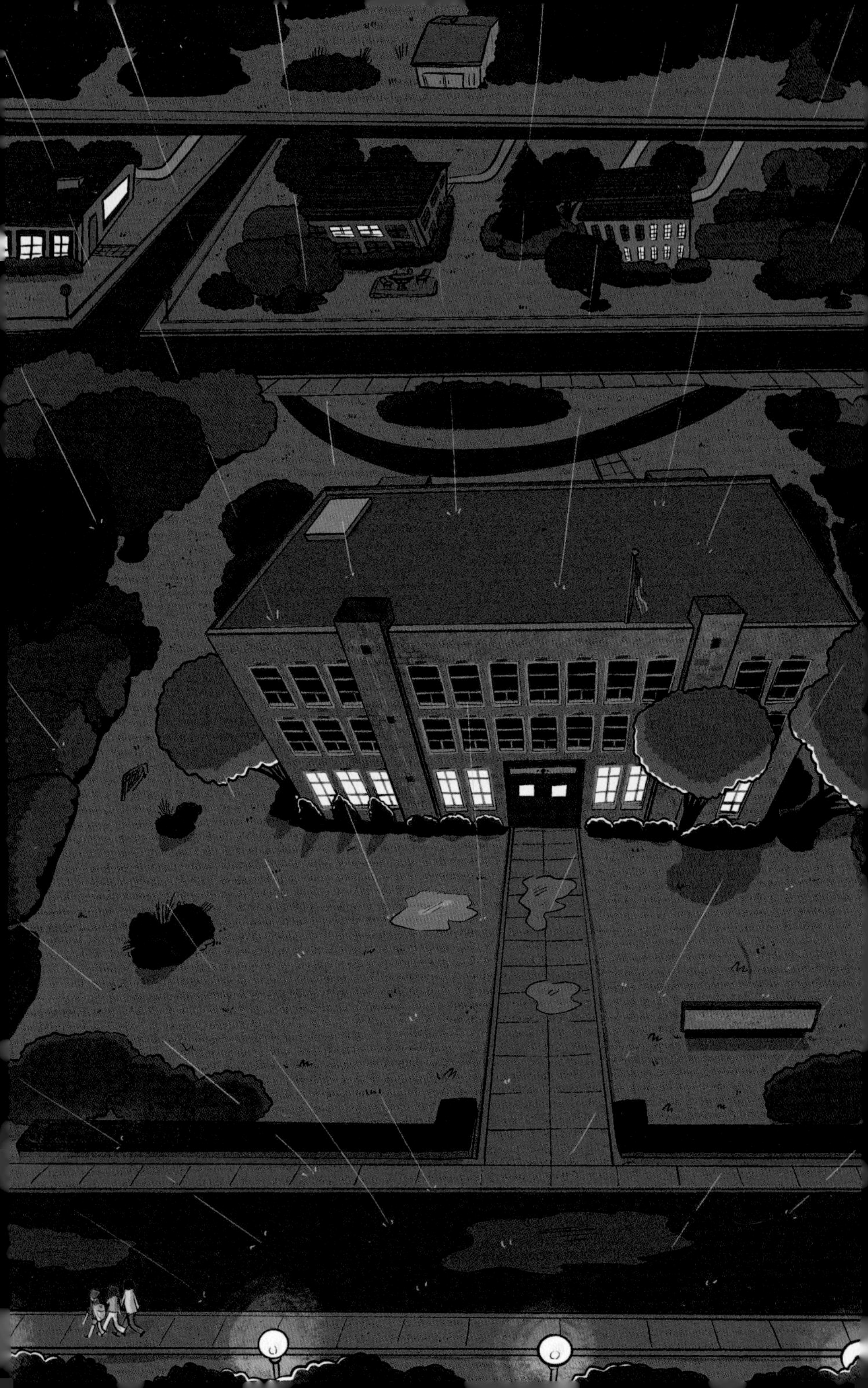